Th[illegible]

Co[illegible] Kitchen

Jane Linfoot writes fun, flirty bestselling romantic fiction with feisty heroines and a bit of an edge. Writing romance is cool because she gets to wear pretty shoes instead of wellies. She lives in a mountain kingdom in Derbyshire, where her family and pets are kind enough to ignore the domestic chaos. Happily, they are in walking distance of a supermarket. Jane loves hearts, flowers, happy endings, all things vintage, most things French. When she's not on Facebook and can't find an excuse for shopping, she'll be walking or gardening. On days when she wants to be really scared, she rides a tandem.

@janelinfoot

www.facebook.com/JaneLinfoot2

@janelinfoot

www.janelinfoot.co.uk

Praise for Jane Linfoot

'Just like the perfect wedding cake, Cupcakes and Confetti is beautifully crafted and wrapped in romance'
Heidi Swain, bestselling author of *The Cherry Tree Cafe*

'A pure delight...fabulous, fun and unforgettable'
Debbie Johnson, bestselling author of *Summer at the Comfort Food Café*

'Simply stunning'
A Spoonful of Happy Endings

'Gorgeous book with characters full of heart, and an impassioned story to make you smile'
Reviewed the Book

'This author packs a punch'
My Little Book Blog

'Loved this book. The main characters are vividly drawn...the writing is fast and feisty'
Contemporary Romance Reviews

'With every book I read I fall more in love'
Booky Ramblings

'Jane Linfoot has got out the mixing bowl and whipped up a truly gorgeous story...A deliciously scrumptious treat'
Rebecca Pugh, bestselling author of *Return to Bluebell Hill*

Jane Linfoot

The Little Cornish Kitchen

A division of HarperCollins*Publishers*
www.harpercollins.co.uk

HarperImpulse an imprint of
HarperCollins*Publishers*
1 London Bridge Street
London SE1 9GF

www.harpercollins.co.uk

A Paperback Original 2018

First published in Great Britain in ebook format by Harper*Impulse* 2018

A catalogue record for this book
is available from the British Library

ISBN: 9780008260682

Set in Birka by Type-it AS, Norway

Printed and bound in Great Britain by
CPI Group (UK) Ltd, Croydon, CR0 4YY

To M, Anna, Indi, Richard and Eric,
Max and Caroline, and Phil xx

"You know, Adelie penguins, they spend their whole lives looking for that one other penguin and when they meet them, they know. And they spend the rest of their lives together."

Josie Geller, *Never Been Kissed.*

1

The Deck Gallery, St Aidan, Cornwall
Siren song and crashing waves
Wednesday

'Would you like some mini macaroons to go with your complementary samples?'

The biscuits on the platter I'm holding out to guests are shades of sea blue and lavender, and I'm down to my last few. As I was the one who spent the afternoon in my brilliant friend Sophie's farmhouse kitchen, sandwiching soft buttercream filling into so many hundreds of them I lost count, I already know how delicious they are. They're a perfect complement to the products we're here to celebrate, and so light I bet you could easily eat a dozen and still feel you'd like more. Although Sophie, whose event this is, stopped me before I tested that theory to the max. At times, she was watching me so closely she might as well have done the job herself. But with my serious lack of cooking skills I can hardly blame her. It's not my fault, I just haven't ever had a kitchen of my own to practise in. It's no secret. If I come within a yard of a Magimix it's more likely to result in a blitzkrieg than a bake off.

As Sophie glides in behind me she hisses in my ear. 'You're doing a fab job, Clemmie, almost onto the fun bit now, I owe you for this.' Hopefully she means we're almost at the part where it becomes party rather than work.

'You're not joking there.' I laugh and take my chance to down another raspberry vodka in a pretty flowery tea cup and snaffle a macaroon to soak it up. Then I brush the crumbs off my boob shelf. If you'd told me when I flew in from Paris yesterday that within twenty-four hours, I'd be out in public dressed as a mermaid I might have got straight back on the plane. But the more cocktails I have the less I care about the public humiliation. Three hours into the event I've almost forgotten I look like I've got a tail rather than legs.

Sophie turns up the volume again as she moves in on the next guests. 'The macaroons are home-made to echo the natural simplicity of the Sophie May skin care range.'

It's not just sales talk. With ingredients like chamomile and seaweed the products really are every bit as amazing as they sound. Her main seller is a hot wash cleanser that makes you feel like you've been for a full facial. It's such a revelation it took her company from nowhere into department stores across the country in a matter of months.

Did I mention her amazing husband, Nate? He's the one who handles the sales and marketing, and is currently schmoozing the VIPs on the gallery's outdoor deck. Nate's been in charge of this evening's invitations too. Even though he's managed to ask most people in Cornwall as well as 'everyone who mattered' from the rest of the world, he's been slightly less amazing at the detail. Sophie had factored in at least an hour to clear the professional guests before the locals arrive. But the journo from *Time Out* is still taking pictures of the macaroon towers as the entire team from Iron Maiden Cleaners clatter in from the High Street. Despite being from London he's picking his jaw up off the bleached wood floor at the sight of six dry cleaning assistants in their short, bondage-style uniforms. Right now, it's starting to look less like a tasteful promotion of gorgeous new packaging designs, and more like a free-for-all in a dominatrix bar.

Sophie assesses the damage and waves in a girl with a teapot in each hand. 'Top up for our guest in the flak jacket, please.'

Not many women could carry off a pastel jump suit, especially one the same colour as their cosmetics boxes. But in the palest mint blue, with her choppy blonde layers and clear complexion, Sophie's a walking, talking, breathing embodiment of her range. There isn't a whisper of the sooty eyed fourteen-year-old Goth she once was. Add in her four children, aged from ten to tiny, and her life really does look like she plucked it from the Boden catalogue. Of all our childhood friend group, she's the one who reached for the stars and grabbed them all. And doing that took a lot more straight talking and butt kicking than her wholesome glow suggests. But so long as she holds off ordering people around until the press leave, she's pretty much cracked it here.

As we turn to the next guests, I'm taking the biggest steps my cinched-in mermaid skirt will allow, and beaming over my remaining macaroons. 'Sophie May is all about nurturing and wellbeing ... treating yourself ... becoming the freshest version of you.'

I may only have arrived back in my hometown St Aidan yesterday, but my lines are already polished. And the best part is, they're all true. If these products hadn't been phenomenal I'd never have agreed to dress up in character. Let's face it, I get enough jokes about my long Ariel coloured hair as it is.

Bigging up the ocean connection was Sophie's daughter Milla's idea. She's always loved that our little group of friends used to call ourselves 'the mermaids' when we were kids. Milla became an honorary junior mer-member when she was born ten years ago. As we're all here to help with the launch, and Sophie still had our light-as-air aqua silk bridesmaid's dresses in her wardrobe, the rest was easy. Add in a few yards of tulle and fish netting nipped in in all the right places. Throw in shells, strings of pearls, a rock-pool full of dried starfish (assuming that's how you measure them), some glitter stick and a few strands of the all-important seaweed, and the end result is Plum, Nell and I wandering around looking like we've crawled up from the beach and got lost on the way to the 'Under the Sea' Disney party.

The next pair of guests are heading towards the door, but they have their Burberry bags open ready as they spot more goodies. As these are the ladies from *Marie Claire* and *Vogue*, they have near-goddess status. Sophie loads them up with swag, then passes them a flowery cup and saucer each. 'One last cocktail before you go? Peach, champagne and elderflower, or raspberry vodka with rosemary and grenadine?' She waves in the tea pot girl.

Ms *Vogue* smiles as she sips her drink and rearranges her windblown bob. 'It's a whistle stop visit; I'm afraid we've mostly been outside enjoying the sea views and talking to your *delightful* husband.' No surprise there. Even though he'd never look at another woman, Nate is particularly swoon-worthy and super attentive in all the right places.

Ms *Marie Claire* waves immaculate pale brown nails at the ragged layers of my skirt – or should that be my tail? 'The mermaids are a lovely touch. But there's one last question we *have* to ask before we go.' Her voice drops to a whisper and she leans so close her Black Opium cloud makes my head spin. 'Is it true that your algae scrub treatment is used by Kim Kardash—?'

Apart from the pink glow to her cheeks, Sophie has been unruffled by her high-powered guests. But she's dipped behind them now, and she's making desperate throat-cutting signs.

I'm not the best at thinking on my feet, but Sophie's agonised stare has me jumping in so fast I cut Ms *Marie Claire* off in mid name-drop. 'We're absolutely not at liberty to say.' No idea where that came from. But I'm pretty damned impressed with my speed.

Ms *Marie Claire*'s eyes are popping. 'You've signed her *confidentiality clause*?' She claps her hands together triumphantly. 'Don't say anything more, that's everything we need to know. We'll be in touch next week about a feature.'

Sophie's nodding frantically now, gesturing me to carry on.

I'm racking my brains trying to remember what's upmarket London-speak for 'great'. Or anything English would do. All I can think of is *chouette,* which is French for 'owl', but means 'cool'. 'Lovely ... sick ... fabulous ... jolly brill ...' As the words flood out, I'm getting throat cutting signs from Sophie again.

By the time my rush has subsided, Ms *Marie Claire has* downed her drink, taken a sea life 'selfie', and as they hurry off to catch their train, I'm already up on Instagram.

I shake my head at Sophie. 'Shit. They were decisive. What was all that about?'

Sophie gives a guilty squirm. 'We don't *actually* supply Kim. I just couldn't bring myself to throw away the chance of so much national exposure.' Her face breaks into a grin as Plum and Nell swish across to join us. 'Fab team effort here, we've just nailed *Vouge* and *Marie Claire*. And as it's so long since we've had all you mer-girls together in one place, I need a picture myself.'

When I say Sophie and I go way back, I'm not exaggerating. I mean all the way to our mums meeting up at the 'Mums and Bumps' group when they were pregnant. Plum and Nell were very late to the party because we only met them at Tumble Tots. Our whole childhood we danced, played, went to the beach, fought, had picnics and grew up together running wild over long lazy summers. Some of us have gone away and come back again. But somehow we're all still here for each other, and still the firmest of friends.

Sophie slides out her phone. 'At least you won't be on Insta in a bikini top made from scallop shells, which was what Plum originally planned.'

Plum was born 'Victoria', but that was never going to work on a round, rosy-cheeked toddler, so to us she's always been Plum. She pushes back her dark silky hair and squints down her slashed silk neckline to her non-existent cleavage and lets out a groan. 'Shells were my only hope of making my mer-boobs look bigger.'

Sadly, as fast as she shed her chub I gained it. These days Plum is Topshop skinny but I'm Bravissimo all the way. While some of us struggle to zip up our large size 14s, her skimpy size 8s billow in the wind. But even if she looks every inch the hungry artist, in reality she's anything but. The gallery we're in now was a disused chandlery until Plum got her hands on it soon after leaving art college. She stripped it out to use as a studio, and over the years has turned it into a thriving business selling pieces for other artists as well as herself. Although, obviously, it doesn't quite have the multi-million turnover of Sophie May.

After a swift glance round the lofty white room and the six-foot-high seascapes, Plum turns back to me. 'A quick warning now the local crowd's arriving. Word on the street is you're back to move into a penthouse, Clemmie.' There's a mischievous glint in her eye. 'Most people's money is on the snazzy new apartments at Rock Quay.'

If you want to keep your life private, don't come to St Aidan. Although I've timed my trip to catch Sophie's launch party, my main reason for returning is because the sitting tenant's moved out of the flat I inherited by default years ago. But even if I'd got my hands on a mansion, I'd still have no intention of sticking around.

I can't help my grin at how wrong the St Aidan grapevine is. 'It's more of an ancient attic from what I remember. And believe me, I won't be here for long.'

Plum winds a strand of hair around her fingers. 'Bangkok still buzzing? Or is it Stockholm? Or was that Prague?'

I can't blame her for not keeping up. 'It's actually Paris and it's great, thanks – for now.' There's no point saying any more. Plum, Sophie and Nell are so in love with St Aidan's jumble of pastel coloured cottages clinging to the hillside, they couldn't exist anywhere else. They're all as settled as I am rootless. They can't imagine living without the echo of the waves rushing up the beach, and the familiar clink of the rigging on the boats bobbing in the harbour. If I explained non-stop for a month, they'd never get that for me St Aidan isn't enough. That after half a day away from Paris, I'm aching for the broad boulevards and big elegant buildings and the round-the-clock roar of the traffic. They don't get that the world beyond here is huge. And they totally miss that when Paris dulls I'll move on and feel the thrill all over again somewhere new. Even though my jobs are what they call 'shit' ones, and my career trajectory is non-existent, at least they allow me to move. To be free.

Nell comes in for the last macaroon. 'So what are you doing this time?' She's a hot shot accountant, who admits the lure of her job is the salary not the excitement. So, she's always up for hearing my more outlandish work stories.

I start to take a deep breath but stop halfway. In the five years since Sophie's wedding, my dress must have shrunk in the wardrobe. A lot. 'At the moment, I run errands for Maude, who teaches at the Sorbonne. I open her jars of fish soup. Buy her artichokes from the market. Top up her Post-it note supplies. Check she hasn't got lettuce stuck in her teeth when she leaves the flat. Stuff like that. She's addicted to tea and needs Liptons on the hour. And a Porn Star Martini on the dot of five.' I worked my way round the world doing bar work, but lately I've progressed to personal assistant positions. And this one sounds a lot more awful than it is. There's time to dash out between brews. I get Friday afternoons off when Maude goes to her masseuse. Best of all, the job comes with a room and a view. When I stand on tiptoe and wrench my neck I can see the Eiffel Tower from my window. You've no idea how magical it is to look out at that shadow of crisscross of pencil lines in the day, the trace of pin prick lights in the dark.

'Even better, I've got a few weeks paid leave while she's away on a research trip, which is why I've made my dash to Cornwall now.' I'm beaming because this is the first holiday pay I've ever got my hands on. The circle of faces is much less impressed than I'd anticipated. I don't quite get why, but I'm staring at a mix of puzzlement and despair.

When Nell breaks the silence, she's sounding bright and the subject change is jarring. 'Well, the good news here is our St Aidan's Singles scene is buzzing, so it's great you'll be around for that. We're doing Strictly Single Tea Dances at the Harbourside Hotel, Scare Yourself Shitless Ghost Walks, Under the Table Gin Tasting at the Hungry Shark, and our Whale Watching Weekend boat trips around the bay are always brilliant.' That's the other thing about Nell. Since her break-up a couple of years ago she's thrown herself into the Singles' Club.

How things change when you're gone. 'There are whales in the bay?'

Nell's brow furrows. 'Not exactly. But the trips are proving better than Loctite as far as couples go.' The only problem is, she's so immersed in organising everyone else, so far she's failed to grab a man for herself. She lets out a low laugh. 'Leave it to me, we'll give you a reason to stay in St Aidan, Clemmie.'

What was I saying? My appalled gasp is so huge and unchecked, this time I almost do split my dress. 'Hold it there. Count me out of *any* couply activities. I'm a hundred per cent *NOT here to hook up.*' The life I live is just for me and I don't need complications. The few guys I went out with at college were all more effort than fun. Which doesn't mean I don't have loads of friends, a lot of whom are guys. In fact, as more people are arriving, I'm bobbing up and down non-stop waving at people over Sophie's shoulder.

Nell's not going to be put off. 'Fine, skip the singles' events. But there are some really nice, genuine guys in our group. It can't hurt to introduce you ... to one or two?'

If I thought dressing up as a mermaid was bad this is worse. I put up my hand. The one thing I've learned in Paris is if you want respect, good service, and halfway decent artichokes, there's no point coming over all nice and friendly. It's the 'don't mess with me' 'mean bitch' expressions that get the un-burned baguettes. I scrunch my face into my best French scowl. 'No activities, no introductions, is that clear?' I don't wait for a reply. Apart from anything else, I'm bursting for a pee. Not that I'd planned to use the loos tonight given how thoroughly we did up the tail ties. But those mismatched tea cups hold more than you'd think. 'And now I'm off to the Ladies'.' As I grin at Nell to show her there's no bad feeling so long as she's got the message, I notice her mermaid shell crown is completely skew whiff. Looks like I'm not the only one who's over done the fruit cup. I turn around, throw my foot forward to stride purposefully away, hit my tail tie, then begin to topple.

'Whoops, steady there!' Sophie and Plum catch one arm each and gently ease me upwards until I find my balance point.

Plum's scratching at the seaweed dangling from her pearl head band. 'Maybe next time we do this, we need *elastic* rope around our ankles?' For an artist, she's very analytical.

I can't believe what I'm hearing as I set off again. 'There's going to be a *next* time?'

When I reach the loo, it turns out my fears about finding my pants are completely right. Put it this way – real mermaids are damned lucky they can pee in the sea. I have so much tulle and fish net to untangle before I can go, and I don't put half enough effort into getting it back into the right place again. As I shuffle back into the gallery my tail's as saggy as if I've collided with one of those heaps of abandoned nets down by the harbour. I feel more like a *Strictly* dancer who got caught in a wind tunnel than a silver-tailed siren as I press myself against the rough white-washed wall as a group of guys pass, all waving their tea cups in appreciation of Plum and Nell's costumes.

Despite my firm stand, as I arrive back, Nell's providing me with a running commentary of everyone in trousers I don't already know. 'That was Blue Watch, arriving from the fire station. And I'm sorry but the total hottie in the suit by the Cleanse and Polish stand is someone I don't know.' She sends Sophie a querying glance.

Sophie scans the crowd. 'Hot and then some. I think he's something to do with some property consortium.'

'And?' Nell's waiting expectantly. 'The least you can do for a jawline like that is check the guest list.'

Plum and Sophie both start peering at their phones, but Plum's first to look up.

'Got him. At a guess that's Charlie Hobson, he's down here as "local developer".'

Nell's got a gleam in her eye. 'I may have to Google him on behalf of the singles' group. Whale Watching would pass a whole lot quicker with that kind of dark charisma in the bows.'

'Dark being the important word there.' However much he

looks like he strode straight off the pages of *GQ* magazine, as expressions go, objectionable doesn't begin to cover it. If I was at sea with that particular long face I'd have to jump ship.

Sophie shakes her head at me. 'And the big blond man by the door is George Trenowden, our legal whizz. He's single but as he's your solicitor too, I take it you won't throw a wobbly if I introduce you once the crowds thin out.'

I ignore the jibe because it will be useful to meet him after years of only communicating by letter. 'Great, I'm seeing him about the flat first thing tomorrow.' Although I couldn't feel less enthusiastic about that.

Sophie laughs. 'No need to look so worried, he gave up eating mermaids years ago.' Her brow wrinkles. 'Do you want me to come with you to hold your hand?'

I can't think of anything better, but I didn't like to ask. 'Aren't you busy?'

She whips out her phone again. 'Let's check the family spreadsheet. Milla's at school, my mum's taking Marco and Matilde, so that only leaves Maisie.' Her face breaks into a grin. 'It says here that tomorrow morning is officially booked out for *hangover recovery*. So, Maisie and I are all yours.'

'In that case I'll celebrate with more macaroons.' I'd hate to see *any* go to waste after all the effort I put in. And I'll risk another cocktail too. I point myself towards the drinks station. 'Anyone like anything bringing over?'

Nell perks up. 'If you strike up a convo with the lush Mr Hobson you could tow him back with you. We always need more men at events.'

I pull a face. 'As if.'

Sophie checks her phone. 'Don't spoil your appetite, the bakery is bringing in food soon.' She's forgetting, when it comes to me and eating there's no such thing as too full.

As if to cue the start of the party, the Serenity Spa music that's been wafting around us cuts out, and after a beat of silence the Sugababes start belting out 'Push the Button'. As I dance my way through the crowd, I'm careful to stay well away from any suited shoulders. But I'm only halfway to the edge of the room when there's a shout: 'Pies are ready!' The next thing I know the crush of bodies is enough to lift me off my feet. By the time I've grappled my way to the refreshment table I'm breathless. I grab a handful of macaroons from what's left of the tower, then close my eyes to savour the moment. As the sweet almond deliciousness melts onto my tongue a low voice rumbling in my ear brings me crashing back to reality.

'Do pasties always cause a stampede in St Aidan?'

As I open my eyes a glimpse of a grey jacket cuff has me spitting out my buttercream. 'Only the hot ones.' I'm silently cursing because I've landed next to the one guy I meant to avoid. Up close his eye lashes and his scowl are both blacker than they were from a distance. If I'm swallowing hard at the sight of his slightly loosened tie knot and the open top button of his shirt it has to be because I don't come across many guys dressed for the board room. In the bars where I serve drinks if you meet a James Bond lookalikey he'll probably be in fancy dress. To judge from Charlie's glower, either he hates product launches, or he's rocking the male equivalent of the resting bitch face. But there's something so raw about the moody shadows under his cheekbones that for a second my heart squishes.

'I suppose canapés haven't reached Cornwall yet? Personally, I'd rather stick with these.' He couldn't sound more bored but as he waves a macaroon at me his frown deepens. 'Did you know you have a starfish stuck in your hair?'

When someone really doesn't get the irony, you have to take the piss. Especially when you're kicking yourself for being ridiculous enough to let the word 'sexy' flash through your head when the man in question really isn't at all. 'That's where I store my starfish until I'm hungry. It's what mermaids do when they come ashore.' I know I'm getting way too far into character, but he's the one who's missing the joke here.

He gives a bemused stare as he wolfs down his macaroon then holds out his hand. 'Well, great to meet you, *and* your surviving starfish. I'm Charlie Hobson, I work for Bay Holdings.' His heartfelt sigh suggests there's nothing 'great' about this for him.

Unlike Nell, I'm not falling over to introduce myself to random strangers, especially not ones who are faking their enthusiasm, so I dodge his hand. I'm not that impressed by corporate credentials either. But on behalf of local mermaids, I reckon I should be pushing this. 'So which "bay" would that be?'

'*All* the bays.' As he takes his hand back and picks up a leather zip folder from the table there's finally a glint of interest in his eyes. 'Wherever there's development potential we'll maximise it. We're working our way around the coastline.' He makes it sound chillingly methodical. Scary news for locals *and* sea creatures then.

Nell's giving me a double thumbs up as she threads her way through the crowd towards us. From her excited bounce, she can't have any idea how dull Charlie Hobson is.

I grab a stack of macaroons and a tea pot, fill some tea cups, and manage to loop my fingers through three handles. 'Great, well enjoy the rest of the party, Charlie, is it?' I'm saying this ironically too, because it's obvious he wouldn't know a good time if it hit him on his perfectly chiselled designer-stubbled chin. 'And good luck with whichever bays you decide to plunder.' It's a bit heavy on the well wishes, but as a parting shot it's got a nice ring. I'm aiming for a tail swing and a grand exit without spilling the cocktails. But as I swish around, there's a tug on my thigh, like a rope tightening. 'What the ...?'

A deep growl echoes my cry. '... hell are you doing?' Mr Hobson is holding his zip folder at arm's length, and the further he lifts it up, the more my netting lifts too.

I let out a hiss. 'Your man bag's caught on my netting.'

No idea how Nell does it, but in two bounds she covers the length of the room. 'Just give it a pull, Charlie, that should set her free.' She's skipped the intros and gone straight to ordering him around. 'Go on then.'

'Or we could ...' I'm squeaking, still hanging on to my biscuits and cups. 'Is it too much to ask to unravel it gently?'

Nell shakes her head. 'Leave it to *us, we've* got this. One two three, *go* ...'

As Charlie wrenches at the folder the yank he gives is big enough to pull a lifeboat ashore. My cocktails fly out of their cups as I lurch, let out a yelp, then my entire tail pulls free. It sails through the air, skittles a tea cup and demolishes the remains of the macaroon tower as it thumps onto the table. I stand open mouthed as the macaroons explode off the walls and skid across the floor.

'Jeez.' Charlie Hobson's personal gloom cloud has turned thunderous.

'Sacré starfish.' Even though I'm staring down at the skimpy skirt of my bridesmaid's dress, without my tail I feel strangely undressed.

Plum's already here, tutting and whisking the net up off the table. 'This wouldn't have happened if we'd used elastic.'

Then Sophie gives the tail a shake. And a few moments later, they've wrapped it around me, and twisted the fastenings back into place. 'There you go. Good as new.'

Nell's bobbing about picking up macaroons, oblivious of the developer disapproval. 'And I thought you said you weren't going to hook up with anyone? Now, Clemmie, are you finally going to introduce us all?'

From what I've seen so far I'd advise running a mile from Mr Hobson, not getting to know him better. But I know when I'm beaten so I grit my teeth and get on with it. 'Charlie, this is the one and only Sophie May whose event this is, Plum owns the gallery, and Nell is St Aidan's most prolific event organiser.' Hopefully that covers it.

Nell's straight in there. 'Lovely to meet you at last, Charlie. Can we offer you some product samples?'

I smile at Sophie to cover up Nell's blatant manoeuvre. 'Mr Hobson's big on coasts, if you've got any unspoiled coves I'm sure he'll be happy to take those off your hands. Cosmetics not so much.' I make it sound jokey for Sophie's benefit, but I flash Charlie a dead eye so he knows it's not.

Nell ignores me, senses Charlie's hesitation and goes in for the kill. 'You could always take some for your wife ... or your girlfriend? That's what the other men have been doing.'

Charlie puts up his hand. 'No, I'm good, thanks.' If Nell pushes far enough to ask if his mother might like some instead, I suspect he might implode.

Nell raises an eyebrow, digs down into her tail nets, and pulls out a leaflet. 'In which case you may like to take this?'

Someone's got to wind this up, and I suspect it's going to be me. 'You'll have to excuse Nell, she's a bit of an evangelist. When it comes to the Singles' Club, she's St Aidan's fairy godmother, feel free to ignore her.'

Charlie looks like he can't wait to escape. 'I'm definitely not searching for a partner. But if you insist, some cleanser for my mum? Or a few more macaroons?' Of three hundred guests, he's the only person to take the swag and make out he's the one doing *us* a favour. And still look miserable about it.

'Our pleasure.' Despite the knock back, Nell looks triumphant as she hands him his goodies.

He holds up his bag. 'Thanks, it's been great to meet you all, but I have a dinner meeting to get to.' He's wheeling out the fake 'great' again. The flicker of a smile on his lips is probably because he's ecstatic to leave, but even that doesn't reach his eyes. He turns to me. 'Can I offer you a lift home – seeing as I defrocked you?'

There's no harm in telling it like it is. 'Thanks, but I don't actually have a home. In any case, I'd probably rather swim.' I'm clinging onto my mer-persona but being completely true to my human self here as I give him a goodbye wave.

Nell watches his back all the way to the door, then turns to me. 'You two have a lot in common.' She narrows her eyes. 'Both defiantly single, both macaroon obsessed ...'

He also has the biggest scowl this side of John O' Groats. Which is only one of the hundred reasons I have to close this down. 'That's where it ends, okay? Shut up now, clam face.'

And that's my first evening in St Aidan. Which is exactly why I can't wait to leave.

2

In Trenowden, Trenowden and Trenowden Solicitors' office
Peeling paint and sticky breakfasts
Thursday

'Your grandmother was a great believer in matriarchal lineage.'

You know that thing where you've no idea what someone's talking about? As the solicitor's words float past me I gaze at Sophie, who's effortlessly managed to nail looking cool and in control. Even though it's barely nine and she's bouncing Maisie on her knee, there's not a crinkle in her perfectly pressed pale blue chinos, or the hint of that humungous hangover she's penciled in for. Sophie's the only person I know who could juggle a baby and a fistful of carrot sticks and still keep her top pristine white. I stare past her through the small paned window to the cottages clustering along the harbour's edge. As the morning sun sparks off the water I blink away the shadow of a headache, curse those tricksy cocktail cups, and force myself to concentrate. 'Sorry?'

Behind the desk, George Trenowden lets out a sigh. We only managed to wave at each other last night, but in the office, he's way bigger than he looked across the gallery. This big blond bear of a guy apparently handles so much business for Sophie they're on bestie terms. Even though Trenowden, Trenowden and Trenowden have been managing the tenanted flat since it was left to me all those years ago, the only other time I came to their office, the Trenowden I saw was a generation older and in Penzance. Although I'd say wrenching our hands off with his hand shake when we arrived came across as more painful than friendly. Despite my fingers still being in recovery, I'm crossing them tightly, hoping he was out on the deck when I lost my netting last night.

Even worse, what if he's looking across the desk, and doing that thing where he can't help seeing last night's mermaid outfit superimposed on top of the flowery cotton dress I put on earlier, mistakenly thinking it was spring? This is why fancy dress should be banned. And why I make sure I move often enough to leave the embarrassing stuff behind. With any luck, in a minute he'll say something I can understand.

'The flat your grandmother left you, which is finally vacant? The reason you're here?' He cocks a pale eyebrow at me, checking I'm back in the room. 'I understand Laura chose to pass it on to you rather than her grandsons.'

I shrug, fix my gaze on the toe of my suede ankle boot and spot what looks a lot like a soggy rice crispie cluster. Hurrah to Sophie's kid's and their overflowing cereal bowls, although organic and soaked in almond milk doesn't help me here. As for the shoes, I know mine will be the only feet in St Aidan not in flip flops or baseball boots, but I had heels welded to my feet when I was fourteen so I'd look less dumpy. Even if St Aidan is a heel wearer's minefield of granite steps and sand piles, for the short time I'm here I'll work with them. And where do I put a piece of stray breakfast in a solicitor's office? As I pick it off and close my hand around it, I'm wishing I'd kept my *I'd rather be shoe shopping* sleep shirt on, if only to express how much I'd rather be anywhere else than here.

It sounds ridiculous to say that me and my late grandmother weren't related, but that's how it is in my head. Mostly I know Laura from her neat pointy handwriting on parcels that arrived on every significant day throughout my childhood. She must have been one of those people who are great at buying presents because the contents were usually spot on. But the excitement was mostly eclipsed by how tetchy they made my otherwise happy mum. When Laura died and the flat unexpectedly came to me, I was too busy partying to take much notice. The rent covered the maintenance, the solicitors handled everything, and up until now I've managed to pretty much dodge the reality of being a property owner. As for the rest of Laura's family details, I'm deliberately in the dark. For my whole life, I've made it my business to know as little about the Marlows as I can.

'I'm not sure about her other grandchildren, she wasn't my actual ...' I tail off, then as Sophie sends me a smile, I try again. 'Apart from when I was small I never really knew her.'

My biological dad chose to jump the channel rather than be with my mum and me, but as the old saying goes, I didn't miss what I never had. My mum was the best. With the two of us in our little cottage there really wasn't space for a dad. And that's why my extended mermaid family have always been so important to me. Then when I was five my mum fell in love with a man called Harry who *was* worth the trouble, so Harry's the one I count as my real father. When someone has your back every moment while you're growing up and beyond, that top trumps absent DNA a thousand times. Which is probably why I feel like a fraud sitting here now, claiming something that doesn't feel as if it should be mine.

George clears his throat and smiles at me. 'By the way, no ill effects after yesterday, I hope, Clementine?'

I smile back, cringing inside, hoping I don't have the foggiest what he's talking about. 'Ill effects?'

His face cracks into a grin. 'St Aidan Sirens' Charter, rule sixty-seven, stealing tails is strictly forbidden.'

Shit. So, he is looking at me and seeing a mermaid. And he must have seen my 'worst moment' too. I grit my teeth, but before I can mumble a reply, Sophie jumps in.

'No sea life was harmed during the launch party. You know how stringent our wildlife and nature policies are, you drafted the damn things. Shall we move on now?'

'Sure.' George sounds reluctant. 'They were fabulous costumes though. I'll pass that on to Charlie Hobson too. He'll be very relieved to hear you survived and won't be suing.'

Oh my days. I could have done without a name check for my grumpy accidental tail stealer. I can't blame George for letting his mind wander off his legal job first thing on a Thursday morning, but someone needs to get this man back on task before I expire with embarrassment. 'Weren't we talking about matriarchy?' Maybe I was listening after all.

'Right. Thanks for the reminder, Clementine. Passing property down the female line is well documented, but the point in your case is, whatever her son's actions, Laura didn't want *you* to be short changed. Looking through the papers, it's obvious she wanted the best for you. And she was also wise enough to let the flat on a long tenancy, so you only took possession and had the deeds transferred into your name when you were mature enough to handle it.' He sends a glance Sophie's way to check she's approving. Although, if she wasn't, realistically she'd have butted in by now and shut him up. 'So now the tenant has finally moved out, I assume you're here to pick up the keys before we finalise the legal side?'

Sophie's nodding enthusiastically enough for both of us.

Although I've known about this for the best part of fifteen years, it's as if I'm staring the enormity of it in the face for the first time. And being called Clementine is so rare it actually makes me feel like he's talking to someone else rather than me. Not that I mean to behave like a spoiled, ungrateful bitch, but there's something holding me back. I frown and drag in a breath. 'I wasn't ready for a key. Not quite today.' Although realistically, if not a key, what was I expecting? 'Actually, I'm not sure I want the flat at all. Now it comes to it, I don't even want to go there.'

George's forehead furrows as he takes in the level of my reluctance. But then he smiles the kind of smile that stretches all the way through to his voice. 'Don't worry, knowing the background I completely understand. If you'd rather sell, the market's strong. We could arrange for the contents to be cleared, and handle the sale for you?'

Better and better. 'Okay …' I'd got my head round spending a couple of weeks in blustery old Cornwall, but this way I can head straight back to Paris and ease my itchy feet.

George picks up a picture from the desk and starts to rub

some invisible dust off. 'The flat's a little tired, or as the agents say, "ripe for restoration". But with those open vistas across the bay, no doubt buyers will be queueing up.'

'It has sea views?' The mention of restoration had Sophie quivering, but her last lurch of excitement is so large she almost launches Maisie over the desk. '*Where* is it exactly?' She whips round and fixes me with the same 'ravenous wolf' look that took her cosmetics from her kitchen table to John Lewis best-sellers in under ten years.

I give a clueless shrug. 'Somewhere between the harbour and the sea front. The last time I was there I probably wasn't tall enough to see out of the window.' I went there as a child, before Laura moved to be closer to her son. I can picture a velvet chair the colour of a flamingo. A musical box. Serious amounts of cake and icing. Then my mum pulling me across the cobbled quayside, hurrying us back up to our cottage up the hill.

George puts down the photo and looks up. 'It's a top floor flat in Seaspray Cottage, the rambling pile at the far end of the quay.'

Sophie lets out a shriek. 'Not the place with peeling paint and the long ocean facing balcony?'

'That's the one.' He nods.

She rounds on him. 'Shit a brick, George, if you'd told me that I wouldn't have let Clemmie mess around for weeks. I'd have had her on the next plane home.'

He's laughing at her now. 'However much you bully me, I can't tell you *all* my secrets.'

She sniffs. 'You never actually tell me *any*.' Then she turns to me. 'Are you bat-shit crazy, Clemmie? Of course, we'll take the damn keys. You're looking, not committing, okay?'

The reminder of commitment sets my alarm bells jangling. 'What about repairs? And common areas? And meter readings?' If I sound absurd and random it's because these are my mum's questions not mine. In the depths of my bag there's a crumpled reality-check list she wrote out for me before she left for South America. If I'd intended to use it, I'd have read it more carefully.

George blows out his cheeks. 'The Residents' Committee handles most things. They've been a bit fierce with their rules over the years. But let's deal with the detail down the line.'

Sophie catches my appalled groan. 'Sweat the boring stuff later, Clems. Only when you have to. Do you have the keys?' Then her hand shoots out across the desk, George's drawer opens and the keys drop into her palm before I've stopped choking. She jingles them at George as she shoves Maisie and I towards the door. 'Expect us back in half an hour.'

'Lovely to have you in the office, Clementine.' Before you can say 'soggy cereal', George has my hand and its contents in the kind of power press that could crush molecules.

Whatever the theories on disappearing dark matter, when I get my palm back it's entirely crispie free. Maybe George won't be quite so pleased when Maisie's breakfast resurfaces on his designer suit.

He calls after us. 'Make sure you work your magic, Sophie Potato. St Aidan could definitely do with another mermaid.'

As Sophie propels me past the empty desk in reception, I let out a shocked squawk. 'Did he just call you Sophie Potato?' That was her name from when we were kids, because she refused to eat anything other than Smash. It went nicely with Nellie Melon and Victoria Plum.

She lets out a laugh. 'First rule of great business, keep your enemies close and your solicitor closer. He can be quite playful once he lets himself go, those childhood names of ours are a great way to get him to loosen up. When he hears you're Clemmie Orangina, there won't be any more of this Clementine shit. Have you noticed how much he sounds like he's got a poker rammed up his butt when he gives you your full title?' There's no room for a reply, because she's spotted a cardboard sign that's propped on the desk where the receptionist should be sitting. She snatches it up. 'Yay, Trenowden, Trenowden and Trenowden have a short-term vacancy for a front of house assistant. Their usual treasure Janet is off because her daughter's had twins. How auspicious is that? Talk about good timing and heaven sent all rolled into one.'

I'm picking up my jaw off the floor as she rams the sign into her changing bag. 'Tell me you're not stealing their sign?'

Her grin is inscrutable. 'Borrowing's a better word. Winning for Beginners, watch and learn. No point leaving the job ad lying around when the perfect applicant is already in the building.'

As I screw up my face, I'm squeaking. 'You've got four children, a factory, and a marketing team. How do you have time to do extra hours?' Sophie has always been big on moonlighting, and huge on ambition. But even for a high achieving workaholic, adding this job in is ridiculous.

She lets out a laugh. 'Not me, silly, this one's got your name all over it. It'll be a perfect fit while you refurbish the flat. Let's face it, you're going to need to earn something to pay for paint. And seeing as it's temporary, you won't feel trapped.'

Considering George just gave me the perfect get out for the flat, she's jumping ahead to a place I don't intend to go. 'Who said anything about decorating?' Apart from anything else, the biggest area I've painted in my entire life is my nails. And although I like a colour change every day I have trouble with them if they get too long.

'Not meaning to be ageist, but the flat's bound to be old-person magnolia. A quick lick of warm white and the occasional feature wall will add thousands to the sale price. You *have* to do it.' The determined set of her jaw tells me it's pointless to object. 'More importantly, think of all the hot guys who come to see George. Once you're behind that desk, we'll find you a keeper before you can say, "Power of Attorney".'

I thought I made it clear last night. 'Don't confuse me with Nell here, I'm not the one who's heartbroken, lonely and on the lookout. I'm single because I love my freedom. I just spent three months *not* hooking up with ten million Parisians, I don't see anyone from tiny, dull St Aidan changing my mindset.'

She lets out a sigh. 'Globe trotting's great when you're twenty. But perpetual motion isn't the answer to inner happiness and harmony when you're the wrong side of thirty.'

I have to tell her. 'Quite apart from the Hygge shit, you sound as "stay at home and boring" as my mum.' She used to love me travelling because it's what she wanted to do but never did. But since I passed the big three zero she comes out with Sophie's mantra so often she sounds like she's on repeat.

'That would be your amazing mum who's so un-adventurous she's currently spending six months on a Peruvian mountain top?' Her triumphant nod as she pushes through the exit door says she thinks she's won this round.

'They're visiting hillside villages not climbing peaks.' She and

Harry have gone to spend six months working on an out-reach health education programme.

'You know what I mean.' Sophie grins over her shoulder at me. 'And right on cue to prove my point about George's handsome client base, look who's coming.'

'Oh shit.' My headache was easing, but a full-frontal view of Charlie Hobson speeding towards us across the cobbles has my brain hammering against my skull again. When I party in Paris I can't find people afterwards even if I want to. Here in St Aidan, it's not even nine and the guy I'd hoped never to see again is right under my nose.

Sophie jumps in. 'Hello, Charlie, how are you this morning?'

He wiggles his eyebrows at Maisie but by the time he looks up again he's frowning at his phone. 'Running late, but thanks for the party last night.' As he pops his head round to where I'm skulking behind the changing bag he still hasn't cracked a smile. That far-away, empty look in his eyes has to come from too many dodgy deals. 'No tail today? Did someone do a better job of stealing it than me ... or did you decide Friday was a good day to be a human?'

I can't believe what he's handed me here. 'Actually, it's Thursday.' I pause for the words to sink in. 'In which case you're probably a day early for your appointment.'

He pulls a face. 'Thanks for reminding me.' He flashes a glance at Sophie. 'Any confusion, blame the cocktails. Next time you serve dynamite in a tea pot maybe you should warn the guests.'

Sophie rises above that and narrows her eyes at me. 'There you go, girl, you're a natural.' She turns her focus onto Charlie. 'Put a word in for Clemmie with George, she's first in the queue to be his new receptionist, just what he needs to put his customers at ease.'

I purse my lips and stay silent. The only way to deal with Sophie in her 'conquer the world' mood is to go with her. Then clear up the wreckage afterwards.

'I will – even if she does make me mix my days up.' He sighs, then as he swings through the door to his appointment his face finally creases into a grimace rather than a smile. 'Although any day's a great day for a deal.'

I groan and wait for the door to close. 'Did he really say that? And there goes proof that looks and personality don't always go together.' Although Maisie seems smitten. And when he finally managed that sardonic wince he did have those creases in his cheeks that make your knees give way. And teeth. Beautiful, not-quite-perfect incisors. 'Imagine if you had to face that every morning, you'd be so queasy breakfast would be impossible.' And damn for letting that slip out.

Sophie raises an eyebrow. 'Queasy? What kind of queasy?'

I push my hand on my stomach to stall the churning and swallow hard. 'No, you're right, it would take more than the thought of ugly buildings to put me off my pain au chocolat.' I think I got away with that. Swooning at alpha males is what we take the piss out of, not what we do. Like everyone else on the harbour, I'll blame the cocktails.

Sophie's frown is rivalling Charlie's. 'According to Nate, the Hobson signature move is to buy up rows of cottages one by one, then bulldoze them and shoe horn super-expensive flats into the plots. No doubt about it, he's here to price out the locals and destroy our village.'

'Trouble on legs then.' Although I suspect I knew that already.

She nods. 'The man's a wrecker. He does exactly the same with large detached villas.'

'Everything we *don't* want here.' I'm surprised how fighty and defensive I feel considering how happy I usually am to wave goodbye to the place.

Sophie's nostrils are flaring. 'He's hell bent on buying up St Aidan one brick at a time. Although obviously, we aren't going to let him.' She gives me a significant stare. 'We could do with keeping close tabs on him, if you fancy building on your acquaintance. However crass he sounds he's not short on smoulder.'

Sometimes I think she's deaf. 'Absolutely not.' It comes out *so* loud, I have to back pedal. 'Thanks all the same. Now how about seeing this flat?' And who'd have thought I'd be rushing her into this?

3

At Seaspray Cottage
Thunderstorms and Surprise Rainbows
Thursday

'So what do you think, Clemmie? Can you remember any of it?'

Sophie and I are standing outside Seaspray Cottage with our backs to the turning tide as we take in the peeling render, the slender bay windows, and a slate roof that's shining like hammered silver against the cornflower sky. The paintwork is weathered to the colour of the beach and the letters on the name board are so faded the only way we know we're in the right place is the balcony above that looks so precarious it could be held up by invisible hooks to the sky. As we make our way towards the front door the slant of the steps makes me stagger.

'When George said "past its sell by date", that was an understatement. It's shot to frigg, end of story. Time to walk away?' I wasn't expecting to be proved right quite this soon.

Sophie sounds thoughtful. 'A lot of people think patina is

characterful. In any case, the cottage is bound to get all the weather because it's placed to get the views in three directions.'

I'm scrunching up my face as I wrack my brain. 'I don't remember it being at a dead end.' Somehow the cottage is marooned beyond the quayside where the road runs out into a small path across the dunes that cuts through to the sea front. With every wind gust the sand's blowing up the beach, over the low boundary wall, and drifting into the garden that extends back beyond the sides of the cottage. Although it's small in scale, with its three storeys and repeating windows, it's larger than it looks at first.

Sophie's suppressing a smile. 'As it's so close to the sea I'm guessing the name is more real than romantic.'

Worse and worse. 'You mean the water actually blasts against the windows?' Not that I was enthusiastic to begin with, but imagining cold brine hammering on the glass on stormy days is making my shivers seismic.

She laughs. 'Don't worry, it's only Seaspray Cottage, not Splash House or Tidal Wave Towers.' Shifting Maisie in her arms, Sophie fishes in her bag for the keys. 'Now we've come this far we might as well go in and see the dereliction inside.'

Instead of the anticipated struggle with a rust encrusted lock, the key turns easily, and the door swings open without a creak. Then as we step into a pale buff hallway filled with splashes of sunlight the familiarity is so jarring my feet stop moving before I've stepped off the neat coir door mat.

'The smell's just the same. How strange is that?'

Sophie wrinkles her nose and somehow manages not to crash into my back. 'Fresh salty air ... and the beeswax on those ancient floor boards?'

My words come slowly, as if I'm dragging them from very far away. 'With a hint of rosemary and thyme ... because that's what grew in the herb patch at the side of the cottage. They used to mix the leaves into the polish.' There isn't time to wonder how I know that because I'm darting forwards again. 'And there's the staircase, at the end of the hall.' Even though I can't see past the first flight of steps, I already know. 'On the way to the top floor it winds so tightly the steps run out to nothing at the edge. And there are creaky bits on the landing where the boards groan.' Like timbers on an old ship. Wasn't that what Laura used to say?

Sophie's giving me a searching look. 'The paintwork's better in here too. Are we going for a look?'

My diffident shrug is misleading. The weird thing is, I couldn't stay away now even if I wanted to. I'm trying to play down that there's an invisible force drawing me upwards. 'We might as well. Before we do the sensible thing and leave.' My fingers are already stroking the silky smoothness of the bannister rail.

I wind my way up two floors so fast that by the time Sophie arrives, panting from carrying Maisie, I'm already at the landing window that opens onto the balcony, staring across the expanse of sand to where the sea is glinting way down the beach.

'I'm ignoring that stupendous view for now. Here you go ... flat six.' Sophie waves another key, and one click later the door on the left of the window is ajar.

I hold my breath as I tiptoe in. Then as I look around at a room crammed with cosy sofas and tables and shelves full of books I let out a gasp. 'Oh my, the same furniture's still here, it's like I've flipped back thirty years.' Whatever I was expecting, it wasn't to step into a time warp. Although up until this moment, just like with the thyme, and the creaky stairs, I'd mostly forgotten. And obviously now I'm seeing it as an adult, I'm appreciating the whole arty Bohemian patchwork of the room that I never saw as a child. 'It's still got the same cosy warmth, but I never realised it was quite this pretty or perfect.'

Sophie's patting a threadbare silk cushion, and fingering the corner of a stripy crocheted throw. 'Somehow I assumed it would be empty. We were wrong about the magnolia too.'

I'm blinking at the paint colours. There's raspberry and peacock and emerald and purple and orange and turquoise, although they're so worn and faded they merge like a water colour painting. 'It's like someone's tried every sample pot in the range.' Although that's wrong, because every clash works perfectly. I push through a scuffed turquoise door into a tiny hall and on into the next room, where the paint I can see in the gaps between an entire wall of pictures is shades of cerise.

Sophie follows me, nodding. 'Antique pink for the bedroom, you can't argue with that. And a high painted brass bedstead covered in silk quilts, how comfy does that look?'

I'm with her on that but I don't reply because I've already moved on to the bathroom. I let out a cry when I see the freestanding bath, then smile at the high cistern hanging on the wall above the loo. 'I had to climb up on a stool to pull that chain, and then run like the wind because the flush sounds like thunder. And those claws on the bath feet used to give me goosebumps.' We pass another smaller greener box room, and go back through to the living room.

Sophie's shaking her head in awe at the mismatched rugs. 'This makes me want to ditch neutral and be more adventurous with colour.' Her farmhouse is a mix of understated taste and expensive perfection, all in tones of white. Understandably, it took her and Nate years of effort and shit loads of cash to achieve. It probably only looks *so* beautiful and effortless and calming and uncluttered because every last knob, cushion and curtain tie has had the arse designed off it. 'So what haven't we seen yet?'

My hand's already on the door knob at the other end of the living room. 'I think this must be the kitchen.' Then, as I go in and take in the shelves filled with bowls and bright coloured plates and mugs and dishes, and the rows of hanging saucepans over the range cooker, it hits me. '*I know* what's missing here today. Laura loved to cook, so the flat was always filled with the smell of fresh baking.'

Sophie shifts Maisie onto her other hip, and leans across the windowsill to peep through one of the round topped windows. 'Amazing, you can see all the way to the houses at the end of St Aidan bay from here.' She turns to the rectangular table, squeezed in the centre. 'And look at those mismatched chairs and those fabulous patterned tiles by the sink.'

I can't help grinning. 'George mentioned it was worn out, but you have to love the petrol blue paint, and the hotch potch of cupboards, and the way that apple green dresser is properly distressed from years of use.' It's also groaning under the weight of a thousand recipe books. I run my hand over the work surface between the pottery sink and the cooker and shake my head as the memories come rushing back. 'This was where I used to sit when I helped Laura make butterfly buns in flowery paper cases.' Although mainly I was interested in licking out the mixing bowl. It's funny, although it's decades since I thought about that, I can imagine the vanilla sweetness of the buttercream and the crunch of the hundreds-and-thousands sprinkles as if it was yesterday.

'Probably the last time you went into a kitchen, was it?' Sophie gives me a gentle dig with her elbow. 'Until you stuck those macaroons together yesterday?' The mermaids never pass up an opportunity to point out how shit I am at cooking, although I get that from my mum. She's so bad Harry's in charge at home, and before Harry we relied on stab and zap and pitying neighbours. Even so, when it comes to eating, mum and I are equally enthusiastic. You only have to look at my Insta pics to know that. #gateauxofinstagram. The last four months I've made it my business to visit and test out most of the patisseries in Paris. I let out a sigh as I think of those fabulous glazed fruit tarts and my favourite *mille-feuille* custard pastry stacks, topped with the prettiest feathered icing.

I wander back through for a last look at the living room. As I perch on the edge of a velvet chair and stare out through the double doors that open to the outside from the living room, Sophie sinks down on a sofa bursting with cushions, and drops Maisie onto her knee.

'Tempted to go out on the balcony?'

'No chance.' I peer at the gaps between the sun-bleached planks. 'I'd rather sky dive, at least that way I'd be falling *with* a parachute.' I let out another sigh, because I hadn't expected to care about some rotten wood, let alone be disappointed at not getting to stand out there and feel the wind whipping through my hair.

Sophie sends me one of those searching glances of hers that pierce right through you. 'So has coming here made you change your mind about rushing into selling?'

I'm playing for time here, avoiding the issue. 'Have you noticed how the sea changes colour? It was way greener as we came in.' Now we're done, I'm strangely loath to leave. The dreamy part of me would like to forget about going back to give George the keys and sit up here and watch the sea all day. But the firm and practical voice in my head is shouting at me very loudly, telling me to get the hell out of here and leave George to sort the sale.

Sophie frowns. 'It's strange. When we arrived, I expected to have to work my butt off doing the hard sell. In fact, I haven't said a thing, yet there you are in your red flowery dress, looking like you've been here all your life.'

I owe it to Sophie to be honest. 'Actually, now I'm here I don't know what to think.' I've tried to take an over view rather than zooming in on the small stuff, but now I'm closer I can't help focusing on the parade of tiny wooden penguins marching along the shelf edge in front of the books. I don't even feel my arm move, and my hand has landed on the blue painted box next to them.

Sophie leans to see. 'Is that the musical box you told me about?'

My fingers are already twisting the winder on the back. 'Remember those musical jewelry boxes with the spinning pop-up ballerinas in net tutus that Plum gave us all when we were kids?'

Sophie laughs. 'The ones that played tunes from the *Sound of Music*? Mine was *Climb Every Mountain*, Nell had *Doh a Deer*, yours played *My Favourite Things*, and Plum had *Edelweiss*. Plum had to keep hers shut because she used to cry buckets every time she heard it.' Sophie can recall the tiniest detail.

'And this one is ...' I'm bluffing. Unlike Sophie, I haven't got the foggiest what I'm going to hear. But I open the lid and the tune comes tinkling out.

She gets it on the third note. *Somewhere Over the Rainbow*? That fits in perfectly with all the colours somehow.'

Like everything else, now I'm hearing it, it couldn't have been anything else. 'And there's one of those blurry Kodachrome colour photos that makes the world look so old.' I overcome my reluctance to intrude, but as I pick the photo out of the box I see a blurry dark auburn woman cuddling a toddler with a mass of ginger curls and a blue dress with butterflies I recognise from the picture on my mum's dressing table. 'Oh my, that's me. And I think that must be Laura.' Laura's face is so full of love as she looks down on me I'm swallowing back a lump in my throat.

Sophie's hand lands on my arm and she squeezes. 'Pictures of generations are lovely. It couldn't be any more tender, could it?'

I sniff and rub my eye. 'How could I ever have forgotten how comfy it was to be wrapped up on her knee?' All that love from years ago, and it's rushing back, warming my chest.

Sophie's first sympathetic pat gives way to a triumphant shout. 'And finally we get to find out where your red hair came from. But jeez, just think, if you'd had your way and had George send in the clearance people straight away, you'd never have found that.'

'You're right.' I'm feeling confused.

She jumps up so fast poor Maisie shoots her arms out. 'That settles it. You can't walk away. Not until you've had a look through everything.'

I let out a long groan. 'But the place is rammed.' The picture is like a gem, but even with the promise of more treasure, the thought of so many rooms packed with someone else's possessions is overwhelming.

She brushes away my protest. 'If we all come to help, it won't take long.' She's happily including Plum and Nell in her offer too. 'This is way more fun than any Bumps and Babies or Singles' stuff. And once you know exactly what bits of your history are here, then you can make an *informed* choice about what to keep. And *then* throw the rest away if you must.' This is what Sophie's like. When she gets that dynamic gleam in her eye, there's no point blocking her. Even if she is pushing me towards the door. 'We'll see George now, and take it from there.'

'Great,' I say, as I linger on the stairs, meaning anything but. As for this particular bit of history, however heartwarming a picture of me with Laura is, there are other parts where I'd rather not be digging. For every lovely bit the blank parts I don't know about are way scarier. If I'm feeling ambivalent, it's because however astonishing the riot of colour and the amazing space is upstairs, it's not a neutral place. It's like a step into the unknown because there's no knowing what will turn up. What's certain is, if I choose to spend more time here I'll need to be prepared to be brave. For someone who habitually runs away, I haven't had much practice at manning up. And I'm not entirely sure I want to start.

Sophie is hanging back, examining the letters on the tenants' post table. 'There's one here addressed to a Mr Hobson.' There are times when I wish she was less thorough.

'It won't be the same one we know.' My hand is on the door handle, and I'm already looking forward to the breeze off the sea battering my cheeks.

She wrinkles her nose. 'As Nate was saying, Bay Holdings are getting everywhere.'

Which sounds like one more reason for me to get as far away as I can, as fast as I can.

4

In Laura's flat at Seaspray Cottage
Bacon and salty dogs
Friday

A lot can happen in a short time when Sophie's on the case. When we get back to the office, George advises leaving it a week or two before I make a final decision on the flat. One wise man, and the pressure's off me. Then I spend Thursday afternoon doing a trial on the front desk at Trenowden, Trenowden etcetera. In fact, the name is misleading because it makes the office sound way more busy than it is. As soon as I'm on the other side of the desk I discover that in the St Aidan office there's only George, me and whoever is in for appointments. By five thirty I've learned how to push enough buttons to work the phone system – three – and managed to convince George I'm not going to frighten his clients away. He offers me enough hours to keep me in takeaways and we agree to flexible temporary, with a day's notice on either side. For someone as wary of commitment as me it's a comfortable arrangement. Luxurious even.

I turn up and keep his chair warm for the whole of Friday morning, discover three hours' commitment is do-able, then nip to the bakery to buy a BLT cob for lunch and wander along the quay to Seaspray Cottage. I'm planning a quiet afternoon of pottering, then the girls are popping in later, after work.

This time I manage not to fall up the steps on the way in and second time around it's way less unnerving letting myself into the flat. I grab a plate from the kitchen and find my favourite velvet chair. Then because it's so warm I unlock the window leading onto the balcony, and open the door a crack.

I'm basking in my sun spot, trying how it feels to be somewhere so huge with so much lovely stuff that's entirely mine. For someone whose lived out of a backpack for the best part of fifteen years it's an alien concept. And yet with the luminous light and the vibrant colours and the beautiful fabrics it's a wonderful place to be. The kind you never want to leave. It's a bit like the time we all went off to a high-end spa in Bath for Sophie's hen weekend. The suite we booked into was so blissful we were pinching ourselves to make sure the downy four posters and palatial bathrooms were actually real. At the flat, while I'm tingling because there's so much space, it's also deliciously cosy and familiar. As I soak up the warmth and the place wraps itself around me, in my head I'm testing out how it would feel to stay here forever. Then I crash back to reality and the ton weight of responsibility that comes with it. The live-in rooms that come with my jobs are usually tiny, but the up side is that the bills and the leaky showers are someone else's problem. When the most I've ever had to maintain is a suitcase, five rooms and a hall is a lot to get my head around. And that's before I even get on to service charges. I'm mulling and agonising, munching on my sandwich stuffed with salt 'n' shake crisps, having occasional panic spasms every time I think about meter readings, and watching the walkers down by the water's edge when a sudden scrabbling outside makes me almost drop my baguette. By the time I've licked the mayo off my fingers there's a big grey dog scratching at the door.

'Where the heck have you come from?'

Short of being dropped from a helicopter, I can't think of an answer to that, although it crosses my mind he's living dangerously. There have to be less precarious places in St Aidan to stand. From under his grey floppy fringe he's staring at me with the kind of brown soulful eyes that melt your heart in two seconds. Or maybe less.

'Hey, mate, eyes off my lunch.' However much I'm melting, I'm too hungry to share.

He bounds, barks, slobbers on the glass. Then he starts barking again, except this time in a crazy 'won't take no for an answer' way.

I'm yelling over the din, shaking my head at his Bambi legs and scrabbling claws. 'Watch out, the planks are rotten, please stop jumping or you'll fall through.' I put my plate on the side table, and as I wrench the door open he bounds straight past me. 'Nooooooo.' I let out a wail as he heads for my sandwich but I'm too late. His nose is practically at elbow height, the table might have been made for him. Two gulps later, the plate is empty and my sandwich is ancient history. Then he flops down in the doorway and rests his chin on his paws.

'Hey, don't go to sleep there, I'm really not up for a rescue dog.' I'm staring down at him, working out my next step, when a pair of bare human feet come into view. 'You might not want to walk there. Those boards could collapse at any moment.' Feeling like I'm stuck on repeat, I follow the jeans upwards, and hit a soft checked shirt. Then as I come to a rough jaw and some very crinkly dark eyes, I let out a long sigh. 'Charlie Hobson, what the ...?' Of all the guys on all the balconies, and this one had to turn up on mine. Or rather, Laura's.

'Clemmie, what a surprise. I hope Diesel isn't making a nuisance of himself.'

I take a moment to let my galloping heart rate subside to normal. 'Not too much but he's just arrived. So far he's only wolfed my lunch.' I'm working hard at making my smile ironic when it hits me if gravity gets the better of him, he could disappear too. 'Unless you've got a death wish maybe you'd better come in ...' He's the last person I'd *choose* to invite into the living room, but it has to be a better option than scraping him up off the garden wall in pieces.

One hop, he's over the dog and we're standing on the same rug.

As the delicious scent of expensive body spray drifts up my nose, I take a big step backwards. 'Now you're both safe maybe you can clear up why you were risking your necks on my balcony?' As soon as it's out, I'm cursing the slip.

Charlie's narrowing one eye. '*Your* balcony? We're from the flat next door, the balcony's shared. Do I take it from this you're the mysterious absentee landlord?' He shakes his head. 'George is a dark horse. He could have told us we were going to be neighbours.'

I try not to baulk at the word and put on my best 'office' voice, which is still way lighter than his. 'In a place as small as St Aidan, confidentiality is crucial.' George gave me 'the talk' when he took me on, along with a complementary tube of super-glue to apply with my lip gloss. If this was anyone else, I'd let my smile go. Faced by Charlie's humourless expression, I stay tight lipped. 'Apparently, the tiniest piece of information in the wrong ear will be around the town faster than you can say "compromising situation". And obviously, we can't have that.' It would have been useful for me not to be *so* much in the dark here too. At least then I might have avoided the heart attack I almost had when Charlie invaded my space.

Charlie pulls down the corners of his mouth. 'If you've landed the job at George's, we're going to see a lot of each other, I'm in there seeing George most days.'

I try to look less disappointed than I feel at that news. And in line with company policy I don't press him to find out why the heck he needs to spend so much time visiting his solicitor. 'Just don't expect me to talk to you at the office. With George's list of banned topics, "Hello, can I offer you a coffee?" is the most I'm allowed to say.' Which is probably damned useful given he's not exactly easy to talk to.

Charlie's eyes are boring into me again. 'So you won't be asking me how many sugars then?' If there were the merest hint of a smile, it could be jokey. But there isn't.

I don't smile back. 'Nope, that's definitely off-limits.'

'Two.' He gives a sniff. 'Just so you're prepared. Keep that on file, please.'

I can't ever remember not smiling for *this* long. Even the pharmacy queue is jollier than this when I'm waiting to pick up Maude's arthritis medication, and that's full of ill people. 'Sweet tooth?' Although I already know that from the way he hit the macaroons the other evening.

He pulls a face. 'I'm anyone's for a piece of cake.' Then he lets out a sigh. 'That's why Diesel was confused before. We used to pop in here most days for tea with Jenny, your former tenant. Her rocky road slice was spectacular, that's the reason Diesel was hell bent on battering the door down.'

'You actually knew her?' I'm intrigued, because thanks to George and his obsession with discretion, I haven't even got as far as extracting her name from him. Although it's hard to imagine anyone as tense and gaunt as Charlie 'popping in' for 'cosy chats'.

'Jenny was an author, but she was more an old friend of your grandmother's than a tenant. She lived over near Rosehill, but she never stayed over, she just came here every day because the views helped her write. The arrangement suited them both. Jenny used the place until you grew up, and the peppercorn rent went towards any repair costs.' Despite the sullen expression Charlie is as open as George is guarded.

The more he says, the more my mouth drops open. 'Go on ...'

'The building wasn't ever in the greatest shape.' There's a questioning frown playing around his forehead as he grinds to a halt. 'But surely George will have told you all this?'

I give a sudden beam to cover up how much George hasn't said. 'Absolutely. But it's always helpful to get another viewpoint. And she left because ...?'

Charlie's long sigh is presumably for the loss of his friend, not her cake. 'She was getting on, the two flights of stairs became too much, and she moved south to be closer to one of her sons.'

He rubs his chin. 'The balcony is perfectly safe by the way. It runs all along the front of the building, so both our flats open onto it. It was repaired before I moved in last year, it's all in

George's files, the cost was shared between us. You do know about that?' He's giving me a searching stare. 'Believe me, *I* wouldn't forget a bill that big.'

'Too damned right.' I try to look the right amount of appalled. Which is hard when I don't know if I'm reacting to a hundred pounds or a hundred thousand. 'Remind me to go out there and party. Very hard. I need to get my money's worth before I leave.'

He seems to give a jolt, but a breath later he's back to reaching over for my empty BLT wrapper. 'Did you say Diesel ate your sandwich? Give me a minute, I'll make you another.'

All I have to say here is 'No' and I can wave him off along the balcony and out of my day. I know I should be jumping at the chance, if only to let my heart rate get back to normal. Even if he looks grave enough for a funeral plan brochure when he sways he's still disarmingly close. Another step back, and I'll topple onto the sofa. On the other hand, the growls coming from my empty stomach are loud enough to have come from Diesel.

However he doesn't allow me to squeeze in even a two-letter word before he bashes on. 'I don't have bacon, but there's thin sliced ham on the bone, homemade plum and sultana pickle, and some kind of crumbling cheddar matured in a slate cavern. There's crusty cobs too, and salad. I could throw a ploughman's picnic together for us.'

I try not to make too much noise as I suck back my drool. Then just as I'm gritting my teeth, resolving to say 'No' I catch a hint of a smile playing around his lips and my mouth is moving on its own. 'Great. Sounds brill.' And that's that.

I hold my hands up and admit I'm a slave to my stomach. I also know he's way too decorative, serious and sure of himself for me to ever hang out with. And I might be a teensy bit of a hypocrite too, accepting snacks from strangers I'd rather run a mile from in normal circumstances. But however off-hand he appears, Charlie Hobson has spilled a pile of proverbial beans, and I can't help thinking there could be more he can tell me about my grandmother.

But by the time I've worked this lot out, Charlie's long gone. And Diesel has relocated to the sofa with the best view down the beach.

5

In Laura's flat at Seaspray Cottage
Real ale and home truths
Friday

'So how about you, Clemmie, what's your story?'

When Charlie arrives back he's trundling a double-decker hammered metal trolley along the balcony on super-chunky industrial wheels. As I help him ease it through the living room doors I see it's laden with everything he promised and more, plus hand glazed plates and mugs, and scarily spare cutlery that's so on trend and triangular it's hard to tell which are knives and which are forks. There's also serviettes, fruit juices, and a cluster of chilled beer bottles, pebbled with condensation. It takes approximately ten seconds to load up our plates. Then as he sits down he drops in the question, and I immediately fill my mouth and the next half hour with so much eating that I can't possibly answer.

I catch glimpses of him over the top of my crusty bread as I chew, and it flashes through my head that if he were on Tinder, every woman out there would swipe 'Yes'. Including me. Which is way more ridiculous than it sounds, because I'd never go on Tinder. And who knows why the hell the 'sexy' word keeps flashing through my brain when there isn't a suit anywhere in sight today.

'Anyway, Clemmie,' he says eventually, 'are you going to tell me where you fit in at Seaspray Cottage? Or are you just going to swim off into the ocean and make me think eating a ploughman's lunch on a patchwork sofa with a mermaid was all a dream?'

'Me?' I grab my fourth beer, wrench the top off and glug. 'What's this I'm drinking?'

He peers at the bottle. 'They're a mix. That one's local brewery, Roaring Waves' answer to a German Pils. But watch out, they have a tendency to make your legs disappear without warning.' The low noise in his throat could almost be a laugh. 'Although you're probably used to that sensation.'

I almost drop my bottle. 'Are you implying I get drunk a lot?' He's not getting away with that.

He shakes his head and blinks. 'No, just meaning the way your legs and your mermaid's tail are interchangeable.' There's that almost-smile playing around his lips. 'For a mermaid settling on land, you couldn't have found many flats closer to the sea than this one. I can't understand why you wouldn't want to stay.'

Even if he's not laughing outwardly his tone is mocking. 'Come on, I didn't take the piss when you turned up with your high-end boys' toy lunch wheelie.' That has to be the most macho item ever, I'm betting he grabbed it from Groupon. That or he found it down the harbour and it's meant for trundling fish around. 'And while we're on the subject of toys and size, please tell me you aren't going to set up one of those monster Australian-style barbie's on the balcony?'

He gives a sniff. 'For someone uninvested, you're coming over as very territorial.'

I screw up my face, and take another gulp of my drink. Considering I'm not a beer person, it's going down very fast. 'It all comes down to the "settling" thing. The word actually makes me shiver, that's just how I'm wired. From the way I feel now, I'm guessing I'm destined to swim around the world forever.'

He pulls down the corners of his mouth as he gets up and strides towards the door. 'How about cake to soak up the alcohol? I'll see what I've got next door.'

I'm psyching myself up for a second feast on wheels, but when he comes back in he's only carrying a plate. 'No sweet trolley then?'

He gives a guilty shrug. 'If there's cake in the flat, I eat it. Two measly bits of chocolate brownie is all I could find. Sorry they're so tiny.'

'Small, but delicious.' It must be the beer making me gush even though I'm trying to stick to understatement. The square I'm sinking my teeth into is dark, sticky and so delectably chocolatey it clogs my throat. And small is taking a man-sized view. I wave the remains of my pretty massive slice in the air as I struggle to talk through the cocoa haze. 'It's such a shame there's no such thing as cake take-aways with home delivery. I'd always rather ring for gateaux than pizza.'

He narrows his eyes. 'Gateaux in Cornwall? You'll be lucky.'

'Sorry, I'm mixing up my languages again.' And coming across like an arse. 'I just flew in from France.' And now I'm sounding even worse.

His eyebrows lift. 'Anywhere nice?' At least he seems to be overlooking the pretentious prat part.

I try to play it down. 'Only Paris.'

'Quite a landlocked place for a mermaid.' He sends me a sideways glance. 'But, honestly, I can see why you'd rather be there than here.'

I smile at the recognition. 'I make do with the rain instead of the sea. There's nothing quite like wet city pavements shining with reflections from the street lights and the traffic. As soon as my job restarts I'll be back there and loving it.' I hesitate for a moment. 'Gateaux and all.'

His frown is thoughtful. 'In which case, maybe it's a good time to mention – if ever you want to sell the flat, Diesel would love some extra space to expand into. Obviously, I'd be offering you a top price.'

As he hears his name Diesel's tail thumps on the sofa cushions. It's as if he's adding his weight to what Charlie just said, while I'm struggling to believe what I just heard. I'm taking a breath, gathering my words to reply. If he was anyone else it would have to be 'yes' a thousand times over, for every reason. Let's face it, before he turned up I'd just spent a full half-hour freaking out at the thought of an electricity bill so I'm not quite sure why my stomach feels like a popped balloon as I look out at the frill of the waves running up the beach. And then suddenly I get it.

'So this explains it. You send your dog to eat my sandwich, so you can offer me lunch and muscle in on buying my flat?' My voice is high with indignation. What's more, I'm furious for allowing myself to eye him up when what he was really here for was to get his hands on Laura's property.

He screws up his face. 'Really, Clemmie, that's not what happened.'

I let out a snort. 'Fill me with beer then push through another of your deals? That's low, even for lowlife like you.'

There's a flash of pain in his eyes, then he takes a deep breath. 'There was no pressure, I was simply trying to be helpful if that was what you wanted.'

'Helpful my *arse*. That was pure opportunism.' I'm not even sure it's the right word. Worse still, I've got this sinking feeling I'm probably shooting myself in the foot here. But there's something about the bare faced gall of the man that's made me so angry. If he was the last punter in the world, at this moment I wouldn't sell to him.

'If you choose to see it that way, that's your problem.' He's not even bothering to defend himself.

To reclaim some dignity, I go back to my best clipped office tones. '*If* there's a sale, George will handle it, I'm sure you'll be the first to know.'

He shakes his head. 'We've already discussed how sharing George is.' He just gives yet another sigh and carries on. 'As I said before, the building needs work. We've got extensive roof repairs scheduled for autumn.'

I'm not sure why he's telling *me* this now. 'Great, I'll cross my fingers it stays fine for you. Let's hope you don't get too much of that rain I was talking about earlier.' I take another swig of beer. My excuse to myself for accepting lunch was to get information, and this far, apart from an offer to buy the flat which floored me, I've got approximately zilch. 'Remind me who's in the other flats?'

Charlie's reply is fast and businesslike. 'Two are let to short-term tenants, and two are let out through Airbnb to holiday makers.'

I'm frowning, tapping the bottle on my teeth, still not getting it. 'All good. So, your point is?'

'There's not a lot left in your peppercorn rent pot after the balcony repairs. And the cost of the roof will be shared between all the flat owners.' He's drumming his fingers on the chair arm now. 'So if you did plan to stay, I'm simply flagging up that you'll need to find ten grand before the autumn.'

I gasp so hard I almost swallow the bottle as well as my next gulp of beer. 'Ten grand?' My bank account's never seen that many noughts. As far as my finances go, I earn enough to get by, put a little aside, then I travel. Then I stop and work again. It's called living in the moment, and this far, give or take a bit of juggling, it's always worked out fine.

Charlie nods. 'It's not a huge amount, but you might need to dip into your capital.' He's talking like I'm loaded, and staring like I'm not keeping up. Which, to be fair, is right. 'Capital, meaning your savings?'

The second he starts talking English again the penny drops. 'Ah, those.' Right now, I've probably got a couple of hundred to tide me over for when I move on from Paris. 'Of course.' It's strangely levelling. One minute I'm struggling because I've got so many choices of what to do with the flat and I don't know how to handle it. The next I'm fighting to keep it away from Charlie. Then I'm back to way worse – there is no choice, because the only option I can afford is to let it go. Except now I feel like I've had something huge taken away from me. Which I know is a ridiculous way to feel, when only a couple of days ago I wasn't even going to bother to visit the place.

Charlie's face gets the closest to a smile I've seen today. 'My point is, you'll have plenty of savings if a sale goes through. Subject to tax liability, obviously.' Yet another downside to entertaining a 'decorative developer' in your living room. If he carries on like this, we'll be onto mortgages in no time.

I'm about to put my hands over my ears when there's a clatter out on the landing.

'Clemmie, we're early ... we brought bubbly ...' As the door pushes open, there's a hollow boom, and a cork shoots past my nose.

6

In Laura's flat at Seaspray Cottage
Cotton wool and feisty talk
Friday

As Charlie dashes off along the balcony, insistent on going for 'proper' champagne glasses, it only takes one half-raised eyebrow from Nell before Diesel's slinking down from the sofa and turning circles on a rug. Sophie settles Milla and Maisie into his place, then flops down beside them herself

I'm counting on my fingers as I snaffle one of Milla's banana chips. 'Aren't you two short here, Soph?'

'Nate's taken Marco and Matilde.' She sneaks a look at her phone. 'Let's see, they've got Water Polo, then they're going on to Spanish for Smalls and taster Tinies' Yoga.' Seeing these two have barely hit nursery, her 'what the heck' expression is probably entirely justified. 'So how's it going here?'

Nell's staring at me in awe. 'Swimmingly, I'd say. *You* didn't mess about, Clemmie.'

I pull a face. 'It's not what it looks like.' Claiming 'the dog ate my sandwich' is too close to those lame excuses for lost homework. I try another tack. 'Charlie happens to live next door, he dropped round with lunch and an offer to buy the flat.'

'How lucky is that?' Nell asks.

Sophie's less impressed. 'What the eff does he think he's playing at?' She looks like she's about to explode.

I give a shrug. 'You can ask him yourself, he's here with his flutes as we speak.' As I take the slender glasses from him and put them on the table I'm telling it like it is. 'There can't be many neighbours in St Aidan who will wheel in lunch *and* be happy to share their crystal, then try to buy your home before you've even had chance to move in.' We might as well bring this into the open.

Sophie flashes him a disgusted glance then fixes him with one of those stares of hers that bore right through you. 'So, are you going to explain yourself, Charlie?'

His gaze flicks over all of us. 'Now might not be the best time. I'll leave you to drink your fizz in peace. Things to do, places to be, and all that.'

'I bet you bloody have.' Sophie growls as he trundles the trolley towards the door and calls Diesel.

Plum peeps into the kitchen, then comes over to pour. 'The flat's as much of a gem as Sophie told us. Small, yet perfectly formed.'

Nell narrows her eyes as she passes round the fizz. 'As said by the woman who has an entire chandlery to rattle around in. It couldn't be more cosy, but five of us just arrived and you can barely tell we're here.' A grin spreads across her face between sips. 'It would be fab for more intimate singles' evenings.' Since she's taken charge of the club, Nell sees every venue, public or private, in terms of its party potential.

Plum sniffs. 'Probably why Mr Hobnob Holdings can't wait to get his hands on it. No doubt he'd want to rip the guts out of the place.'

'Ewww.' The thought of workmen with sledgehammers smashing Laura's lovely coloured walls makes me wince. Although it might have been a less dramatic reaction if I'd had more food and less beer. That's the trouble with lunchtime drinking. It makes me so thirsty my fizz barely touches the sides before it's gone.

Sophie's eyes flash. 'It doesn't have to be like that, Clemmie. You don't *have* to accept.'

I sigh. 'I damn well won't sell to him, but I might have to sell to someone. He's explained the situation. If I keep the flat I need to find a bomb to fund joint repairs.'

Nell cocks her head. 'Exactly what size incendiary device are we talking here?' The accountant in her always insists on the price down to the last penny.

I hesitate and lean forward for a refill. 'Ten grand by September. Maybe more.' That thought is enough for me to down my next glass too.

'Shit.' Plum lets out a whistle. 'In that case you're probably stuffed.' It's not mean, she's simply taking a realistic view of my finances. She understands because she stretched to the limit and then some to get the gallery going.

Sophie shakes her head. 'Not so fast. You and Plum might not be best friends with your bank managers, but Nell and I are better placed.' Her multi-million turnover can blind her to what real life's like for the rest of us.

Nell looks thoughtful. 'We could tide you over?'

I blow in frustration. 'It's awesome of you to offer, but even if I wanted to keep the flat, I couldn't accept. I'd have no hope of paying back a loan that big on what I earn.'

'Can your mum help?' Plum knows we're on shaky ground here.

I pull a face. 'When Mum and Harry laughingly call their trip the "Spend the Inheritance Tour" it's not a joke. They're volunteering, but it's the kind you pay for.' My mum was always sensitive about me getting this place, but at least it gave her the green light to enjoy her savings. They plan to spend the lot while they're fit enough, see the countries she never got to because I came along. 'This is the last place I'd ask them to change their plans for.'

Nell pulls a face. 'Leave it with us. If there's a way to keep you here, we'll think of it.'

I'm biting my thumbnail as I agonise, because I don't want to lead them on. 'I probably do want to sell, because I can't think how the hell things would work otherwise. But it would be nice to have a choice.' I can't remember being anywhere that made me feel so instantly secure and comfortable. I know I'll always be a wanderer, but it would still be amazing to keep this place as a safe haven. Although that's probably not a luxury my empty bank account will run to.

Sophie lets out a snort. 'You can't be backed into a corner by a man with a hostess trolley, even if he does have beautiful glasses.' She holds her flute up to the light, then finishes the half-inch of fizz she accepted. 'So are we going to make a move? I'm taking this lot home for supper, if you're hungry?'

Nell grins. 'Or even better, come with Plum and I on the Singles' All the Sixes evening. That's six bars in six hours.'

After so many bottles of real ale I can't think of anything worse. 'Since when did you want a boyfriend, Plum?' We've always been the two who are entirely happy on our own.

She laughs. 'Definitely not looking for one of those, but Nell's pub crawls are too good to miss.'

As I stand up and stretch, my head feels like it's filled with cotton wool. 'I'd barely begun to look around when Diesel and Charlie arrived. Maybe I should stay here tonight.' Note to self: getting pissed in the afternoon and ending up a prisoner in the attic is off-the-scale bad. But at least this way I avoid staggering down two flights of stairs when my legs feel like they belong to someone else, *and* I get out of a night out with the dreaded Singles' Club. That's a result all round. Although I have to admit my half-drunken self is feeling a sudden pang for what I'm about to give up here. 'Make the most of it while I can, and all that?'

Nell frowns at me. 'For one time only, we'll let you off the singles' event. So long as you have us all round for brunch tomorrow.'

Plum's staring out of the doors to the balcony. 'Good idea. I'm missing this view already and I haven't left yet.'

Sophie's on her feet. 'I know exactly what you mean, Plum. It's the kind of place that makes you want to come back again and again. Way too good for Charlie Hobnob.' She's scooping up Maisie from the sofa. 'We'll bring the food, Clemmie, be ready. Brainstorming begins at eleven sharp tomorrow. This is one fight I promise we'll win.'

So, it's official. We're going into battle. That's Sophie all over. But right now, all I can think of is making my way to the pink haven of the bedroom, and crawling under the quilt.

7

In the flat at Seaspray Cottage
Ice cubes and cold feet
Saturday

I'm standing on the balcony next morning, breathing in the sharp salty air, watching the figures along the water's edge and the sand clouds whipping up the beach. It turns out ten minutes of having your face blown off is a great way to wake up even if it makes your hair go wild. I'm just about to go inside when a shout drifts up from the garden.

'Hi, Clemmie, how was your first night at Seaspray Cottage?'

Peering down, I catch sight of a grey wagging tail, then Charlie comes into view, craning his neck to look up, blinking in the sunlight.

'Great, thanks.' I'm not telling him that once I'd slept off the beer and champagne, the waves crashing up the beach kept me awake until the tide went out again. Give me the lull of traffic and police sirens any night. 'How did you know I stayed?' As if me standing out here at the crack of dawn wasn't enough of a clue.

If it was anyone other than Charlie, I'd swear he let out a chortle. 'I reckon the whole of St Aidan hears when you pull that flush of yours. I'm assuming it was you in the bathroom in the night, not intruders?'

Shit. If the sea making it impossible to sleep wasn't enough to put me off the flat, Charlie Hobson counting every time I visit the loo takes away all the enjoyment of my first night ever with my very own bathroom and spare bedroom. Although I'm determined not to let myself get used to it, a whole flat all to myself, not sharing a loo, with rooms to wander through is beyond awesome. 'Off for your morning walk?' Hopefully that'll take us somewhere less cringeworthy than him knowing how often I pee.

That sounds like another half-laugh. 'Diesel and I had our morning walk hours ago, this is our lunchtime one.'

Damn again. When did it get so late? 'Jeez, I'd better go.'

He steps backwards and looks out along the quayside. 'Nell and Sophie are on their way now. It looks like they're carrying the entire morning's output from the bakery.'

'Thanks for the running commentary.' As nosey neighbours go he's scoring a straight ten here. My 'against' list is getting longer by the second.

'You're welcome, any time.' He's missing the irony again. 'By the way, there's no need for you to shiver out here doing your Bridget Jones impersonation. There are some silk dressing gowns hanging behind the door in your bathroom.'

I'm gobsmacked, but I ignore the urge to run. Instead I give my long cardi an extra tug downwards and face him out. 'How the hell do you know that?' Even if my pants were on show – which they're absolutely not – I've no worries about minimalism or over-exposure because my granny knicker shorts almost reach up to my boobs.

He's already backing off along the path towards the bay. 'Laura's tenant did a lot of tidying before she left, we saw the bath robes when Diesel and I were round for tea one day. Anyway, we must go.' No doubt he's rushing off before Sophie comes close enough to collar him. 'Enjoy your lunch.'

I give the girls a wave, then dip inside. By the time they burst in from the landing I've had time to dive into yesterday's dress, flick on enough eyeliner and mascara to make it look like I have actual eyes rather than slits, and use up the whole of my handbag perfume.

'Shall we eat at the table in the kitchen?' I rake my fingers through my hair and bundle it into a bun with a scrunchie, then do a double take because that's not a sentence I've ever said before. One night staying in a flat that's almost all mine and I'm already sounding like I shop at Waitrose.

'Good idea, then Matilde can do her colouring while we chat.' Sophie leads the way and pulls out the fuchsia chair for her. 'Your favourite colour, how lucky is that Tilly?' She pulls a face. 'Four kids in, I've decided you can't fight gender stereotyping. Tilly was screaming for pink as they brandished the forceps.'

As Tilly slips off her unicorn backpack, scrambles up and spreads out her felt tips, it hits me I must have done the same thing at the same table when I was Tilly's size. As Plum slides in to draw her some butterflies to colour, Nell's getting her apple juice and waffles, and I'm plumping her cushion, making her comfy. When I think of how much love we all have for Tilly, it reminds me of the look on Laura's face on the photo in the musical box.

She must have done a lot more with me than I realise when I was small. Love comes from so many different places, but having it in our lives makes us who we are. For a second I'm overwhelmed by the feeling, and it's like an unexpected gift to be back here having a chance to revisit everything Laura gave me.

'Coffee's the priority.' Nell throws a pack on the worktop, and fills the kettle. 'Let's hope you've got a pot here, Clemmie.'

Sophie's unpacking the bags onto platters she's found on the dresser. 'We've also brought every kind of breakfast pastry the bakery makes.'

'Yummy.' I'm bobbing in and out of cupboards and scouring the shelves for plates and mugs. 'It's a bit of a lucky dip, but here you go, one cafetière.' As I slide it along to Nell, I come across a cutlery pot next to a knife block, and pick out a handful of bone-handled knives and silver spoons.

'It looks pretty well stocked.' Sophie's taking in the cupboards rammed with utensils.

I'm smiling because the collection of crockery is enormous, yet so random. 'So long as you're not expecting to find any two items the same, I reckon we could stay here for a month without needing to wash up.'

As Nell opens the packet the smell of ground coffee drifts into the air. 'And any time you want matching sets, you can always plunder the flat next door. Charlie seemed exceptionally willing to share his designer kitchen collections.'

I'll ignore that suggestion. 'We had no need to borrow those flutes, there are shelves of glasses here.'

Nell wiggles her eyebrows. 'No harm in accepting help and cementing neighbourly relations.'

'Knock yourself out, Nell, but after yesterday, for the time I'm here, I'm going to be the kind of aloof neighbour who keeps my distance.'

Nell's nostrils flare, which is a sure sign she's pissed off. 'You might want to think of the Singles' Club here, not just yourself.' She seems to be ignoring that he turned her down flat on that one.

I grin. 'So you *have* got the hots for Hobson after all?' Then knowing she'll deny it on principle even though I'm teasing, I move on to explain. 'First, he wants to get his hands on the flat, now he's claiming he can hear every loo flush through the wall so blanking him is the only way to save mega-embarrassment.' As a cover-all reason for why I'm avoiding him it's almost worth the shudders of remembering he knows when I wee.

Nell sniffs. 'You might want to keep him on side when you hear what we've hit on for your fund raising.'

Sophie frowns at Nell. 'Best to talk about that *with* coffee.' She stoops down to reach the bottom section of the dresser. 'You really have got *all* the equipment here. Your very own picnic basket too, can we have a peep?'

'Looks like a two-person set from the size. You might have something cute and matching after all.' Nell was never this 'couple' obsessed before her break up. She'd shoot us down in flames if we suggested it, but the way she goes on, even if it's subliminal, there has to be a gap in her life that needs filling.

As the wicker basket hits the table, my scalp tingles. 'That's not for picnics.' As I undo the buckles a glimpse of blue gingham lining spins me back to when I was small. In my head, I'm standing on a stool so I can reach the work top better, searching through a pile of cards to find my favourites. And I know without looking what's inside the basket. 'It's full of Laura's recipes.'

As I swing the lid of the basket upwards it's like opening a window onto the past. 'She used to copy out the recipes she liked most.' I'm flicking through a mass of colourful hand written cards, all with scribbled notes and sketches in the characteristically pointy writing, with cut out magazine pictures and photos pasted on too. 'Oh my, that Pavlova on the flowery tablecloth ... apple pie in a summer garden ... the most delicious looking syrup tart. Maybe I came here more often than I remember.' My mouth's watering.

Nell's laughing as she pulls out a card. 'If you were making salmon en croute and soufléed spinach omelettes as a kid, how did you not end up on master chef?'

Sophie lets out a groan. 'Strawberry and lemon sorbet with mint leaves looks gorgeous.'

Plum's leaning over her shoulder. 'And look at the colour of that raspberry one. This is making me *so* hungry.'

'Sorbet?' Nell jumps forwards with a cry. 'Hold that thought, I've just had a lightbulb moment.'

I'm going to have to move this on before my hunger pangs get the better of me. 'Forget about me holding anything other than a cup of coffee and a pastry. Can we *please* have some breakfast?'

'Absolutely.' Nell swings by with the coffee pot, then pulls up a sky-blue chair. 'And Soph and I can talk you through you the finer points of our plan.'

'What?' I'm mainly interested in how authentic the filling is in the almond croissants. It takes two minutes of ecstasy as it melts on my tongue to discover. It's amazing.

Sophie brushes a chunk of cinnamon whirl off her chin, and leans over to break Tilly's second chocolate waffle into pieces. 'We put our thinking caps on last night and came up with the perfect answer to your cash flow problems.'

'Bank robbing?' It's the only solution I've thought of, and I had hours to wrack my brains while the sea kept me awake.

Sophie's wearing the same rise above it expression she uses when the kids are being especially tiresome. 'This flat of yours is perfect as a micro venue. And Nell has a database of people in her club all instantly contactable on Facebook. It's a no-brainer – merge the two, and you've got your very own instant "pop up" event.'

'Then hear the cash registers ring.' Nell had to add that bit. 'People are happy to pay for something exclusive. To be honest mostly they'll be ecstatic to try something different.'

I take a custard slice, bite into it, chew. And I'm *still* not getting it. 'Can you explain that again, please? In English this time.'

Nell leans forward. 'I've messaged around my Singles' Club inner inner-circle and they're all up for an "evening" at yours.' Who knows what her finger wiggle speech marks are hinting at there. 'In fact, it's so popular, there's already a waiting list.'

Sitting with my jaw sagging open is such a waste of a good mouthful. 'What on earth would they *do* here? Sit and knit?'

Plum jumps in excitedly. 'That's another great idea we missed when we brainstormed.' So, they've definitely been discussing it in detail.

Sophie takes a breath and begins again. 'All Nell's friends are looking for is a couple of hours to relax and enjoy the views. It's a spectacular setting, the quirky decor makes it totally unique.

And with your flawless customer service skills, if you throw in something lovely to eat, you're in a perfect position to give them a fab time they'll be happy to pay for.'

I'll concede she's right about the flat, even if she is over playing the positivity to the point of sounding like a lifestyle manual. But they're forgetting something. 'I don't *host* parties, I go to them. This is way beyond me.'

Sophie gives my arm a squeeze. 'Why do you *always* undersell yourself? Don't worry, you do whatever you feel happy with, and we'll cover the rest.'

Which is lovely, but there's one huge hurdle they seem to be overlooking. 'So are you going to order in takeaways, or are you planning to use caterers?'

Nell's tutting. 'For maximum profit, cut out the middle man. If *you* provide the food, *you* make on every side.'

'Me?' I'm so horrified I let my custard slice drop onto my plate. 'I'm a bar person, I serve *liquid*. Lemon slices are the only food I touch. And I don't actually make anything edible, even for myself, because I don't have the skills and that's what chefs do.' Let's face it, in most of the bars I've worked in food was the last thing on anyone's mind.

Sophie's voice is soothing. 'You follow cocktail recipes no problem. Simple snacks and nibbles are only one step on from that. We'll do a trial night and see how it goes, okay?'

'How about "NO"?' Suddenly I'm not hungry any more, they've put me right off my breakfast. Which is a total waste, given the stack of pain au chocolats I'm staring at.

'One crucial word from earlier ...' Nell's eyes are sparkling. '*SORBETS!*' She holds her breath for dramatic effect for long enough to finish her coffee. Then starts again. 'Sorbets will be easy *and* effective. They're fresh and *very* seasonal. Realistically they're one step away from ice cubes, and you dish those out all night long without blinking.'

'And you've got loads of pretty glasses and cups here to serve them in too.' Plum's nodding, as she shuffles through the handful of cards she's plucked out. 'They couldn't be more simple. All you need is fruit, sugar, a food processor and a freezer.'

Which already sounds like a very long list to me.

Sophie beams. 'Brilliant. It's so lucky we found Laura's basket. Before this the best we'd come up with was tapas or nachos, but all the recipes we Googled had the "extra effort" marker and way too many knives on the skill symbols.'

I'm secretly shuddering at the thought of *any* knives *or* effort.

'That's decided then.' Nell's clasping her hands together to stop herself from full blown cheering. 'We're all set for an original and delicious Early Summer Sorbet Evening. I'll put the word out. Does Monday at eight work for you?'

I manage to hold in my scream. 'Isn't that rushing things a bit?'

'Not if we're talking ten grand by September.' Nell's never one to pull her punches. 'I'll give the whale watching a miss. That gives us all day tomorrow to sort the small stuff.'

Which from where I'm sitting sounds like no time at all.

'Don't look so anxious, we'll all help.' Sophie's patting my hand, but frankly if she'd been this sympathetic earlier we wouldn't be in this mess. 'At least you've got the recipes here. You did say you wanted to leave your options open with the flat. This might let you do that.'

'It's fine, I'm not worried.' It's only a bit of a lie. I know we're careering towards a complete car crash here. But the fastest way to prove this isn't going to work is to let the disaster happen. Then we can walk away knowing we've all tried our best and failed. The sooner we get this nightmare over, the better. 'Although ...'

'Yes?' Nell cocks her head at me.

I'm fingering the recipe cards, looking at the familiar handwriting. It won't happen again, so we've got one chance to credit her. 'As we're using all her recipes, could we call it Laura's Sorbets?'

Plum's eyes light up. 'Making it personal is the perfect way to remember her. Laura's Lovely Sorbets?'

I'm laughing. 'Even better. I think she'd like that.'

'Great.' Sophie's already on her feet. 'What are we waiting for? We'll pick up Milla from dancing, and then we'll hit the shops and go to mine to practice.'

8

In Trenowden, Trenowden and Trenowden Solicitors' office
Sorbet and melting ice caps
Monday morning

'Morning, Clementine, good weekend?' As he breezes past my desk to his office, George's greeting sounds like he's on autopilot.

'Great thanks.' Even if he was taking notice, I'd spare him the details.

As I staggered away from the market stall with Sophie on Saturday afternoon, under a fruit mountain so huge I could barely see the toes of my kitten heeled pumps I'd decided to go with the flow. By the time we reached Sophie's kitchen, which is literally the size of a barn, I was relaxing into it. The minute we added in Laura's name it stopped feeling like I was being press ganged, and I began to feel part of the mission. In spite of my huge reservations and doubts, I began to enjoy myself.

Sophie's a whizz at multi-tasking. Somehow she managed to sort French plaits for Tilly, wade through a marketing report, pass Maisie her organic carrots and chickpeas, stop Marco from crashing his ride-on tractor through the bi-fold doors into the courtyard outside, and shout instructions at me and Milla too. After an afternoon of doing as I was told at her polished concrete work surfaces, I'd liquidised so much fruit and dipped in and out of her stable-size freezer so many times, I swear I'll be making strawberry sorbet in my sleep forever more. But at least I'd nailed the technicalities and learned how to operate a hand blender without sending a tidal wave of fruit puree up the walls.

The up side of trialing recipes is we all got to taste the sorbets. Pause for a brief sorbet swoon there – the icy crystals hitting my tongue was like an electric shock to my brain. Out of nowhere I could remember sitting at my little table on the balcony, hulling strawberries, with Laura sitting on the planks beside me, her legs outstretched. Me holding her hand, as we hurried out to the ice cream kiosk to get wafers. Standing them up like sails in our sorbet balls. Then later I found the splashy blue and orange flowery fabric of the dress she'd been wearing that day in a patchwork cushion on the sofa. For someone who usually has trouble remembering much beyond last Tuesday, it was a revelation.

By Saturday tea time, we'd made our selection from the samples, bought more fruit for making the full amounts, and trundled it up the stairs at Seaspray Cottage. All without bumping into Charlie. Why did I ever think this was going to be hard?

Then on Sunday, Nell, Plum and I spent the afternoon at the flat, tweeking the sofas and side tables into party order, cleaning the loo, and sorting out the best cups and glasses to use, and still finished in time to go for a hot chocolate at the Surf Shack along the beach.

So now I'm tapping my heels under George's reception desk, flicking through this morning's appointments on my screen, willing lunchtime to arrive so Plum and I can get back and crack on with the sorbets.

'How are you getting on with the flat? I hear you've moved in.'

Shucks. So much for autopilot. This time around George is full on warm and interested, with a disarming smile to match.

'Yes, all fabulous, thanks for asking.' My throat constricts in panic. I skip straight over the Airbnb people underneath who could have been bonking for England all night on Saturday. Does he know about the flat because he's put himself down for the Laura's Lovely Sorbets event? I might be softening to the idea of twenty strangers invading Laura's living room in return for a discreet yet extortionate cash payment. But I'm damn sure I'm not up for my boss seeing me fall flat on my face when it goes all kinds of wrong, even if he does have kind crinkles at the corners of his eyes. 'I'm not up to speed here because I've been away, but do you go to Nell's singles' events?' Hopefully I make the crucial question sound super casual.

George's smile fades in a second. 'Hell, no.'

'Jeez, I'm *so* pleased to hear that.' And that gave too much away. This calls for some serious back pedalling. 'Any particular reason? I've heard they're excellent, even for people like us who are happy with their "alone" status.'

For a moment, he looks confused. 'I do long hours here, then take work home.' Now he's found an answer he looks happier. 'Socialising isn't on my radar, probably how I've avoided getting pushed into it like everyone else has.' Although it's on his radar enough to know it exists.

'Great, well I'd better get on.' I need to wind this up, before I get into any more deep water. 'This human works best on Monday mornings if coffee is added. Are you ready for one too?'

'I thought you'd never ask.' The grin that spreads across his face at the offer of a caffeine hit makes his previous one look arctic. 'Only joking, why not let me make them?'

'That's what I'm here for.' Obviously, I don't want him at my sorbet evening, but all the same I can't quite work out why Nell hasn't snapped this one up for her singles' group. With lines like that I'd say he has all the makings of a 'keeper'.

Despite being a twenty-four seven workaholic, it turns out George is just as shit as me about the Monday thing. Four coffees on for each of us, with no visit from Charlie, we finally get to lunchtime, and I'm free to go and make sorbet. Ten hours from now the micro-venue theory will have been tested to destruction, and my life will be back on its old course again. All I have to do is hold my nerve and get through to midnight.

Two hours later, Plum and I are up to our elbows in pureed raspberries in Laura's kitchen, looking out across the blue sparkling water of St Aidan Bay as we sieve the last double batch.

Plum counts them off on her fingers as she juggles the containers in the freezer, which is rammed. 'Strawberry, pear and rosemary, lemon, lime and peppermint, water melon, orange and mango, cucumber and mint. There's just about enough room to squeeze the raspberry in here too.'

'As Sophie says, they're gluten-free, dairy-free, suitable for vegetarians, pescetarians, vegans, celiacs and lactose intolerants.' Now they're almost done, I'm feeling dizzy, excited and so uptight I'm squeaking when I should be talking.

Plum laughs. 'Sophie *would* say that. Better still, they're bloody delicious, those recipes of Laura's are on point.'

'I can't believe it was so easy. If this is cooking, bring it on.' Even if I'm joking, I'm still stunned at what we've done. If Laura could see me now, somehow, I know she'd be happy.

Plum scrapes the last of the dark ruby mixture into a shallow dish. 'I had a flick through the recipe basket earlier. Nothing's too complicated to make, but everything in there looks seriously yummy.'

'Which kind of reminds me ...' Edible being everyone else's description of the man in question, not mine. 'Do you think Nell's interested in my neighbour?' I can't quite bring myself to say his name. When I think of him trying to wrestle the flat away from me I'm livid. But then I catch my stomach disintegrating when I think about the way he looked at me afterwards.

Plum wrinkles her nose and rubs her finger round the rim of the bowl. 'Nell would never admit it. But she does get extra animated whenever he's around.'

I've no idea why I wish she hadn't said that. 'I'd noticed too.' It's good to get this out in the open.

'Then she always claims it's on other people's behalf.' Plum rolls her eyes as she sucks raspberry mixture off her finger. 'She loves it when she gets couples together at her events. But she always holds back herself.'

I let my lips curl into a smile. 'Maybe we'll have to give her a helping hand, one of these days.'

Plum grins. 'A bloody great push more like.'

It's funny how differently our lives have all panned out. When Sophie was brave enough to have Milla on her own not long after uni, none of us imagined ten years later she'd have Nate, her business and three more children. Plum and I were always the ones to prioritise life not relationships. Whereas Nell was the one who always had a boyfriend in tow, from the age of thirteen onwards. She settled down early and bought into the whole mortgage and the house on the estate with way more bedrooms than they needed, only to have it all crack up. Last year, quite abruptly, she and Guy decided they'd be better apart than together. He moved to Glasgow, and that was that. One weekend she was enjoying a married mini break in Bridport. The next she had her house on the market and was flinging herself into singles' karaoke at the Hungry Shark.

Somehow the parade of wooden penguins has migrated from the living room shelf to the kitchen table. Okay, they didn't move on their own, it was me. That's another thing I've remembered. Laura used to move them around. I pick one up and rub its white painted stomach. 'Nell definitely deserves a second chance to find her special penguin.'

Plum's eyes light up at the reference. 'Oh my, remember Drew Barrymore and *Never Been Kissed*? How many times did we watch that film when we were teenagers?'

I laugh. 'Enough times to know the scenes off by heart. And for you and me to decide the bit about spending our lives looking for one penguin to stay with forever with was bollocks.'

She wrinkles her nose. 'Josie Geller getting her penguin at the end was still one of the best movie snogs ever.'

'Even though I'd hate to be tied down personally, it still gives me teenage goosebumps when I think about it.' It's great to be able to admit this to Plum and know she won't ever try to hook me up with anyone. 'So what's the story with George? How come *he* isn't press ganged into going to Nell's events?' I may as well ask now we're here. Then we've covered everything.

She laughs. 'George goes his own way; we all gave up on him years ago.' She adds the empty bowl to the huge stack next to the sink and slides the last dish into the freezer. 'So what's next? Shall we clear away, then go for the booze?'

I turn on the tap. 'Good idea. At least with washing up and Gin Fizz, I'm back in my comfort zone.'

Plum picks up a tea towel. 'And there can't be too many sinks in the world with a view straight out to sea. Which is a good thing, because looking at the number of dishes, we're going to be here forever.'

It turns out that she's right. By the time we get back from town it's late afternoon. We're on the landing letting ourselves into the flat, when the door across the way swings open.

'Charlie, lovely to see you.' I'm over compensating here. He's the last person I want to meet when our bags are clinking with enough gin and soda for twenty, plus helpers.

'Diesel and I thought you might like some tea?'

I'm kicking myself for staring at his bare feet and tanned ankles. 'Errrr ...' My mouth gapes. As I try to work out the best excuse I let my eyes rise, and notice he's carrying a loaded tray.

He's too quick for me. 'Great, it's all ready, *and* we have brownies. Just showing there's no hard feelings after yesterday. I'll grab another mug for Plum.'

I pull a face at Plum as he disappears. 'Because obviously the six shelves of mugs at ours won't be enough.' As for who's the hard feelings are, he doesn't say. I'm guessing if he was the one apologising, he'd come out and say it. In which case this is him saying he's forgiven me for calling him an 'opportunist'. Or was it an 'arse'? I refuse to be forgiven for telling the truth, so those brownies had better be amazing, or it could all kick off again.

'He probably wants all the mugs to match.' She drops her voice to a hiss. 'And while he's around, it might be a good idea to come clean about tonight.'

I glance at my phone and my stomach leap frogs. 'Shit, three hours from now they'll be arriving.' As I look through into the living room and imagine twenty guests filing in from the landing my squeak rises to a shriek. 'How the hell will they all fit in? There's nowhere near enough chairs for everyone, it's going to be like playing Sardines.'

Plum sniffs. 'Maybe Nell has over extended with the numbers, but with the singles' the more they're squashed the better they like it.' She winks at me. 'Close encounters and all that.'

'Whatever floats their boats.' I shudder at that thought, then hold the door open for Charlie as he wanders back across, with Diesel two steps behind. 'Let's have tea in the kitchen.' I'm saying it so often it's feeling like a habit. This way we avoid Diesel dropping chocolate crumbs on the rug, and I can take a look in the freezer while we're there.

As Charlie pours the tea and offers the cakes round I whisk a brownie off the plate and sink my teeth into the dark sticky slab. After a few minutes of cocoa swoon, I screw up my courage to speak. 'So I'm having a few people over this evening.' I'd planned to sound brighter and more airy, but my throat is clogged with chocolate. As I point to the embarrassingly large cluster of Gordon's bottles poking out of the carrier bags and amble across to the freezer, it strikes me I need to make it clear he's not getting an invitation. 'Gin and *home-made* sweets for some *very, very, very* close friends.' Okay, I'm only bragging about the 'home-made' thing because I'm over the effing moon with what we've pulled off here. And hopefully he'll get that the 'close' bit excludes pushy neighbours. As I open the freezer door a crack, I'm praying the jammed-in dishes don't dislodge and come cascading out.

'Sounds like a chilled kind of evening.' Charlie's giving Diesel a bone shaped biscuit from the tray. 'By the way, I'm not being mean with the brownies, but chocolate's bad for dogs.'

'All the more for me then. Excuse me a sec, I'll just check on the sorbets.' That's another sentence I'd never planned to say in my entire life ever. Feeling very like someone else's mother – obviously not mine, as she doesn't cook – I lift the cling film and peer into the raspberry mixture. 'This looks a bit weird, I was expecting it to be solid.' I'm already regretting my boast. As I stick my finger in and find it's still as runny as when we put it in, I let out a scream. 'Waaaaahhhh, it's still liquid, this can't be right?' I turn to Plum.

Plum blinks at her phone. 'How long's it been in?'

It feels like hours. 'It froze solid in half this time when we tried it out at Sophie's.'

She comes and pokes at the others. 'Shit, none of it's anywhere near frozen.' As she purses her lips her eyes are popping out. 'There's no way this is going to be ready for tonight.'

Charlie's frowning over his tea mug. It's hand thrown, with grey and blue and white in random stripes. Plum was right, they're all a teensy bit different but essentially they do all match. In the most on-trend, guy-type of a way. Which kind of suggests he'd fit in very well with a proper 'Waitrose' woman. 'Anything I can help with?'

I send him my most ironic beam. 'Seriously, I doubt it. Not unless you can explain why an entire *sodding* freezer full of *sodding* sorbet is sloppy when it should be frozen?'

He looks like he's holding back one of those cough-laughs of his. 'I think you just answered your own question there.'

'Well thanks a lot, that's *really* helpful.' As I look at his superior sneer something inside me snaps. I don't even care that I'm shouting. 'I've got no effing idea when the hell I'm doing here. All I know is in a couple of hours a whole load of people are going to descend on me expecting to eat sorbet, and this far all I've got to offer them is smoothies. So, unless you've got something useful to say, cut the jokes please.'

His lips are twitching. 'Hang on, there's no need for a full-scale melt down.' His smirk's gone now. 'What I meant is, if you put a massive amount of food into a freezer it'll take longer to freeze than a small amount, that's all. It's the laws of physics.'

Physics? 'Still not helpful.'

'But maybe I *can* help. I do have an industrial size freezer next door. That should chill your sorbets to perfection in no time.'

'What?' Now I *am* listening. Somehow it's no surprise he's got this kind of kit. A freezer like that could save me here, but before I get my hopes up I need to check that it's not just more bullshit. 'Just a minute. How did you get one of those up the stairs? Or even fit it into the flat?'

He's back to looking super pleased with himself without actually smiling. 'My flat's a *lot* bigger than yours. And the builders craned the fridges in when they were doing the balcony work.' He pauses for a second. 'It's got a fast freeze option.'

I feel like my fairy godmother's flying over the area. 'Really?' This time I don't bother hiding my enthusiasm.

'It's a shame you weren't here, or we could have craned a new one in for you too.'

Oh my days. 'I'm not sure I've actually got the room.' The man is so out of touch. If I'm having to flog sorbets to pay for roof work, I'm damn sure I can't afford super-sized fridges. What's worse, when I look around for a space to put anything tall, the kitchen suddenly feels minute rather than cosy.

'So ...' He's staring at me expectantly. 'What are we waiting for?'

Plum sends me a 'WTF?' grin as she slides some trays out from the gap beside the dresser. 'Best not waste valuable chilling time.'

I know I secretly vowed never to set foot next door, or talk to the neighbour, let alone accept favours from him. But sometimes a situation is so desperate you can't hold on to your principles. And this is one of those times.

9

In the flat next door
Fur balls and shaggy rugs
Monday afternoon

'There you go. I can pretty much promise your sorbets will be ready by the time your friends get here.' Charlie swings the giant freezer door closed. 'Don't forget to come for them in good time. They'll need twenty minutes to soften up again before serving.'

When he implied his freezer was enormous he was seriously understating. As for his flat, it seems like the top floor of Seaspray Cottage has been divided into 'minute' and 'effing enormous'. And no prizes for guessing which half he's got. Or how the whole beautiful backdrop of perfection only makes him look ten times more magazine-ready than he does anyway.

The space I'm staring round at is humungous, and there's so much wall to wall white and natural wool and hewn wood I'm guessing he's used the same super-expensive decorators as Nate and Sophie. Although the flashes of stainless steel and hi-gloss in his kitchen area are a masculine variation. Instead of being flat like Laura's, the ceilings rise up to follow the roof line, and the roof lights punched through them let the sun flood in and outline spectacular rectangles of blue sky. It's all a bit stark and startling for me, but Diesel has flopped in the centre of a massive grey rug almost as shaggy as he is, so at least someone's relaxed into it.

'So now your sorbets are in safe hands, how about a tour?' Charlie looking pleased with himself is probably justified, although how he does that without the ear to ear grin the rest of us would use is anyone's guess.

I try to force my face into a less bemused expression. 'You mean there's more?' The room we're standing in has to be at least the size of a football pitch. I've no idea why Diesel needs exercise when he lives here. A walk from one side of the kitchen living room to the other probably equals more steps than I do in a week. I shiver as I imagine Charlie and his wrecking ball approach to restoration obliterating the flat next door too. Realistically, compared to this it might provide him with enough space for a tie store.

He's poised to go. 'There are bedrooms, en suites, and acres more living area. I thought you'd be interested to see the different aspects?'

I'm feeling speechless enough as it is. More of the same and I might not recover. As for the way his ripped jeans are pulling across his thighs, there's no way I can see where he sleeps *and* keep my thoughts clean. I can't afford distractions like that when I need to focus on tonight's very important job.

'We're good, thanks.' I catch Plum's scowl as her Converse collides with my heel and adjust my answer. 'Some other time maybe ... perhaps when Nell's here?' Hopefully that'll satisfy Plum.

Realistically, if Mr H makes Nell glow, when she sees his flat she'll illuminate. Or maybe even explode entirely. I know I almost have.

As Plum wanders forwards, it's obvious she's going to make the most of *her* visit by exploring to the max, no holding back. When she reaches the hewn wood island unit her eyebrows shoot upwards. 'Wow, look at these.' She's so far away by now I need binoculars to see what she's talking about.

Charlie shakes his head. 'You spotted my clutter. Everything's supposed to be in cupboards, but somehow I can't bear to put those little guys in the drawer.'

Plum's yelling down the room at me. 'Penguins, Clemmie, in a little line. Just like some others we know. How funny is that?'

Not at all, I'd say. 'Very Josie Geller.' That's as much as I'm giving her.

Charlie's eyebrows shoot upwards in surprise. 'Another *Never Been Kissed* fan?'

'Shit.'

Plum recovers from the implications faster than I do. 'You know that film too?'

He rolls his eyes to the roof window and a passing cloud. 'Growing up with four sisters it goes with the territory. And let me guess, you can recite every line too?'

Worse and worse. Luckily, Plum's under the spotlight for this one. 'Too right.'

I know it. Any minute now we'll be on to the final scene. Discussing *that* snog here would be beyond cringeworthy. I jump in. 'So, remind me why the hell you want to buy the flat next door, when you've already got one this massive?' As subject changes go, it's a country mile away from anywhere I'd intended to go.

But anything's better than standing on Mr Hobson's shag pile reliving Drew Barrymore getting her knickers pashed off to a Beach Boys soundtrack.

Charlie blinks, and curls up his toes as he considers. 'I'm going to level with you here, Clemmie. Wanting to buy flat next door is less about the space, and more for the sake of completion. I'm very focused and hugely patient. However long I have to wait, I always get what I want in the end.'

I take it back. At least if we'd stuck to Josie Geller and tongues down throats I'd have understood. Whereas what he said there is developer-talk that makes no sense at all, served with a side order of bloody mindedness. And even if he is freezing my sorbets, I'm still determined when it comes to Laura's flat he's not going to get whatever completion he's after.

He picks up my reticence and changes tack. 'Actually I need a home entertainment space. That would be a great addition to any penthouse.' If he knew how 'Hugh Heffner' he sounds, he might not say that.

As for Plum, she's left us to it and gone off on a hike right past the kitchen and she's already halfway across the dining area beyond. Much longer, she'll be a dot on the horizon. 'Hey, is that a cat?' She's always been the same, in situations like this she can be such an embarrassment. 'Talk about adorable. Come and see his eyes, Clemmie, they're completely China blue.'

Far from resenting the intrusion, Charlie's lapping it up. 'That's Pancake, my mum's Ragdoll, and she's actually a girl. She's staying for a couple of nights while my mum's away.'

However frosty I feel towards Charlie right now, when it comes to a pale fawn fluff ball, my reservations go straight out the window. Despite my heels skidding across the polished boards, I run the length of the room. As I arrive panting next to Plum, my insides squish. 'Wow, how cute are you?' Obviously, I'm talking to the cat here. No question, Pancake's adorable, especially when she looks up from the grey wool designer cushion she's curled up on and allows us to scratch her head. 'So how do she and Diesel get on?'

Charlie pulls a face as he sidles up to us. 'They have their moments. So long as Pancake stays in her sun patch, Diesel leaves her alone. Lucky for me, she doesn't move much.' He sniffs. 'Now you've got this far, why not let me show you the rest? Then you'll understand how well the top floor would work as one space.'

I ignore Plum's imploring look. 'Sorry, we really do have loads to do.' Drinking Darjeeling with a barefoot neighbour in my kitchen is bad enough. Being exposed to his bed linen and his waterfall bath taps is a bridge too far. Especially when he's so blatant about coveting my bit. And that's before we get to how hot he is. I set my sights on the distant door and start to march, and three steps later I hear Plum shuffling behind me, then the thump of Diesel's tail on the rug as I storm past him.

Charlie's calling after us as we spill out onto the landing. 'Any time you're ready for the sorbets help yourselves ... the door's always open. Feel free to use the ice maker too.' One man and his industrial fridges. You have to laugh at guys and their gadgets, even when they are saving your proverbial bacon. It goes without saying I'd rather be using any other freezer in St Aidan.

As we reach the kitchen, Plum grins at me. 'What a nice man, he's left us the chocolate brownies.'

As I sink my teeth into my third slice, I can't help feeling I'm being bought here. 'Nice guy my bum. If he'd said about making this flat into a bloody gaming room earlier, I'd have taken the damn sorbets somewhere else.'

Plum laughs. 'You know that's bollocks, Clems.'

And the annoying thing is, she's right.

10

In Laura's flat. Laura's Lovely Sorbets Evening
Soft scoops and quiz nights
Monday

Two hours later, it's all hands on deck for the mermaids. The plan is for Nell to meet up with the Sorbet Singles at the Surf Shack, then bring them along the beach and up the stairs altogether. Sophie's dashing in and out to the balcony, rearranging cushions, enthusing about the sunset, trying to be the first to see the group arriving. Because that's how driven and 'in charge' she is. And Plum and I are sloshing gin into big jugs, prodding sorbet dishes, and running from window to window in between squeezing lemons and slicing limes. 'Nice dress,' Plum says, trying to distract me as she clinks ice cubes into glasses. 'And I love the lippy.'

I've swapped my navy and white office spots for my favourite floaty flowers. And for my lips I've ignored the clash with my hair and picked my cranberry rose to complement the jewel colours of the flat. And it's 'matte all-day', because something tells me this is going to be a very long night. But I'm so scared, I reckon I stopped breathing at least half an hour ago. 'Cool dungarees,' I croak back, checking the lines of waiting bowls and glasses on the table for the hundredth time, and shuffling the waiting baskets of mint leaf and fruit garnish. Even though she has more pairs of overalls than there are days of the year, Plum's the only one who can tell the difference. Obviously, the nuances are in the rips and the paint stains. I pinch myself one final time to check that I'm not in the middle of a bad dream. 'This really is happening, isn't it?'

Plum comes over and pulls me into a hug so tight her dungaree buttons make imprints on my boobs. 'Don't worry, Laura's sorbets are amazing. It's all going to be fab.'

Then Sophie's shouting from the living room. 'They're here! Go, go, go! Pop the soda and bring out the fizz!'

I know I'm the drinks person. But when I have the first tray loaded and pick it up the glasses are rattling so badly due to my shaking that Plum takes pity and wrestles it from me.

I'm patting her back as I follow her through into the living room. 'Oh my gosh, we forgot music.'

She grins at me over her shoulder. 'Chill, Clemmie. Put on your vintage French mix, say "Hi", then as soon as everyone's got drinks we'll make a start on the sorbets.'

Which is how I end up waving an endless stream of strangers in through the door, blinking at the blur of names as they file past. Did I really hear Dakota? And marvelling at their chorus of 'Wows'. All to the accompaniment of Charles Trenet singing 'Boum !'.

'Great tune.' Nell's waggling her eyebrows as she comes up the rear, translating as she squeezes in behind a hunk in a Hawaiian shirt. '*When our hearts go "boum", love wakes up.* The way everyone's hearts are banging after all those stairs, this could turn out to be a very amorous evening.'

I can't take the credit. 'It's a total lucky fluke.'

'No such thing.' She lifts a Gin Fizz from Plum's tray as she wedges herself in the only spare square millimetre between my favourite velvet chair and the patchwork sofa. 'And here's to a great evening.'

As a measure of how full the living room is, a game of Sardines would seem like a luxury. I wriggle my way back to the kitchen trying not to notice how many toes I step on along the way, then begin scooping sorbet into glasses. We're serving three courses, the first in plain glasses, the next in a variety of pretty glass bowls, and the third in Laura's colourful selection of tea cups. I'm concentrating so hard on getting my scoops even that somewhere between the tenth scoop of blurry red strawberry, and the fortieth scoop of ice green mint and cucumber I actually forget to worry. By the time I've added teaspoons and a sage sprig to all of them, I'm almost enjoying myself. The second I finish Sophie whisks them onto trays, and she's off.

By the time I've collapsed against the work surface, and gulped down a glass of soda, she's back again, with an encouraging smile.

'You can tell by the silence how well the sorbet's going down. I've opened the balcony doors to let the breeze in, but roped it off so people don't wander out.' She pulls down the corners of her mouth. 'I know Charlie's being a sweetheart with his ice-maker, but he won't want singles gatecrashing his quiet evening in.'

I join her by the kitchen doorway and together we peep out at the guests. A woman with cropped blonde hair, a teensy waist and a yard of bare midriff snakes her arm around the Hawaiian-shirted shoulders of the guy I saw coming in. As she leans towards his sorbet spoon with her mouth wide open, I grin at Sophie.

'I guess it very much depends who's wandering into Charlie's flat. If someone friendly like her walked in off his balcony I can't see him grumbling.'

Plum laughs as she arrives with her own empty tray. 'Jealous?'

'Too right.' I have to admit it. 'I'd kill for a waist that small.'

Plum's straight back at me with a teasing nudge. 'I wasn't talking about her.'

Sophie frowns. 'She doesn't look twenty, let alone twenty-five. Although I'm guessing Nell wouldn't have let her come if she wasn't. She's very strict with her age criteria.'

Plum nods at the couple. 'What did I say about close encounters? If things carry on there you'll be in line for a "cupid" award on your first night.'

'A what?' It sounds horribly as if an assessment's involved.

Sophie smiles. 'Don't look so nervous. Nell awards a "cupid" whenever a get-together ends up with a "get together". It's part prestige, part statistical. Apparently, it's a great way of working out how effective events are.'

Since we were small, Nell's always turned every activity into an opportunity for calculations. When we collected shells on the beach as three year olds, while the rest of us piled them in buckets and on sand castles, Nell was counting them. It's strange how our personalities showed so strongly when we were young. By the time we were five Plum was drawing everything in sight and Sophie was organising anything that moved. There was a time when we were teenagers when we thought that she was so brilliant that we were holding her back. But then we worked out she needed us to boss about as much as we needed her to sort us out. Out of all of us, I'm the only one who never showed a talent for anything in particular. I might have travelled a long way in miles, but I've made very little progress with my life. Although I'd never admit it to the mermaids, it's sad that I've never been good at anything.

Plum gives a sigh. 'Nell actually has "Cupid" award league tables.'

'Please tell me you're joking?' I groan, although realistically it needn't bother me with my one-off evening.

Plum shakes her head. 'Not at all. In fact, the regular events with the highest cupid scores are always the most popular. For obvious reasons.'

This time my groan's for Nell. 'The sooner we get her a new partner the better. Then she can give up being sad and singles obsessed and get on with her proper life.'

Plum wrinkles her nose. 'There's nothing sad about Nell from where I'm standing.'

Sophie turns on her. 'Nor should there be, we've worked our butts off and delivered her a stunning event in next to no time.'

Nell's got a triumphant shine to her eyes as she flattens herself against the bookcase and makes her way around the room edge towards us. 'The sorbet's going down a storm. And everyone's blown away by how quirky and colourful the flat is.' She waggles a sheaf of papers at Sophie. 'Here, I brought you the quiz.'

Sophie jumps for the sheets, then dips into the kitchen for her bag. 'Ooo, this is me, I've raided Tilly's felt tip box for pens.' She strides as far into the living room as she can, which is approximately one step. Then she claps her hands and puts on her 'don't mess with Mummy' face. 'Okay, quizzes coming round. Grab a partner, or work in twos, threes or fours. Anything goes, *so long as everyone joins in*.'

I'm mystified and horrified in equal measure. 'What's this?' I know zilch about anything so party games are my pet hate, especially when participation's non-negotiable. And Sophie's sounding insistent.

Nell waves away my concern. 'Don't worry, you're excused. Quizzes are a singles' tradition. We even do them when we're whale watching or out on walks. Collaboration's excellent for pair bonding, and not everyone hates trivia as much as you.'

I'm glad she remembered. 'How do you not run out of questions?'

It seems like a valid point, but she ignores it. 'It'll give us breathing space to circulate with more drinks and get the next round of sorbets ready.' She has to be talking metaphorically about the space because truly, there isn't any.

'Okay, I'll look after fizz and scooping.'

Which is exactly what I do, with as much washing up as I can manage in between. Sophie's apologising for the endless stream of glasses she's bringing in, but for someone like me who's used to working a busy bar, that part's a picnic. When I finally have a second to look at my phone, it's already eleven, and the guests are sighing over cups filled with raspberry and mango ices.

As I make my way to the open door, dip under the silk scarf and slide out into the soft darkness of the balcony for a few seconds of quiet, there are so many compliments drifting past me I'm almost blushing: '… sooooo pretty, I could eat them all over again' '… saving the best 'til last' '… the icy mango is orgasmic …'

I know I've had so much help, but there's a warm feeling

spreading through my chest that's due to much more than too many gins. It isn't over yet, but for now I couldn't be any happier. I can't help a flutter of excitement when I think Nell, Plum and Sophie's crazy 'pop up' idea might actually work.

Even though the sorbets are going down brilliantly, Nell's full-on coupling strategies are doing less well, and that's what everyone's here for. From where I'm standing it looks as if the evening's coming to a close with the women swaying on the rugs scraping the pattern off their china cups, and the guys flopped onto the chairs and sofas doing the same. At least with fewer people standing up, there are air gaps between the bodies. Although at this stage of the event, with Plum making the rounds with the last serving of gin fizz, that's not such a good thing. As far as couples in clinches go, it looks like I'm going to miss out on my Cupid.

A sudden crash makes me look along to where light from Charlie's flat is pooling out onto the balcony through his open doors. There's another bump, and as I see the blurred shape coming towards me it clicks. 'Pancake?' As a pale brown fluff ball hurtles over my feet there's an anguished squawk, a soft swish of tail brushing against my leg, then a cloud of claws and splinters as she does a ninety degree turn and flings herself into the living room.

I open my mouth to shout 'watch out for the cat' to the sea of legs inside, but a much larger shape comes clattering along the balcony. 'Diesel, sto——-p!'

His paws, tongue and ears are all flapping, and he covers the length of the balcony in three strides. As he skids towards me he changes course, comes to a momentary halt in a heap in front of my doors. Then with one massive bound he leaps into the flat after Pancake. As I dive after him to warn people, I'm already too late. He's forging a path across the floor, felling women as he goes. As Diesel's tail disappears into the hall, the guests are toppling off their heels wailing as they wave their arms. Squealing as they fall. Crashing into side tables, sending gin glasses flying. Cups are arcing through the air, clattering as they hit the wall. People are landing on top of other people at angles, in random piles.

As I pause to gasp a lump of raspberry sorbet smacks onto my boob, slithers down my skirt, and squishes onto my strappy sandal. I'm crouching at floor level, scrabbling to clean it up when some familiar tanned toes arrive next to mine. I get as far as the ankle bone, then follow the faded jeans up to a T shirt and a flash of tanned torso.

I close my eyes as my head spins. Then I shake my head and make myself focus. 'Charlie. How can I help?' My heart's beating double speed and sinking at the same time, and I'm almost throwing up.

His brow knits as he stares around at the mayhem. 'I came to ask if you'd seen Diesel. But obviously, he's not here.' He hesitates as he spins to leave. 'If you'd said you were having an orgy I'd have stayed at my end of the balcony. You do know this isn't acceptable?'

I stagger to my feet. 'What's unacceptable is your dog galloping through my living room breaking up my party. And in case you're wondering, Pancake's here too. And it's not a sex fest.'

Nell appears in the hall doorway, hauling Diesel by the collar. 'Is this your missing boy? The cat's hiding under the bath, we've closed the door until she feels safe to come out.' I've no idea why she's being so polite.

'Jeez, Diesel.' He looks satisfyingly shell-shocked.

As I look around, the piles of bodies on the sofas and chairs are realigning. Where a second ago I was staring at a mass of limbs, some of the women are making themselves comfy on guys' knees.

Nell's beaming, and as she crosses the room and hands Diesel over her cheeks are definitely extra rosy. 'No harm done, Charlie. Diesel certainly got people mingling, the floor hasn't been this empty all evening.' She grins round at the guests, who, to be fair, look completely unbothered to be stacked on top of each other. 'As an icebreaker that was even better than musical chairs. We must try it again some time.'

Charlie shrugs, but he's staring at my mouth. 'Did you know your lips are exactly the same colour as that lump of sorbet running down the wall?'

'And?' I work bars, I take banter without flinching. So, there's no reason at all why I should be feeling hot around my Peter Pan collar. I'm wracking my brain for a way to serve the cheek back tenfold when I remember if it hadn't been for Charlie's mega-freezer there wouldn't have been sorbet or a party. So, I bite back my anger. 'Get Diesel out of here, we'll let you off the tidying.'

Nell chips in. 'The club usually clears at events. Washing up is a very interactive way to end to a night.'

'Plum and I have got this covered. It's mostly done anyway.' I'm looking for a way to say that now the party's been literally flattened I'd like to be left on my own.

And damn that Charlie's still there. Hanging on Nell's every word. 'Club?'

I'm on it in a flash. 'Most of my friends are unattached, Charlie, obviously, there's some crossover.' Sometimes the best way to hide something is to draw attention to it. 'Remember Nell's Singles' leaflet? The one you weren't interested in?' The one that definitely isn't *anything* to do with tonight.

'Sure.' His tone says he's not buying it. 'Well whoever you are, try to leave quietly. The Airbnb flats are let tonight and the local Tourist Board are trying to keep the ratings high. You've already caused enough mayhem for one evening.'

I might be on shaky ground, but I'm still wide-eyed at his nerve. 'Excuse me? I just saved those Airbnb guests from your dog and cat falling off the balcony and sailing past their windows to their deaths. That would get way more one stars than murmurs on the landing.' If I was warm before I'm blazing now.

He's standing his ground, still hanging onto Diesel. 'You've got some reading to catch up on. The Residents' Code has clear guidelines on late entertaining.' He couldn't sound any more up himself.

I'm open mouthed that he's twisting this. 'I'm a resident too. What about me *not* having neighbours' livestock stampeding through my living room?'

Sophie's breezing over, and her 'don't eff with mummy face' just got fiercer. 'Let's pick this discussion up again tomorrow.' It's an order not a suggestion and her finger is wagging inches from Charlie's chest. 'If *YOU* go home *IMMEDIATELY*, along with your dog, we'll bring you some sorbet. How does that sound?'

I can't help shrieking. 'Don't offer him pudding, *we're* in the right here.'

Nell's shoving me in the ribs and making cutthroat signs. 'Excellent idea, do we have a deal?'

'Fine.' Charlie's mumbling as he turns and pushes Diesel out onto the balcony then staggers after him.

Plum disappears with a handful of crockery she's picked up from the floor, and comes back with a serving bowl piled with scoops of sorbet. 'Who's taking this?'

There's a rush of outstretched hands, all eager to deliver Charlie's sorbet, but before she's knocked over she spins round and whips the bowl out of reach. 'You can't all go.'

'Who got the lowest score in the quiz?' I ask, already knowing it wasn't Ms Midriff.

But there's a flash of disgustingly flat stomach, and she's already snatched the bowl away from Plum. 'That was me. I didn't answer any.'

Sophie's mouth hangs open as the girl dips out onto the balcony. 'Oh my God, did you see that? She grabbed, *and* she lied. If this was Milla's party, she'd be on the naughty chair.'

Nell's laughing. 'Single Street's not for softies. If you see something you like, you've got to grab it before someone else does. Like Dakota did.'

Sophie wrinkles her nose. 'That's her *real* name?' As she and I exchange glances we're equally disbelieving.

Nell laughs. 'I haven't checked her birth certificate.'

Sophie's right back at her. 'I thought not. It's not just a fake name, she *has* to be under age too.'

Nell shakes her head. 'No, she talks about her thirtieth. I'm guessing that's what gym time can do for you.' She winks at Sophie. 'Or maybe she uses your rejuvenating cleanser?'

I pull a face at Plum. 'If Charlie's getting the friendly one, I might end up with a "Cupid" award after all.' Anyone else but her, I wouldn't have minded. Although I'm so annoyed with him, I'd happily have delivered the sorbet myself and tipped it over his head.

All round it's a shitty end to a disastrous evening. Like the cherry on the calamity cake. And with sorbet up the walls and every guest either falling over or squished, this must be the crappiest singles' night ever. I'm bracing myself to receive Nell's Golden Toilet award. Let's face it, she has to have one.

11

At the Surf Shack
Out of the blue
Tuesday afternoon

'Isn't it great to have the Surf Shack as your corner café?' Sophie says as I come out into the late afternoon sunshine the next day carrying a huge tray.

The Surf Shack is St Aidan's most ramshackle building, made from a thousand bits of wood randomly hammered together. It also serves the fattest, most delicious sandwiches on the sea front, as well as the best coffee, which is probably why it's popular with surfies as well as being our own go-to place for breakfast, lunch or tea. Today it's perfect to pop into on our after school potter with the kids along the water's edge. I've been inside to order while Sophie settled the children, and as I make my way across the wide wooden deck the bunting above is flapping against a deep blue sky.

I laugh. 'Having The Surf Shack two minutes along the sandy path from Seaspray Cottage isn't the best news for my waistline.'

If my finances weren't on lockdown, I'd be here for every meal. Then probably grow out of all my clothes.

Even though it's perched on what has to be the prettiest sand dune in Cornwall, and at high tide the breakers come rushing up the beach and splash onto the deck, I can't help thinking it's not my corner café in Paris. But if I'm missing my tiny table on the pavement with the metal chairs so close to the traffic that sometimes the waiter can't hear to take my order, I'm not about to mention it.

'Milla, we've got wraps here if you want a break from dancing.' As Sophie calls to her across the decking, Milla takes out an ear bud, tosses back her curtain of blonde hair, and nods. Then goes back to tapping out her steps beyond the tables.

I shout to the littlies. 'There's tomato, lettuce and cheese, or hummus, carrot and coriander, Brin's made them specially for you.' As I put the board of wraps down on the slatted table Tilly and Marco come running, take one in each hand, then go back to their pile of shells and stones and seaweed. Hopefully this way they'll miss that Brin's made me and their mum a hot chocolate with squirty cream and mini doughnuts on the top. Although Sophie insisted on having hers with oat milk to make it healthy. We've also got clandestine muffins underneath our serviettes. Blueberry for our five-a-day, and gluten-free to avoid bloating. Obviously, I'd have preferred double chocolate, but with the kids here we have to set some kind of good example.

Sophie eases Maisie into a high chair, puts her bib on with one hand and empties cucumber and cheese cubes onto the tray with the other, then glances at Milla. 'This deck is too much like a stage for her to waste time eating.' Sophie's obviously forgotten.

At Milla's age, she'd insist on coming down to the beach every day in summer so she could dance on the jetty. Only back then she had her songs on a Fisher Price kiddie cassette player, and the fishermen who passed used to sing along to Madonna while Sophie did her 'Like a Prayer' dance in her swimsuit with a sequined skirt held up by knotted elastic.

She sits down, nibbles a doughnut behind her hand, takes a slug from her bucket sized cup, and turns to me with a grin. 'So have you recovered from last night?'

I wince. 'I shudder every time I think about it.' I'm honestly feeling so humiliated, for most of the day I'd have been happy for the floor to open up and swallow me. There's a twang of disappointment too, because before Diesel arrived it was so close to wonderful I was almost imagining we could have another event. 'The first time I invite anyone round anywhere, and mostly they end up skittled.' It's one more reason for leaving town and never coming back. As if there weren't enough already.

She sighs, takes a monster bite of muffin behind her serviette and pushes a cucumber stick towards Maisie. 'It wasn't your fault Diesel rushed in. Sure, they were sad about their lost sorbet balls, but people still had a great time.'

I wouldn't go that far. 'Even if he did save us with his freezer, I'm furious with Charlie. And Pancake's still at mine too.' When I went out to work I found her litter tray outside my door and two gourmet food pouches. Probably left as Charlie went to run Dakota to her pre-dawn session at the gym. Although there's one piece of good news on the Dakota front. Charlie might hear Laura's loo flush but mercifully there wasn't a single groan through the wall from his flat last night. I'm thanking my fairy godmother that his master bedroom must be at the other end of the building. As for me waking up for the first time in my life with a fur ball snuggled in the crook of my knees – comfortable doesn't start to cover it. Suddenly all the stories about crazy cat women make complete sense.

Sophie shakes her head. 'It's a good thing you don't mind animals. What's not so good is the news coming off the grapevine from my cleaning team.' The way she pauses for effect it's obvious there's a biggie coming. 'According to Denise from Dainty Dusters, Charlie's the one who runs the Airbnb flats he was talking about last night. Apparently, they just started cleaning for him there.'

I put aside that Sophie lives in the kind of home where the cleaners arrive in a mini bus. 'What the *heck* does that mean?' I'm indignant and apoplectic all at the same time. 'Trust Charlie Hobson to ruin my hot chocolate.' Then I realise I'm shouting and giving our game away, and clamp my hand to my mouth.

Marco's head jerks up. 'Do we get chocolate too?'

Sophie pulls a face. 'The cocoa's very bitter, there's organic apple juice here for you, that's much sweeter.' She pushes a carton towards him then turns back to me. 'That's not all. Denise's cousin's a cleaner down near St Austell. According to her, Charlie was all set to get married at a country house near Polperro back in 2009, but his fiancée called off the wedding. It was the same weekend her daughter got married there. That's how she knows.' That's at least thirty miles across the county, so the cleaning world gossip-line must be well oiled.

I shrug. 'Okay, so he's got a sob story. But he trashed my evening and he wants my flat for a gaming room. I'm still livid.'

Sophie's wearing her 'super patient mother' expression. 'It's not about sympathy, I'm looking at the wider picture. I'll ask around to find out more about the Airbnb. If he's making moves on your flat, we need to understand what makes him tick.'

We both look up to see Nell winding her way between the galvanised chairs. She throws down her mini backpack, slips off her padded waistcoat, and pulls up a seat.

'So what am I missing?'

Sophie laughs at how eager she sounds. 'We found out Charlie Hobson's probably reluctant to join in with the singles because he was left standing at the altar.'

'Wow, hunky, hot *and* broken hearted.' Nell blows out her cheeks. 'Poor guy.'

I let out a long sigh because Nell arriving is making yesterday's disaster spring to life again. 'And I'm really sorry for disappointing all your friends last night. At least now we know the "pop up" venue idea is dead in the water.' Drowned and sunk. End of story. 'So I'm back to plan A – sell and disappear, before twenty angry party goers run me out of town.' Ideally selling to anyone but Charlie. Although realistically a flat with a ten-grand bill coming up and the most intrusive neighbour in St Aidan isn't going to have buyers stampeding.

Nell frowns. 'What part of "successful evening" don't you get? You're two hundred pounds better off than you were this time yesterday.' Bottom lines are the only measure she knows.

I'm gawping at the amount, but I don't understand. 'You did give everyone a refund?'

Her brows knot. 'Why would I do that when they all loved it? Better still, you got three "Cupids".'

I'm not sure why my heart sinks. 'Dakota got laid *three* times?' It's even worse than I imagined.

Nell shakes her head and winces. 'No, not Dakota, she's way too fussy to commit. But don't knock her, she's very helpful and a great asset to the club. And it's not all about sex, either. Cupid awards are for follow-up dates not hook-ups. Three is the score so far, but it's still only tea time. It could well be more.' Her disgust has turned to a delighted beam.

Sophie's clasping her hands together. 'Isn't that brilliant?'

'Abso-bloody-lutely.' Nell's punching the air. 'As a percentage guest-to-couple ratio the success is entirely unprecedented for any previous club event.' Nell's only ever two words away from drifting into analysis and becoming completely unintelligible, but even if I don't completely get it, there's still a shivery thrill zipping up and down my spine.

Sophie's eyes are gleaming as she brings us back to reality. 'Forty-nine more events like that, Clemmie, and you'll have your ten grand. With three events a week, you'd reach your target in four months.' You can almost hear the cash registers beeping in her business brain.

After years behind a bar I can do maths in my head too when it's the right sort. 'Forty-nine events with twenty guests? That means I'd need to find another nine hundred and eighty people who like sorbet.' My heart's sinking again, because put like that it's completely unattainable. 'Surely I've run out of gullible punters already?'

Nell's smile has turned smug. 'That's the beauty of social media. I've already had feedback, and everyone from last night is up for another event at the flat.'

Sophie's almost quivering with excitement. 'We need to think what to do next.'

I have to make a confession. 'Actually, despite last night's disaster, I was looking through Laura's recipe cards over lunch.' Coffee and croissant, because I didn't have time for breakfast. And I'm too much of a professional to drop pastry flakes on George's reception desk. 'I found out meringues only have two ingredients. Seeing the sorbet making went so well I was thinking I could try making those.' Some people drool over savories but I'm not one of them. And I loved Laura's meringues. She'd pipe them onto sugar paper and stick the halves together with buttercream. It all came rushing back to me when I saw the photos on her card. How I'd get meringue mixture right up my arms when I tried to lick out the piping bag. Putting out the pale blue bun cases while Laura made the buttercream. Me sticking the halves together, then arranging them on the three-tiered cake stand with flamingoes on that's standing on the dresser now. How they were dusty and delicious and so light I could put them away faster than Sophie's macaroons. I even managed to remember there was some special patriotic celebration where we made pink and blue ones too.

Sophie's face lights up. 'Yay! Pavlova, Eton mess, chocolate meringues. Prosecco would work well with those. Celiac-friendly, suitable for everyone except vegans and people with egg allergies. It's great you're so up for this, Clemmie.'

Laura's Pavlova pictures were making my mouth water earlier. 'Remind me what Eton mess is?' I'm almost as excited as Sophie.

Sophie's counting off her fingers. 'Broken meringue, whipped cream, berries and bananas, works well served in a glass. You can add lemon and ginger too. Or mascarpone.'

'Whoa. We're supposed to be keeping this simple.' Even if it sounds delectable, that's already six more ingredients than I'd planned.

If she'd eaten an entire Pavlova to herself Nell couldn't look any more ecstatic. 'Meringue's a crowd pleaser.' Her smile broadens even further. 'I'm running these as Singles' Club events for insurance purposes, but you need a proper title if we're doing this a lot.' It's great she's talking as if it's all of us.

Sophie's tapping an ice blue nail on the table. 'Clemmie's Cornish Kitchen sounds snappy?'

Even though I'm breathless with excitement, hearing my name in the mix makes the bottom drop out of my stomach. 'Definitely not "Clemmie", I prefer to stay anonymous.' Or better still, not here at all. Except I definitely want to be here for the meringues, especially if there's tasting.

Nell's going again. 'The Cornish Kitchen?'

My heart rate's steadying. 'Or ... The *Littl*e Cornish Kitchen? True to what it is.' Better still, keeping expectations small.

Sophie's nodding madly. 'Yes, yes, yes.'

Nell's buzzing so much she hasn't even scraped the squirty cream off her hot chocolate yet. 'That's good for starters, although we're getting ahead of ourselves here. The word's out about how much fun the sorbet evening was. My inbox has been pinging all day with messages from friends asking for a re-run so they can come too.'

I'm staring past the rope at the edge of the deck, and across the glittering turquoise expanse of the bay, asking myself what the hell I'm letting myself in for here. Then I suddenly remember. 'Ooops, sorry. Scrub the sorbet, the freezer can't cope.'

Nell's agonising. 'I'm sure if you asked Charlie, he'd be only too pleased to let you—'

I cut her off in mid flow: '*Absolutely NOT*.' Quite apart from me not wanting to owe him, after last night's disapproval the less he knows about parties at mine the better. Especially if we're about to embark on a Pavlova fest.

She's not letting it go. 'It seems a shame, when sorbets are such a winner and there's so much demand. And he does need to make amends for last night's total train wreck.' Her hand's shading her eyes as she looks out along the beach. Then she drops her Aviator sunglasses from the top of her head and I can see myself reflected in mirror lenses the colour of the sea.

My voice is squeaking with stress. 'I thought you said last night was okay?' When exactly did it change from amazing to shit?

'There are two sides to every story.' Her eyebrows wiggle fleetingly over the top of her glasses frames. 'Unless I'm mistaken Mr H and Diesel are on their way back from their stroll as we speak. We'll see how contrite he is and take it from there.'

I turn to Sophie for support, but she's fully absorbed cutting up Maisie's cheddar. A second later, Diesel's bounding up onto the deck, making a bee line for me.

I pull away as his tongue hits my face. 'I washed already, Diesel thank you.'

Nell's laughing. 'Hey, you've made a friend for life there.'

'Or maybe he's hoovering the crumbs off my chin.' As he moves on to the high chair I haul him away. 'No, Diesel, Maisie doesn't want your wet nose in her ear either.' He's not exactly under control here.

Nell's hissing at me without moving her lips. 'Nice to see our friendly developer scrubs up just as well when he dresses down.'

As I shake my head and hiss back, I'm still hanging on to Diesel. 'Surely it's not warm enough for cut offs and flip flops?' It's the flashes of stomach between the short T-shirt and the low-slung belt that are getting me.

Sophie jumps in to cover for us. 'Hi, Charlie, great afternoon for a walk.'

He takes the steps in one jump then saunters across the deck. 'What's this, a mermaid's chocolate convention?'

She's straight back at him with a snipe. 'Sirens against inappropriate construction. You don't qualify to join us on either count.'

He ignores the jibe. 'If the cake's as good as last night's sorbet, I'm in. What goodies are you hiding under those napkins?'

I send him a scowl. 'Cut the "C" words please, the kids are having a nutritious tea.'

Too late. Marco is piping up. '*Ple-e-e-ase* can I have cake and chocolate?'

Charlie reacts fast. 'Strong guys stick with carrot. Every time.' He peers at the table. 'And juice. And salad, obviously, because it's so good for muscles.' He crosses to high-five Marco, who high-fives back then returns to his pebbles.

Sophie's biting back her grin. 'Help yourself to a wrap, Charlie.'

He wrinkles his nose. 'Thanks all the same, but I'll pass on those.'

I cough. 'I take it you've come for Diesel?' I hold out his collar. 'One dog. Returned. *Again.*' Hopefully he'll get that however slobbery and lovable Diesel is, I'd like this to be the last time.

Charlie clips a lead on him. 'He can't keep away from you.'

I sniff. 'I had noticed. Pancake's still at mine by the way.' Just flagging it up.

'Great.' He looks about as happy as if I'd stolen her. 'I've left more cat food by your door, along with a copy of the Resident's Code. Page three is very clear about noise and disruption.'

I'm blinking at him with the shock. 'Unbelievable. So, the man who spends all day inflicting the noise of bulldozers on Cornwall lends me his copy of the effing *Silence Rule Book*?' After last night's guests leaving more quietly than nuns going to vespers, I was hoping we'd be sidestepping this bit.

He doesn't rise to my shriek. 'That's the one. Put it this way, Clemmie, if St Aidan were a train, Seaspray Cottage would be the quiet coach. And that's how I intend to keep it.'

I can't believe what I'm hearing. 'So what kind of coach do bonking Airbnb guests banging the headboard against the wall all damned weekend travel in? You might be blissfully unaware of them in your poncy penthouse, but they're on the train too. Sort *them* out first, *then* come and pick on me.'

He drags in a breath. 'Let's put this another way. Some of us have spent a lot of money buying seclusion, so let's clear this up. Non-stop student parties will *not* be tolerated. End of.'

Of all the luck, I get the joyless neighbour who hates fun. 'You need to lighten up here *and* get real. That wasn't a wild party, it was a *handful* of friends enjoying a quiet evening in.' If we'd been at his place they'd have fitted in his broom cupboard. It only looked a lot because Laura's flat is tiny.

Nell's straight in to back me up. 'It was a soiree not a party. And you might need to know, Clemmie does have a few more friends who'll be dropping in to catch up and try her sorbets while she's still around.'

I'm not backing down on this. 'As you say, it's best to clear this up now.'

And finally, Charlie's voice rises. 'What is this ... class of ninety-five reunion?'

'We were a very big year.' Nell's holding her line. 'And we'd hate to disappoint old friends. Three more evenings should knock it on the head.' Nell's got her eyes fixed on Charlie's face, gauging his reaction. 'Or maybe four.'

Indignant of St Aidan just about covers it. 'And I suppose you're expecting to use my freezer for all of those?'

Sophie's straight in there, taking the wind out of his T-shirt. 'Absolutely not, Clemmie's super grateful for you stepping in yesterday. But *my* industrial freezer makes yours look like a toy. So, we won't be needing your fast-freeze facility.' I can tell how much she enjoyed saying that.

Nell's beaming. 'We'll make sure we eat our sorbet quietly. So long as we don't rattle our spoons too loudly, I can't see you'll have anything to grumble about.'

'Great.' Now we've left him with nothing to grumble about, Charlie's backing off the decking. 'If there's any spare sorbet, I don't mind helping out with that.'

I'm shaking my head at the gall. 'I take it you'll keep Diesel at yours when my friends are round? And Pancake can stay at mine as long as she wants.'

Sophie's shaking her head as he and Diesel bounce back down the steps. 'So, not contrite at all then?'

As we watch Charlie and Diesel amble off down the sand, Nell's smiling. 'We'll handle him, don't worry. You have to admire a man who's totally driven by his stomach but still has abs to die for.'

Sophie's rubbing her lip. 'A tendency for muffin envy *and* a weakness for sorbet. We should remember that.' She's grinning at me. 'So now you've got a flat *and* a cat. Who'd have thought?'

I have to keep her right. 'Both *strictly* short-term.'

Nell's laughing. 'Whatever next?'

'I learn to cook meringues?' Even I can't quite believe that will happen. But if I don't try, I'll never know.

She's straight back at me. 'Brilliant. I'll bring you some eggs. You can get started right away.'

12

In Laura's kitchen
Breaking eggs
Wednesday

If you're in St Aidan and want newly laid eggs, Nell's your woman. As promised, she's back round at the flat before I have time to say 'fry up'.

'Two dozen?' I say, taking the stack of boxes from her. Twenty-four eggs sounds a lot. 'So who laid these?' Although I haven't had them before myself, I know Nell always likes to personalise her egg deliveries.

'Daisy, Fern, Bracken, Hilary and Nigella.' She wiggles her eyebrows. 'And a few of their very close friends.'

Nell's parents still live at Forget-me-not Farm, the small holding where she grew up alongside a variety of sheep, cows, pigs, horses, and chickens, and that's where she gets her eggs from. As kids, we used to love the cosy stone-built farmhouse, where the kitchen always smelled of her mum's freshly baked bread and meat pies, and the higgledy piggledy hay barns with the animal stables underneath. As teenagers, if we weren't at the beach we'd hang out in the meadows at Nell's, spending the long summer days feeding baby calves, helping bring in the hay and build the wood pile, splashing in the stream, or sprawled on the grass making daisy chains.

Nell's enthusiasm for home reared pork, her tendency to eat for England, that penchant for checked shirts, and her ability to make large groups of animals or people do exactly what she wants, all stem from her days at the farmstead. When she and Guy bought their own place on the edge of the housing estate her first priority was a garden suitable for keeping chickens. Once she found it, the hen house she built was so perfect it even had fairy lights. When she downsized to a tiny cottage in St Aidan after the split what upset her most wasn't Guy leaving or losing lovely her home. It was that her Buff Orpingtons and Speckledy hens had to go back to live with her parents.

As I open the first egg box and run my fingers over a smooth brown shell even six eggs looks like an awful lot. I stamp on the doubts, and try to sound like I'm on top of this. 'I've been watching people breaking eggs on YouTube.' Confusing doesn't begin to cover it. Who knew you needed knives and bottles and a whole stack of bowls, and that's just to separate the whites from the yolks.

'See how you go, shout when you need more.' Nell's backing out onto the landing. 'Are you sure I can't tempt you to an evening of Singles' Scrabble at the Yellow Canary? Dakota's not coming.'

However happy I am to hear the last part, for once my excuse is real. 'I'd better put the time in on my meringues.' Or more correctly, watching videos where people make them. How hard can it be, mixing egg whites and sugar? So long as I prepare in advance, one secret session should be enough to crack it. No pun intended. Let's face it, if I'm hoping to fit in three Little Cornish Kitchen events a week between now and September, I need to sort this and fast. By the time I go to bed, I've found a new heroine. She's called Cressida Cupcake and even though some of the YouTube comments complain that she doesn't give amounts for her recipes, I'm confident she's talked me through everything I need to know.

As soon as I'm back from work the next day, I stick my eighties mix on Spotify, gulp down my croissant, then I grab a pinny just like Cressida's and an egg cup and a saucer. The moment I set to work separating, I know I've done this before with Laura.

'Move over, Mary Berry, there's a new kid in the kitchen.' By the time I put my bowl of yolks to one side, and tip my dish of egg white into the mixer, I'm bopping round to Billy Ocean singing 'When the Going Gets Tough'. I set the mixer off at slow speed, and within seconds I'm speeding it up exactly Cressida Cupcake did, and dancing to 'Don't Leave Me This Way'. By the time I'm listening to '9 to 5' and pouring in the sugar, nothing seems to be happening, but I'm enjoying myself anyway. Three tracks on, I'm staring at a mass of white sticky stuff. I'm confident I'll be nailing it any minute, and it's hard not to feel on top of the world singing along to Bonnie Tyler. Very loudly. It has to be ready by the end of the track because it's been whisking for what feels like hours.

'"I'm holding out for a hero .... and he's got to be strong ... and he's got to be up for the f-i-i-i-ght ..."' As I crescendo and belt out the word 'fight' at the top of my voice and brace myself for the next stage of the operation, something cold and wet hits my thigh. I catch my breath, then look down. 'Diesel?'

A moment later, Charlie's head appears round the kitchen door. 'The French windows to the balcony were open, I knocked and you were calling out for a hero, so I came on in ...'

Who the eff would say something like that? 'Sorry, I didn't hear you.' I grab my phone and turn down the volume.

He's staring at me. 'Not surprising, it's good you turned that down, I came to tell you people can hear you singing all the way down to the Surf Shack.'

There's no answer to that other than to laugh. 'And here's me thinking getting caught mid-song by a wanker is the worst it gets.' So, I move on to my announcement: 'Actually, I'm making meringues.' This has to be my worst Waitrose shopper sentence yet. Although to be fair, Cressida Cupcake sounds like she might shop at Waitrose, and she's pretty damned impressive. 'Although the mountains aren't as high as I was expecting yet.' That doesn't sound quite right, but I'm a bit distracted by him moving in so close I can see the individual hairs in his eyebrows.

He peers into the bowl. 'Have you made meringues before?'

Something about his doubtful tone brings out my bullshitting side. I wipe my hands on my apron. 'Obviously. Only like, all the time. Here, let me show you this trick, it's totally gravity defying.' Not to mention gobsmacking. This is the one all the YouTubers do. You tip the bowl full of meringue mixture upside down over your head, and the trick is, thanks to the hugely sticky nature of the meringue mixture, it stays there. I know it's entirely stupid, and I'm totally not competitive, but a tiny part of me wants to make up for my waist being ten times bigger than Dakota's. There's no way she even *thinks* of meringues with a teensy bum like hers, let alone makes them herself.

'Is it stiff enough?' He's frowning over my shoulder now. And obviously totally oblivious he's sounding like a line from an actress and bishop joke.

I overlook the shocking innuendo, tilt the whisk, and with the kind of flourish Cressida Cupcake would be proud of, I whip round to face him and whoosh the bowl into the air and over my head.

'Ta-da!' I fix my gaze on his face, so I get every last millimetre of reaction. But what I'm reading isn't awe, it's horror.

'Shit, Clemmie!'

A second later, I feel a light slap on my head. Next thing I'm blinded by a curtain of white sludge. 'What the fuck ...?' The lumps slither down from my forehead, drop off my chin, hit my chest and slide into my cleavage and onto my skirt.

There's an awful 'I told you so' note to his voice: 'I'd say gravity won out there.'

I scrape the egg white out of my eyes with my fist. 'Jeez, that wasn't supposed to happen.' Diesel's licking my dress, but my groan isn't for that. 'And my hair's totally covered.'

Charlie's lips are twitching. 'Isn't egg white a conditioner? Do you want me to check on Google, see how long to leave it on for?'

I drop the bowl on the table, feel my way to the sink, and scrape as much off as I can. 'Oh my days, it's *so* sticky.'

As he hands me a towel his phone rings. 'I'll take that call later.' He's actually chuckling to himself as he taps his screen, which is a first. 'It's Dainty Dusters ringing about a sparkle clean for the ground floor flat. I reckon we need them a lot more here than there though.'

'What the hell's a sparkle clean?' It's a relief to take the attention off me and my fuck-up. Whatever it is, I'm sure Cressida Cupcake's kitchen has them. All the time.

'It's Dainty Dusters name for the deep cleans they do for tenancy changeovers. The ones with added shine.'

'You deal with those?' *Downstairs?* It sounds unlikely.

He's shuffling and looking down. 'Bay Holdings are multi-faceted, any property issue, we'll cover it.'

Which still leaves me in the dark but does bring me onto something else. 'For someone so multi-whatsit-ed, you don't seem to work much.'

He narrows his eyes. 'Says the woman who's home making meringues in the afternoon ... and having parties – sorry, soirees – more evenings than not.'

Damn. 'But I already told you, I'm on paid leave.' Except he didn't know *all* of that. As soon as it's out, Sophie's in my head ordering me to keep my mouth shut.

'Really?' He's suddenly super interested, then he back-pedals. 'Good for you. How long's that for?'

'For as long as my employer's in Geneva.' I'm feeling smug that the truth is so unclear. She has emailed saying she could be extending her visit beyond the planned three weeks. But time's whizzing by, and I've still not started to look through Laura's flat yet. It's all so overwhelming. Every time I promise myself I'll begin I always end up wandering along the beach instead. Or reading Laura's recipe books on the balcony.

'Remind me what you do?' I ask, scraping meringue mixture out of my hair and flicking it into the sink as we talk.

'I'm at the front end of a development company, acquiring the sites. I hang out with the local agents and solicitors so I'm first to know when land and property hits the market. Then once I've bagged the sites and sorted the designs, the building team comes in, and I move on to find the next.'

I'm thinking of the new flats everyone assumed I was moving in to. 'So you get places like Rock House?' They're fabulous apartments in a converted warehouse on the quayside.

His sniff is dismissive. 'There wasn't enough in that one for us. We like to play for bigger stakes.' He narrows his eyes. 'A lot of what I do is a waiting game. It's about standing back, assessing the profitability, then knowing the perfect moment to move in.'

'For the kill?' It's no surprise he can be so hard-nosed and calculating. Those soft faded jeans and unthreatening bare feet are definitely sending out the wrong message.

He pulls a face. 'I'm an honest speculator, Clemmie, not a predator.' Like those two words ever go together.

My laugh is hollow. 'I'm not sure Sophie would agree with that.'

'I'm sure she wouldn't. But then she's in no position to be judgemental.'

I push the towel up and screw my head around so I can see his face. 'What do you mean by that?'

He shrugs. 'They'll have made a tidy sum renovating that farm of theirs.'

'But that's their *forever home*.' All their effort, it couldn't be anything else. 'How the hell do you know this stuff when you're the new kid in town?'

'I only moved in recently, but I've been around a while. When Nate was chatting at the party, he sounded much more interested in profit than longevity. I actually looked at their place when it was up for sale a few years back.' He lets out a sigh then moves on. 'Shall I clear up in here while you get washed and changed? Then I'll show you where you're going wrong with your meringue peaks.'

'Sorry?' I'm so horrified by the implications for Sophie, I miss the last bit.

'I'll show you what to do, pass on a few tips, so next time, those meringues of yours stay in the bowl.' He hesitates. 'If that's okay with you?'

Let's face it, right now I'd give anything to get perfect peaks. Even if it does mean hanging out all damned afternoon with Mr 'killer-deal' Hobnob. 'Thank you. That would be exceptionally useful.'

Wait 'til Nell hears this. Hot, heartbroken – her words – *and* he can bake. I can't help feeling this is big news for St Aidan's singles' scene. For anyone who can tempt him onto it. And overlook his ability to suck the fun out of life. And who doesn't mind his profiteering side.

13

Still in Laura's kitchen
Another crack at breaking eggs
Wednesday

You know that sweet sticky marshmallow creme called Fluff? Imagine buying ten jars and massaging it all into your hair. And you still won't be close to the cleanup I'm facing in the bathroom. By the time I'm egg- and sugar-free, I've scrubbed off every scrap of makeup and most of my nail varnish too, and my legs are pink and hot from the shower. If I spend another two hours blow drying my hair and making myself into my very best self, Mr Hobson will get bored and leave for sure. And let's face it, my priority here are meringues. End of. So, the second I've toweled my hair, I pull on a clean dress and add a flash of lippy. As I hurry back bare-faced the kitchen looks like meringue-gate never happened. If this is how he cleans, I've no idea why Charlie H would ever call in professionals.

He's standing by the scales, sugar in a bowl, eggs already separated. 'I'm wiping down the whisk and bowl with vinegar. A speck of egg yolk or dirt, and your egg whites won't stiffen. Put the whites in and start off slowly.'

It's like having YouTube in my kitchen. Only better. With a delectable, yet indefinable scent of hot guy, which obviously, I'm ignoring. And I think he's tactfully told me where I went wrong with my last mix. As for leaving off the makeup – not that I wear it for the benefit of guys – that was a good call, because he hasn't even looked at me yet.

'So how come you're a meringue expert?' Even as I ask, the penny drops so loudly I'm putting my proverbial hands over my proverbial ears. There's one screamingly obvious answer. 'Are you gay?' And damn that my heart has plummeted and hit the floor.

The corners of his eyes crinkle. So, he can do amused. Approximately once a century. 'Sorry to mess with your gender stereotyping assumptions, but I'm a hundred per cent straight. I just had the kind of mum who thought teaching me to cook would make me more marketable for a future partner.'

I laugh, to cover that I'm mentally punching the air, even though I'm totally not in the market etc. etc. 'So that didn't work out either did it?' I might as well be honest. He didn't exactly hold back about Sophie.

He gives a shamefaced shrug. 'I still prefer to have my puddings cooked by someone else.'

'Good luck with your hunt for a doormat.' I'm gleeful that Dakota doesn't look like she could make a pudding to save her life, without knowing why. I'm pacing myself for a long afternoon here. 'Would you like to listen to my eighties mix if I keep the volume down? A hundred blockbuster hits. They should just about last until we're done here.'

He looks less delighted than I anticipated. 'I'm probably okay, this shouldn't take long. Look in here, this is the texture you're aiming for. Don't over beat or it'll get too dry and foamy. You can start to add the sugar now, a spoonful at a time.'

I can't believe how fast this is going. 'It's already smooth and glossy.' It's so different from first time around, I let out a whoop. 'Oh my, and there are peaks too.'

He dips a teaspoon in. 'A few more minutes of beating. As soon as all the sugar's dissolved, we're good to spoon it onto the trays.'

My mouth drops open in surprise as I see them ready with greaseproof paper cut to size. 'Ones you prepared earlier?'

He nods. 'The oven's on too. I've left a note of the temperatures and times, but all this is on your recipe card anyway.' His pause says I should have read Laura's notes more carefully. 'You can spoon them out ... there's enough mixture for twelve, keep the sizes equal.' His face breaks into a half smile. 'Unless you'd like me to hold it over your head again?'

'Thanks for the offer. But I'd rather not.' My first few blobs of goo are such a mess he has to know I've never done this before, but he's polite enough not to comment. By the time I've filled the tray I'm plopping them out so fast I could give Cressida Cupcake a run for her money.

He's rinsing his hands at the sink. 'Okay, into the oven for thirty minutes, then turn it off, open the door and leave them in there until they're cool.'

'I think I've got that.' I'm standing, watching him leave, when his phone goes again.

He waves as he slides it out of his pocket. 'If in doubt, read your recipe. Good luck, and remember to save me one. This is Dainty Dusters again. I'll take it this time.' Which sounds very much like 'over and out' to me.

Once he's gone, I pick up my own phone and take a picture of the twelve white blobs – because for me this is iconic. Then I open the oven and slide in the tray. Thirty minutes, from start to finish. I'm already drooling in anticipation. But I'm also feeling like there's a big gap in the kitchen. Which is ridiculous when I should be whooping that my grumpy neighbour's left the building. Or at least gone to his own bit of it.

In the next ten minutes, I discover the downside of cooking – it makes you a prisoner in your own home. Usually I might waltz off along the beach or pop up the hill for a mug of tea with Plum. But when there's something in the oven, you have to stay at home and look after it. Which for a non-cook is a bit of a shock. I suppose back in the day this is the bit where Laura would sit with me at the table, and we'd look through the recipe basket, or she'd tear up scrap paper and let me draw. Sometimes I'd stand on a chair, and Laura would fill the sink with foam and let me wash out jam jars. Or if the sun was out we'd take Fairy liquid out onto the balcony and blow big wobbly rainbow bubbles and watch them get whooshed off towards the sea.

I wander through to hang up my towels and clean the bath, then nip into the bedroom to check on Pancake. She's made a nest in the dusky pink quilt and wedged herself up against my pillow. As I walk in she doesn't lift her head or open her eyes, but the way she extends one paw and flexes her claws is a cool kind of greeting. When I hear the soft burr as she begins to purr, the sound's so cosy that I curl up in the battered velvet chair beside the bed just so I can listen. Then to stop myself falling asleep too, I reach for a book.

Whereas the kitchen dresser is stuffed with every recipe known to woman, the bedroom shelf is bursting with handicraft hardbacks. Judging by the weaving and dying manuals, books on patchwork, embroidery, dressmaking, upholstery, découpage, macramé and knitting, Laura must have been crafting non-stop. I'm flicking through the pictures, then when I reach the end I'm tipping the book upside down and giving it a thorough flap. Just in case there's a note tucked away.

When I was in Sixth Form, I found twenty pounds tucked deep in the inside pocket of a vintage peplum jacket, weeks after I bought it from a second-hand stall at a festival. It kept us in vodka kicks for at least three weekends. Which is probably why I've accepted I need to be meticulous about going through every inch of the flat. Who knows, I might find a rare Penny Black stamp like the ones we searched for so expectantly when we were kids. One mention on *Blue Peter*, and we were ransacking our houses, much to our parents' horror. Plum actually went as far as taking up her bedroom floor boards in case one had fallen between the cracks. Luckily her mum's an artist and her dad's a child psychologist, so they put it down to creative thought and self-expression. Whereas if I'd expressed myself by ripping up the carpet my mum would have had a hissy fit.

Then I come to a canvas folder full of the kind of knitting patterns you get on those birthday cards with comic captions. For every pretty knitted twin set I flick past, there's another ten where it's impossible to believe humans consented to wear this stuff. I'm falling off the chair laughing at three guys in the most awful Christmas balaclavas in the world ever, then I flip the pattern over, and suddenly I'm staring at a slim orange Kodak wallet. For a second I forget to breathe.

'Other people's holiday snaps. Or Laura's even.' Pretty meaningless unless you were there. But they're as fascinating as the knitting patterns for the period detail. Then as I let my fingers slide across the matt orange paper and under the flap my stomach leaves the building.

There aren't any negatives, it's not a set. It's just four or five irregular sized colour prints. With the blood roaring in my ears, I steady my shaking fingers and ease them out.

'A woman in a white dress with red flowers with two small boys and a big sand castle.' I'm murmuring to myself as I flip the photo over: *St Aidan, summer '68*. That neat pointy writing is definitely Laura's. And she looks a lot like a younger version of the one in the picture from the musical box. I'm not sure if I'm weak or excited. But I know I couldn't stand up if I tried.

The next is those same two boys sitting on a bench, their grins hidden behind vanilla ice creams with chocolate flakes that are almost as big as them. No date or place this time, but the fragment of the roses on their mum's dress is caught in the corner of the frame. Those same curly iron benches are still there along the sea front, only they're painted sky blue now not cream.

The only details I ever remember knowing about the man who got my mum pregnant were that he was *twenty-four when I was born, and called Rob*. I go through another four pictures, all variations of sand and the same boys, spreading them across the quilt as I go.

I'm doing the maths in my head, trying to think how big boys are when they're six. It might fit. As I pick up the last photo of two boys splashing in the shallows, one with a stripy bucket, one wearing some very under-inflated arm bands, I'm shivering. I turn it over, knowing it's my last chance, and yes. There's more pointy biro: *The day Robbie learned to swim.* 'Bingo!.' Or rather, holy shizzle!. This really wasn't meant to happen.

I've never wanted to know anything about my dad. Even though half of me came from him, given he was the kind of person who'd leave a pregnant woman, I've always tried to ignore the part of me that came from him. It's better to have a blank space in my self-knowledge than for it to be filled with something bad. When I started flicking through those books finding pictures of him was the last thing on my mind. But now I've got one in my hand knowing for sure it's him, I'm frozen. And I can't look away.

I grab my phone, take a photo of the picture, then spread my fingers out on the screen to zoom in. As the photo expands the face I'm looking into could almost be mine at the same age. My entire body feels about two seconds away from imploding when there's a shout from the hallway.

'Clemmie, what the hell happened?'

Shit. It's Mr H, and I'm not sure I know where to begin to answer that question.

'Did the timer fail?'

'Timer?' It comes out as a croak. Now that *would* have been a good idea. I consider standing up and on balance decide not to bother. 'I'm with Pancake ... come through.' It's not only my legs, my voice is all over the place too.

As Charlie appears in the bedroom doorway, he frowns, then leans across the bed to tickle Pancake. 'I brought cream.'

My stomach must still be in my body because it just flipped over. 'How are the meringues?'

He pulls a face. 'Fine ... so long as you like your cinders well cooked.'

I feel as crumbly and wrecked as those meringues. 'Damn. I totally forgot. I'm sorry.' It's half whisper, half rasp.

'Are you okay?' Something about his concern makes my insides crumple even more.

'I just found a picture of my dad.' I nod towards the photos fanned across the bed.

Charlie's frown is puzzled. 'I'm guessing he liked ice cream.' He moves in closer. 'You're very alike. A whole family of redheads too.'

'Shit, I hadn't even noticed the hair.' I was too busy looking at our eyes and our cheekbones, and our mouth shape and our foreheads. 'It's a shock to know I'm related to a family of full-on ginger nuts.' It's also a surprise to realise how little mum has to do with my face. The Marlows must have super strong genes. As well as wanting to spread them around.

'It can be very emotional discovering where you come from, seeing your parents when they were small.' He squints at me then pulls out a tissue from the box on Pancake's side of the bed and puts it in my hand. 'Here, have a hanky.'

'Why would I need a ...' Then I put my hand to my cheek and find he's right. As I mop my eyes and sniff I'm kicking myself for inviting him through. 'It's all *Blue Peter's* fault for feeding us so much bullshit when we were kids. If I hadn't been searching for bloody Penny Blacks, this would never have happened.'

His hand comes to rest lightly on my shoulder. 'You did that too? I spent so many holidays as a kid hanging round the Post

Office sales windows, trying to spot sheets of stamps with imperfections so I could auction them for millions at Christies.' He does his half cough. 'Then I discovered property development gave better returns for less time.' His forehead wrinkles again. 'You have seen his picture before?'

I shake my head. 'Nope. Never. Not that I know, anyway.'

His voice rises. 'Shit Clemmie, this is two thousand and eighteen, not the bloody dark ages. Why the hell not?' Then his face falls. 'Sorry, I shouldn't have asked that.'

The thing is, I want to tell him. I want everyone to know what a bastard my dad was, and that I've been a-okay wonderful and better off without him. 'It's not complicated. He didn't want my mum *or* me. Why would I want to know *anything* about *him*?' I collect the photos, stack them into a pile, and slide them back into their folder. It's hard to reconcile a boy with ice cream up to his ears who did his first strokes bobbing about in the bay as the same guy who walked out on my pregnant mum. 'I actually wish I hadn't found these. And I won't be looking at them again, because that's not a door I want to open.' It's the same promise I've been making to myself my whole life. Which is exactly why I should have gone with my first instinct and stayed away from the flat. 'So did you mention cream?'

His worried expression hasn't completely gone, but he's sounding upbeat. 'If you're up for making more meringues ...?'

'Hell, yes.' If I'm going to do this a hundred times more I need to get this.

And there's another hint of a smile. 'In that case I'll show you how to whip cream without accidentally making butter.'

With the mountain of Pavlovas lining up on my horizon,

that's an offer I can't refuse either. Not that I can tell him that. 'I'll remember the timer this time.'

'And while we're waiting for the meringues to cook, I'll show you how to use up the yolks making lemon curd in a bain marie.'

Shucks. Cressida Cupcake never mentioned that.

14

On Plum's deck
Chickens and eggs
Thursday

'So now you've perfected meringue's, Nell can go ahead and take bookings for next week.' Sophie licks the hazelnut crumbs off her fingers and reaches for one with pink pomegranate syrup swirling through it. 'Little Cornish Kitchen, here we come. I'm so proud of you for this, it's a phenomenal effort, Clemmie.'

Sophie and I are sitting out on Plum's deck, sipping tea and dipping into giant plastic cake boxes filled with my try-outs, deciding which to include in the final line up. She might be proud of me, but I'm effing delighted with myself. Who'd have imagined I'd ever be able to make meringues? Although once Charlie showed me the basics, I couldn't resist trying *every* variation in the basket. I moved on to scour the recipe books too, but Laura had all the best ones on cards. No surprise there.

'And it's so funny that when I got right to the bottom of Laura's basket, one of her Eton mess recipes used lemon curd too.' I lick the mix of lemon, meringue and raspberry off my spoon and close my eyes as I let the flavours melt onto my tongue. 'At least that saves me having a produce stall on the footpath outside the cottage.' I can imagine how well that would go down with Charlie and his Residents' gang. With Diesel tearing up and down it wouldn't last five minutes.

Sophie's brow furrows into her best business frown. 'If there's any spare lemon curd you can always sell it to the singles. I'll print off some labels and put the word out for jars at the school gate.' She purses her lips. 'And how's the running total going?'

I'm doing a Nell wiggle with my eyebrows because I can hardly believe it myself. 'The next evening should take us past the thousand pounds' mark. All from sorbet.' Although to be fair, the last two weeks we've made it by the bucketful. And a lot of the customers have come back for seconds and even thirds. And we've kept the music down, and Nell trained the guests to tiptoe up and down the stairs in silence – she has a talent for making people do just what she asks.

Sophie high-fives me. 'Brilliant or what? We'll get you to your target, no worries.'

'Yay!' I high-five her back. The thought of keeping this going for ten times as long complete with variations might be mind boggling, but I'm completely caught up in the challenge. I go to sleep thinking about recipe cards, and that's what I think about when I wake up too. If Charlie Hobson happens to march his way into my brain, which inexplicably he does from time to time – much to my horror – the thought of chomping on a spoon heaped with cream and meringue is enough to drive him away.

Inside the gallery beyond the tall glass doors, Plum is wrapping up a miniature sea scape painting for a customer. As soon as she's seen the customer out, she hurries to join us. 'Okay, I'm here. Let me at these puddings!'

As I pass her a mini Pavlova I can't help feeling thrilled with myself. 'Start with this. We decided individual ones would be easier to serve.'

'Wow.' She scrapes a dollop of cream off her meringue stack with a strawberry, then digs in her spoon. 'This one's definitely made the shortlist. So, when did you become a meringue ninja?'

It's hard to think of myself as an expert at anything, particularly in the kitchen. 'I've been whisking nonstop between sorbets. If they're in air tight containers they stay fresh so I've cleared a space in the box room. That way I can make them in advance.' And hopefully be less frantic. When it comes to meringues, thanks to Laura and Cressida Cupcake, I do seem to have *all* the knowledge now. Although without Charlie's input I know I'd still be struggling.

Plum scrapes out her dish, then begins on an Eton Mess in a china mug. 'You've done more clearing at the flat?' She gives me a hard stare. 'And did you come across any more treasures?'

I wouldn't describe the photographs I found last time as that. 'No strings of diamonds yet. Just lots of bags of wool and fabrics.'

Sophie's nostrils flare. 'And how about the pictures. Now you've had time to think it over, have they made you want to find out more?' If she's insisting on confronting the big-news issue, at least she's sensitive enough not to personalise it.

'Actually, I've decided it's best not to poke the bear.' I'm thinking cans of worms, balls of snakes and sleeping dogs here. 'If a five centimetre photo makes me bawl my eyes out for no reason, I'm better not going there.'

Plum looks anxious. 'You haven't thrown them away?'

I shake my head. 'They're buried deep in a drawer now.' I let out a sigh. 'There's still one picture on my phone though if you want to look.' I know she will. I can't bring myself to open it, so I hand it to Plum.

'Oh my.' She spreads her fingers across the screen to enlarge it, and lets Sophie see.

'Well, well, well. Who'd have thought?' Sophie's not often this lost for words. 'Remember that picture of us the day we covered Plum's mum in sand when we were about three then all sat on top of her laughing?'

Plum nods. 'That's the one I was thinking of too. It's not just the features that are similar, it's your expression.' She pulls in a breath. 'Although maybe it would be more surprising if you *didn't* look like each other.'

I might as well tell them where I stand on this. 'Every time I see that picture it's like someone's walking on my grave. I had one gap in my life for a dad and Harry filled it. This really isn't where I want to go.'

Sophie's got her fake bright voice on. 'And we're totally with you, whatever you decide. We'll take our lead from you on this.' She flashes a smile to match and reaches in for another meringue. 'So what's this, Clemmie? How the hell do you know how to do *piped* meringues *and* perfect whipped cream?

Plum butts in. 'The last we heard you were tipping egg white all over yourself. Have you been taking *advanced* classes?'

I have to come clean on this. 'It turns out Charlie has enough cookery skills to be in the *Bake Off* tent. And he's been sharing in return for Pancake's board.'

Plum's mouth twitches. 'This *is* an afternoon of surprises. So, Pancake's *still* at yours?' She looks vaguely horrified.

'It's not all bad. When she insists on lying next to my head her purr drowns out the noise of the sea. So at least I can sleep when she's there.' With the warmer weather and open doors, Diesel has a knack of sneaking in to cosy up on his favourite sofa, so I've often got him too. Which seems to be missing the point somehow. But whatever. 'Charlie's always dropping by to bring yummy meals too.'

That makes Sophie sit up. 'What kind of yummy are we talking here?'

I shrug and try to remember the labels. 'Trout royale, potted shrimp and pasta pearls, duck and bamboo shoots, Florentine with pollack.'

She sniffs. 'Luxurious but very fishy. I thought you preferred sweet stuff?'

I laugh because she's got it so wrong. 'These are Pancake's dinners not mine.'

'Bleugh, that's so *not* funny.'

Plum grins at Sophie's disgusted expression. 'So the top floor's turned into an access all areas pet haven.'

'Pretty much.' Charlie padding around barefoot to sort out Pancake is a small price to pay for Pancake's purr, even if it does give me heart failure from time to time.

'Which reminds me.' Sophie's arching her eyebrows. 'George's receptionist, Janet, was at Bumps and Babies with her daughter's twins. I went for it and asked if she could explain why Charlie's got Dainty Dusters all over every flat at Seaspray Cottage apart from yours.'

I let out a wail of frustration. 'I bet George has super-glued her lips the same as he has mine.'

Sophie's smiling her superior smile. 'I was careful not to make things awkward for her. Apparently, if you want to know who owns the flats you can apply to Land Registry.' Sophie pulls a face at that suggestion. 'But for a short cut, simply ask George for copies of the Residents' Committee minutes. According to Janet, all the details of ownership changes for the flats are noted in there.'

Plum punches the air. 'Brilliant. There's nothing secret about those. If you'd been interested he'd actually have sent you those already.'

Sophie's got her 'I told you so' face on. 'I suspect you'll find that Charlie's been quietly buying up the flats one by one over the last eight or nine years.'

'Oh, shit.' Plums peeling the melted chocolate off a meringue, and staring past the roof tops out at the sun glistening on the turquoise sea below.

My chest feels like it imploded. 'So if he gets his hands on my flat he'll own the whole building?'

Sophie shudders. 'Exactly. And after that he can do whatever he wants with the site.'

'Bloody hell.' It's barely a whisper. Suddenly his wrecking ball in my flat seems like nothing. I get as far as imagining him standing in a cloud of dust and rubble where Seaspray Cottage once stood and feel sick. For me and for Laura.

Plum pushes back her hair. 'So the stakes just racked up a notch. It's a damned good thing you've got these meringues sorted, so we can get straight on with raising your cash. It's even more important we don't let him back you into a corner where you've got to sell.'

The more I cook in Laura's kitchen, the more I remember what we did together. Every day I'm there more memories pull into focus. It might be an apron hanging on the door, or a pattern on a saucer that emerges from the depths of a cupboard. But the more I find, the more connections I feel to the place, and the closer I feel to Laura. And the less I want to let it go.

Sophie's leaning forwards urgently. 'You need to get onto this straight away. Talk to George first thing tomorrow.'

Plum's brushing icing sugar off her dungarees and eyeing me cooly. 'It feels like this could be a good time to launch Operation Cupid Dust?' She turns to Sophie. 'We were thinking about bagging Nell the partner of her dreams. This is the perfect time to do it.'

I manage not to choke on my pomegranate swirl meringue as I gasp. I know we'd mentioned Nell liking Charlie ages ago, but somehow I'd forgotten.

Sophie cocks her head. 'What have you two been hatching without me?' Our whole lives, she's always hated being left out. 'More importantly how do you two fiercely independent women know *anything* about matchmaking *or* relationships?'

I ignore that and catch Plum's eye. 'Nell *so* deserves a cupid's dart of her own. We've been waiting for the right moment.' I'm lying through my teeth and forcing myself to sound enthusiastic. If I'm feeling vaguely sick it has to be down to mixing my meringues.

Plum laughs. 'By which we mean we're going to give her a damn great shove in Charlie's direction. Do them both a favour with their love lives and get an insider's view of Charlie's dealings at the same time. It's a no brainer.'

I'm nodding madly. 'Apart from Nell lighting up like a beacon every time he appears, they've got *so* much in common.'

The way Sophie's wrinkling her nose she's really not buying into this. 'Like *what*?'

I've no idea why her voice went so high there, but I'm winging it here. 'Where shall I begin? They both love profit. And checked shirts. He ticks her pet box with his dog and part-time cat. And they've got the whole chicken and cake thing going on too.' I haven't done badly there considering I hadn't prepared.

Plum squints. 'What's that last bit?'

'He's a master baker, she has *all* the eggs.' My grin's triumphant as I turn to Sophie. I might as well go for it now I've come this far. 'Did we tell you he knows about Adelie penguins mating for life? That's exceptional for a guy. The more we think about it, the more it's obvious he's her "one".' I'm even shocking myself with the great case I'm making here. I mean, with my lifestyle choices me lusting after him is bonkers. If I did pull him, I'd never have the nerve to follow through, even once. Whereas, Nell's got enough experience to land him and keep him. Which is exactly what we need here. At least for long enough to find out what he's up to.

'Well I'm glad you see it like that.' If Sophie's shaking her head it's only because she didn't think of it first.

I'm throwing it all in now. 'And he smells nice. Very nice. I wouldn't be recommending him if he didn't.' Probably better than any guy ever, if I'm honest. Whatever scent he fills my kitchen with, it's a lot more than hot meringues and vanilla. 'So what's not to like?'

Sophie's voice is all screechy again. 'You can't *seriously* think you match life partners on the basis of shirt fabric?'

'Why ever not?' I'm taken aback she's being so negative when she's usually so upbeat. She needs to get a bit more 'Hygge' about this.

Plum's laughing. 'I agree, Clemmie and me aren't experts when it comes to boyfriends.' She's not kidding there. We've possibly had a total of three between us, and the best of them lasted a month. 'But we're very creative, and really, how difficult can it be?'

Sophie rolls her eyes. 'I'll leave you two to sharpen your love arrows then. And I'll get on with the menu.' She gets out her phone and starts tapping the screen furiously. 'So that's finalised. Strawberry Pavlova with pink swirls, chocolate and mocha meringues and Eton mess with raspberries and lemon. At least we all agree on that.'

Which leaves Plum and I staring at each other, because we haven't talked about it at all.

15

At the office
Talking Italian
Friday

As I hurry back down the cobbles to the quayside and the office next Friday lunchtime, the sweet scent of strawberries drifts up from the cake boxes I'm cradling in my arms. Primed by Sophie's six early-morning texts all reminding me what not to forget, I bagged myself a ten-minute slot with George at one. Which left me just enough time to rush up to the bakery. After Sophie's bombshell yesterday about Charlie owning most of Seaspray Cottage I know I should be saving every penny. So, if I went wild picking enough tarts from the glass case at the bakery to get extra cakes and complementary serviettes, I'm viewing it as an investment. I know I shouldn't be feeling awkward about tackling George about Seaspray Cottage, but a hit of deliciousness with our coffee will make the talking easier.

Pushing the door to Reception open with my bum, I shout to the kitchen where I left him making coffee. 'Are the drinks ready?

I hope you're up for a monster custard fest.' I ease the cake boxes onto the desk, confident he loves his flaky pastry and cream horns as much as I do.

There's a click but it's not from the kitchen. Instead the door to George's office opens, and as I hear the unexpected sound of voices, my stomach wilts.

'I'm so sorry, I didn't realise ...' I bundle the boxes behind my computer screen then stand rigid hoping this isn't a super-important client. With any luck my brightest Customer Service smile will cover my custard gaffe.

'No worries.' George raises one eyebrow at me, then returns to the guy he's ushering towards the door. 'Thanks for calling in, I'll definitely let you know what Clemmie's response is.'

I gulp as I hear my name. 'Er ...'

George fires a fierce glare at me then waggles his hand up by his ear in the 'call me' gesture and nods at the client. 'The minute she gives me an answer, I'll get back to you.'

My heart lurches. If this is someone else willing to buy the flat, it couldn't have come at a better moment. Whoever this guy is, his cowboy boots are almost as scuffed as mine. He's halfway to the door when he hesitates. 'Thanks for your time, Mr Trenowden. I'll say *buon appetito* and let you get on with your lunch.' If he's hanging round expecting us to share he'll be disappointed. 'Whatever cake is coming your way, it smells amazing.'

As his face breaks into a smile, my stomach lurches again, and next thing, I'm gabbling. 'It's the tarts, the strawberries are very ripe.' There's something unnervingly familiar about his broad cheekbones and tousled curls. And when our eyes collide, his irises are inky blue with green flecks. 'They're from

Crusty Cobs, if you want some. On the right up the hill, you can't miss it.'

There's another flash of forest green as he blinks. 'Thanks for that. I hope you left me some. Catch you soon.' His smile splits into a grin, then he swings out.

I clamp my hand over my mouth making sure he's gone. 'What kind of a poser talks Italian in Cornwall?' As I flip up the lids on the cake boxes I can't quite move on from the feeling that he stole my actual teeth.

'It's probably because he's just flown in from Italy.' George heads for the kitchen, and soon comes back with two steaming mugs of coffee.

'Where in Italy? It can't be Milan, because when I was there a while back guys had their combs out all the time.' I'm easing towards question time by being chatty.

'Ravenna.' George takes a deep breath and pulls up a chair opposite me at the desk. 'Were those dreadlocks on his head then?' The poor man is so *not* streetwise.

'I'd say it was more 'festival hair'.' I'm getting a blank look from George. 'Two days no brushing does that.' It does to me anyway. 'Dreads take more work.'

'Right. Glad we've sorted that one out.' He runs his fingers through his own inch-long hair as if he's testing it for knots. 'Thanks for buying the cakes. For the next part you might need to sit down and take a bite of the biggest, sweetest pastry you can lay your hands on.' Considering he's ordering me to stuff my face he's looking a lot more serious than he should do. And I thought I was the one who's supposed to be softening *him* up here.

'In that case ...' I take a cream and strawberry puff and devour half of it in one bite. 'Did I hear Señor Buon Appetito mention *me* back there?' Hopefully talking through my crumbs makes the question seem less of a big deal.

The pause is so long there's time to finish the whole pastry and pick every last flake off the desk top too. I feel completely mortified for jumping in. Of course it's not me, there must be other people called Clemmie. Sinking my teeth into a strawberry tart is the perfect way to hide how much of a dumb-ass I feel for leaping to the wrong conclusion entirely.

George's frangipane slice is still un-started in his hand. 'There's actually no easy way to say this. It *was* you he was talking about, yes.' He blows out his cheeks. 'That was Joe Marlow.... your half-brother?'

Fuck. The realisation hits like a smack in the face. 'You're joking me?' A strawberry slithers down my dress and onto the carpet under the desk as I lurch, but I'm too gobsmacked to follow it. Thank Christmas my ditsy print dress is as forgiving for strawberry stains as it is for hiding bulges.

Considering George is a hard-nut solicitor, he looks like this is hurting him as much as it's hurting me. 'We'd notified him via Laura's trust that you'd taken possession of the flat, and he's come in wanting to make contact. I didn't want to let him know who you were when he was here in case you'd rather not meet up.'

For once, I'm hugely grateful for the whole super-glue approach. Not to mention George's quick thinking. 'Not. No. Shit. Contact's the last thing I want. You have to tell him that. And thanks for not giving the game away before.' I let the remains of my tart slide onto the desk. 'Why the hell would he come all this way though?'

George shrugs. 'It could be to embrace family. Or he could be intending to challenge your right to the flat. Technically, it's still part of the estate for the moment. Either would be legitimate options given the circumstances.' His frown deepens. 'You must have noticed though, you did look very alike. Especially side by side.'

I shudder. 'What?' even though I'm screeching I still don't sound anything like as horrified as I truly feel.

George's tone is very measured. 'It's not beyond the bounds of possibility that *he* recognised *you*.' He blows out his breath again. 'He's here until Sunday. I'm sure it'll be fine, but to be on the safe side stay off your balcony over the weekend.'

'Good idea. Thanks for that.' It's very sweet of him to be concerned. If Nell hadn't scheduled two last minute All Laura's Pavlovas evenings, I'd hide under the covers until Monday.

'Oh, and by the way, there are three of them.' George stares at his flan slice wistfully. 'Altogether.'

'Three of what?' I'm in too much of a daze to keep up.

'Half-brothers. Although only one's here now.' He's nodding. 'Joe, Jack and Jordan. Not necessarily in that order.'

I let out a sigh. 'Better and better.' I'd only just got my head around the shock of seeing Laura's son in two dimensions on the photo. Coming face to face with his living, breathing, talking, three-dimensional offspring is the kind of mind-blowing I don't need. Not just today, but ever.

George sits up and sends me the kindest smile. 'Anyway, we don't want to waste valuable cake eating time talking about *them*. Remind me what we're here for. How I can help?'

I could hug him for being so calm and professional. Instead I pick out a tiny piece of strawberry, and watch as he finally gets to chomp on his slice.

'Almond sponge.' He closes his eyes and as he chews an ecstatic expression spreads across his face. Then the outside door clicks, and he opens them again. 'Bugger. Excuse the language, but some days my planets do seem to be in the House of Horrors not the House of Indulgence.'

There's a very familiar cough, and five seconds later, Charlie's standing by the desk, hands in his jean pockets. 'So who did I just bump into out there on the quayside? He had eyes just like yours, Clems. And the kind of hair tangles you had that time yours was full of star fish and seaweed.' He pauses and stares at me very hard. 'You do remember that night?'

As if I'd forget. 'My long lost mer-brother just washed up from the beach. It could have been him you saw.' I might as well come clean here, but at the same time I don't want to make it a huge deal. 'I'd rather *not* meet him again. In fact, I didn't meet him properly this time. So, if he comes looking please don't tell him where I am or which one's me.' I could do with texting the girls too.

Charlie tugs at his hair. 'You aren't serious?' He scours my face to check. 'Shit, you *do* mean it. Talk about complicated. Are you hiding out then?'

I hate sounding melodramatic. 'Put it this way, I won't be answering the door this weekend.' Except to a crowd of Pavlova fans, obviously. I need to move this on to somewhere less excruciating and more jokey. 'Luckily I'd stocked up at the bakery just before. With this lot on board I won't need to leave the office for at least a month.'

He takes the bait. 'So let me guess ... is it Fabulous Friday, or Office Cake Day? Or did someone turn forty?' He comes in for a closer look. 'Okay, no candles, so I'm guessing it's not a birthday?'

George sends me a mischievous twinkle. 'Crusty Cobs are doing *All you can eat* cake offers.'

The mention of *All you can eat* confectionary, and Charlie's tongue is hanging out so far it's practically touching the desk. 'That's a huge amount of patisserie even by my standards.'

I laugh. 'Buy six, get two free, what's not to like?'

George can't resist the tease. 'Sorry, only for workers stranded in offices. Roving developers have to make do with afternoon tea at the Harbourside Hotel.'

Despite my resolve, the dents under Charlie's cheekbones get the better of me. 'He's winding you up. You can try *one*. But I know what you're like, I've seen you inhale meringues, so don't eat them all.'

His nostrils are quivering as his hand hovers. 'Thanks, I'll go for the brownie.'

'No surprise there, Hobson.' However fast he hoovers sorbet, it's no secret that sticky chocolate is his favourite. Every time.

He takes a bite and his pupils go dark as he chews. Then he stops eating for long enough to send me a half grin. 'Hey, Egg head, now you've got the hang of meringues how about I teach you brownies for your next trick?'

George laughs. 'They were talking about your "meringue on the head" incident in the Parrot and Pirate last night. You're a local legend apparently.'

I let out a horrified squawk at how fast and far news spreads. 'How the hell did that get out?' I did tell Nell, Plum and Sophie, but they're totally water-tight with secrets. Only one other person knew about it, and I'm fixing him with my hardest stare.

Charlie's face crinkles. 'Oh, jeez, that might have been me.

When I let Dainty Dusters in downstairs for their sparkle clean, I told them about the mess they *weren't* having to clear up upstairs. I'm sorry, I assumed they'd be discrete.'

It's only thanks to Denise sharing her indiscretions with Sophie that we're here now, so I'm not going to dwell on it. Instead I turn to George. 'I thought you didn't go out?'

George looks mystified. 'Who said that?' Then a smile of recognition spreads across his face. 'I avoid singles' nights like the plague, but if apple crumble ever comes onto the menu at one of these seconds evenings they do at yours, I may have to reconsider.'

I'm opening and shutting my mouth in panic. George just jammed enough references into that sentence to hang me. It's lucky that as yet Charlie's too absorbed in his brownie to react. There's only one topic that's startling enough to save me here. I might as well go for it.

'So moving on from cake ... seeing as we're all here together ...' I wait until they've both looked up from their serviettes. Then I launch. 'Who owns the other the flats in Seaspray Cottage?'

George swallows, clears his throat and locks his eyes on a spot six inches to the left of the kitchen door handle. So that's him out of the game for now.

I jump in again and this time I fire my question directly at Charlie. 'Weren't you the one who mentioned that the Residents' Committee keeps an up-to-date list of owners for admin purposes?' I send a silent thank-you winging across the airwaves to Janet, because without this gem of hers I suspect I would still be hitting a brick wall. Since the day Charlie wheeled lunch over on his hostess trolley, he's splurged so much information he can't have kept track of it all. 'So it must be common knowledge rather than confidential.'

George's expression lifts, but before he has chance to speak, Charlie's in there.

'It's not a secret, and now is an ideal time to clear it up. All the flats in Seaspray Cottage belong to me, except for Laura's. Okay?' He's trying to sound ice cool, but the waver in his voice says he's anything but.

'Thanks for being so straight forward about that.' My gratitude's wholly ironic. Somehow I'm trying to tie this in with the guy who's been wafting in and out of my flat these last few weeks, pretending – in between the worst bouts of territoriality – to be a bestie. Which he patently isn't, because if he were he'd have been open about this from the start.

'I prefer not to shout it all over town.' There's a concerned note in his voice. 'Gossip travels fast, and usually to the wrong places.'

I'm with him on that. 'As I know to my cost. I'd be happier if the whole damned area didn't know I tipped egg white over my own head.' I won't forget this in a hurry. 'Just saying.'

Charlie rolls his eyes and his lips twitch. 'I'm sorry about the meringue leak.' An apology is a first. His voice goes grave again. 'But there's a lot less at stake with that than with the cottage.'

I stand up, put my hands on my hips, and drag myself to my full five foot four plus stacked heels. 'Are you talking down to me here? Because if you are ...' I'm about to tell him where to get off when he stands up. And suddenly he's towering above me. Worse, as he gets to his feet there's a rush of air and the smell of his body spray hits my nose head on.

'You were saying?' He's staring at me expectantly.

Damn. Now *all* the words have gone and I'm left mumbling. 'It's not important.'

He's still waiting. 'Well, if you're sure you've nothing to add there and no more questions, thanks for the brownie. I'd better be on my way.'

Questions? Did he actually offer to answer those? From the blur of his feet, I'm getting the impression he's running away. As fast as his Timberland deck shoes will carry him.

As I watch him hurrying across the harbourside, I suspect it's every bit as bad as we suspected. Or worse. Which means I'm definitely looking after 'the enemy's' cat. And accepting cosy cake making tips from a guy who probably shouldn't be anywhere near my flat. Let alone have the run of my kitchen.

As I slump back down into my swivel chair I'm looking at four yummy tarts with perfectly arranged berries, all begging me to eat them. And I'm not hungry at all.

16

In the garden at Seaspray Cottage
Manicures and navigation techniques
Sunday

The one good side of a weekend in hiding is that it finally drives me round to the back of Seaspray Cottage. Before this I've only glimpsed the garden from the round topped windows on the half landings on the stairs or from the walled herb patch at the harbour side of the house. But late on Sunday afternoon after I've unstuck every last meringue crumb from the sofa cushions from last night's Pavlova party, and put out all the bowls and glasses ready for another round this evening, I've got five minutes to spare.

It took me ages to get going this morning. Instead of my usual routine of going out on to the balcony to be whipped round the face by a brusque breeze off the bay and coming inside completely awake three minutes later, I had to stick my head under the cold tap, but the tingle just wasn't the same. When the time comes for my late afternoon break, when I would usually sit barefoot on the decking in the sun, rest my feet on the balcony rail and watch the people down by the sea while I sort out my nail polish, I'm missing it even more.

By five I'm gasping for some fresh sea air, so before I think about starting to chop fruit and whip cream, I grab a can of Red Bull and a bottle of Rimmel 60 Seconds, slip down stairs and creep out onto the front step. First I check the shimmer of the sun on the water – glistening – and the colour of the sea – mottled turquoise with patches of dappled navy blue. Then I check there's no one – namely Joe Marlow – coming along the dunes. Once I'm sure the literal coast is clear, I dart around the side of the house, and make my way along the worn herringbone brick path with sand drifting across the cracks. Once I'm through the creaky picket gate that leads to the back of the house I can let my guard down. The grass is soft under my feet and as I make my way across a broad lawn towards a row of fruit trees decked with blossom, the garden is achingly familiar.

It's funny. After almost three weeks here my memory triggers are all food related. As I look at the line of fruit trees now, superimposed on it there's a garden table and chairs, a flowery table cloth fluttering in the breeze, and a pie. Lemon meringue pie. With Laura's home-made pastry, draped over one of those wiggly flan rings, and shiny yellow tangy glazed filling, and the kind of meringue that's soft and toasts in the oven. It used to be my favourite. How much I loved the toffee taste of the soft meringue is only coming back to me as I stand here. Once, I even tried to use the shiny silver flan ring as a crown but it dug in my head. And the flowery table cloth is on the pie photo on one of the recipe cards. I know enough about cooking now to appreciate lemon meringue pie takes a lot of making. But one day, I promise myself I'll be able to do it.

I find a splash of sun under one of the trees, spread out a tartan rug, and pop open my can. Kicking off my sandals, I flash a quick coat of Chic in Chelsea varnish onto my finger and toe nails. Then I lie back looking up at the patches of blue sky between the emerging apple green leaves while I wait for it to dry.

The tide is coming in, and I'm listening to the rush of the sea on the beach beyond the house as I sort out my plan for the coming week in my head. Pavlova evenings are good because I'm making the meringues myself. But I still want to pay Sophie and Plum back for the time they're putting in to help me on the nights. Plum's happy for me to do some afternoons at the gallery, and Sophie's asked if I'll go with her and Maisie to Sensory Babies. Nell on the other hand doesn't want anything. She's just ecstatic to have something bright and new to liven up her singles' calendar.

My phone beeps. It's a Facebook message from her:

Yay! Another two Cupids from last night. xx

I'm not sure if that's good news or not, but I type an upbeat reply:

Woohoo, pairing off at this rate you'll be running out of members. x

Even if that might be good down the line for local wedding shop Brides by the Sea, this might not be the best short-term outcome for me and my renovation fund. She's straight back with her reply:

You'll have to move onto candlelit dinners for two. Lol xx

Even if I'm loving the image of a table for two laid on the balcony, me cooking an entire meal for anyone is laughable. I'm chuckling so hard at the idea I almost miss the click of the gate. I roll onto my side just in time to see Diesel's grey paws and Charlie's flip flops and boarding shorts coming into view.

'Catching up on your zeds after last night?' He's smiling over the top of the large box he's carrying. 'We spotted you out here on the way up the stairs.'

I might as well break it gently. 'Actually, I'm painting my nails ready for tonight, so mind you don't smudge my toes, Diesel.' I push myself up to sitting. 'Thanks to you making me a local legend, the entire class of ninety-five or whenever it was want to taste my Eton mess. I'm going to be having meringue parties for weeks to come.' There's no harm making him think his big mouth is to blame for the latest round of disruption.

He glances at my feet. 'Nice colour. Do your fingers and toes always match, then?' He's unnervingly interested in all the girlie stuff.

'It's Chic in Chelsea, I chose brown to go with tonight's hazelnut meringues. And, no, I couldn't leave the house if my toes and hands weren't the same.' I'm haphazard in many ways, but not this. Not that I'm actually going out, but he'll know what I mean. And somehow he's neatly avoided my firing line too. I'd meant to give him hell the minute I saw him.

He drops to his knees and slides the box onto the grass. 'I came to explain ... about the flats.'

Even if he has the grace to look guilty, I'm not letting him off this one. 'What is there to say? Bay Holdings owns the entire place apart from my teensy corner.' And I need to suck that up. 'But it would have been more civilised if you'd volunteered that information rather than having to have it prised out of you with thumb screws.' As I look around I can almost hear the rumble of the waiting bulldozers, but I'm not going to be hypocritical. 'I might not necessarily be here to see it, but I hate to think of this lovely garden being obliterated by blocks of new flats. I can't think anything Bay Holdings would do here would be an asset to St Aidan.' A gust of wind whips through the branches over our head, making the blossom fall like confetti.

He takes a deep breath. 'Seaspray Cottage is nothing to do with Bay Holdings. I'm the one who's been buying the flats. I bought the first by accident when I had some – er – unexpected capital.' As he looks up at the clouds scudding across the sky he swallows and for a second a shadow crosses his face. When he carries on his voice breaks slightly. 'Diesel and I came to stay for a week, the flat was for sale. He loved the beach, so we snapped it up for weekends.'

There's a date sticking in my head. 'Was that round 2009?' His face is the giveaway. Somehow the flash of anguish in his eyes sends such a twang through my chest I want to pull him against me and rub the pain away. Which is ridiculous when I should be giving him the hardest time I can.

'Yes, nine years ago. Diesel was still a puppy.' He blows. 'The rest came our way one by one after that. I should have told you, I would have told you, but I've always tried to keep it quiet. As an outsider, there's always the danger some local will muscle in and hold me to ransom.' He pulls down the corners of his mouth.

'It's the developer in me getting the better of my human side. We moved in here full-time after we bought the top floor flat.' Note the way he's making Diesel sound like he's a fully paid up partner in all this, as if it makes Charlie less to blame.

Not that I've met many, but I wasn't aware speculators *had* better sides.

He shrugs. 'It's true Bay Holdings develop to maximise returns every time, but they always do it superbly. In a place like Sandbanks they'd easily fit a couple of dozen flats on a garden this size.' He notices my face. 'No need to wrinkle your nose either, they'd be beautifully designed to respond to the site. And probably low energy with a minimal carbon footprint too.' He's certainly not stinting on the jargon.

'So where have all the daisies gone? The lawn used to be full of them.' I've got a vision of the grass spattered with white that's not blossom petals. Laura doing this trick and turning the daisies upside down so the stalk came out of the yellow centre of the flowers.

He's staring at me like I'm gone out. 'The gardeners are contracted to use weed and feed. It could be that.'

No surprise there, then. 'Weed killer's not very green. Don't you allow random daisies in Developer-ville?'

He shrugs. 'We go for clean edges. If we want weeds, we do a full blown wild flower meadow. But they can easily look a mess.'

I roll my eyes, because we're so far apart here. 'And heaven forbid we should have messy daisies. Although I might be raising this with the Residents' Committee.' It's an empty threat though if it's five of him against one of me. But it might be fun to consider the potential of annoyance tactics.

He takes an exasperated breath and begins again. 'Obviously, as an individual I'm more flexible than the company.' And no doubt able to work his butt off to sound more plausible too. 'Now we're talking about it, I just want to make it clear. If you were ever thinking of selling, you'd be the one calling the shots. You could impose any conditions you wanted.' His sigh suggests he's not ecstatic about that.

'Such as?' He hasn't been straight forward this far, so I'm struggling to believe him now.

'You could stipulate sale conditions, like the house being retained or the garden not being built on. The choice would be yours.' He's put a lot of thought into making this easy for me. 'Obviously, restrictions would impact on the price, but I'd always expect to pay over the odds for the last flat in a building. I'd give you a damned good price and more.'

'Right.' It seems like a bit of a U turn. I'm not sure I can trust such a change in his attitude.

He gives Diesel's ear a tickle as if to emphasise how nice he is. 'And to apologise for my bad judgement over this, I've bought you something useful.'

I was surprised before, but my voice shoots upwards at this. 'You're bribing me?'

'Open it.' He taps the box with a wry smile. 'It's definitely without strings. When you see what it is, you might not mind.'

'I'm not sure about this.' But I'm tearing off the brown paper anyway. 'Oh my. A food mixer?' I'm appalled and relieved in equal amounts.

His smile is so unexpected it belts me so hard in the stomach it almost winds me. From the width of it he's very pleased with himself. 'A Smeg one, in raspberry pink. With all the attachments, most cooks would die for one. I'd have lent you mine, but black wouldn't fit in with your kitchen at all.'

I'm not sure anyone ever bought a non-cooking nomad a less appropriate gift. Which somehow makes it easier to accept as I lift the top and peer into the box. 'Thanks, that's super thoughtful, it's a fab colour.' And probably eye-wateringly expensive too. I try to think of something intelligent to add about the extras, but I can't even begin to imagine what they'd be used for. I'm guessing I'll to have to leave this with Plum when I go back to Paris. But on the plus side, if my crowdfunding fails and I do end up having to sell the flat to him, I can always knock the price of the mixer off it to keep my conscience clear.

His grin is sheepish. 'Laura's vintage Kenwood really isn't up to the industrial quantities you're using it for. And I have to admit self-interest here too. We'll *both* get the benefit when you graduate to cakes and pastry.'

I have to ask. 'So when are you planning on moving on to *them*?' It sounds a lot more complicated than the plain old brownies he suggested in the office, but I'll have to know about pastry before I can make lemon meringue pie. And I do love a cupcake.

'If you have a free afternoon we can start this week?' He looks up at the tree. 'This is a pear we're sitting under now. The crop isn't usually huge because of the wind off the bay. That's why the fruit trees are planted along the south facing wall, for the shelter. But it would be nice to use any pears from the garden to make a creme patisserie tart when the time comes.'

Aside from pastry complexities, for someone who lives in the moment, fruit sounds a very long way away from blossom. 'When will they be ripe?'

His brow furrows as he thinks. 'Late summer.'

I need to make my excuses here. 'Sorry, I'm not great at committing in the long term.'

He shakes his head as he laughs, which is something else that knocks me sideways. 'August will be here in no time, it's only a few months away.'

And now he's really misunderstood. 'I'm not talking about summer, I'm talking about being tied down later this week.'

'You're so funny, Clemmie.' This time when he laughs his eyes go so dark my mouth waters. 'I never met anyone quite like you before.'

I'm laughing back at him. 'Think of me as a breeze wafting through. As for tying me down to anything as concrete as a sale, good luck with that one.' Unless I'm truly desperate, I'd always let things slide rather than make a decision.

He's still smiling, and this time he's torturing me with a view of those teeth. 'I prefer to think of you as a mermaid. So long as I find enough of the right kind of star fish, I'm sure I'll be able to tempt you when the time's good.'

I stop imagining how his incisors would taste if I ran my tongue over them, and go for my least ethereal, most earthbound voice. 'Don't count on it, mate.' I'm taking a swig from my can to indicate the conversation's over when I hear a creak from down the garden. As I peer past the honeysuckle arch, I catch a glimpse of mussed up auburn hair and ripped jeans, and let out a yelp. 'Shit, Hobson, you left the gate open.' I drop my voice to a whisper. 'It's Joe Marlow, I'm stuffed here.'

'Damn.' Charlie's voice is low. 'Sit tight, don't worry, I've got this.' A moment later his hip thumps down next to mine.

As his arm flops around my shoulder, I let out a loud squawk. 'What the ...?'

His arm clenches me tighter and his breath is warm in my ear as his scent engulfs me. 'Just look him straight in the eye, leave the rest to me.' Then he looks up and clears his throat. 'Hello, there, anything we can help with?'

Joe jumps up the steps to the lawn, and strides towards us. 'I'm looking for Clemmie Hamilton. She moved into my grandmother's flat on the top floor a few weeks back?' What a shame those athletic genes passed me by. And it's significant he's talking about the flat as Laura's not mine. Although I can't blame him for that. He's got a lot more right to it than I have.

Charlie hesitates. 'I'm Charlie Hobson, and this is my girlfriend.' It rolls straight out.

My heart is already banging so loudly, Joe has to hear, but with that gem it does an extra lurch. 'Were you in Trenowden's yesterday?' As my cheek is crushed against Charlie's soft cotton shirt, I might as well join in here. 'I was the one shouting about cake fests in Reception. Did you find the Crusty Cobs shop?'

Joe scratches his head, then smiles as he gets it. 'Yes, thanks for the tip, the tarts were great.'

I'm on a roll here, so I nod at the box. 'Charlie's just bought me a food mixer. Hopefully from now on I'll be baking my own.' All bollocks, but I'm getting right into character. And hopefully being *so* obvious he won't see me as myself at all.

Charlie's fingers give my arm a double squeeze. 'I'm Clemmie's neighbour. Shall I tell her you dropped by? Or when you'll be coming again?' That genius stroke from Charlie goes halfway to making up for leaving the gate open.

Joe pulls a face. 'I'm off now, but she knows I'm looking to catch up. Let's hope I'll be luckier next trip. I haven't fixed a date yet, but I'll definitely be here for longer next time to get properly back in touch with my roots.'

My heart sinks at how thorough and committed he sounds. 'Maybe see you again then.' As I watch him make his way back along the garden I can't help thinking I could have done with either of those genes too. The moment the gate clicks shut I shrug out from under Charlie's arm. 'Thanks for jumping in to save me there.'

'You're welcome. Any time.' He realigns his legs and rests his elbows on his knees. 'Was that an actual ginger man-bun then?'

I roll my eyes that this would be his first comment. 'I think it was.' I push back my hair and rearrange my breathing and get onto more important stuff. 'I'm digging a hell of a hole for myself here, and I'm feeling awful for lying. But realistically I never intend to let him catch up with me.' I glance at my phone. 'And I'd better get on too.'

Charlie's eyes narrow. 'So you definitely aren't up for the long lost family happy reunion thing?'

I push my foot into a sandal, and fumble with the ankle strap. 'That doesn't work for everybody.'

He rubs a thumb over the stubble on his chin. 'It's your call, obviously. But that family is fifty per cent of who you are. It's a lot to cut yourself off from.'

This has to be said. '*I* wasn't the one who did the cutting off, *I* didn't actually have a choice. But I've never been anything other than fine as I am, and I'm damn well not going to change that now.' I'm shocked at how snappy it's making me feel. 'And did you *have* to do the whole girlfriend thing back there?'

He grins as he gets up. 'It worked, didn't it? And we're both back to our single status now, so no harm's done.' He grasps my hand and hauls me to my feet, then picks up the box. 'Ready to go?' He whistles Diesel.

I know there's no point wishing I could wind the clock back. But if I could go back to that first day in George's office, and not come and see the flat, I might do it that way. I never imagined one pocket handkerchief apartment in Seaspray Cottage could open up such a can of worms. Before it life was simple and straightforward. I existed. End of. Now there are new complications every day. Pavlova parties being the tip of the proverbial complication iceberg. And I really didn't sign up for any of it. But now it's happening, unless someone can point me in the direction of a time machine, I need to ignore the nightmare it's become and push on through to the end of it. Wherever that might be.

As we wind our way back up the stairs, there are a couple more things I need to check out with Charlie.

'So what about this evening. Are you up for another helping of meringue?'

He laughs. 'Of course.'

'And how did you get on with Nell?' I've been dying to ask this. Sending her along the balcony to deliver his free puddings is the main Operation Cupid thrust. Although how I'd cope with the insane jealousy of seeing my bestie with her hands all over Hobson, I've no idea.

He raises an eyebrow. 'Who?'

'Nell ... the pretty one with short blonde hair and the gingham blouse.' Maybe more details will jog his memory, and hopefully he won't confuse blonde with Dakota. 'She brought you last night's party carry-out?' Although to be fair Nell did boomerang back very fast.

He gives me a blank stare. 'Is it the wrong answer to say I was looking at the meringue?'

I roll my eyes. 'Well tonight please at least try and chat when you take the tray from her. She's an accountant, you both have pound signs in your eyes instead of stars. You'll get on, and she could do with a break.' Hopefully that will appeal to this compassionate side he seems so keen to prove he has.

'So what's in *your* eyes then, Clemmie?' He pauses as he reaches the top of the last flight. 'Star*fish*?'

I laugh as I wander along the landing. 'Maps of ocean currents, stuff like that. Turtles and dolphins guide themselves by the earth's magnetic fields. Mermaids are similar.'

He pushes through the door from the landing and I follow his back. Then he looks at me over his shoulder and his face breaks into another grin that splits my chest in two. 'Ooops. Navigational slip.'

'What?' Even top flight mermaids get confused sometimes, and I've got no idea what he's talking about.

'Spot the deliberate mistake. We're in the wrong flat. Mine not yours.'

Jeez, what a day. 'In that case I'll turn my sonar on and see if I can get us to next door.'

If I thought about the full Freudian implications, I'd be appalled that I'd just accidentally followed him back to his place. As it is, there's no point making a big deal out of nothing. Although to be honest I'm not that surprised I can't find my way back home.

I've got my own flat, a job, a resident cat, a half-brother in pursuit, I'm fancying the pants off the most disgusting and unsuitable guy out when I'm the last person who would ever contemplate a relationship, worrying about development in a place I don't even want to live. These are all alien concepts to me. And to top it all, I now actually own a food mixer. As free spirits go, is there anything more depressingly domestic? No wonder I'm confused. It's like I'm inhabiting someone else's life, not mine. Seriously, I need to get myself back to Paris, and get reunited with my old and proper self before anything worse happens.

17

In the courtyard at Hawthorne Farm
Car boots and baby-led weaning
Monday

Sophie's shout comes floating from the kitchen. 'Rhubarb!'

I have to be honest, after an entire afternoon at Raining Stars Sensory Babies even a random word like rhubarb seems sensible. As I rest my bum on the sixteen-person dining table in Sophie's outdoor courtyard, and watch Marco and Tilly haring round me in their Cosy Coupé cars, my stomach muscles are literally killing. Sadly, I can't claim it's from a Dakota-style Body Pump gym workout because I haven't done one. My pain is all from trying to hold in my hysterical laughter earlier because no one else in the village hall was cracking a smile. The class coordinator rolling round under a silk parachute popping puppets through holes while we all sang along. The Little Green Frog Song lyrics projected onto the ceiling. A bubble machine. Chaser fairy lights. And ten babies, all howling.

It's a huge relief to be home again, standing by with a bath sheet while Maisie flings her food. I flinch as a broccoli floret whizzes past my ear, and pick a sticky lump of banana out of my hair. 'Please, no more missiles for Maisie's high chair tray, this is already worse than paint balling. Why is she throwing the food not eating it?' At eight months, old Maisie's a crack shot, but I'd be happier if she was firing her snacks into her mouth, rather than at me.

Sophie's finally reconnected with her sense of humour because she's laughing. 'Baby-led weaning is about fun not calories. Anyway, I was suggesting rhubarb for you, not Maisie.'

I let out groan as a handful of mashed potato splats down my dress. 'Red Bull and BLT's are good for me, thanks. I'll leave the healthy options for your poor kids.'

Sophie rolls her eyes. 'Keep up, Clemmie. How about rhubarb as the theme for the next Little Cornish Kitchen event? You brought Laura's basket along so we can decide on new menus remember?' Since I've been searching through the cards, this time around my list of ideas is so long I'm hoping she'll help me choose.

I wrinkle my nose. 'Summer sorbet and meringues are stuff-your-face irresistible, but rhubarb feels like a minority interest.'

She's shaking her head. 'That's the trouble, living abroad you get *so* out of touch. Rhubarb's totally on trend. Truly, it's the new quinoa.'

I shudder as I think of the tasteless little balls I came across nestling next to my roasted squash when I accidentally got the wrong order at the Yellow Canary one night. 'Kale and seaweed haven't peaked in Paris yet. Not in the patisseries I visit anyway.'

She's still just as enthusiastic. 'We've got shedloads of rhubarb in the veggie garden, so it's free. That's extra important now you've smashed the three thousand pound profit barrier. You've got a great following now. People love coming to your flat because it's like a themed pub, only real. I suspect you could serve Pot Noodles, and they'd still flock up your stairs.'

I perk up at that. 'Pot Noodles are a good suggestion. Last time I checked, they did seventeen flavours. We could watch ironic films while we ate them.'

'Wo-ah, minor interest *and* grunge is not where the money is. Believe me, I've paid for the marketing surveys.'

If she's onto boring strategy talk, I need a diversion. 'Actually, there was a bit of a disaster at last night's event ...'

She takes a breath. 'There's no such word in business. View every set back as a new opportunity.'

Business hardly describes my scramble to get some cash together, even if I do get a curious thrill when I check my totals. Who'd ever have believed I'd be doing my own accounts and getting almost as obsessed with columns of figures as Nell.

But getting back to reality. 'I accidentally delivered a Pavlova into a guest's lap. And he'd asked for extra cream too.' Mortifying didn't begin to cover it.

'Oooo, shizzle.' The smile playing around her lips suggests she's regretting missing out on the action. 'Remember Gravy-gate?'

'As if I'd forget.' Me tripping and colliding with the replacement gravy urn en route to the condiments table was the trough of my teenage glass collecting career. Back then the Crab and Pilchard did three meats and all you can eat vegetables for the bargain price of £1.99. Back when bargains *were* bargains, as Harry would say. Two parties of ten, their chairs *and* the carpet, all doused in catering Bisto. And a cleaning bill that mounted up to more than

I'd earned in two years. 'Whipped cream on one pair of Levis and a tapestry cushion wasn't a hundredth as bad as that.' I was lucky the manager let me off for being a good worker, or I'd still be paying it back now.

Her eyes narrow. 'It's not like you to make a slip up?'

There's no point dancing round what happened. 'He dropped his quiz pen a long way down the side of the sofa and when he pulled it out he was also waving a picture of my mum and ... a guy.'

One eyebrow shoots up. 'Your dad?'

I sigh. 'I assume it's him. I wouldn't care, I've looked through every damned book in the place since I found the last pictures because I was *so* determined not to be tripped up again.' I close my eyes and shake my head. 'Apart from dropping meringue in the poor guy's crotch I didn't let on it was a significant photo. And the guy was very chilled about the mess.'

Sophie's nostrils are twitching. 'This *could* work for you. People love the chance of a spectacular stuff up. And I bet he wasn't short of attention afterwards either.'

Sometimes it's annoying she's so right. Plum should be the one with the innate sense because her dad was the child psychologist. Before he buggered off when she was six Sophie's dad was a long-distance bus driver. One day he took a coach load of holiday makers home to Chester-Le-Street and never came back.

I grin. 'Nell texted. So many women rushed to help the unfortunate guy he had multiple date offers, so she gave the event three cupids.' I'm not in the market for gorier details.

'So are you going to show me the photo?'

I dip in the pocket of my dress for my phone. As she taps the phone screen her face falls. 'Shit. They're on the beach ... she's very hands on, isn't she …? I mean, your mum always seemed so respectable … and uptight …' Her voice diminishes to a whisper then stops.

I may as well fill in the blanks. 'Put it this way, she'd never have let me out in a bikini that small. And if she had and I'd draped myself over someone like that, I hope one of you would have been kind enough to tell me to either back off or get a room.' Last night when I saw it I felt like I couldn't breathe. Then my shock turned to indignance, and now I can't criticise enough.

She crinkles her face. 'I completely see why you lost control of your pudding.' She pulls me into a hug. 'Well done for holding it together.'

'How can a simple photograph be so upsetting?' I actually felt like I had a noose around my throat.

Sophie's screwing her eyes up in an effort to take in the detail as she scrolls around the phone screen. 'Your mum looks so young and pretty – and from her body language I'd say she's very happy. In love, even. So, it wasn't just a holiday fling either. Your birthday's September, you were conceived closer to New Year than summer.'

'I've spent hours staring at it.' Pretty much all night, on and off. 'For thirty odd years where I came from has been a blank space I refused to think about. Now suddenly there's this real live couple who even look like they like each other.' That's a euphemism. It's obvious they can't keep their hands off each other.

'It's only one snapshot. But that picture has a very different feel from what you've always understood.' She sniffs. 'We always had a special bond because our dads both left us. I'm sure my mum has some pictures of a time when she and my dad were happy too. Or she might have done if she hadn't burned them all.' She rolls her eyes and shakes her head. 'But maybe it's time for you to ask your mum about it?'

I sigh. 'I can't start grilling mum when she's on the other side of the world and emailing once a month from an Internet cafe, if I'm lucky. She's always got really upset talking about my biological dad, I'm not sure I'd be comfortable talking about it even in St Aidan.' In my head, I came from a one night stand. And my mum couldn't tell me what my dad looked like because it was dark. But she knew him just enough for Laura to be there with her buns and her musical box and her pointy writing and her presents. Not forgetting her legacy and her recipes. And now I'm remembering more, it's becoming obvious I spent a lot more time at the flat when I was small than I'd realised.

Sophie opens the basket on the table and from her stare there's something profound coming. 'It's one picture from before you were born, and you can't change the past. But if you knew more details, you *might* change your view of it.' She leaves it at that and starts flicking through the recipe cards. 'Crumble, fizzy jelly, fool, mousse, self-saucing pudding. However badly that guy in the photo behaved, his mum was certainly a whizz with rhubarb.' She smiles at me over the top of the card she's tapping against her chin. 'Not that that makes up for anything. We both deserved better than our biological dads gave us. Not that I let it hold me back any.'

I totally agree. 'Me neither.'

Sophie purses her lips and her eyes go all flinty. 'I was so damned determined to show mine I could make a success of my life without any help from him.' She stares around at the vast

L-shaped living room and kitchen areas with their wide doors pushed back, and along the low roof of the children's bedroom wing beyond. 'I probably have him to thank for every last polished limestone floor slab in this place. And the business too.' Although we both know he's not around to see any of it.

'Too right.' I have nothing to add. I lived my life with no reference to the guy who impregnated my mum, so he didn't influence me at all. 'So guess which neighbour lent us a spare pair of jeans?' I say, quickly changing the subject before it gets too heavy. I don't wait for her answer because there only is one. 'And Nell was so long picking them up, Plum had to go and hurry her up. When she got next door, she overheard Nell and Charlie having a deep convo about some kind of easing thing.'

Sophie looks puzzled. 'Was it *quantitative* easing by any chance?'

'That's the one. Does it get any raunchier?' Even if I'm biting back the jealousy, I'm not going to waste rubbing it in with Sophie.

Sophie's left eyebrow is slightly raised. 'Do you even know what that is?'

'Hell, no, but it sounds fabulously dirty. And at the end Plum said they were joking round about Nell going back to the kitchen and "getting fiscal".'

Sophie pulls a face. 'Bleugh. Sounds like a match made in innuendo tax haven. Seriously, this one's going to take more than a shared interest in accounts' jargon and leftover Pavlova, Clemmie.'

I've no idea why Sophie's still being so dismissive. 'Which reminds me, about my other news.' It doesn't exactly, but it's a good way to move on to those drinks we still haven't had yet. 'Charlie showed me how to make those nasty tasting brown things you like so much. I've brought some to have with our tea.' I'll be for the high jump if I mention the 'B' word with the kids around.

Sophie's eyebrow is working overtime this afternoon. 'Considering he lives next door he and his dog spend a lot of time hanging out at yours. *And* he buys you presents. Maybe you're the one he wants to "get fiscal" with?'

I laugh because she's reading this so wrong. 'It's no secret, Diesel's the womaniser. Or at least he prefers women's company to men's. And all Charlie wants is to buy my flat, to the point he's so desperate he can't let me out of his sight in case I sell to someone else. That gift was simply a measure of how much he effed up on his quest. Considering what he did the gift should have been way bigger than a food mixer.' It's completely straight forward. Once you understand what drives Charlie, it all falls into place. Although I'd never exploit it, it's good for him to face up to his mistakes and pay for them.

'And what about the cookery lessons?' She's certainly screwing me down here. '*We* could help you with those. Or are *his* brownies better than ours?'

I smile as I realise. This is Sophie being competitive and also feeling shut out. But at the same time, there's a strange part of me that wants *him* to give me those lessons. I'd never say, but I like that he wants to come and do it. And even if he rarely smiles and just gets on with the job there's something deliciously shivery about having him there in the kitchen. I'd hate to have that taken away. 'It's definitely better if someone runs me through the method, that way I have less disasters, but I want to save you mermaids for the more important stuff. As he's there and he's free, it makes sense to make do with second best for the baking. And the recipes are all Laura's.' I hope that's enough to stall her. 'Shall I make some tea then? I left the "food that shall not be named" on the island.'

As she raises a hand and heads for the kitchen her eyes are shining. 'The tea's all ready. Sit down, there's something I want to run past you while we have it.' Her glow is nothing to do with my brownies either. That's the sparkle she gets when she's empire building. A couple of minutes later, she's back with a tray and a pile of serviettes where the brownies should be. She pops a handful of fruit pieces in front of Maisie, and slides a brochure across the table to me.

'Estate agents?' It's so glossy the reflection is too dazzling for me to see the picture. 'So you're opening a shop?' Not that I'm a property expert, but Bradley's dark blue livery has been round the area so long I recognise it immediately. Although when I get past the glare the picture looks more like a hotel.

Her eyes are wide and her voice has dropped to a whisper. 'Our favourite house in the world ever has come on the market.'

I bat away one of Maisie's flying grapes, not getting what Sophie's talking about. 'Keep going.'

She's quivering. 'You remember the castle on the cliff road we used to fantasise about living in when we were kids?' This is how inclusive she was back then. She even used to dream on our behalf.

I'm staring at her. 'I always wanted to live in my home-made wigwam on the dunes. Or in one of those beach huts at the far end of the bay.' Probably so I wouldn't have to walk back to our cottage up the hill after a day on the beach. 'Didn't I?' A lot of the time she claims she knows what was in my head back then better than I do myself.

She sends me a disgusted sideways eye roll. 'You *can't* have forgotten Siren House. We used to look up at it from our favourite spot on the beach and plan how we'd all move in there together when we grew up ... because it had ten bedrooms and Prince Charming castellations?'

As I flick through the photos the views from the beach below are evocative enough to jog even my sluggish memory. Despite the dilapidation, its towers are the closest St Aidan ever got to Disney. 'It looks pretty run down.' Even to a beginner like me that much is obvious.

Her body is tense with excitement. 'That's a plus though. We could *never* afford it if it was in good condition.'

I let out a wail. 'You're not seriously thinking of buying it? What about Hawthorne Farm?' I can't begin to imagine the cash they've poured in or the sheer human effort it's taken to transform this place from the tumble-down barns they bought to the designer luxury we're sitting in.

'Siren House is the *one* place we'd move for.' Her voice goes all dreamy when she says the name. 'Nate's always loved it too.'

As she picks up the brochure, even though the polished stone is warm under my bare feet I can't hold in a shiver of surprise. So long as you overlook the splodges where Marco's run over Maisie's mango slices and broccoli florets, what's here makes the homes in *Country Living* magazine look ordinary. It couldn't be more different from the higgeldy piggeldy fisherman's cottages we grew up in. The bedrooms there were so tiny if we stood in the middle and stretched out our arms we could touch the walls. And I'm not talking teenage arms. That was when we were seven. And those walls were mostly made out of planks of wood. Our parents did those places up with fledgling DIY skills and very little else. Not that I think about it much, but when you see how differently we've ended up it's startling to remember we began in the same place.

Sophie pulls a face. 'It's probably way out of our league, auctions can be tricky.' Her voice is husky, but she sends me a grin. 'But they're having an open viewing so we might as well go. You and Plum can come with us too.'

'Why would I look around a castle?' I've sailed past thirty and so far I've avoided even signing a lease.

'Because you can? For old time's sake? Because eight eyes are better than four?' Her grin broadens. 'Jeez, this is *Siren* House we're talking about. *One* of us mermaids belongs there.'

Everything she's got here, and she's still not satisfied. Whereas until Laura's flat came along, what I own would have fitted in the boot of Tilly's toy car. And most of that was nail varnish. I know I was reluctant at first, but with every day that passes, despite the pictures I'm coming across, I love Laura's little flat more and more. It's almost as if as I remember all the lovely things we did together, I'm getting wrapped up in her love all over again.

I push the serviette mountain towards Sophie. 'Here, try one of these.' If anything can shut her up when she's talking bollocks, it's chocolate. 'Give them honest marks, please. Out of ten.' When it comes to cocoa-orientated vocabulary, Marco's got X-ray hearing. Any discussion's going to be limited.

As she disappears behind her tissue from the noises it's hard to believe she's doing anything other than blowing her nose. When she emerges, she's smacking her lips, and sniffing. But in terms of marking, judging by her digits in the air, she's not impressed.

I can't help my grumble. 'I know I asked for a true ranking, but two out of ten's a bit harsh.' I was counting on for four at least. It took me ages to measure the damned things into millimetre-perfect equal squares because I know what a perfectionist she is.

She's laughing and shaking her head. 'I haven't given points yet. You're squawking about my double thumbs up.' She wipes away the evidence from the corners of her mouth then digs in for another napkin. 'The judge needs another taste. This far I'd say "delectable".'

I'm laughing. 'Better than rhubarb then?'

Marco's blue and dayglow yellow chequered police car has come to a halt by my abandoned cowboy boots and he's glaring at me through the rear window. 'Electable ... that's mummy's other word for yummy.'

I can't keep my grin in. 'That's great news for me then.'

He lets out a howl of protest. 'But I can smell *cho-o-c-o-la-a-ate*.'

As his yell pierces my brain, I can't think why I've been agonising over jelly, crumble or jam themes and missing the obvious.

As I clamp my hands over my ears and beam at Sophie over the top of his car roof, my head is banging but he's forced an idea into my brain. 'Stuff rhubarb. For now, anyway. I'm not ruling it out forever. For the next theme we'll do "what Marco said".'

If these brownies are hitting the spot, that only leaves two more recipes to conquer. I'm already thinking of chocolate fudge pudding and orange chocolate roulade on the recipe cards. I know that could have come straight out of Waitrose shopper's head. But my mouth is watering so much I don't care.

Sophie's voice is thick as she talks through her cake. 'Yay! I'll go with that. Little Cornish Kitchen, Love for Laura's Chocolate here we come.' She drops her napkin low enough to flash me a grin. 'So long as you remember to turn up at Siren House at two tomorrow, we're all good.'

Which is great. But we can't always do what Sophie says, because it wouldn't be good for her. So, while she's wiping Maisie's latest mango explosion off her powder blue Converse I slip a piece of brownie into Marco and Tilly's car boots. Carefully wrapped in serviettes obviously. And send a plea to any passing unicorns to make Sophie come to her senses before tomorrow.

18

The open viewing at Siren House
Chocolate roulades and sizing up the opposition
Tuesday

'Are you sure it okay for all of us to traipse round? Every other time I've visited a house like this, I've paid to get in.'

There's no getting away from it. As we get out of the car on the wide gravelled forecourt at Siren House, it's looking shockingly close to a stately home. I'm still gawping at the lions by the humungous stone gateposts and the stone urns dotted along the sweeping drive. And close up with its mellow coursed stone and its small paned sash windows the building is a hundred times more imposing than ever it was from the beach.

Sophie brushes away my concerns as she marches us past a line of parked cars towards the wide front door which is ajar. 'Open viewings are all about tactics, it's great to confuse the opposition by turning up in a crowd. The agents don't mind at all because it bumps up their numbers.' It's Sophie all over to have her fighting strategy in place from the start. And it also explains why she was so keen to have us in her posse.

I'm scouring the line of car's making a big thing of examining the shrubbery checking if Charlie's is parked up. 'Nice box bushes.'

Sophie frowns. 'Since when did you know about planting, Clemmie?'

'Box is a French thing, there's a lot of it in Paris.' It's pure luck that it's the one plant I know. I'm peering down the side of the house, but when his car's not there either my chest deflates. At least my banging heart can go back to normal speed. Although with the anticipation of bumping into him around any corner, my body's so flooded with adrenalin I doubt that will happen.

Plum's getting in the mood as she hurries after Sophie. 'We could be a consortium. Or Clem and I could be your interior decorators.' She's right in character with her paint spattered overalls.

I stare along the roofline and take in the towers at either end. 'With all those ramparts it's more the kind of place Kate and Wills would live than any of us.' Even Sophie.

Sophie rolls her eyes at me. 'You do exaggerate, as crenelations go they're minor. Come on, let's look inside.'

We leave Nate to sign us in and wander off around the ground floor picking our way between the other viewers, through rooms that are faded yet sun filled and surprisingly warm.

Plum's nodding approvingly as we hover by the tall French windows. 'The light is fabulous, it must be the reflection from the sea.' Despite the dingy paintwork, the rooms have a luminous quality.

Sophie's smile is blissful as she stares out to the horizon. 'Isn't it wonderful the way the garden ends and the sea begins? And there's a zig zag pathway and steps so you can walk straight down to the beach.'

Now Nate's caught us up he's tapping walls, peering up the chimneys and frowning at every crack and crevice in the downstairs reception rooms. So, we women head off for a quick tour of a massive kitchen and a maze of pantries and boot rooms, then make our way back to the hallway. As Sophie bounces up the wide staircase she's already acting like she owns the place. Although against the sludge coloured walls her aqua and white stripe T-shirt looks way too pristine to belong here. As we reach the landing Sophie and Plum are both breathless, I assume with excitement. Even though I should be in practice with my regular two flight climb at Seaspray Cottage, I'm panting from running to keep up with them.

Plum tugs at a piece of peeling wallpaper in the bedroom. 'This place is almost as run down as mine was when I bought it.'

As she leads us into the next vast bedroom Sophie's eyes are bright. 'The knack is to look beyond the dirt and clutter and see the rooms as they *will* be.' She closes her eyes. 'Think neutral colour palettes, natural fabrics from sustainable sources. Log fires, jute runners, unbelievably chunky hand-knitted throws ...'

I can't help a teasing prompt. 'Don't forget Mason jars. You'll need a shit-load of those to make an impression in this place.'

Sophie's missing the joke. 'I've been counting up as we walked round, I'm pretty sure I've got enough.'

As Plum chimes in she sends me a wink. 'I'm feeling beech furniture made by Nordic artisans, Icelandic sheepskins, Scandinavian scented candles ...' She's been exposed to Sophie's Hygge home thoughts even more than I have.

Sophie's eyes snap open. 'That's my exact vision – with a bit of bothy thrown in too because by the time the builders are done the Scottish Island influence will have hit us full on. When I close my eyes, I can hear this place crying out for a happy family to live a simple cosy life and connect with nature.'

Somehow the simple vibes are passing me by. And the cosy ones too. 'I can see that Hawthorn Farm connects with nature, but where's the nature in this house?'

She laughs. 'Now you're being silly, Clems. Here we'd practically be living *in* the ocean. You can't get any more natural than that.' She points to the window and the sea beyond that's glittering blue all the way to where it smudges into the sky. 'It's the views and that connection with the sea we're really here for. And if I get my dream castle at the same time, I can live with that.'

I have to concede on this. 'I have to admit it is amazing looking out on the ocean all day, every day.' I used to prefer city rooftops and traffic. But each time I look out at it from Laura's I feel luckier and luckier to be there. Looking straight out across the bay gives you so much space to breathe and to be. It's almost as if for the first time in my life I'm feeling every colour change of the horizon, noticing the clouds scudding across the sky, the dippers on the beach. Now I've woken up to the water and its moods, it draws me to watch and I can't stop.

Sophie's nodding at me. 'It was spending time at Seaspray Cottage that made me remember what I was missing. Plum looks out on the sea, Nell gets a teensy glimpse from her bedroom. I'm the only one of us who hasn't got a sea view.' It has to be the *only* thing we have that she hasn't. And now she wants that too. Although I can't blame her. When I arrived back six weeks ago

I had no idea how mesmerising and addictive that view would become, or how much time I'd spend, day and night, looking out. Or how I'd love the flat more with each passing day.

I'm trying to remember how she sold us her move inland. 'But you love Hawthorne Farm because it's sheltered. And looks out on fields. And because it's brill not having neighbours.' Back then she cited coastal pollution and wild flower meadows as reasons for leaving St Aidan. There was a lot of talk about rolling land and buttercups. And waving grass being so much better to look out on than dreary old St Aidan bay with its washed-up plastic bottles and acres of boring old water.

She's shaking her head. 'There's the whole beach to play on here, and I'm *so* ready for a move back to civilization. Even if the house here isn't as big as I'd hoped, I'm sure we can work with the space limitations.' As for the size thing, all I can say is hanging round warehouses and factory units and having an entire barn for a bedroom has totally messed up her spatial awareness.

Plum's nodding as if she completely understands this bit. 'It's funny, some cottages are like tardises. This looks huge from the outside, but once you're inside it's almost snug.' She has to be deluding herself if she's saying that.

As someone whose entire flat would fit in the back porch, I can't honestly join in about how it's not big enough. 'I'm liking what I overheard the agent saying about the name. It's lovely to think of the original owner changing it to Siren House after he heard mermaid song drifting up from the sea.'

Sophie's eyes are dreamy. 'It's as though the house was completely made for us. After a whole lifetime anticipating what it was like I was worried I'd be disappointed, but now I've seen it I want it even more.' It's official, she's totally smitten.

Plum wrinkles her nose. 'A premium site like this won't come cheap, then there'll be mahoosive renovation costs on top.' Having done up her own place, Plum knows.

Sophie pulls a face. 'We need to move fast, I'll have to do some spectacular juggling *and* sweet talk the bank.' If anyone can make this happen, she can.

Plum shrugs. 'You'll be talking gazillions.'

If my eyes are popping I can't help it. This makes my own shortfall seem teensy. But then I'm not bonkers enough to want to buy a castle.

There's a familiar voice coming from the doorway. 'Gazillions. And then some ...'

As we all whip around to see Charlie's half-smile peering round the door edge, Plum is the first to get her shit together. 'Hey, Charlie, what are you doing here?'

I knew he had to turn up, but my knees are still sagging now he has. And even though I'm opening my mouth hoping to say something super intelligent, nothing's coming out.

Sophie's looking daggers at him. 'Apart from lurking and eavesdropping?'

He almost laughs. 'Same as you I'd guess, assessing the potential. Although where you're mentally moving in, I'm imagining flats in the grounds. Or even across the whole site.'

The colour drains from Sophie's face, but she's lightning fast with her decoy. 'In that case you'll have to fight Clemmie for it.'

He pulls down the corners of his mouth. 'It would make a great party house, and get the class of ninety-five out of my hair.'

His lips are twitching as he turns to Sophie. 'Or, if you're ready to hang up your Hunter wellies and get out your bucket and spade you could swap it for Hawthorne Farm.'

Sophie's desperate to head him off. 'Don't you have some baking to be getting on with? Perfect chocolate roulades won't happen in one tutorial, you know.'

Charlie looks at his watch. 'Jeez, Clemmie, what are you doing *here*? You said you'd be at yours ready to start at three.'

I'm not the only one running late here. 'You said *you'd* be there too.' I'm wondering how we've spent so long looking round.

As he turns to Sophie, I could swear he's biting back a grin. 'The serious contenders will all be back for a second viewing. With their surveyors rather than their besties next time.' He's got arrogant piss-taking off to a fine art.

Sophie isn't done. 'If you ever get around to teaching Clemmie to make cupcakes, Milla would love some for her birthday. Or is rainbow buttercream beyond you?'

Charlie sends me a sideways smirk. 'Ganache is tricky, rainbow we can do no problem. Does she prefer it pastel or bright?'

'We can?' I hope he's not winding us up, because Milla will be counting on this.

Sophie's right back at him. 'I'll ask and let you know.' She's giving him her best 'eff you' grin. 'I'll tell you when we see you. *At the next viewing*.'

As he backs out of the room, I suspect he's choking back his coughing laugh. 'See you in ten then, Clemmie. Unless you'd like a lift?'

'I'll come back with Plum, thanks.' If we're spending the rest of the afternoon in my kitchen, I don't want to be distracted by being jammed up next to him in his car too. Although I'm forgetting the humungous car he drives is so wide the passenger will have to shout to have a conversation with the driver. As it is, I'm furious with myself for looking forward to the baking for anything more than the chocolate pudding.

Just when we think he's gone he pops his head back around the door. 'And if you're seriously wanting to leave your comfy pied-à-terre and live in a drafty castle, Clemmie. For the record, I think you're mad. But just say the word, and we'll talk offers.'

We stare at each other in silence until Plum crosses to the door and checks the landing. 'Okay, he's gone.' She tosses back her hair. 'Shit, what *is* he like?'

I'm shaking my head. Me finding that mix of teasing arrogance super hot is *so* not helpful I'm actually ashamed.

Sophie's eyes flash. 'It's bad enough what he's doing at Seaspray Cottage. If we've got to go head to head with him for Siren House too, I'm damned sure this isn't going to be a clean fight.'

I exchange glances with Plum. 'We can't rely on Nell delivering leftover puddings. We have to take Operation Cupid to the next level to find out what he's really up to.'

Sophie's squinting into the sun, pursing her lips. 'I don't mean to be pushy, but ...' This is how she excuses herself when she totally does. 'Stuff Operation Cupid, Operation Siren's what matters now.'

I can't help smiling. 'Are you going to explain the difference?'

Her face is intense. 'Drop the no hope romance with Nell and instead we'll *all* target him socially. Coming at him from four directions we'll be way more effective. Especially if there's alcohol involved.'

Plum's nodding. 'So we wait for him to get pissed, then listen to his drunken boasting?'

I hate to pop their balloon. 'Great. Except him turning up at the product launch was a complete one off. The only time he goes out is to wine and dine his estate agents.' Not that I stalk him. But over the last few weeks I couldn't help notice. And if I felt pleased and delighted about this, I'll keep that part to myself.

Sophie's looking at me like I'm missing the point. 'But there's the real difference. With Operation Siren, we don't wait around, we *make* things happen. Step one, we *have* to get Charlie to an event.'

Plum's mouth is set in a determined line. 'Exactly. And there's one person in the perfect position to make that happen.'

I look up expectantly. 'Yes?'

And damn that they're both looking at *me*.

19

In the flat at Seaspray Cottage
Colouring in and blunt instruments
Tuesday, three weeks later

The next couple of weeks pass by in a chocolate blur. As June ends, the weather gets warmer and there are more people to watch on the beach. Last Sunday there was a good forecast and by the time I woke up after my late night the town was already heaving. When I made my way up the winding cobbled street to the bakery to get my morning croissants if it hadn't been for the smell of salt and fishing nets blowing up from the harbour I could almost have been in Montmartre.

After a serious amount of Laura's Love for Chocolate evenings we slide in some Rhubarb Laura's Way nights so it doesn't go to waste. It turns out Sophie was right on that one. The rhubarb runs out before the punters. So, then we move on to White Chocolate Sin Chez Laura. Although now I've started on chocolate there are so many delicious recipes I'm dying to try, I feel like I could go on with Laura's Chocolate Box variations all the way through to autumn. Which may yet happen. The word from Geneva is that my holiday pay has dropped to half and Maude has extended her stay by another month. If I was less busy I might mind. As it is, I've barely got time to reply to the email. My escape route is still there, it's just been delayed a little. The truth is, right now I'm loving the flat so much and enjoying the baking, the 'moment' I want to be living in is this one. Which probably explains why the news that I've got to stay longer in St Aidan doesn't send me into the panic it once would have. If I ever do think about having to leave, there's a knot in my stomach that only goes when I forget about the future and relax back into the here and now. It could be down to the sun. Although to be fair, I loved the bluster of spring. And the if thought of winter rain and sea spray hammering on the windows sends a shiver zinging down my spine, these days it's a shiver of anticipation not horror.

As the long summer days take hold, on any afternoons I'm not baking to get ready for events, Charlie and I fit in recipe trials. What with that guy and his sugar addiction, he's more than willing to trade his tuition skills for the results. After the way he kicked off about the rules at first, I'm always holding my breath, waiting for something to go wrong, but involving him is a fail-safe way to keep him on side. Hopefully, if he puts his energy into recipe planning he'll forget about scuppering my supposed social life. Fingers crossed, if he feels like he's in charge, he won't complain. If we've baked something spectacular, he understands that all my friends will want to try it as much as he does. And the regulars at the evenings come so often they are like friends now.

Charlie's pretty damned organised when it comes to his stomach. He usually arrives ready prepared, with ingredients in a bag for whatever he fancies making from the current short-list of Laura's cards. Whether it's raspberry and white chocolate blondies or squidgy chocolate pear pudding, melt in the middle chocolate pots or berry white chocolate cheesecake, he's always up for demolishing the results. And in the same way the arrangement is never actually mentioned, there's also this kind of silent, unspoken understanding that I'll try every recipe with him first. The theory is, so long as we are super careful about not making too much noise with the evening do's, the massive amounts of chocolate endorphins pumping through Charlie's veins will take care of the rest. And so far, they have.

It's the strangest feeling. After a whole life never clicking with anything, here I am, making puddings and loving it. And other people are loving them too. Sometimes I'm so proud of what I'm doing I feel like my chest could burst. Although that could be down to my buttons being tight due to too much tasting.

As for how I've got this far and managed to keep my hands off the hot Mr Hobson ... in a way, it's been easy, because the swooning and somersaulting tummies are all on my side. There isn't a glimmer of a spark from him. It's like baking with a super beautiful stone wall who happens to have the occasional good line in developer banter. So long as I keep the lusting the other side of the kitchen table and keep my hands off his delicious forearms/butt/delectably tight thighs, he's definitely none the wiser. Even his half-smiles are so rare, I write them on the calendar. Let's face it, if I was going to sleep with anyone, it would only ever be on a one-off basis, and I'd be crazy to choose someone so close to what is feeling more like home every day. There are afternoons when all I want to do is scream. But mostly I've got this.

However much I try to kid myself, this is Cornwall not the Med. We don't have wall-to wall sunshine every day. This particular afternoon the clouds are scudding across a sky the colour of a battleship fleet. The beach is empty apart from the occasional flurry of lapwings and the rain is hammering so hard the sea is dimpled with the splashing. As I stand in the open doorway to the balcony watching the iron-grey rollers crashing up on the sand, the salty sting in my cheeks is reminding me that the cottage name is completely right. I'm shivering and pulling my cardigan closer when there's a sudden rush and, a second later, Diesel's skidding to a halt on the wet decking, and forcing his way past me. Followed close behind by a slightly more polite Charlie.

He shakes a slick of rain off his forehead and holds up a carrier bag as he strides into the living room. 'I was hoping you wouldn't mind a break from chocolate just for today. We still haven't made cupcakes, and Milla's birthday can't be far off?'

I'm surprised he remembered. 'It's next week.'

He sniffs. 'Sophie never got back to me about the icing colour.'

That's because Sophie wheedled private viewings for their second and third visits to Siren House, hoping everyone except the agent would assume they hadn't been. Apparently with auction property it pays to keep your opponents in the dark about how interested you are. I'd be dead meat if Sophie thought I'd breathed a word. 'Milla would like bright rainbows, I asked her myself.'

Charlie's eyes narrow. 'I hear Sophie's gone all 'cloak and dagger' on us. She skipped the open viewing at Siren House and snuck in a couple of evening visits instead.'

'How the *hell* do you know *that*?' After the lengths she's gone to keep her intentions secret, Sophie would be appalled.

As he shrugs there's a smile lilting on his lips so that'll be another tick on the calendar. 'The appointments book was open at the Siren House page when I called in to the agent's. I couldn't help seeing who'd viewed.' He makes it sound like the book jumped up, hit him in the face and forced him to look. And he's showing his teeth as well.

I can't help protest as I follow him and his bag through to the kitchen. 'That's low, I didn't think you'd stoop to cheating.' His chocolate mousse might be to die for, but morally he sounds as bad as Sophie fears. I have a momentary thought about how much I'd like to shake him, which doesn't end well. It's always best if I don't think about snogging his face off.

He gives a dismissive sniff. 'It's hardly classified information. And I'm the one who's put in the *years* making friends with the agents.' His eyes narrow. 'Don't knock it. There was a lot bigger surprise than Sophie on that list.'

'Who was that then?' I'm suddenly seeing the benefit of spending most afternoons baking with someone so keyed into the developer hot gossip line. Realistically, my local speculator knowledge doesn't extend beyond Charlie. But to Sophie whatever information he's about to spill could be liquid gold. This is a side of Operation Siren I hadn't anticipated.

He's watching my face intently. 'Apparently, your long lost half-brother Joe is also in the frame for Siren House.'

'What?' I'm so shocked I almost swallow my tongue with my gulp. 'Not Joe Marlow?' He can't be? Can he? If wanted to put the brakes on mentally undressing a developer, it wasn't like this.

Charlie nods. 'It's definitely him. He flew in last week, had three viewings with professionals crawling all over the place, then flew out again.' For once, he's justified in looking super pleased with himself. Although I still haven't worked out how he pulls it off without grinning.

'Shit. That sounds serious.' My stomach feels like it's been kicked. Hard. When I finally find my voice it's a whisper. 'We *can't* let him buy it.' For every reason.

Charlie pulls down the corners of his mouth. 'Auctions are very unpredictable. You never know who's going to be there, or how much they'll bid on the day. And Joe did say he wanted to get back to his roots.' He lets out a sigh and gives me a nudge. 'Who knows, I might not be Sophie's biggest rival after all. This could be all your fault for letting him into the secret about Crusty Cobs' delicious strawberry tarts.'

'At least Joe's been and gone again without chasing me down.' And I know I'm not a permanent resident and my mum's on the other side of the world, but when it comes to the Marlows I feel very possessive about St Aidan. This should be our place, not theirs. I hate the thought of them muscling in, especially at Siren House.

When I finally pull my focus back into the kitchen again, Charlie's already put the oven on, and he's tipping his bags out on the table. This is what he's like. Walking in, taking over, staring at me over his shoulder like it's already his kitchen. 'So it seemed like a good time to invest in colouring, piping bags and pipes, and more vanilla essence.' For all I know, while *I'm* trying my hardest *not* to imagine waking up next to him, *he's* probably fantasising about refurbing my flat and plotting where to hang his cinema screen.

'Great. Thanks for those.' Not that I'm going to comment, but here's someone else who thinks in industrial sizes and quantities, judging by the gear he's bought.

He's stacking icing sugar, sugar, flour, butter and cupcake cases beside the array of bottles and packets. 'I take it you've got eggs?'

'Absolutely. Free-range too, best in St Aidan. Nell's such a star bringing those. You really should get some.' I'm not passing up the chance to sing her praises. I also haven't forgotten Sophie and Plum are expecting me to deliver him to an event sometime soon. Considering how many puddings Nell's taken him it's a surprise he hasn't perked up more at her name. And I should be feeling less glad about that than I do.

He's giving me a sideways glance as he turns and slides the scales across to me and pulls out a recipe card. 'Catch up, Clemmie. All my Airbnb guests have had farm eggs in their welcome packs for weeks.' He bashes on, as if he hasn't noticed me picking my jaw up off the floor. 'Okay, this is a standard sponge mix, two eggs and equal weight of butter, sugar and self-raising.'

I get in before him. 'And no need to say it, I won't forget to sieve the flour.' And while I'm doing the weighing seeing he's already cottoned on to Nell's eggs, I might as well go a bit further. 'You do know Nell would be super sympathetic to get together with. After her break-up, she's in the perfect position to empathise. Especially with someone who's has their heart ripped out and trampled all over.'

It comes out in the best way I can think of putting it. But basically, despite our differences he's been treating this place as his since the day I arrived. He saw me tip egg over my head, and cry when I found the photos of my dad in the knitting patterns. We've bumped elbows over chocolate, pistachio and nougat semi freddo, and talked endlessly about the consistency of crumble. If I can't hint there could be a way back to happiness with my bestie I don't know who can.

He unhooks the sieve from the rack and passes it over. 'Remind me who this person with romantic issues is?'

Sometimes you can't avoid being blunt. 'You. Obviously.'

He frowns at me. 'Now cream the butter and sugar and whip until it's really white and fluffy. Then add the eggs then the flour.' His frown deepens. 'Me? *Why* me?'

It occurs to me I might need to apologise. 'I'm sorry, but I know about the wedding getting called off. And now I do know it's not like I can un-know it. And it's even worse with all this baking we're doing together.' I take a gasp. 'It doesn't get any worse than being left at the altar, but there are so many lovely women out there who'd never betray you in that way. Surely it's worth giving yourself a second chance – with the right person.' Hopefully he's getting that he could trust Nell on this. And if not, that a singles' event would be a great way forward.

'Hang on here.' He lets out a snort. '*Whatever* you're talking about, St Aidan's cesspool central's certainly been working overtime on this one.'

I'm shaking my head vigorously. 'Not at all, this came from a very reliable mutual contact. Don't worry, your secret's totally safe with me.'

An 'appalled of St Aidan' expression spreads across his face. 'And exactly *how many* other people are saying this?'

I'm mentally checking off the Dainty Dusters staff. I've seen at least six arriving in the mini bus at Sophie's. 'Don't worry, the source is fastidious and very discrete.' There's a cleaning clue there if he wants to pick it up. 'It won't go any further than us.'

'Shit, Clemmie.'

Before he can say any more and actually explode, I point to my butter and sugar mix to distract him. 'Creamy enough?'

He drags in a breath and shakes his head and closes his eyes. Then he opens them again and nods at the bowl. 'See how it's changed colour from yellow to white? That means it's ready to crack in the eggs. One at a time.'

'Great.' I'm pushing my luck here. 'Which brings us back to Nell.'

For a second he looks like his eyes are going to pop. Then he lets out a sigh. 'You do know about George?'

'No? What about him?' As to why we ended up talking about George when we were actually talking about Nell, he's lost me there.

He pulls down the corners of his mouth. 'You'll have to consult your fastidious friend on that one.'

'Hell, that's not fair, how would I know stuff when I'm never here.'

He lets out a grim laugh. 'That doesn't appear to have held you back digging the dirt on me.' He gives another sniff. 'You're meant to put the eggs in without their shells, Clemmie.'

'Damn.' That wasn't meant to happen. I pick out the pieces of shell from the bowl. Maybe he can be ironic after all.

He's still peering into the bowl, poking about looking for egg shell. 'So why is George not invited to your parties? I know for a fact he's desperate to be included.'

'I have it on the best authority that George doesn't socialise.'

When I catch his doubtful gaze, I add weight to my argument. 'That came straight from the horse's mouth.'

The corners of Charlie's mouth turn downwards. 'Well either you've been talking to the wrong horse, or your equine friend hasn't been entirely straight with you.' He looks at me from under one raised eyebrow. 'You can fold in that flour now. Use a metal spoon not a wooden one, don't over stir.' He's already opened the paper cases and he's spreading them onto a baking tray.

My voice is soaring. 'I asked George, he told me. You can't get any more straightforward with the pony than that.' At least this far I'm managing to keep the Singles' Club well out of this.

He's pulling a face. 'If there was crumble involved, I'd put money on him turning up for that. Throw in some crème anglaise and you'd double your chances.' He scratches his head as he thinks. 'Whatever he told you, I'd say it's in both our interests to get him along.'

I can't believe he's being serious. 'How much mixture in each then?'

He picks up a teaspoon, and drops a dollop into the paper case. 'Not too full, it's going to rise remember.' He narrows his eyes. 'Although thinking about it, a crumble party at your place might be too intimate for comfort. As George is your boss, it might have to be at mine.'

I can't quite believe what I'm hearing, but I'm straight onto it. 'So you'd be there too then?'

He gives me an incredulous stare. 'You're not going to ban me from my own party, even if you do look after my cat.'

I keep on spooning, trying not to get too excited that he's just handed me what Sophie and Plum had ordered. 'Just checking, that's all.'

His voice is rising with excitement. 'Parties are what my flat is made for. I suggest a whole load of puddings, and lots of people to eat them. A hundred say?' There's no holding him back. 'And my mate Rory at Huntley and Handsome wine merchants is doing great deals on Freixenet this month.'

If page three of the Residents Code just went of the window, I'm not about to say. I'm blinking at him. 'Come again?'

He's wiggling his eyebrows. 'Now we *can* tell you've been away. Freixenet is Spanish cava, it's the new prosecco. I'll get it if you like.'

This is getting way too complicated for my columns of figures. 'Actually, Nell picks up my wine supplies in her car. She's besties with Rory, too.' More so since we dreamed up the Little Cornish Kitchen and started dishing out huge quantities of alcohol at least three nights a week. As for the complications, they're huge. But if I deliver Charlie into a social situation, then it's up to Sophie and Plum where they go from there.

'You're the one with all the friends, so it would still be your party rather than mine.' As he rubs his hands his excitement is about a lot more than being about to get the mixing bowl. 'You could roll three of your class of ninety-five nights into one, give your friends a blow out, then we'd get two nights off as a bonus.'

Looks like I've accidentally got a result here. 'Laura's Seconds at Seaspray.' It's out before I can stop myself. 'Giving my parties names is a little thing of mine. Maybe you'd better lick that bowl now?'

The way he takes it from me, you'd think it was years since he had one, not yesterday. 'Twelve minutes, Gas Mark Seven. And while we're waiting for them to cook I'll run you through how to make perfect cupcake buttercream.'

I can't help smiling. Don't ask me why. 'Much more of this, I'll be turning into Cressida Cupcake.'

He freezes, spoon halfway to his mouth. 'You *know* Cressida Cupcake?'

I feel a bit silly. 'Not personally. Only on YouTube. People complain that her amounts are all over the place, but I totally love her anyway. She's *so* far ahead of everyone else, I watch her all the time.'

His face splits into the biggest smile. 'Cressie's my little sister. Well one of them, anyway.'

I'm flapping my hands in front of my face having a total fan girl moment. 'Ooo. Shit, did I just say her quantities were crap?' When I sink down onto a chair because my legs went all wobbly, I can't help wishing he'd smile like that at me.

He laughs. 'Don't worry, she knows that's a weakness.'

I can't wait to find out. 'Does she *actually* shop at Waitrose? And does she sparkle clean her kitchen every day?'

He's still laughing and it's such a good sound. 'It's not actually her kitchen on YouTube. Sorry to disillusion you, but she's not the tidiest person. And she hates cleaning. But she does shop at Waitrose, or at least she does when she's at our mum's.'

I punch the air. 'I knew it.' It sounds stupid, but I'm desperately trying to hold back from pressing my entire body against his, not for my normal lustful reasons but in the vain hope that some of Cressida's cooking magic might rub off on me. As the sun comes out and pours into the kitchen, it lights up the Granny Smith green of the dresser, so I concentrate on that instead.

Luckily, Charlie's missing quite how much I'm swooning here on all fronts. At least he seems to have recovered his colour from earlier. If I'd known that alluding to something that happened years ago was going to make him so furious or so pale, I'd never have gone there.

He gives me a nudge. 'Wake up, there's a rainbow over the bay and you're missing it. How fitting is that?'

I manage to hide how much he made me jump, and decide to skip the joke about how I could do with finding the proverbial pot of gold. As I stare at the luminous band of colour arcing across the slate sky, I just soak in the beauty of the moment. If there's a pang at the thought I might ever have to let go of this wonderful view of the ocean, I do my best to push it away. Eventually, I drag myself back to what we're doing. 'Okay, so spill. How do we make this spectacular icing?'

It's hard to believe it but he's still grinning. 'Easy. Make separate batches of pink, blue and green buttercream, put a dollop of each into the piping bag. Then squeeze.'

'It's that simple?'

He laughs. 'Don't sound so surprised, it's cooking not rocket science. And you do know you're a natural?'

I'm blinking at him because I've no idea what he means. 'Natural eater, definitely.'

He rolls his eyes. 'Some people are born cooks. You're one of them.'

I'm shaking my head and laughing at the same time. 'Charlie Hobson, I always suspected you were full of shit. Thank you for finally proving me right.' When my cheeks go pink they really clash with my hair. But hopefully he'll think I'm just warm from the sun, not totally ecstatic that he couldn't have given me a bigger compliment.

He gives me a strange sideways stare. It's so funny when people can't see the truth, even when it's staring them in the face. As for my Little Cornish Kitchen, it's getting more precarious by the day. Even if it's like three events in one, having a party at Charlie's is really pushing my luck.

20

In Charlie's flat at Seaspray Cottage
Second chances
Friday

'However annoyed I am with Charlie for *everything he* has done and will do, his flat is fabulous for a party.' As Sophie says 'everything', the wave of her hand is so huge she could be laying the blame for every inappropriate development in the south west at his door.

Sophie's usually right with her gut feeling, and despite the stunning rainbow icing trick he pulled off for Milla's party last week, she still couldn't trust Charlie less. I have to admit when it comes to Mr Hobson, I don't know what to think. It sounds hypocritical seeing as we're in his flat – but then tonight was his idea not mine. On the one hand, there's the developer who was less than straight about the flats here, who's fighting my bestie for Siren House. Yet on the other, there's this guy with a lovely dog – currently curled up on the sofa at mine – who makes my knees feel nonexistent, who couldn't be any more helpful when my egg custard's curdling. Someone who's also *actually* related to Cressida Cupcake. I know he's got the capacity to be a scheming bastard, but sometimes I end up overlooking that simply because his face is so haunted and beautiful.

When Sophie's talking fabulous party flats, she's not wrong. Her hand wave also encompasses Charlie's vast open living room, which is thronged with people all enjoying the *Laura's Seconds* party. Right now, they've all got dishes in their hands, and they're all digging in and making the most of the expanded choice of puddings at this super-sized evening. I've had such an amazing week choosing which of Laura's recipes to include and the table groaning with all her favourites is such a tribute to my wonderful grandmother. It's as if Laura's quietly cheering me on in my quest to save her flat.

Nell cut down on Charlie's original expansive numbers so I don't have my cover blown. My priority is to stop Charlie finding out that I'm doing this for money rather than the love of entertaining, so I'm sending silent messages to every enchanted mermaid in the area to look out for me on that one. As long as we don't have any hitches, this 'non'-event should give my renovation fund a mahoosive boost. Even though we've got four times the guests we'd usually have next door, the result is way less crowded.

Once again, Sophie, Nell and Plum have all pulled together to add the final touches. Plum's lent us her giant outdoor storm lanterns and the balcony is festooned with fairy lights last seen on Nell's chicken coop. Behind the puddings, the table is decorated with Mason jars filled with cow parsley and buttercups gathered by Sophie from her fields. We've got the familiar French playlist going, and as 'Boum !' moves into 'Le Mer' and 'Rien de rien' the atmosphere is relaxed yet buzzing.

Plum turns from where she's ladling the last of the custard into jugs from a huge vat on the hob. 'So is our plan on schedule?' Nell engaged Dakota, who needed very little persuasion to take personal charge of making sure Charlie enjoys as much cava as she can persuade him to knock back. Part two comes later when we'll all be on hand to hear him give his secrets away.

At this point in the evening most people are ready for a new glass, and Sophie carries on pouring Freixenet cava into flutes as she replies to Plum. 'I've already more than made up for missing my Soul Nutrition class.' For someone who's supposed to live completely in the moment Sophie's such a schemer. As she's currently working her way through her fourth helping of melting chocolate pudding drenched with cream and custard, it looks like she's found better ways to feed her soul than meditation. And she's ditched gluten-free too.

'And?' I can't wait to hear what she's got to say.

She raises her eyebrows. 'I didn't want to say earlier in case it put you off your serving, but Charlie collared me on my way in. He said Joe has been in touch with him about joining forces for the auction.'

'What?' I grab a bar stool and sink onto it before I fall over.

Plum drops her ladle and she hurries across. 'It happens a lot. They pool their resources to win the auction, then Joe would take the house and Charlie would take the garden.'

Sophie's shaking her head. 'And we'd get nothing?'

Plum's frowning. 'It could just be a wind up. Psychological warfare.'

I feel like I've been kicked in the guts. 'Either way it's a total betrayal.' With anyone else it would be bad. With Joe Marlow, it couldn't be more upsetting. But it's a stark reminder of what Charlie is. I really shouldn't be taken in by the chocolate brownie side of his character.

Sophie's expression is pained. 'Charlie said if I wanted to talk, I knew where to find him. But there's nothing to discuss, can you imagine the garden obliterated by his flats?'

Plum lets out a long whistle. 'So there's lots to nail down later then. We needed this event even more than we thought.'

I could do with a triple helping of queen of puddings just to get me back on my feet. 'Bloody developers. All that matters to them is the bottom line.' I hardly dare to bring the subject up now. 'So how's the sale of the farm going?' They've had lots of viewers, but this is the first chance I've had to ask if they've got any serious interest yet.

Sophie pulls a face. 'We've priced to sell and the agent's making it clear we'd be willing to do a deal for a fast exchange of contracts. But there aren't any firm offers yet, and it's difficult with the auction only three weeks away.'

Plum sighs. 'Not too many people have the kind of loose change lying around that they'd need to buy your place. Would you dare to borrow against the company without a sale on the farm?'

Sophie's shudder is so big it's visible through her fifth spotless apron of the night. 'When we took big risks to build up the business we didn't have four kids. I promise myself to be level headed and keep the family in a good place. Then I remember how wonderful it would be to live in Siren House, and sensible goes out the window.' Even without Charlie's game playing she's tearing herself apart over this. 'Much more important though. You've busted your bum making puddings, Clemmie, so where's the reason we're all here?'

Plum and I stare at each other. It's true that since the last chocolate evening on Wednesday, I haven't stopped. And if I'd ever wondered what humungous sixteen place dining tables were good for, tonight I found out because Charlie's has really come into its own. We've put the puddings out in two waves, and guests have come along and served themselves then come back for extra helpings. And then some. I've been holding my breath to see how the puddings have gone down, but the trifles have been just as well received as the banoffee pies, the cheesecakes have had as many gasps as the sticky toffee puddings.

As I get up and refill a jug with a slick of thick cream, I'm looking across the room. 'If you want to find Charlie look for Dakota's dress. It sticks out a mile, despite only being the size of a small hanky.' Not that I want to be bitchy. Or unsupportive to other women. But bright pink. Off both shoulders, off the bum, *and* off the back, with frills. She couldn't have chosen anything more out there. And the worst thing of all is, she has the body and the confidence to rock it, and more. And right at this moment, I'd happily claw her eyes out.

And the second worst thing, which kind of makes my fashion-heart bleed, is that her sky-high cork wedge sandals are almost identical to the ones I'm wearing. Which I always thought were unique because I bought them from the Montreuil flea market in Paris. And obviously, mine worn with my floppy ocean blue knee length spotted dress look like nothing next to ones worn by someone whose tanned bare legs stretch all the way up to their neck. And muscular ones at that. It's so unfair I actually get a little bit of sick in my mouth.

Plum rolls her eyes. 'She's very tactile, isn't she? I'm sure body slamming Charlie up against the bookcase for the entire evening wasn't in her job description.'

Sophie gets another two bottles of cava out of Charlie's floor to ceiling wine chiller. 'On another subject entirely, Nell and George were chatting when he first arrived and I couldn't help noticing their shirts were almost identical.' As she pops the first cork she grins. 'Should we be reading something into *that*?'

I turn and make a space for the cream jug on the table. 'They weren't *that* similar. Nell's is *River Island* and it's covered in random ruffles. Anyway, you were the one who said checks *weren't* a basis for a relationship.'

Sophie stops pouring. 'I know. But for the fleeting moment they had their heads together they looked very close, that's all.'

At least I can safely put that theory to bed. 'Forget that, Nell's been circulating all evening. And George has been on his stool at the island unit talking to a couple of guys he crews with when he sails. They've been chugging their way through crumble and custard all night.' I know because I've been feeding them. Seeing as they're the only non-paying customers here it seemed like a sensible precaution. If George is busy with non-stop puddings, hopefully he won't have time to mingle and stumble across the awful truth that other people have paid. I've also been keeping a close watch, waiting to pounce on any evidence of whatever scandal Charlie hinted at. It's been the same at work too. For someone who's usually chilled and laid back, I've actually had a hell of a week. Not only have I had to make a gazillion puddings, I've also been on high alert watching George for clues. Although this far he's given away precisely zilch. So, my nervous exhaustion has all been for nothing.

'You've totally excelled yourself here tonight, Clemmie.' Plum says as she pulls me into a little hug. 'We're almost on to the main business of the evening now.'

My inside is all warm with the praise. 'Thanks, babe. What are we going to do?'

She narrows her eyes. 'As soon as people have finished eating, I'm going to mix things up a bit.'

Sophie's eyebrow shoots up. 'How exactly?'

Plum's grin is wicked. 'Ice-breaker musical chairs.' She pauses to do her jazz hands. 'Truly, we can't let a matching dining set for sixteen go to waste. A few riotous rounds of the St Aidan Singles special should give us all ample opportunity to prise a few secrets out of Charlie.

I'm not convinced. 'Isn't musical chairs lame and prissy?'

Plum's laugh is low. 'Not the way this lot play it. Nell tweaked the rules a while back to get the maximum number of permutations of different people sitting on each other's knees. It's the perfect way to round the evening off with a bang and squeeze some extra nuggets out of Charlie.' She looks at me. 'Find Plastique Bertrand on your playlist. That's the kind of wild we need here. Then they like to move on to up tempo Blondie tracks and The Killers.'

'Great.' As I grab my phone and start shuffling through Spotify, I can't help noticing. For someone who admits to the occasional Singles' pub crawl, Plum's very informed. Although I'm not sure

I ever came across a game of musical chairs before that included sitting on knees. The ones I've played were more about disappearing seats.

She turns to Sophie. 'You prise Dakota away from Charlie, then Nell, Clemmie and I will take care of the rest.'

Moments later, Plum's abandoned her custard and she's humping the first leather and stainless steel dining chair around into the main party area, and calling for Nell. One sniff of the game, and a load of the chaps rush over to help. Before we know it, the island unit is covered in empty dishes and glasses, and we're looking at sixteen chairs lined up back-to-back down the centre of Diesel's favourite rug, and they're filling up with enthusiastic guests.

Plum sidles up to me, talking out of the corner of her mouth. 'Okay, we'll do a few dummy runs to get them into the swing. Then we'll sit Charlie down ... and *kerching*!' She gives me a wink. 'All ready?'

As she moves off Nell's taking up a position at the far end. The minute all the chairs are full, I switch on Plastic Bertrand and the whole room erupts. Crazy doesn't begin to cover it. Everyone is belting round the chairs whooping and waving their arms.

I mouth at Plum. 'What the fuck?'

She pulls a face, and bellows in my ear. 'It's so much fun they can get a bit over excited.' She lets it go for a few more bars then yells again. 'Okay, stop the music.'

As Plastic Bertrand breaks off in mid-syllable, there's a tremendous scuffle, not to mention a few flying fists. Eventually, the scrum eases back, and we're left with sixteen people on chairs and sixteen more sprawled on top of them. There are legs and arms flailing in all directions with Nell holding court at the far end.

'Okay, for the next bit, the choice is yours, but it must be consensual – snog, secret or surprise.' She lets out a low laugh. 'Or all three if you want. But as soon as the music restarts, stop the snogs and surprises, swap places, and we'll go again.'

As I glance at the writhing mass of bodies I groan to Plum. 'Jeez, look away now, this is hideous. However much Sophie needs her secrets, I'm not going to dare to go in.'

Plum laughs. 'You will. Pass the phone, I'll do the music.'

I do as I'm told. As the crazy starts up again I shout into Plum's hair. 'I'm all for anarchy but is it good for the Little Cornish Kitchen to be aligned with this kind of riotous?' I'm suddenly feeling very protective of our creation.

Plum shrugs. 'We're here to do whatever it takes. The minute Sophie gets Dakota separated, I'll get Charlie onto a chair then you and Nell can dive in and see what he comes out with.'

We're on to Blondie now, and Debbie Harry's singing her heart out. Charlie's nowhere in view, and George and his crewmates haven't ventured into the melee yet. But by my reckoning most of the Singles' Club have had every other eligible member on their knee and then some.

Waiting for Dakota to be un-glued, Charlie to be sitting down and me or Nell to be near him is like one of those maddening cracker games where you have to get all the balls into holes at the same time. Half an hour later, I'm despairing of it ever occurring then suddenly the unthinkable happens. I've no idea how the hell she's detained Dakota, but Sophie's waving her arms. As the music stops, Plum's shouldering Charlie into a gap and onto the knee of a woman who looks from her big calves and sweat band like she heads up the hockey team. Plum gives Charlie a second to listen to whatever secret she's telling him, then presses play. As Charlie falls back onto his own dining chair, we're one move away from landing Nell or me in his lap.

As the music begins and everyone starts haring around the room, I catch Nell's eye. 'You go first?' Once Charlie's crushed under my weight, I'm not a hundred per cent certain I'll be able to resist a full-on pash and go in for a boring old secret instead. After all the puddings I've made here, whatever he spills had better be good.

Then suddenly, the Killers break off in midline, and somehow it's like time stops. I'm standing staring down at Charlie, he's smiling up at me turning my toes to syrup. There's no time to wonder where Nell is because there's a huge shove in my back and the next thing I know I'm disentangling my hair from his stubble and hanging on to the most muscly shoulders.

His voice is low in my ear. 'I think we might have been set up there.'

It's a relief that's the worst he suspects. 'Really?' My head's spinning and I'm aching for the music not to start again. Ever.

His voice is low again. 'My secret is I don't mind at all.' Jeez, he must be so drunk.

I gulp and laugh at the same time.

'If you'd like to snog me I'd like that. That's two secrets already.'

I've got a nanosecond here to decide at most. I swallow, and take a huge breath. Then his hand comes around the back of my head, and without me doing anything at all my lips are dipping towards his. The butterflies in my chest are going so wild I'm in the middle of worrying I'm going to throw up here. Then there's a sharp tug on my hair, my arm is wrenched out of its socket and the next minute I'm sailing through the air. As I sprawl backwards onto Diesel's shaggy wool rug there's a flash of flamingo pink. As I stare upwards a skimpy fuchsia frill wraps itself around Charlie's ears, and a bright blonde head descends as Dakota goes in for the kill.

Her bright red lips suck onto Charlie's face and I let out a groan. 'Oh my days, it's not even as if her lippy matches her dress.'

'For frigg's sake ... are you okay, Clemmie?' Plum's Converse leap in next to me and she grabs my hand and hauls me back up onto my wedges.

As Debbie Harry starts singing 'Heart of Glass', everyone on the chairs leaps up again. Sophie's in there hauling Dakota off, and firmly helping a wide-eyed Charlie to his feet. As I coax my feet into action and we stagger towards the kitchen island, Sophie catches us up and flings her arm around me.

She's talking through gritted teeth. 'That woman is out of order, if this was my party I'd eject her.' Her voice is high with indignation. 'Those were tai chi moves she used there. That's meant to be for inner mind and body balance, not bashing people up, I've a good mind to report her.'

Plum's smiling. 'If you were in charge, Soph, you'd have barred her the first night for snatching puddings, remember?'

They're so cross on my behalf, I haven't the strength to add to it. I feel like someone pulled out half my insides and ran off with them. But at the same time, maybe I was saved from myself there. Talk about in the heat of the moment. That was a moment so heated I managed to overlook I was about to snog the face off the drunk guy who's got so much integrity, he's helping my half-brother screw over my best friend. And if I had gone there, the balcony would have been out of bounds forever more due to the embarrassment. All of which is true, but doesn't stop me feel any less gutted.

Plum's brushing invisible specks off her paint splashed denims. 'It looks like Nell's taking that as a cue to start clearing up. From the cluster of volunteers around the dish washer area, it looks like the ship's crew are getting a late but very warm mass welcome.'

I scour the room, and give a silent curse. 'There's no sign of Charlie or Dakota.'

Sophie's straight onto that. 'Clearing off the moment there's work to be done. No surprise there then.' She gives a disparaging sniff, but this time she's wrong. On normal baking days, even though there isn't a dishwasher, Charlie sticks around until every last spoon has been put away. Although as this is more our party than his, this isn't strictly his mess to clear. Anyone not in the kitchen area is bouncing around by the chairs, yelling at the top of their voices, thumping the air to the Killer's 'Mr Brightside' chorus.

Jealousy, turning saints into the sea ... It's like they're playing Charlie and Dakota's song. It would be *so* Dakota to shove Charlie into the nearest walk-in wardrobe so she can slam him up against the wall in private. Let's face it, from the secrets he muttered to me back there, he has to be off his face. When the song gets to the part where *she's touching his chest, now he takes off her dress*, I clamp my hands to my ears so hard all I can hear is a noise like the rush of the undertow out in the bay.

By the time I let go, Sophie's tapping me on the shoulder. 'Clems, are you okay?'

I shake myself back into the room. 'Yeah, sure.' I add in a grin to cover that I'm anything less than fabulous. 'Just having cocoa overload, I definitely over-did the caramel brownies.'

She directs a knowing nod towards the kitchen. 'What I was saying about all the checks ... look at George and Nell over there, sorting glasses. They're in their own little world.'

At first I can't believe what I'm seeing, then the penny drops. 'Phew, this is my lucky day. That's Nell keeping George away from the paying public, I'd best go and help.'

'Or maybe, don't bother ...'

As I dash towards the sink area, Sophie's words fade behind me. I know she's only trying to save me from clearing up because they insisted they were going to do it. In any case, it's time I checked in with George.

'Hey, how's it going?' The crew have drifted off to join in the dancing, leaving Nell and George washing up glasses and dipping into the last giant queen of puddings bowl.

Nell scoops a mouthful of soft meringue and jam off the spoon. 'Brilliantly. Everyone's loving it, the musical chairs melted some glaciers I'd thought would stay frozen forever. And this is the most delish queen of puds I've ever tasted.' Even for upbeat Nell, she's sounding extra enthusiastic. Although having tried thirty compulsive crazy seconds of it, I completely get how musical chairs forges links. As she dips in again her voice is clogged with jam and custard. 'What's your secret?'

I shrug. 'I used brioche instead of breadcrumbs.' That was Charlie's tip.

George laughs and dips in too. 'So strictly this is a Marie Antoinette version?'

'Nice take, George.' I nod and wiggle my eyebrows at Nell.

'Mostly I reckon it's down to the fabulous free-range eggs.' Once upon a time that line was meant for Charlie, but if he's not here it's a shame to waste it.

George passes me a fork. 'Seriously, you need to try this.'

Nell rolls her eyes. 'Of course she's tried it, she made them, dumbo.'

'Except I haven't actually tasted this one.'

George looks exceptionally pleased with himself. 'There you go then. Dip in.'

I'm about to do exactly as he suggests when Sophie sweeps over.

She whips the fork out of my hand. 'Come on Clems, out of the kitchen.'

'B-b-b-ut ...' My mouth's still open in anticipation of pudding.

She's got a firm hand on each of my shoulders. 'This way, there's a large glass over here with your name on.' She's already powering me past the chair line. 'I insist ...'

'I should really look after George.' I know we're not at work, but I still feel responsible for him.

Sophie's growling in my ear. 'Take it from me, George is in very good hands.'

Which brings me neatly back to Nell. 'What a woman. She certainly saved me with her quick thinking there.' I make a mental note to make her a batch of chocolate brownies as a special 'thank you' for that one.

I must be knackered and over wrought, because I have another little moment, this time fanning my face. I'm tired or else this Freixenet stuff that Sophie's just handed me another glass of is way stronger than the ice cream pink bottles suggest. This time the lump in my throat is because I'm so happy that I can actually make brownies. All by myself. To think that when I first came to Seaspray Cottage, I couldn't make any of the things I've made tonight. Not that I'm shouting about it, but I think Cressida Cupcake would be thrilled by what she'd inspired me to do. But most important of all, I hope Laura would be too. She's the person I truly have to thank for this. With everything I know now, it's hard to imagine what it was like to be that 'clueless in the kitchen' person who walked into Laura's flat all those weeks ago. I'm still not Nigella, but I'm way better than I was. So much so, when I have my dreamy moments between client calls at the office, I imagine a Little Cornish Kitchen that doesn't end. A Little Cornish Kitchen that would let me stay in the flat I love, with all the happy times I remember. Being here has not only let me discover what I'm good at. It's also what I enjoy. When I'm here in Laura's little kitchen it's as if I've finally discovered who I am, I can be the person I'm meant to be. And I so want to find a way to hang on to this.

Then I remember that sometime soon an email will come from Geneva, calling me all the way back to Paris be the person I was before. To pick up again where I left off. For tonight I'm not letting myself think about that. I know I used to love that spangly view of the Eiffel Tower in the dark. But now I love the lights of the fishing boats bobbing out to sea, and the arc of twinkle where the lights sweep around the bay just as much. Actually, a whole lot more.

The minute Charlie's flat's back to sparkle clean standard, I'll pad along the balcony and spend half an hour before bed counting the stars over the bay with Diesel. Then later when I curl up in bed there will be a soft salty wind wafting through the open window. And Pancake will sit on my hair as she's taken to doing lately. And she'll purr in my ear until morning so the roar of the waves doesn't wake me.

And just for tonight, because I've smashed it with my puddings I might just allow myself to pretend that life could stay like this forever.

21

In Laura's flat at Seaspray Cottage
Lost dogs and kimonos
Saturday

This is why I rarely let myself dream – because the reality is so often a letdown. When I got back to my end of the balcony last night, Diesel had disappeared. Nothing sinister. There was a scrawled Post-it note from Charlie, saying they'd gone for their evening walk. Charlie, Dakota and Diesel, I take the threesome as a given because however irresistible Dakota is, Diesel still needs to pee. And realistically she didn't get legs like hers by refusing any bit of exercise that came her way like I do. So, they probably had to have a break in their wardrobe action. Yay to that. The thought of them together made me feel like vomming. Although that could also have been down to necking the best part of two bottles of fizz and finishing off way too much trifle.

I used to like star gazing on my own, but that was *before* I'd had a dog's head resting on my shoulder, sighing, groaning back to all my remarks about the moon and the reflections shimmering on the water. Once you've been spoiled with that kind of doggy company, doing it on your own isn't half as magical. So, I left the living room door ajar in case Diesel needed to take refuge again, then I wandered through to the bedroom where I found that Pancake had puked up a fur ball on the rug. Which was exactly what I meant about the good times lasting. Let's face it, any happy cloud built on a foundation as insubstantial as puddings was bound to be fleeting.

When I open my eyes next morning, I assume from the pale light that it's early. I take in the raindrops splashing through onto a dark puddle on the bedroom floor in front of the open window and grope for my phone which tells me it's eight o'clock and pissing down in St Aidan. Then I remember the whole reason for the party – Operation Siren – failed spectacularly due to Charlie leaving the scene.

On the up side, I bought quadruple quantities of croissants and pain au chocolat from the bakery yesterday afternoon as a hangover precaution. And I can have my wake-up blow out on the balcony while the kettle's boiling. Swinging my legs out of the high bed, I pull a cardi over my sleep shorts and vest, grab a brolly and make my way through the hall. As I reach the living room door, I'm met by a cold black nose and a rough grey head.

'Diesel, so you *did* come back. I don't blame you for wanting to hide out in a groan free zone.' I push my way through to the kitchen, and give his ears a rub as I fill the kettle. 'Come on, let's go outside for a blast, then we'll have coffee.'

I'm crossing to the balcony doors, when I hear a grunt. As I turn to the patchwork sofa, the pile of throws on it heaves, and as a hand comes out I let out a squeal. A second later the heap of blankets parts and Charlie's stubble covered face appears. 'Did someone mention coffee ... and what's that about groans?' He scratches his head and crumples up his face. 'Why are you carrying an umbrella, Clems?'

As I stare down at my stumpy legs sticking out of my pyjama shorts I'm kicking myself for not putting on my flea market wedges. Then I notice the crumpled pile of denim on the floor by the sofa and catch a flash of tanned skin between the folds of alpaca rug, and I forget all about sandals.

My mouth is dry, but I have to check. 'Sorry, where do you stand on underwear?' However much I should, I'm not up to tackling him about what the heck he's doing with my half-brother Joe and Siren House. As for the snog that never was, I'm going to act like he's forgotten it.

There's a smile playing around his lips. 'That sounds like a trick question.' From the slices in his cheeks he's finding this a lot more amusing than me. 'You need to be more specific.'

I swallow hard. 'If those are your jeans on the floor, I'm hoping you wear it, that's all.'

He laughs. 'At a guess I'd say my boxers are marginally larger than yours.'

I'm trying hard not to think about them. And failing. 'Damn. Back in a sec.' What seemed fine for a moment on the balcony is way too skimpy when there's a half-naked guy in my living room. It's like every fantasy I've had over the last few weeks has come to life but now it has I'm completely unprepared to deal with it. I dash to the bathroom and unhook one of Laura's flowery kimonos from the back of the door. It's the best way to stop the virtual version of myself leaping on top of the quilt pile. Not that

I wear them often. When you travel light like I do dressing gowns aren't top of the 'to pack' list. Even if this one's a bit voluminous it's a perfect, instant cover up.

As I go back into the living room Charlie narrows his eyes. 'Is that Laura's robe?'

Moving across the room the peach silk splashed with cornflowers is almost weightless. 'I'm borrowing it for the next two minutes, while I wave you and Diesel off. Then it'll go back on the bathroom door where it belongs.'

He pulls down the corners of his mouth. 'No need to feel guilty, everything here was meant for you. From what Jenny said Laura chose what she left behind very carefully.'

I'm brushing the comment aside. 'It probably suits me better than Joe or his brothers.'

Charlie frowns. 'It's a perfect match for your hair.' As it would be for Joe's too. And Laura's. I'd have felt too uncomfortable borrowing it on the first day, but now I've got to know her better again I'm certain she wouldn't mind at all.

I'm used to crushing the ginger jibes then moving swiftly on. 'Yeah thanks, two shades of marmalade. More importantly, why the hell is the guy with the monster sized bed sleeping on a vintage sofa in the flat next door?' We had to get round to this sometime. Not that he's bragged about bed size, but somehow humungous goes with the territory.

He pulls in a breath and has the decency to look guilty for approximately point one of a second. 'Sorry to sound like a lightweight, but I didn't want to stick around to watch my Mies van der Rohe icons get tested to destruction.'

If he was talking French, I might understand better. 'Your *what?*'

'The musical chairs were limited editions. They're authentic thirties originals.'

'Fuck.' It's a morning for dry mouths, and it's a lot more than a hangover. 'So they cost shitloads?' I know I'm coming across like Nell here, but sometimes it's best to know.

Charlie's eyebrows lift. 'A few grand each.' I try not to notice that as he pulls the covers up his chest is bare.

My squeal is a mix of horror and disbelief. 'Jeez. And St Aidan singles were jumping all over them and you didn't stop them?' And damn that I'm rattled enough to let that out.

He shrugs. 'I didn't want to spoil the party.'

This gets more and more awful. 'I'm *so* sorry. As far as I know they all survived.' It just goes to show, if you pay enough you get looks *and* strength. And I'm thanking my lucky stars he missed my singles slip. If I wasn't on such thin ice, I'd give a dig to point out how much mayhem he was responsible for last night. Picking up what he once mentioned about Seaspray Cottage being a train, yesterday's would have been the bar and disco coaches, with rugby teams on board.

He sighs. 'There's no point being precious. They were bought to be used.'

That's one way of looking at it. 'Well, you must be ready for that coffee.' After coming so close to trashing his priceless furniture the least I can offer him is breakfast. Although it turns out a kimono isn't that suitable even if you're only crisping croissants. Baggy sleeves might be fine for Geisha-ing around in Japan, but in St

Aidan they're picking up every pastry flake. I've already had near misses trailing them in the sink and Pancake's potted shrimps.

By the time Charlie follows me through to the kitchen, he's reunited with his jeans. My mouth's watering so much I'm swallowing back the saliva as I try not to watch him doing up his shirt buttons. Then it hits me. Sod dining chairs, I need to find out about Dakota. So far he's conveniently concealed a huge chunk of shagging time behind a smoke screen of designer furnishing. Not that it's any of my business.

I put some plates and mugs on a tray and aim for my best airy tone. 'Musical chairs was before you hooked up. How come you ended up here afterwards?'

His face wrinkles in query. 'Hooked up?'

I hope I've got the right expression. 'With Dakota. That is what you call it when two people meet then bonk each other's brains out?' Even as I say it, I realise it's probably a lot more than just that.

For some reason, there's a smile lilting around his lips. 'Once I finally got away, I thought it was best to lie low, and here seemed like the easiest place.'

I'm confused. 'But why hide?'

'In case Dakota came back to mine ... on the lookout for more of those hook things you mentioned. She's quite a handful.' He puts the cafetière on the tray then picks it up and gives me a hard stare. 'Let's eat where it's comfy. Are you okay to bring the croissants?'

As I follow him through and perv on everything from his ankles up to his butt cheeks in the soft denim, I'm trying to work out if this is good news or not. Like so many things with Charlie it's hard to work it out, but I can't keep banging on about it. I put the plate down on the table in front of the sofa and help myself to a pain au chocolat. Then I drop into my favourite velvet chair and get totally tangled up with the robe. 'I can completely see how the Chinese could hide their dogs in their kimonos. This one is massive, although for breakfast it's less practical.' I make a grab for the silk neckline that keeps sliding open.

Charlie laughs as he hands me my mug. 'Don't say that too loudly, Diesel's already eyeing it up for size to see if he can fit in. Careful, don't knock your coffee over.'

'Good point, thanks.' A spill is the last thing I want. I move the drink and I'm trying to bunch the arm fabric round my wrist when my fingers come across a stiffness in the silk folds. 'There's something here in the droopy bit of the sleeve.'

Charlie laughs. 'So you *have* got a Pekingese in there after all? Even more secrets, then.' He catches my eye, and doesn't let go.

With cheeks this hot clashing with my orange wrap I can't not retaliate. 'This one isn't a *drunken* secret though.'

He's staring at me with a mix of smoulder and intransigence. 'I was sober.'

'Yeah and I'm a Chinaman.' If he carries on blinking at me like that my stomach will wilt to nothing, so I turn back to my arm. 'It's definitely not a dog in here, it's more like a card.' I'm struggling but I can't find how to get to it.

Charlie gets up. 'Straighten your elbow so the sleeve hangs down, I'll see if I can find my way in.' He's pretty deft. Two seconds later he's holding up a folded piece of paper between his fingers. 'There you go, it looks like a letter.'

There's an unnerving tingle where our fingers graze as I take it from him, but I'm puzzling because the round regular hand writing is familiar. Birthday cards, shopping lists, my mum's long list of pitfalls to watch out for with the flat. It's as if whoever wrote this went to the same school as her. Then I open it up and see the names at the end and the beginning. 'It's from someone called Jill.' My heart gives a little kick at the coincidence. 'To someone called ...' As I scan back up the page my heart starts hammering.

Charlie's looking over my shoulder. 'Rob, isn't that your dad's name?'

There's a sour taste in my mouth. 'Jill's my mum.' I pass the paper back to Charlie. 'I can't read it. It might be a love letter.'

His hand is light on my arm, and his eyes are dark with concern. 'Shall I skim through it and see what it says?'

'Yes.' As I clamp my eyes shut my mouth tastes sour. 'This is exactly why I shouldn't have come here. If only I'd stayed away ... then you could have had your flat ... and I'd already be back in Paris by now ...'

His hand tightens on my wrist. 'Clemmie, you need to read this.'

A chill creeps down my spine as I open my eyes. 'I do?'

He nods and passes me the paper. Even though it's as old as I am it's still that bluey white colour. And now I look more closely, there's not a letter out of place in the even blue biro writing. The way it flows down the page with every line parallel, it's way too neat for a first draft. Careful planning. Not leaving anything to chance. That's my mum all over. I screw up my insides and pick out some phrases:

... this is breaking my heart too ... I couldn't live with myself if it were any other way ... the hardest decision, but the only choice ... you have to go ... even if we can't be together, I promise I'll always love you ... forever and longer ...

Charlie's arm is round my shoulder, and my cheek is crushed against the soft blue checks of his shirt. When my words come out, they're a whisper.

'It's not how she said. Not at all.'

Charlie's chest expands under my face as he takes a breath. 'It was a long time ago, you can't judge from one letter. It's a few lines and they say very little.'

'But when you read this, it's clear they were talking. And they loved each other. And she's the one who's sending him away. For my whole life, I wrote him off as a total bastard because he legged it the second he found out she was pregnant.' Now there's a glimmer of a chance it might not have been like that, there's a twanging ache in my chest.

Charlie sighs as he lets me go. 'It's the old cliché – there's always two sides. At least now you're old enough and wise enough to understand rather than make snap judgements.'

As I stare at my pain au chocolat, the inside of my mouth feels like sawdust. 'I'm not hungry any more.' It's as if every certainty in my life has been tipped upside down and shaken. It's the same as it was with the photos. I know one piece of paper from thirty years ago shouldn't be this upsetting and once I've had time to get used to it I'll probably mind less. But right now, there are so many questions flying around in my head, and no one here to answer them. My poor mum, no wonder she was always upset when I asked about my dad.

Charlie narrows his eyes as he sits down on the sofa. 'What you need to remember is whatever went on in your past, your mum couldn't have loved you any more, and neither could Laura. You've turned out to be an amazing person, Clemmie. It might be best to concentrate on what comes next rather than what went on before, because that's what you can change. Come on, you're the croissant queen, try a sip of coffee.' However badly he behaves in other areas of his life, when it comes to heartfelt advice he's spot on. And his hugs with the heat of his firm chest against my cheek couldn't be any warmer or more comforting.

'Okay.' I drag in a breath, pick up my cup, and feel very proud of myself for not clinging on for longer. 'Thanks, Hobson.'

His smile is gentle. 'It won't seem half so bad after breakfast.' His face slides into a grin as he nods at the plate piled high with pastries. 'You can't seriously expect me to eat this lot on my own.'

I tug at Diesel's ear as he sidles up. 'There's someone here who's keen to help you. Although you're right, I need my calories. Thinking of the immediate future, there's going to be a mega tidy up to do next door.'

As Charlie's grin widens he's looking super pleased with himself. 'That's all taken care of.' He looks at his phone. 'Dainty Dusters should be cleaning as we speak. If you haven't any other plans, you could always come for a wander along the beach with Diesel and me.'

'A walk?' I'm playing for time and trying to sound less appalled than I am. Given the choice between a walk and cleaning, I'd opt for the inside option. Every time. 'I'm not really an exercise kind of person.' It's one thing hiking a hundred metres along to the Surf Shack with the kids on a sunny afternoon. But Charlie and Diesel look fit enough to be off for a ten mile jog. And the weirdest thing is, now I think about it I'm wanting to go. Not to tackle him about Joe. Just because he's calming and when it comes to my past he understands. Not many people can find the right words for a tough moment. But he does.

He laughs. 'Walking's a great way to clear your head. It's only like one of your blows on the balcony, but you move your legs a bit too. And it's Saturday, it's not as if you're doing anything else.' As usual he's not taking 'No' for an answer.

I'm scouring my brain for excuses. 'I only have cowboy boots. With heels. And I definitely couldn't zoom along like Dakota.'

His face wrinkles. 'What's Dakota got to do with anything?' If he doesn't know the answer to that, I'm not going to spell it out.

'And I have baking to do for Sunday.' Which is tomorrow. Amazingly, there are still more takers for the latest *Chocolate Box* selection. Although after yesterday's bash, an evening at mine will feel tiny. Then I glance out at the steel grey sea and find my best excuse yet. 'And it's raining.'

He's back to his smile. 'Good thing you got your umbrella out. So, that's a 'yes' for the walk. I'll lend you a waterproof.' They're statements not questions. 'And baking reminds me, next week we're moving on to pastry.'

'We are?' I can't quite believe we've finally got there. It's harder to get right, but it opens up so many possibilities.

He nods. 'Once you can make tarts, the baking world's your oyster. That's no bad place to be for a mermaid who's great at cooking. *And* keeping secrets.'

I wave my middle finger at him for the last bit. At times like this I wish he'd bum off back next door and get on with his speculating. And leave this particular mermaid to enjoy a lazy morning in bed.

Although the second I walked into Seaspray Cottage back in April, I swapped peace for shocks and surprises. I can't help wondering what's going to turn up next.

22

At Plum's gallery
The roar of the waves
Tuesday

Surprisingly, I survive my hike along the beach with Diesel and Charlie. It turns out Charlie was right. Summer rain blasting in my face and hammering through the seams of my borrowed cagoule, and a gale sticking my soaking wet dress to my legs prove to be the ideal antidote to finding out my past isn't quite as I thought. By the time I've had a long hot soak in the tub with the claws, the numb pain in my chest has almost gone. A late dash to the Surf Shack for gin slings and a debrief with Plum and Nell does the rest. When Nell says that gin is a depressant I agree to stop after four. Then on Sunday my quadruple chocolate mousse cake with strawberries goes down a storm at *Laura's Chocolate Box* evening. Plus, I score another three cupids from the weekend and my total is getting bigger and bigger. Yay to the lingering magic of musical chairs! And two days later as I'm helping in Plum's gallery and I'm still getting Facebook messages of congratulations for my chocolate marquise I'm racking my brains for any way to make this more permanent.

'So if you're happy to price up the new sea glass stock, it's all here.' Plum points to a stack of open boxes on the desk at the end of the gallery where the craft is displayed.

I wander over, pull back the tissue paper and take out a fine silver neck chain with green translucent glass and silver hearts. 'These are so pretty, they're like wearing a piece of the sea.' I let out a murmur of appreciation. 'And there are key rings with shells and hanging ornaments too.' I already know I'm going to have to buy one.

I'm into the routine of afternoon shifts at the gallery now. So long as the sun's out, I eat my croissant lunch on my way over from the office. Once I've unpacked the latest arrivals, I usually go on to sort out the smaller prints and the cards. As summer moves on and there are more visitors browsing, I usually end up serving the customers who come in for the less expensive things while Plum sorts out the arty enquiries.

Plum's keeping half an eye on the people in front of her pictures as she hitches up her dungarees. 'You know Charlie's upstairs? I sent him to check out my bigger pictures with a view to using some in the entrances of some swanky new flats they're building down near Penzance.'

'Nice work, girl.' I give her a playful punch, then a rueful smile. 'Whatever happened to Bay Holdings horrors?' Although what the hell Charlie is up to with Joe might yet answer that question. We still haven't cleared up exactly what's going on there.

As for Plum's pictures, they come in all sizes from mini to gigantic with price tags to match. Like a lot of artists, she has a favourite theme, and hers is the sea. Sometimes she's painting intricate watercolour details on tiny parchment squares, others she's splashing paint around like Jackson Pollock on canvases so tall she has to work off a ladder. But whatever the scale of her pictures she has this uncanny ability to capture the depth and power of the sea in all its moods. It's as if after living by the coast her whole life, the ocean has become part of her being. When I stand back and study her pictures hanging on the high white gallery walls, they're so extraordinary it's hard to believe that they've been made by the same small girl I built sand castles with on those long hot summer afternoons all those years ago. The swirl of the undertow and the crash of the waves on the canvas feel as real as if you were there in the water.

Plum laughs. 'Charlie hasn't bought yet. But he's talking about commissioning some pictures for Seaspray Cottage, too.'

'Better and better. So long as he comes through.' That's the trouble with Charlie. The second you begin to trust him he does something to make you doubt him again.

She wrinkles her nose. 'We'll have to wait and see. Anyway, more good news is that Nell's out and about doing an audit, so she might pop in too.'

I rub my fingers over a piece of translucent green glass on a key ring. 'Has anyone made any more progress with Operation Siren?'

'Not that I've heard.' Plum waves in the direction of the gallery door, then grins back at me. 'We could have an unscheduled opportunity here though. Nell's just arriving, and I can hear the sound of Charlie's feet on the stairs.'

Nell makes her way along the gallery shuffling in her flip

flops and swipes an invisible slick of sweat off her forehead as she arrives at the desk. 'Jeez, it's too damned hot for VAT today. I was sweating so much I had to nip home to change.' Her vest is loose over her checked shorts and she's flapping the shoulder straps to let the air in. Then she pulls out a handful of papers from her rucksack and puts them on the desk.

Plum picks one up. 'With the latest rush of visitors we've had a run on your Singles' Club flyers. It's good you've brought more.' She turns and whispers into Nell's ear. 'Charlie's on his way down from upstairs.'

Nell's nod shows she understands Operation Siren's back on as she tucks the papers into a neat pile. 'These are new ones, highlighting the summer activities. It's always good to have new people in the mix, even if they're just passing through.'

We're all facing the open staircase and as Charlie's legs come into view beyond the open stair rail, I pretend to examine some sea glass. As I catch a flash of Charlie's bare feet in deck shoes and hard thighs in tight denim I fan myself with a flyer.

Charlie ambles towards us, hands in the pockets of his low-slung jeans. 'So what are you mermaids plotting today?' He squints down at the pile of singles' flyers. 'If you do boat trips I must book us in for one of those.'

Nell pushes a flyer into Charlie's hand. 'The next one's on Sunday afternoon, we call it Whale Watching. Being totally upfront it's a couple of hours on Jed Smith's cruiser with a tasty pork sandwich and a lot more wine than wildlife. My number's here if you've got any queries.'

Charlie folds up the paper and slides it into his back pocket. 'I take it you'll be going?'

'Me?' Nell's puzzled expression doesn't come through in her voice. 'Yes, I'm on every boat trip.'

Charlie's eyes light up. 'Great. In that case, I'll take two tickets.'

If Nell's startled by his decisiveness she hides it well. 'If it's warm we swim off the boat, so bring your speedos – unless you prefer skinny dipping, in which case come as you are.'

Charlie laughs. 'Better and better. I'll bring a towel then.'

I'm beaming at Plum, when suddenly it hits me. He asked for two places, knowing Nell was already going. I have to jump in here to see what's going on. 'Dakota's been before, hasn't she, Nell? She'll keep you right, Charlie.'

Charlie's scratching his head. 'Dakota? Isn't she partying in Ibiza next weekend?'

And I'm back to puzzled. 'You asked for two tickets. If it's not Dakota, who's your plus one?'

That makes him smile. 'It's more A. N. Other than a partner. I'm hoping George will come.'

'*George?*' My voice is high, because I'm so confused. 'Where the hell does *he* fit in?'

Charlie turns to me. 'You saw how much he enjoyed the party, and it's good for him to lighten up. You're going to have to help me persuade him.' He turns to me. 'Obviously, you need to come too, Clems. I can't think why I didn't mention that to start with. And Plum, too?'

Plum puts her hand up. 'Count me out, Sunday's my busiest day at the gallery.'

I'm looking down at my kitten heeled sandals and wiggling my toes. And remembering whatever he's up to with Joe. 'Sorry, I'm out too, girlie shoes and boats don't mix.' It's only the first excuse of many. When I stop to think about it the list of objections is as long as my new maxi skirt. Which incidentally is floaty and purple, with stacks of fringing and two floor to knicker kick splits, which will be getting sewn up if I ever get a minute *and* remember how to sew on the same day. At the knock down price of £1.75, it's my best buy yet from the Cat's Protection shop on the High Street. Although my finances went up the spout a bit when I splurged on nail varnish to go with it. The perfect match was Chanel Frenzy in this gorgeous smokey lilac colour. Worth every penny at twenty quid. But at the same time that's a hell of a lot of meringues.

Charlie's staring at my feet. 'Nice toe nails, Clems. Leave the footwear to me, I'll sort something out. What size are you?'

'Five.' I'm not sure I'm comfortable sharing my measurements with a guy.

'Great.' He's back to Nell again. 'So make that three for the boat trip please.'

Good to know someone else appreciates the colour as much as I do. But I'm back to the objections. 'For me sailing's even worse than beach walking. Dresses really don't mix with rigging.' I have a final brain wave. 'I'll look after Diesel.' If I say it like he does, as a statement not a question, he'll have to take notice.

I'm saved the reply when Nell's phone rings, and she dives off to answer it.

As *you're the one that i want ... whoohooohooo, Honey ... the one that I want* echoes round the gallery repeatedly, I grin at Charlie. '*Grease* was her favourite film back in the day. She had a major thing for John Travolta.' I leave out that she waits so long to answer her phone it usually goes to voice mail, just so she can do the dance moves. Even as I glance over my shoulder I can see her wiggles as she shadows Olivia Newton John's skipping steps. Back then the rest of us were kind enough to overlook that John Travolta was practically old enough to be our grandfather. At least it left more *American Pie* hunks free for the rest of us to share out between us.

He doesn't even give an eye roll before he turns to Plum. 'As for the seascapes, I've seen half a dozen big ones that would work really well. As soon as I've seen the designers, I'll come back to you and we'll thrash out some figures.'

'Brilliant. Wow. Thanks.' Plum's got every right to look ecstatic. Even if Charlie negotiates discounts for buying shedloads, she could make enough from this one deal to keep her going for months. And there could be other flats to hang in too.

Charlie sends her a wink. 'No, I should be thanking you. We like to use local artists wherever we can. Your paintings are so in tune with the region we're counting on them to sell the development.'

I give Plum a nudge and squeeze her arm. Then Nell comes back and high fives her.

'Well done, Plum, way to go.' Then she turns to me and waggles her hand by her ear. 'And that was an SOS call. *For you, Clems.*'

My heart sinks. 'Not a chocolate overdose?' I'm thinking back to Sunday evening, and how hard everyone was hitting the puddings. I'm just hoping she doesn't blow it and start talking about me and my events in front of Charlie.

Nell laughs. 'It's good news not bad. Ben and Rachel, one of my very first couples from the Singles' Club have booked a meal for their second anniversary at the Harbourside. But their baby's getting over an ear infection and they don't want to leave him.'

'So where do I come in?'

Nell's blowing out her top lip. 'They'd like a candlelit anniversary dinner on your balcony.'

It's as if Nell's been peering into my head looking at my dreams. The last time she mentioned dinner for two it was a joke. But lately I've been thinking – where three parties a week might be pushing the Seaspray Cottage rules, smaller more exclusive evenings could give the Little Cornish Kitchen a whole new direction. I know those first sorbet evenings were rough around the edges, but I've come a long way since then. And this way there would be much less for Charlie to object to.

I'm trying not to let the exited fluttering in my chest get out of control. 'If the wind off the sea's a bit flukey I can't promise their candles will stay alight.'

Plum's laughing. 'A well-known hipster tip – night-lights in Mason jars will stay alight in a Force 10 gale. So, that's the candles sorted.' Which possibly also explains why Sophie's got so many of the damned things.

Nell's almost as breathless as me. 'They're bringing their own high chair for Levi. And a travelling cot.'

'Brilliant.' I'm flapping my hands, imagining the twinkle of the lights and the sea rushing up the beach, then it hits me. 'There's only one drawback – I don't know *any* starters or mains.' Talk about getting letting my puddings go to my head.

Charlie's joining in now too. 'Don't forget, Clemmie, we're making pastry later.'

I want to hug him for cutting through my panic. I can do this. 'We could do mini quiches for starters. And strawberry tartlets with sweet crust for dessert. We already know Laura's recipes are fool proof, and we can easily rustle up a couple of other desserts. So, that only leaves a main.'

Nell's looking exceptionally pleased with herself. 'And for that they've requested salmon skewers with a side salad, because that's what they had on their very first date.'

Charlie's straight in there. 'Easy. I can talk you through that. We could even fire up a chargrill at my end of the balcony.' He's obviously forgotten. I told him the day I moved in that barbies on the balcony weren't happening.

Plum's clasping her hands excitedly. 'And Nell and I will help too. Four of us making a meal for two, we should nail it.' They're all as enthusiastic as I am, and I'm loving that they're joining in. I'm also guessing Plum's seeing as much Operation Siren potential in this evening as I am.

'I'll pick up the fizz. Which only leaves one other thing ...' Nell's eyebrows are on wiggle overdrive as she beckons us all closer. Once we're in a tight huddle, listening to her low murmur she carries on. 'Ben specifically requested cupcakes, because he wants to "hide" something.'

Plum's jaw drops. 'Holy shit, he's planning a *proposal*?'

Nell clamps her lips shut. 'You *didn't* hear that from me. But yes.' Her eyes are shining. 'It's so much more special for *all* of us if it happens at yours rather than the hotel, Clemmie.'

'Wow. No pressure there then.' Now we're all crammed together there are teasing wafts of Charlie's scent coming from the faded folds of his T-shirt. *Warm skin on a summer day. Sizzling man on a blistering afternoon.* I take a deep breath, pinch myself so I can really believe this is happening. 'Great. Well, we can't stay here all day chatting, some of us have jewelry to unpack. Not to mention dinners to prepare.'

I pull away from the group then as I glimpse the ginger blur surrounding the guy coming in the door I fly straight back into the huddle. 'Super frig, don't all look at once but sodding Joe Marlow just walked in.'

23

At Plum's gallery
Friendly faces and walks in the park
Tuesday afternoon

'Jeez, when you said total look-alikey you weren't joking, were you?'

Nell takes a small step backwards and peers past Charlie's elbow to where Joe's walking into the gallery, hands in the pockets of his jeans. 'His spotted shirt is almost the same as that blue spotted dress of yours. With at least as many creases too. Okay, I'm going to shut up now. Everyone disperse slowly and act natural.' She clamps her eyes closed, shakes her head. Then she snaps them open and waltzes away for a second round of rubbernecking.

I give her a sharp poke in the ribs as she passes me. 'There's nothing "natural" about your eyes standing out on stalks.'

Plum's hissing at me as she heads for the desk. 'You didn't tell me he was *hot*. Sod the shirt, it's the forearms I'm appreciating.'

I don't believe what I'm hearing. 'You *know* brothers are off limits.' As of earlier this year they are anyway. 'That includes *half*-brothers too.'

A few years back, Sophie's little sister got together with Plum's big brother in a flowerbed outside the Rum and Crab during a New Year's Eve pub crawl. At the time, we were all delighted, then when they got a flat together in London we were literally whooping because it was such a great way to unite the mermaid families. But lately they've been arguing, and that's turned out to be agonising and divisive for everyone. Hence the recent ruling.

More worryingly, Plum and I have never been the type of women who fancy the pants off every second guy we see. We're both much pickier than that. As Plum says, it takes someone spectacular to give her what she calls a 'fanny flutter'. As teenagers when we'd lie on the beach together eyeing up the talent, Nell would be the one pretending not to look because she always had a boyfriend, Sophie would be letting out orgasmic whoops every minute, while Plum and I lay in silence. Plum once estimated that only one guy in ten thousand did it for her, but since I spent six months in Paris without seeing anyone I fancied, I reckon it's more like one in a hundred million for me. Worse still, I can see Joe's pushed her buttons by the way she's pouting without even knowing she's doing it. Although for Plum it would only ever be a one night stand. But even having that thought brings a bit of sick into my mouth.

From the way Nell's wiggling towards us she could be dancing to her ring tone. 'He's at ten to two now and heading this way.' She's singing the words through clenched teeth.

As a trickle of sweat runs down my neck, I've got a split-second choice. Dive for cover and risk being spotted hiding with my bum sticking out a mile behind the rotating card stand. Or do a mahoosive, look-at-me wave and hope I'm not seen as myself. Before I even know I've decided, my arm's in the air. If I was an aircraft marshal on the tarmac at Heathrow, my hand flap couldn't be bigger.

'Hi, Joe, over he-e-e-e-e-re.' As my shout echoes down the gallery and Joe turns our way I step up the wave. I'm halfway through yelling, 'Remember me, I'm Clemmie' when Charlie's deck shoe lands on my toe and shuts me up.

Beside me Charlie lets out a sigh. 'I can't face lying all over again, Clems. Leave Joe to me, I'll take him for a drink.' It wasn't just the lying. Last time also meant squishing me under his arm and pretending to be my boyfriend. No one can blame him for wanting to dodge that. Personally, I can't face shivers like that again either. Although this could be Charlie swooping in to whoosh Joe away before he gives too much away about their Siren House deal.

Plum's hands are on her hips. 'And we'll provide back up. Won't we, Nell?' She's off across the rough hewn boards faster than Diesel after Pancake. Charlie sets off down the gallery, talking over his shoulder as he goes. 'Right, Clems, stand by with the rolling pin and flour sifter. I'll pick up everything we need. Be ready at yours at three.'

Nell grins at me. 'It seems a shame to miss out on the introductions. Would you mind if I ...?' As she hesitates, her pleading expression is as full on as Diesel's when he's asking for cake.

I take pity on her. 'Go on, you might as well.' Let's face it, everybody else has.

The last time a visitor got this much attention in St Aidan was when a shark washed up just along the coast and entire population rushed down to the beach. I remember seeing the Facebook posts when I was in Barcelona. Ten minutes later when Plum comes back, if I didn't know better I'd swear her cheeks had the same glow mine did when Charlie came down her stairs. And it's nothing to do with the outside temperature.

She's rubbing her hands. 'So that went well. Charlie's taken Joe off to The Harbourside for a light lunch.'

Plum's smile stretches from ear-stud to ear-stud. 'I offered to show him around any time he'd like, and to be a friendly face at events.' She pulls a face as she takes in my horrified glare. 'Well, someone's got to keep an eye on him. That would be in a hands-off, platonic, sisterly capacity. Obviously.' Or not so obviously, from where I'm standing seeing she seems to have suddenly got boobs where she never had any.

'So on balance is that a positive outcome? Or not?' Sometimes I don't know what to think.

Nell butts in, waving her phone. 'Oh, and for the cupcakes, special request, came through while we were talking back there. Lemon with blackberry icing. Charlie knows to get the ingredients.'

'Great.' I'm hoping I wasn't overconfident about my capabilities back there – but I'm suddenly wondering how the frig I'm going to pull off the complications of a three-course candlelit dinner?

24

In Clemmie's kitchen
Hand stands and forward rolls
Tuesday

Considering what's coming up later, our pastry afternoon goes very smoothly. I admit when Charlie first empties the ingredients into piles on the table the thought of what's to come has me hyperventilating. But then he looks me in the eye and says, 'Clems, there's nothing you aren't going to smash here. Cressy Cupcake would do this standing on her head, you can too.'

As distractions go, this one's quite random, but I have to put him right. 'Head stands? I can't do effing head stands. Apart from anything else, my dresses would fall over my face.'

Charlie shrugs. 'Like a lot of things, head stands are easier than you'd think. There's an American photographer who took a whole load of selfie portraits doing headstands in skirts. They're great, you should Google her. One time she put camera on automatic, did her headstands, and her dog photo bombed every frame. Maybe you and Diesel could try that?'

Whenever he does long speeches like this I always end up fixating on that vulnerable dent at the base of his throat. That's Charlie for you. By the time he stops talking shit I can't remember what I was worrying about to begin with. It's nothing new though. Since the first day I arrived he's been here, filling the flat with the same white noise. It used to annoy the hell out of me, but sometimes when he's not here, I hate to admit there's this emptiness where he was. Although, let's face it, what with all the cooking *and* coming round at all hours to check on Pancake, he is here driving me to crazy distraction a lot of the time. And even if he's not, Diesel will usually creep in to keep Charlie's place on the sofa warm.

When it comes to great shortcrust, forget gimmicks like ice filled rolling pins. It turns out the knack is to keep the pastry cool and have a light touch. A quick whizz of the Magimix – and whoever thought I'd ever be saying that sentence like I meant it? – then so long as you let it rest in the fridge before you roll it out you're on to a winner. Because we're using mini tins, that makes the rolling out easier. As Charlie says, we'll do the tough calls later. Save the giant quiches for a day when we have hours to perfect rolling the pastry onto the rolling pin and back out over the tin.

Okay, the kitchen does look like a snowstorm, thanks to me going into overdrive with the flour sifter because I was so scared the pastry wasn't going to come off the rolling board. And the blizzard has extended miles past my apron edges and is clinging to my maxi skirt tassels all the way round to my bum. But after puddings for eighty, tarts and tartlets for two is mini. Then we move on to a quick dark chocolate brownie mix, to complement the raspberry tartlets. Although I suspect that's more of an excuse for Charlie to have something sweet to dip his spoon into.

As I'm putting the mini cheese and onion quiches into the oven Charlie dashes out, and when he comes back he's carrying a smart orange paper carrier with dark blue wavey lines running across it.

I make my eyes suitably big. 'So who's been shopping at Riptide, then?' It's the surfie shop up in town which is so pricey I wouldn't dare to put even my nose in, not that there would be anything in there I'd want to buy. I suspect for me the entire stock would fall into the category 'wouldn't be seen dead in'.

He dangles the strings off his finger as he hands the bag to me. 'Don't put them on the table. It's an old superstition. My mum always made us put new shoes on the floor.'

'Shoes?' Now we're onto another random subject when I should be pushing him on the trickier issues.

'You did say size five? I thought glitter Converse might hit the sweet spot between practical and on-trend girlie.'

I'm swallowing back my shock, reminding myself a present is not an excuse to fling my arms around him, especially when I haven't opened it yet. I put the bag down and prise the lid off the box far enough to peep. 'Dusky pink, it's a great colour. Thanks, they're beautiful.' For anyone else but me, that is. The last time I wore flats I was nineteen. After years wearing heels my calf muscles had contracted so much they were impossible to walk in. Even if they're the most shimmery trainers in Cornwall, it's going to take a lot more than flatties to get me onto that boat.

'Dusky blue would have been better for a mermaid, but they didn't have your size. If you need to change them the receipt's in the bag.' As usual he's covered every eventuality with maximum efficiency and the minimum of fuss. 'There's no excuse not to walk along the beach with Diesel now. Although we'll let you off on the days when you're wearing your tail.' He almost sends me a grin for that.

I smile back. 'They'll be fab for running between Metro stops when I get called back to Paris.' It's all bullshit. I'm as likely to run as I am to wear the shoes. Once Sunday's over, I'll slip them back to the shop and get him his money back. As for Paris, there are days when it feels so distant I might have dreamed that I was ever there. But I will have to face up to going back at some point, given all the paycheques that have been landing in my bank account. When I think of swapping Charlie for Maude, it's not the best exchange.

Then as I catch Charlie's crestfallen expression I kick myself and hurry on. 'Anyway, while we're waiting for these tarts and brownies to cook you can tell me how lunch went.' I send him one of Sophie's hard stares because turning up with shoes isn't going to save him from the interrogation that I've been putting off for too long. 'You might like to elaborate on whatever dirty deals you and Joe are cooking up together. It's pointless pretending otherwise – linking up with the guy I'm avoiding to shaft Sophie and Nate feels like a total betrayal.'

He's wheeling out that old familiar eye roll. 'No deals have been done. Dirty or otherwise.'

'So what is going on, why tell Sophie she knows where to find you?'

He drags on a breath. 'There was no deceit on my part. Joe contacted all the developers in the area with a view to sharing the site, but as far as I know no one's taken him up on the offer.

I was simply flagging up to Sophie that she could pursue that option too.'

'Right.' I suppose that gets him off that particular hook.

He turns from where he's leaning on the work surface staring out of the window. 'Joe's still in the picture for Siren House even without developers. He said today he and his brothers have some inheritance they have to spend in the area. So long as they get their finances sorted in time, they'll be at the auction.'

'So you two property moguls had a very chatty lunch then?'

He shrugs. 'I wasn't the only one digging. He was picking my brains about the local market, but he also knows I'm Clemmie's neighbour, don't forget.'

My stomach freezes. 'You told him stuff about me?'

'I had to trade something.' Charlie's only looking slightly guilty. 'He's very keen to talk to "Clemmie" but he still doesn't know that's you. George has made it clear he's got to wait for you to approach him, but in the meantime, he's wanting to find out everything he can about you. So, I mentioned you had a thing for loud French songs and a soft spot for meringues and my cat.'

I can't help my squawk. 'Jeez, Hobson.'

'What?' He's sounding spectacularly unrepentant. 'Anyone in St Aidan could tell him the same. He's staying in an Airbnb up in the town, and weird as it seems, he's lived in France a lot too. And his dad used to be a chef.' He breaks off to peer through the glass on the oven front. 'It's funny. You both do that half close of your eyes when you smile sometimes. And the same "don't mess with me" frown.'

There's a deluge of facts to take in. But my voice shoots up with disbelief at the last accusation. 'I don't frown.'

There's a smile twitching around Charlie's lips. 'Of course you do, all the time. Looking like you're totally not taken in is your trademark thing.'

'So when did you become the expert?' No one ever analysed my facial expressions before, and I'm not enjoying it now they are.

He's laughing. 'You've been directing your disapproving stare at me most days for the last three months, for every reason from me owning all the flats to my matching mug set. It's not my fault if I've become a specialist at reading the fine print.'

I wait until he's looking at me square in the face then fire: 'Fuck off, Hobson.'

That just cracks him up more. 'There you go, that's the Force 10 version you rolled out there.'

'Jeez, we're in *my* kitchen, I demand the right to be as pissed off as I like. What do I have to do to get you to drop this?'

He hesitates, then apparently gives in. 'So ... going back to Joe. Have you changed your mind at all since you found the letter? You don't think talking to him could be a way ... to finding out more about your history?'

I'm not sure how the hell we've arrived here, but I do know a crap suggestion when I hear it. 'If I did want to know more, he'd be the *last* person I'd ask.'

Charlie shrugs. 'He seems like a sound guy, that's all.' And that's so like a man. A couple of Peronis and *everyone's* fab.

This is so unbelievable I can't help shouting. 'You saw him *for lunch*. How was that time to judge *anything*? He's the bad guy here, don't forget, and you're suddenly talking about him like you're best mates.'

Charlie drags in a breath. 'I'm just looking for a way to help.'

I grit my teeth, partly because I know he's right. 'Whatever happened back then, Joe's dad's had thirty years and more to come and find me – and he hasn't. When someone has completely rejected me, I'm not going to lose every scrap of dignity and go banging on their door. I have my pride. No matter how much I'm aching to know the details, I refuse to go crawling to *any* of *that* family.'

He lets out a sigh. 'So you *would* like to know, I'm so pleased you finally confirmed that. It's a healthy way to be, Clems.' There's such concern in his eyes, it's hard to be as cross as I should be.

'Maybe ... I don't know ...' To be honest I hardly know what I feel, other than very mixed up. 'Knowing someone left you, even before you were born, is hurtful. However much you hide it, that hurt stays with you. Nothing can happen now to put that right.' I've never talked about this with anyone else so I'm not sure why I'm sharing this with Charlie. Except more than anyone else, I sense he wants to understand and has the capacity to do so. However, cutthroat his property deals are, deep down I know I can trust him to help me with this.

'Clemmie ...' For a second his eyes are so soft, he looks like he's going to put his arms around me.

There's so much sympathy in his eyes I jump backwards. 'Don't feel sorry for me, I'm fine without him, I always have been. It's different accepting things from Laura, because I knew her. But where the rest of the family's concerned, I can't risk the pain of getting rejected again.' Even thinking about it now is making my stomach churn. The only way I can cope with this is to hide myself away, and protect myself by never exposing myself to any more rejection.

He's got his fingers buried in the pockets of his jeans, and the whites of his knuckles are showing. 'I know it's not any of my business, but I just have this gut feeling that there's more to this than you think.'

'Too right it's not your business.' If I make my growl fierce enough he might back off.

He blows out his cheeks. 'Stuff like this is major. If there's some hidden truth, you deserve to know it. Then you can take that with you and get on with the rest of your life.' The low resonance in his tone is the kind that gives me goosebumps.

I swallow hard. 'How are the tarts?' Despite the warm air wafting in through the open window, I shiver and rub my arms. Then I toss him the oven gloves so I don't have to go any closer. 'You're nearest, you check.'

He opens the oven. 'Firm on top, nicely browned. That's what we're looking for, see?' He pulls them out and slides them onto a cooling rack. 'Congratulations, Clemmie Hamilton, you just baked your first quiches.'

As I see the glossy golden tops and the crinkly pastry edges my mouth pulls into a smile that's so wide I can't stop it. 'Oh my. Pastry has to be the last frontier in domesticity. I'm only a trolley away from becoming Mrs Waitrose Shopper here.'

He wrinkles his nose. 'You know the nearest Waitrose is in Truro, it's not the most convenient supermarket to choose.' Then the corners of his mouth start twitching again. 'Anyway, while we wait for the quiches to be cool enough to taste, if you'd like to build on your success and try a head stand, I'm happy to catch your feet?'

I let out a loud groan. 'How about no?'

He's still going. 'They're very soothing for the brain apparently. Work wonders for stress.'

I shake my head. 'However much you're driving me crazy, it's still the same "No".'

'In that case maybe it's time to move on to the cupcakes.' He's grinning at me now as he uncouples the Magimix bowl and takes it to the sink. 'I don't know about you but I can't wait for a buttercream hit.'

And just for once I totally get where he's coming from.

25

In Clemmie's kitchen
Cupcakes revisited
Still Tuesday afternoon

'So let's have the lemon, and then we'll work out how to make blackberry icing.' There's a sharp smell of citrus as I stir the grated zest into the sponge mixture. As I fill the cupcake cases and pop them in the oven I'm aware that we're venturing scarily off-piste here. There's nothing in Laura's cards because dark berry buttercream hadn't happened in the eighties.

Charlie pushes a brown paper bag towards me. 'Here's the blackberries. I texted Cressy and she said to heat them gently in a pan with a tiny bit of water, then mash and sieve them and add the juice to the icing. And use extra for the garnish. If you do these, I'll wash the bowl ready for the buttercream.' For wash read clean out with a spoon first. I suppose I should be grateful he doesn't put his whole head in there and lick it like Diesel would.

As I stand at the cooker stirring and the warmth spreads through the fruit, the kitchen fills with a rich Ribena scent. A hotline to Cressida Cupcake is beyond awesome even if it is one phone removed from mine. By the time the juice has cooled the buttercream's ready waiting and the cupcakes are plump and cooked and lined up on the rack. I can't help noticing, after all the puddings his face is less gaunt than it was although he still has shadows under his cheekbones that make hollows in my stomach when I see them.

'Okay, here goes.' I turn on the mixer and begin to drip the juice into the icing, then watch as it swirls from pale pink to a deep purple-red.

Charlie nods his approval. 'That's ready for the piping bag. It's a lush colour, and it tastes amazing, you have to try.' He dips a teaspoon in and holds it towards my mouth. 'Remember when we made the rainbow buttercream?'

I slide forward and take the icing from the spoon without thinking. It's only as the fruity sweetness slides down my throat I remember what the First Dates restaurant programme always says about couples who end up feeding each other. My voice thickens. 'There was a rainbow in the sky to match. Is it too much to hope we'll get a crimson sunset tonight?' That was the first and only time we made cupcakes and it was memorable because I put my size five feet in it big time talking about his wedding disaster. Every time I think about the hurt in his face that day I cringe and kick myself for being so crass. However much it's okay for him to meddle in my life, at least I know to keep the hell away from his past now.

He clears his throat. 'You also touched on my wedding that day ... the one that didn't happen ...'

As my stomach drops and hits the floor, my face flashes hot

then cold. 'Don't worry, it absolutely *won't* happen *ever* again, I promise.' I'm not sure if my cheeks are ghostly or crimson. All I know is I want the floor to open up and engulf me.

He winces, then his throat bobs as he swallows. 'Maybe I wasn't as upfront as I should have been that day.' The grate of his voice sends more goosebumps up my spine.

'Absolutely not a problem, the past is the past. Why not have another taste of icing? It really does taste as good as Brambly Hedge.' I dive for a spoon, load it up and push it at him across the table but he doesn't react because he's staring out across the bay.

He takes a breath. 'In a way you were right. The bride did call it off a couple of weeks before. But it wasn't because she'd run off with the best man, it was because she was ill.'

'Oh, crap. I'm so sorry.' Any blood left in my face is draining away. I screw up my face as I work out where she is now and get to the worst. 'She didn't …?' I can't bring myself to say the word die or pass.

Charlie blows. 'Faye was a marine biologist and she'd picked up a parasite on a working holiday in Africa. She put the wedding off thinking we'd have it when she was well again. But that never happened.'

'Oh my days.'

Charlie's voice is low and papery. 'We had a small ceremony at the hospital in London the day before she died. So, we were married, but for barely twelve hours.'

'That's so unbelievably sad.' I swallow back the sour taste in my mouth. Even now, there's so much pain in his eyes I want to wrap my arms around him tight and never let go.

He lets out a long whistle. 'It was all my fault. I'd arranged the holiday for her as a pre-wedding surprise, I insisted she went. If only I hadn't.' His face is so dark with shadows it's obvious.

Oh, shit. 'You blame yourself?'

His voice is trembling. 'There isn't anyone else responsible. I chose it, I encouraged her to go, bought her tickets. It was meant to help with her research. But her losing her life is all down to me.'

He couldn't look any more haunted. Lately he's been smiling more, but they've dropped away and his eyes are brimming with the same empty sadness I saw that first day down at the harbour.

He clears his throat. 'Faye worked in Scandinavia a lot, I was mainly in London. People shy away from grief, they don't know how to respond. When Diesel and I eventually came down here afterwards, it was easier to keep it private. Not to tell anyone.'

'You already had Diesel?'

'I bought Faye the holiday, she bought me Diesel as a puppy, to make up for her being away so much with her work. He spent his first few weeks with us lying on her feet at the hospital.'

He still sounds so desolate and my heart is aching for him. 'So what did you do, how did you even start to cope when it happened?' Even though I haven't ever had anyone I've been that close to, I can't imagine how you'd begin to handle losing the person you're about to share your life with.

The tautness of his face relaxes slightly even though his voice is still a low monotone. 'That was when I taught Cressy how to cook. She was back from uni and somehow my mum's determination to teach her kids kitchen skills had waned with each successive child, so Cressy knew zilch. I was completely numb. I went back home because it was warm and full of sisters and I didn't know what else to do. And every afternoon when Cressy came back from her holiday job we baked together. She was really reluctant, and not very interested. But somehow me teaching her everything I could bake became my temporary mission in life. Our evenings baking together were like therapy. That and taking Diesel for walks. By the time Cressy knew more than me, I was less wrecked and ready to pick up my life again.'

'So it's one of those instances where there's a tragedy yet something good comes out of it.' I'm scraping the tears off my eyelashes, and mopping my nose on kitchen roll. 'Cressy's YouTube clips have got literally millions of views, and all that began with you. You must be really proud.' I give him a punch on the arm, then go back to my dripping nose.

He always looks at his happiest when he talks about Cressy and there's the hint of a smile creeping in now. 'Cressy's great, but I was only a tiny part at the start for her, the rest is down to her own drive and talent. She grabbed every opportunity and magnified it.' He hands me a blackberry and takes one himself. 'It's funny. Baking with you here has been like doing it all over again. I'm sorry if I've come over as dogmatic at times. It's just that helping you was almost like going back in time. Making the same things, nine years later, doing it all over again a second time around has been very therapeutic.'

I'm hoping it's helped. 'Dogmatic? Isn't that Diesel's territory?' Maybe this is him explaining how driven he's been wanting to help me cook. 'However much you've bossed me about, in the end I'm pleased about it too.'

He's laughing at that. 'You should be very proud of how much you've learned from someone who's a bit of a fraud. Soon after Cressy knew more than me, there was a big life insurance payout, and I ended up with Faye's inheritance too. Overnight I became cash rich completely by default. So, Diesel and I came down here and used that for a new start.'

I'm thinking about what Sophie always said. 'So you are loaded but not because of all your fabulous property deals?' For once I miss out the implication they could be dodgy or exploitative.

His wince is rueful. 'All I've done since is work. When you don't sleep, you can fit three working days into one. It felt like I owed it to Faye to make the most of what she'd passed on to me. When you're that driven, it doesn't take too much good luck to make a success. It helped that I have an aptitude for speculation. But I've already told you that a lot of times.' He pauses to give a self-deprecating half-smile. 'Diesel and I took a winter let on a holiday flat in Seaspray Cottage, and it went from there. For a few years, we moved further south, but St Aidan's always felt like home. At night when we're walking along the beach it's as if we're on the edge of the world. Once the beach empties, there's this amazing sense of seclusion and space. Somehow the emptiness brings me a comfort and a peace that I haven't found anywhere else. However spectacular the other developments have been that I've been involved with, the balcony flat here was what we'd always set our hearts on. And getting the whole building bit by bit was my way of safeguarding the place.'

Now I understand why he was defensive about the intrusion, I couldn't feel any more awful. 'Then I came along and wrecked your peace. I'm so sorry, and so ashamed, I promise I'll make much more effort to keep the noise down in future.'

That does make him smile. 'It's fine. In a way, it's been good to be shaken up. Locking myself away, I'd got very set in my ways.'

There's one more question. 'What I don't understand is how you're always manage to look so –' I'm looking for polite way to describe this '– positive?' If disbelieving frowns are my trademark, Charlie has to own looking pleased with himself, even without smiling.

He blows out his cheeks. 'In my business no one wants to spend time with a loser. It was hell at first, but I made myself go out there and act like a winner. If you fake it for long enough, eventually you do it without thinking. You're dying inside, but so long as the shell you build is shiny enough and tough enough, no one would ever guess.'

I finally let my spoon drop back into the bowl. 'You had me fooled. I'm so sorry I got everything so wrong. I promise I'll learn from this.' I feel really small and very silly. Mortified doesn't begin to cover it. Beware the gossip line. Next time I'll check my facts before I fall flat on my face and hurt someone else too. But at the same time, I feel strangely warm inside for some reason that's more than the heat of the oven and the sun outside.

Charlie sighs. 'You could take note ...'

'In what way?' I'm querying, because I wasn't expecting a comeback, other than reassurance that everything was okay.

His stare is grave, as if he knows he about to drop a bomb of his own. 'It pays to know all the details. What happened with your dad and mum before you were born is exactly the same, sometimes half the truth isn't enough. You need to carry on searching until you know it all.'

My nose is stinging again. 'I'll bear that in mind. And thank you for trusting me enough to tell me this.' It's not just his wedding.

What he's told me has made me see him in a different way. How could it not?

His eyes are soft as he smiles. 'By the way, feel free to share this with your friends.'

I blow out a silent sigh of relief that he's taken that decision for me. 'I'll be very discrete.'

'When you lose someone the pain never gets any less. It's so much worse when you caused it. I think that's why I wanted to keep it under wraps for so long.'

His face is more relaxed again. 'So after that, I definitely deserve the buttercream bowl to lick. Sooner rather than later would be good.'

'Great. I'll fill the piping bag.' When I check my phone, I give a gasp of panic. 'Jeez, look at the time, we need to move.' I'm shaking my hands and I can't stop.

Charlie's staring at my hands. 'One hour twenty is enough to finish. So long as you stop flapping and get your butt into gear.'

I know I've been sharing stuff with him. But I can't possibly tell him how much I want tonight to go well. It's like a test to see how far I've come. And if I pass it, there might just be a way forward for me to keep the flat and carry on doing what I love. With all that riding on it, it's no wonder I'm shaking. And that's before I get to thinking how I can help Charlie feel better. But that's so big, I'll have to give it some thought.

26

In Clemmie's flat
Candle light and other inconveniences
Tuesday evening

In the end our candlelight diners are outnumbered three to one, because Sophie won't hear of staying away. She brings Milla who's an expert at baby entertaining after all the practice she's had at home, and a crate load of toys suitable for a five-month-old. They also come with armfuls of meadow flowers to put on the table and in buckets on the balcony, and enough Mason jars to supply a preserving factory. By the time Plum has staggered up the stairs with her giant lanterns and Nell's strung her hen coop fairy lights around, the balcony is all set to twinkle as the daylight fades.

As for that old saying 'boys will be boys', despite all my protests our resident guy goes rogue and insists on firing up his portable lava rock grill at the far end of the balcony. He's also taken charge of the fizz and the ice buckets, leaving Nell and I to make the gin cocktail. We decide on a Bramble, to echo the lemon and blackberry cupcake theme we'll be moving on to later.

As soon as Ben and Rachel arrive and Levi's settled in his chair by the open French window with Milla on the rug beside him waggling her assortment of puppets and rattles, we show them out onto the balcony. It seems that most of St Aidan have heard about the French song mix now because that's what they've asked for. So, with tea-lights flickering and 'Boum !' drifting out on the breeze across the bay they take their seats in directors chairs decked with flower posies, at the curly legged metal table borrowed from the bedroom.

For once, Plum's swapped her dungarees for a snazzy black jumpsuit. As she swings outside with the cocktails Sophie's in the kitchen arranging the herb garnish around the quiche plates, and Nell's scuttled off to the bedroom with and a ring box and a cupcake.

Charlie comes in using the route across the landing, wine bottle in hand. 'Here's the prosecco. I'll take it out with the starters, then I'll be off to light the grill.' With his sharp black trousers and snowy cotton shirt, his usual 'hot' just shot up to 'searing'.

As he passes the kitchen table he catches sight of Sophie's bag hanging from a chair. He screws his head around to read the printing on the large folder that's sticking out from the top. 'What's this? Mood boards for Siren House?' He catches Sophie's eye across the table. 'Isn't that bit premature?'

I can see Sophie mouthing curses behind his head. 'Sophie brought those for us *girls* to look at later. They definitely won't be *your* kind of thing.' If he'd butted in like this last week I'd have felt like throttling him for winding her up. Since he told me about him losing his wife earlier all I want to do is wrap him up and hug him. As for the mood boards, they've been under construction for weeks. Ever since that first visit to Siren House, Sophie's spent every spare minute sticking pieces of wool and paint swatches and photos onto sheets of hand-made paper. Although I'm not entirely sure why she's bothering because everything I've seen so far seem to look like recreations of what she's got at Hawthorne Farm.

Sophie picks a sprig of parsley off her apron and sniffs. 'It's never too early to gather design ideas.' From her frosty expression and clipped speech, she's aiming to shut him down.

Charlie hasn't finished. 'True. But if you haven't bagged a buyer for the farm by now, you'll be pushing it to make the auction at all.'

Whatever I was saying about not wanting to throttle him, I take it back.

Despite the thousands of five star reviews for Sophie May super-concealer foundation, there's a small patch of red on each of Sophie's cheeks as she hisses at him. 'I don't know where the hell you got your information from, but what the frig has it got to do with you anyway?' She looks ready to floor him and I'm with her on that.

I jump in. 'Jeez, we're trying to do a dinner party here. Could you two please fight over Siren House when this is over?'

Charlie tilts his head to one side. 'But the whole point is, Sophie and I shouldn't be fighting at all. The only way we'll stop Joe and his brothers getting *their* hands on Siren House is if *we* join forces.'

Sophie gives a disparaging snort. 'And how's that going to work? The last I heard you were in cahoots with Joe. If this is where you try to get us to back down and leave the way clear for you, you can piss off.' She's growling through her teeth at him.

I'm wishing I'd had time to share what Charlie told me earlier. Although I'm not sure that would have made Sophie any less venomous. When she's set her heart on something, she's always been the same – she's totally blinkered to anything other than her goal.

Charlie's holding his hands up. 'Hang on, just hear me out. As a developer, bottom lines interest me more than individual properties. I looked at Hawthorn Farm when you bought it, but I was going to split it into more units. If you're dropping your price to get a buyer, there could well be more for me in the farm than in Siren House. Especially with the auction price getting pushed up by Joe.'

Sophie's screwing up her face, but there's a hint of hungry glint in her eye. 'So let me check I'm understanding this correctly? You'd be interested in buying Hawthorne Farm?'

His voice is low. 'At the right price, yes. If you've got your decorative schemes for Siren House sorted, I'm assuming you're in the market to do a deal?'

Sophie's nostrils are flaring and her voice is shrill with excitement. 'In that case we need to talk.'

His voice is level and unruffled. 'That's exactly what I was suggesting last week.' As he turns to me, I catch the amusement in his eyes. 'The best place for negotiation is out of the spotlight where the vibe is more laid back.'

I have to pick him up on this. 'Like in the kitchen ... *between courses*?' From the way Sophie's quivering, there's nothing relaxed about this at all. 'You two take a moment and sort out your transaction, I'll go and check if they're ready for their quiche yet.'

As I make a dash for the sanity of the living room, I come face to face with Nell carrying her very special cupcake. She mouths at me. 'What's going on in there?'

I shake my head and blow. 'Nothing major, only Sophie selling the farm to Charlie.'

Nell's voice is high with disbelief. 'You're joking?'

I take a second to reconsider. 'No, I don't think I am. Charlie's the last person we'd expect Sophie to deal with, but she's desperate. But hey, what do we know? Maybe it's sound business for both of them.' We were prepared for a proposal, or a bit of Operation Siren interrogation. Sophie and Charlie metaphorically jumping into bed together, not so much.

Plum's waving at me from over by the French window. 'Okay, stand by for the starter.'

Of all the evenings yet, this is turning out to be the craziest. But right now, I've got four friends and Milla all putting themselves out there for me. If I don't make things work here, going back to being on my own without all their warmth and support is a horrible thought.

As soon as Plum has delivered the next course and Charlie has dished out the fizz and gone off along the balcony to cook the salmon, I head back to Sophie in the kitchen, and squeeze her and Nell into a hug.

Nell's laughing as she breaks off from arranging the cupcakes. 'Hey, don't knock the blackberries off. What's this for?'

I think for a moment. 'For being my besties, and for dreaming up the Little Cornish Kitchen. With us spending time together again, it's been the best summer, I've had the most amazing time.' I know I sound like I've escaped from *Pollyanna* or *Anne of Green Gables* but for once I don't care.

Sophie's smiling. 'And you've done the most amazing things and come such a long way. Your puddings and Laura's recipes have made a huge impact on St Aidan.'

Nell grins. 'You could call it the summer of love. Thanks to you and your LCK, there's a whole lot of new couples in St Aidan.' For a fleeting second I'm counting up how many more cosy couples evenings I might be able to wrangle from the singles' Facebook group.

Sophie tweaks my pony tail and kisses the top of my head. 'We've all had a great time helping.' She gives me a nudge. 'The move to Siren House is all down to you, you know.'

I pull a face. 'I'm not sure I'm ready to take the blame for that one.'

Sophie's Siren House folder is on the table and as she flips the pages over, she's breathless again. 'Did I show you the boards for the guest bedrooms?'

Nell's right there, pouring over the samples. 'More of that piggie stuff? Will every room be the same then?' She can't help that her mind always turns to pork.

'It's hygge, pronounced "hoo-ga", Nellie Melon.' Sophie sighs. 'It's nothing to do with pigs.'

Nell frowns. 'Isn't it all based on the scent of Danish bacon? That special kind of "cosy" you get when you watch *Babe* with a pile of BLT's?'

Sophie glances up at the ceiling. 'Not entirely.' Then the shine in her eyes re-ignites. 'I know Siren House was bit of an impossible dream until now. But if Charlie comes through for us we might just pull this off.' It's the first time she's ever admitted this wasn't a certainty.

Even if I've seen another side to Charlie, I'm surprised at her turnaround where he's concerned. 'Whatever happened to the big, bad developer?'

She shrugs. 'Sometimes in business you have to look at the bigger picture.' Then she goes to the door to check on Milla and turns back to me. 'Talking of which, seeing Levi here made me realise you're missing out on a whole chunk of the market. You should be doing Mum and Bumps afternoon teas.'

They sound very exciting, but I'm not tempting fate. 'As if candlelight dinners aren't enough.' I'll only be chalking this one up as a success when it's over. 'Anything with cake, I'm in. Although it's not exactly child friendly here with so many stairs, so we'll probably have to give that one a miss.' I'm so disappointed I've talked myself out of that one so fast.

Sophie's eyes narrow. 'You'd obviously have to find a better venue. But now you're building a reputation, it could be time to move on from here anyway.' That's a big step to take in.

Nell's got cash register signs flashing in her eyes. 'Sophie's right, we should be using our property contacts to get you a permanent place.'

My voice shoots high with horror. 'Hold it there. The whole thing with pop up venues is they disappear as fast as they arrive. They're like a glimpse of a mermaid's tail in the waves. Here and gone. Just like me.' I snap my fingers to show how fleeting I am. Or should that be how fleeting I used to feel.

Nell's turned on me. 'Bollocks. Your Little Cornish Kitchen is a living breathing part of St Aidan now. You can't seriously throw that away?'

Right now, all I'm thinking of is all Maude's money I've saved up. If I don't go back to work, I'll have to give that back. 'There's nothing I'd love more than to live here doing the Little Cornish Kitchen.' That much is true. 'As soon as I've got my renovation cash together I've got some juggling to do.' The questions have been buzzing through my mind. If I didn't go back to Paris could I do Airbnb here to help my income? Am I really up to sorting out a new home for the Little Cornish Kitchen, and paying for it? But most important of all, can I keep the flat? This is more the size of Sophie's wish list than my usual one, and it also sounds like it needs serious injections of cash I don't have. It's a big jump from the flight out and no commitment job I'd usually be wishing for.

Wanting is an alien concept to me. This far in life I've simply thrown out my metaphorical net, accepted what came along as destiny, and worked with it. Striving for a specific goal is a whole new game that takes way more skill and energy. For the first time in my life I'm wanting grown up stuff. And if I truly want it I can't run away. If I want to keep the flat and the Little Cornish Kitchen, I'll have to stay *and* learn to fight. The only good part is that Nell, Plum and Sophie will be here to help me. And they all perfected the art of getting what they wanted years ago.

Nell's scowling. 'Juggling? What kind of juggling?'

It's too huge to go into here. There must be a fairy god person on hand to get me out of this particular tight spot, because a second later Plum appears in the doorway, with Charlie close behind.

She's got the empty quiche dishes on her tray and she's jumping up and down. 'Wake up, you guys, the salmon's done, we're ready for the salad and the main plates please.'

When there are twenty people crammed into the flat all needing wine and puddings at once there's very little time to worry. With only two it's much more tense, especially with so many of us looking after them. I'm hovering by the French window, worrying in case the sunset's not orange enough, or in case the salmon marinade isn't lemony enough, trying *not* to watch every forkful Ben and Rachel eat. So, when Sophie suggests I join in story time with Milla and Levi, I'm straight on the sofa, followed closely behind by Diesel.

If anything, Levi's even cuter than Maisie in his stripey velour pyjamas with his blond quiff. As he snuggles onto Milla's lap and sucks on his finger there's no sign of the grizzly baby we were expecting. He chortles at the zoo pictures I'm waggling in front of him, then smiles all the way through *Mog and Meg*. By the time we get to the last page of *The Tiger Who Came to Tea,* Ben and Rachel are coming to the end of their strawberry tarts.

Nell beckons me from the kitchen, champagne bucket in hand. 'If Levi can spare you, Mrs, I'll take the bubbly, you can light the anniversary candles and carry the cupcakes out.'

As I push myself up from the sofa there's a loud squawk. As I turn and look behind me Levi changes from cute and snuggly to red faced and screaming faster than you can say 'angry baby'.

I've no idea what to do here other than join in and shout to the kitchen for help. 'Sophie, come quick, Levi needs you.' Given the volume, I'm actually playing it down. The screams are so ear-piercing poor Diesel buries his head under a cushion. 'Sooner rather than later would be good, Sophie ...' I'm putting my hands over my ears to avoid my ear drums bursting when Charlie comes wandering in from the balcony.

His hands are in his pockets and he's completely unhurried. 'I've told Ben and Rach to sit tight for the moment. Anything I can help with here?'

I can't help the sarcastic note in my voice. 'Unless they did childcare diplomas at your speculator school, thanks for the offer, but we'll wait for our expert mum with four kids.' Milla dodges a right hook from Levi and shrinks back into the sofa.

Charlie laughs. 'I don't have diplomas, but I'm here, Sophie's not.' He reaches past me and a second later he's swinging Levi up through the air, nestling him into the crook of his elbow and crooning in his ear to quieten him. 'Okay, little guy, what's the matter?' A moment later, Charlie pulls back swiftly, wrinkling his nose. 'Whoa, problem located, he's only telling us his nappy's dirty. Is his changing bag around?'

'Here you go.' Milla jumps up with a stripy Cath Kidston backpack.

I'm picking my jaw up off the floor as I stare at Charlie. 'How do you know how to change nappies?'

He's looking at me like I'm the stupid one here. 'My sisters have kids and no one's exempt from nappy changing in our house.' Charlie's already in the velvet chair undoing poppers, with Levi stretched out across his knees. 'Once you know what you're doing it only takes a couple of minutes.'

'In that case I'll leave you and Milla to it and go and help Nell.'

When I join Nell in the kitchen she's put her ice bucket down and she's standing by the work top scratching her head.

'Everything okay?'

She frowns. 'I thought I left the special cupcake on a saucer by the bread bin but now I can't find it.'

As the reality of what she's saying sinks in my heart starts to hammer. 'That's the cupcake with the ring in?' I try not to screech.

Nell nods. 'That's the one.'

As Sophie comes back in, I bring her up to speed. 'We're looking for a cupcake on a saucer. You haven't seen it, have you?'

Sophie taps her cheeks as she thinks. 'Cupcakes? Yes, they were scattered around looking messy so I tidied them all onto one plate and added a vintage lace doily. They're over there on the table ready to take out.'

I bolt across to where she's pointing, counting madly. 'Jeez, that's okay. There are still six, so they're all here.' Sophie and her tidying. Given how edgy she is, it could have been worse. We're probably lucky she didn't try to fold them up and put them in the drawer. As disasters go, I'd say mislaying an engagement ring before a proposal ranks a long way above Pavlova-in-the-lap *and* sorbet-up-the-walls.

Sophie's looking alarmed. 'Is there a problem?'

'Nell's hidden an engagement ring in one of them.' I'm staring at six identical cakes, on a circular plate, all with red velvet buttercream swirls topped with a blackberry, desperately looking for any imperfections that would show where Nell's been excavating. 'We're just not sure *which* one.'

Nell's sighing at my elbow. 'I'm buggered if I can tell. I was so careful I've even fooled myself.'

Sophie's gone pale under her foundation. 'Shit. She can't eat six cakes to find the ring. Me and my tidying, I've totally messed this up, haven't I?'

I'm running through the options rejecting them as fast as I think of them. 'Demolish all the cupcakes, make some more icing, find another cake ...'

Nell punches the air. 'I've got it.' As she dashes through to the next room we're right behind her. 'Charlie, a random question here, do you happen to have a metal detector?'

Charlie's standing, legs apart, swinging a dangling Levi backwards and forwards. 'Sure, although we're doing the leopard in a tree hold here and I think Levi's close to dropping off. You might have to help yourselves. It's the high cupboard after the dining room, on the way to the bedrooms. The doors are all open.'

Sophie grabs the cupcakes and as we belt across the landing after Nell she's giving me that hard stare of hers. 'Maybe we need to have a rethink on Charlie. Anyone who's great with babies *and* generous with their hand tools can't be all bad, can they?'

I can't help thinking what a convenient time it is for Sophie to get to this conclusion. Of all the outcomes, I'd never have predicted this one. But there's no denying, it looks like Operation Siren has ended abruptly and in success.

27

In Clemmie's flat
Shag piles and fireworks
The same Tuesday evening

By the time we reach Charlie's hall, Nell's got the cupboard door open, and she's standing knee deep in a pile of wetsuits and surfboards waving a massive metal detector.

The beam on her face couldn't be any bigger. 'Trust Charlie to have a Bounty Hunter Gold Digger. It's a great bit of kit, it should do the job nicely.' On the one hand, it's unlucky that we're having to use one at all, but there again it's damned useful that Nell couldn't be any more at home than when she's got one of these toys attached to end of her arm.

I try not to look beyond her to where the bedroom door is wide open. Although a pale grey quilt with natural throws and a contemporary dark wood bed frame is no surprise given the rest of the apartment. As for the glimpse of free standing tub, I refuse to think of anyone anywhere near that other than Dainty Dusters cleaners.

As I spread the cupcakes out in a line along the floor and stare up at the ring of the Bounty Hunter I'm suddenly feeling over-protective. 'Okay, so *please* try not to squish the icing, and *for chrissakes* don't knock the blackberries off. Charlie might be happy to lend us his tools, but he definitely won't want bramble juice all over his lovely white rug.'

Sophie's on her knees, scrutinising the carpet weave. 'How amazing is this? Un-dyed shearling, hand-woven by empowered artisans, I could do with this on my mood board.' For one day, only I wish she'd forget her bloody swatches and concentrate.

As Nell passes the metal detector over the third cupcake in the line there's a double beep. 'There' you go, that's our baby.'

I grin over my shoulder at Sophie. 'Result! Right, you hang on tight to that one, let's go.' We run the length of Charlie's living room and back across the hall.

As we burst back into mine Milla's at the door with a finger on her lips. 'Shhh, Levi's just dropping off.'

Charlie's stretched out across the corner of the sofa, Levi cradled against his arm, Diesel asleep on his feet. When I take in the softness of his lashes, and the shadows on his face as he gazes down at the sleeping child on his body I'm completely unprepared for the kick in the pit of my stomach and the lump in my throat. That's the trouble with getting to know too much of a guy's back story – they end up messing up your insides.

I hurry back to the kitchen. 'Right, let's get candles in the cupcakes on the big plate, put the special cupcake on a pink plate for Rachel and another on a blue plate for Ben.' By the time I've lit the candles, Nell's back.

She grabs the champagne bucket and two gold rimmed vintage

flutes. 'And finally ... everyone ready? Let's hope this works. Ben wants us all to go out there when he goes down on one knee, then we'll all join in a toast. And Plum's the official photographer.'

By the time we parade out onto the balcony, the stars are pricking through an inky sky and Rachel's pulled a soft cardigan over her floaty cotton dress. Beyond the darkness of the beach the moonlight is catching the lines of the breakers as they suck in and out along the ripples of the water's edge. By the table the fairy light strings are swinging as the wind catches them and the table is pooled in light from the mason jar candles.

As I put down the plates, I'm smiling at Rachel, and looking over the top of her head at Nell. 'I hope it's not too dark.' The cupcake candles are spluttering as the breeze catches the flames. 'Happy anniversary.'

Nell pops the champagne cork, fills their flutes, and slides a fork next to each plate. 'Cheers, and congratulations to you both.'

As we ease backwards to the shelter of the French windows, Nell raises her eyebrows at me. 'Light the blue touch paper ...'

I whisper back to her 'And retreat to a safe distance.'

There's a mutter from the sofa. 'Or better still run like hell.'

Plum's peeping through the window, camera in hand, and Sophie and Milla are there next to her with more glasses and some mini packs of tissues with heart logos on. If Rachel doesn't find the ring soon we might all pass out because none of us is daring to breathe.

Then there's a cry from outside and a whoop that's so loud it can only mean diamonds being unearthed from cake sponge. As everyone rushes forwards and out onto the balcony I hang back. In the distance, I can hear the notes of the musical box playing.

Ben wanted to propose to 'Somewhere Over the Rainbow', but when Milla showed him the musical box, he put his phone away and wouldn't hear of playing anything other than that.

Realistically, proposals aren't anything I identify with. I can see they're exciting for whoever's doing them, but for someone who hasn't ever found a guy I liked enough to call my boyfriend the idea of wanting to be with someone forever is too huge to get my head around. Obviously, Sophie can empathise completely, and Nell's thrilled at her part in this, and Plum's taking the pictures, so they all have to be there. But for now, I'm going to stay inside.

As I glance over my shoulder my gaze collides with Charlie's. He looks down at Levi, and rubs the side of his thumb over one chubby leg. 'Not going out?'

I scrunch up my face. 'You know me, I struggle with the idea of promising further ahead than tomorrow, I wouldn't want to jinx this. How about you?' That's a tactless question and the minute it's out I wish I hadn't asked. From the sad lines around his eyes, he's probably thinking about proposing to Faye.

He pats Levi's knee. 'I'm on taxi duty, and the little guy's out for the count. They want him in the photos, but I'll let him get as many zeds as he can in the meantime.'

I move on to change the subject. 'Nell's brilliant with her matchmaking.'

He almost cuts me off. 'For everyone else but herself, seriously someone needs to step in and help there.' If only he knew. 'We were chatting by the grill earlier. She's great, isn't she? Funny yet insightful, all in the same package.' Maybe without the distraction of puddings she's easier to appreciate.

I'm blocking the jealous twang in my chest, ashamed I'm

wishing he were saying that about me. 'You need to ask her to do her Boy George impression, it's hysterical.'

Charlie's half-grin is guilty. 'Actually it was mostly you she was being hilarious about. She was telling me about the summer you were five and refused to eat anything except custard sandwiches.'

I'm happy to have the piss ripped out of me, but I have to go some way to denying this. 'Truly, I don't remember that, a lot of my childhood is a blank. She probably just made it up or confused me with someone else. But feel free to laugh anyway.'

As he raises one eyebrow he's grave again. 'No, she had every detail nailed, right down to you insisting on Bird's Custard, not her mum's egg version. It was the summer the four of you turned up miles down the coast – the time you all went off to look for your dad. Ring any bells?' His querying gaze is piercing into me.

I let out a snort to lighten the mood. 'I doubt I'd get miles now, let alone when I was five. In any case that would have been for Sophie, not me. It's not a secret, her dad left too.' If I concentrate really hard there's a hazy image of us being driven home from Oyster Point in a coastguard's car. A back seat that smelled of mermaids and damp seaweed. Then when we all tumbled out onto the sea front at St Aidan we couldn't understand why our mums were annoyed. My mum wasn't cross though, she just cried and cried. As a child, there's nothing worse than seeing your parent upset and when you've only got one of them it's way worse. She was still sniffing days later. After that I always avoided mentioning my dad in case I set her off again.

He's staring at me quietly. 'Nell was adamant, Sophie's dad left the year after. So, however you remember it, you must have wanted to know about your real dad at one time.' He drags in a breath. 'This is what I meant about Nell being insightful. She feels this stuff is as important for you as I do, it's good to have back up on this.'

As a measure of how uncomfortable I am with this being dragged up, I'd actually rather be proposed to. However much I wanted to hug him earlier, he's hit a nerve here. I growl in the hope he'll back off. 'Bloody Nora, you were supposed to be barbecuing not doing psychoanalysis. Any other fuckwit conclusions you cooked up alongside the fish?'

At least he has the decency to look sheepish as he sighs and stares hard at Levi's toes. 'Seeing you've brought it up, I think Nell's longing to have kids.'

'Wow.' My eyes pop open so wide they ache. '*She* told you that?' It's not a conversation *we've* ever had.

He blows out his cheeks. 'Not as such, it's more of a gut feeling of how she was around Levi. The look on her face was the giveaway. Between us though, if she's ready for a family the timing couldn't be better.'

I'm picking my jaw up off the rag rug here, because I never noticed Nell anywhere near Levi this evening. Whatever he means about timing, it's significant that Charlie's picked this up. As I gaze at him lying there with Levi snoring on his chest, there's a peculiar spasm in my tummy. Which is totally ridiculous. Me thinking I'd like a baby is my wildest thought yet. It's so absurd it makes my wish list look sensible.

I work my way around to a suitably positive answer. 'Well, all I can say is bring on the boat trip. Sunday's shaping up to be a very exciting day.'

Charlie nods. 'We'll both get to work on the George thing early tomorrow.'

I'm vaguely confused. 'You mean Boy George?'

'No, Clems, not *Boy* George.' Charlie sighs. 'Your *boss*, George, the one you see in the office every morning. We're making sure he comes on Sunday. Tell me you haven't forgotten already?' He looks up as there's a burst of clapping. 'How are they doing out there?'

'Sophie's waving at us to bring Levi out. It must be a done deal because they're all downing champers like there's no tomorrow.'

Charlie eases Levi upwards. 'Would you take him while I stand up?'

At the thought of holding the baby again my stomach leaves the building. 'Me? I can't, I've got no idea what to do with a baby.'

Milla's skipping in, and she stops by my elbow. 'It's fine Clemmie, just grab him round the middle and squish him against you.' She's so close I can feel her breath on my bare arm. 'That's it, you've got him, you're fine.'

I take a step backwards and gasp as I close my arms around him. 'He's heavy ... and very warm ... and who knew babies were so velvety.'

Milla's laughing. 'That's the leggings not the baby, Clems.'

'Come on Diesel.' Charlie gets to his feet, and for the second that he stands staring at us, there's a shadow passing across his face. Then it goes as fast as it came, and he strides across to me.

My legs are welded to the spot. 'Are you taking him back?'

But before Charlie can, Nell rushes in, scoops him out of my arms and whisks him off for a photo with his mum and dad.

28

In Clemmie's flat
Hand knits and dirty tricks
Even later that Tuesday evening

With something as big as a proposal, it takes a while for the excitement to subside. While Charlie makes everyone coffee, Ben and Rachel phone their families and friends. Then they take advantage of the high speed Seaspray Wi-Fi to share their news on Facebook, and the congratulations come flooding onto their phones in a non-stop flurry of beeps. When they post another photo on the Singles' Club page the beeping spreads all along the balcony.

Eventually, Sophie takes Milla home to bed and drops Plum off on her way. And after coming back four times to say their last thank yous, Ben, Rachel and Levi finally head off with Diesel too so Charlie can drive them home in their car, and give Diesel his late-night dog walk on the way back.

Which leaves Nell and me to do the final tidying, which is barely any at all. Once we switch off the fairy lights and blow out the candles, it's just the two of us in the dark with a rug and a director's chair each, a bottle of left over prosecco at my elbow on the table, resting our bare feet on the balcony rail. There's a clicking as Nell winds the musical box. Then she lifts the lid and sets it going. I'm listening to the gentle lap of waves along the bay with the overlay of tinkling notes from the musical box blowing across the beach when I notice a gulping sound next to me.

I look along the balcony for a pale splash of Pancake and call to her anyway. 'Good girl, Pan-pan, we truly appreciate that you saved your fur ball retching for after the proposal.' Considering cat behaviour, that's amazing.

There's a whole lot more choking snuffles. But the giveaway is the huge sniff that's way too big for a cat. As I stretch my arm out sideways and my hand hits Nell's shaking shoulders the sniffs escalate to a low moan.

'Nellie Melon, what's wrong?' As I dip into my pocket for a tissue pack and pull one out her wail is so forlorn I almost find myself joining in.

She takes the hanky, and does a massive nose blow. 'I'll be fine ... in a minute.' She's mumbling through her tears. 'I'm just a bit ... emotional.'

I'm squeezing her into a hug. 'Babe, was it the proposal?' Of all of us, Nell's famed for her no-nonsense, unsentimental approach to life. When the rest of us were crying buckets over weepy films, she'd be rolling her eyes and popping another can. As a kid, she'd be the one who'd grit her teeth when she fell over and cut her knees and refuse to cry regardless of much blood was gushing down her legs. She made it through her entire wedding day dry-eyed and her break-up too. It's not that she's hard-hearted because as a friend she's warm and sympathetic. It's just she just doesn't express herself by bawling. Although it seems like the proverbial flood gates have been opened here.

'It's just Ben's proposal was so beautiful ... the way he told her she made him complete ... and he couldn't imagine life without her...' She's blubbing louder than ever, gulping back the sobs. 'When I walked down the aisle at the register office with Guy... *Somewhere over the rainbow* was playing that day ... that was supposed to be forever ... and now it's all stuffed up and wrecked.'

I remember that too. Nellie was dancing in time to the music, singing along, having such a great time she almost looked like she didn't want the aisle to end.

'But wasn't it a mutual decision to go your separate ways?' When it comes to helping married people the best I've got is divorce jargon picked up from the office. All I know is her howls are a long way from the matter-of-fact split I've heard about. No one else involved, a dignified separation. How did it go? *We've reached a place where we'd be better apart than together. And we both wish each other well.* Not that I'm the greatest at recall, but it sounded like someone put a lot more thought into the wording at the end than at the beginning. As I recall, Nell's wedding promise was a joke about who was going to make the ham sandwiches.

She sniffs. 'That's what we told everyone, and what I believed. But a month later he'd moved in with someone else. Now he's up there on Facebook in a red jumper with a dog and a baby, out on bloody date nights, having a ball doing all the stuff he'd never do with me.'

'Bloody hell, of all the underhand, shitty tricks.' Mostly I'm doing a huge silent 'Jeez' about the baby. 'Where does the knitwear come into this?' Charlie must be way more intuitive than I gave him credit for.

Nell pulls a face. 'Whenever I bought Guy colourful jumpers to make him less mopey he left them in the drawer. He pulled off a no-fuss exit from our relationship when he was screwing someone else and had her waiting open-legged in Glasgow. And you know what's even worse? They've got chickens. *CHICKENS!* Guy didn't even like chickens, and now he's got a bloody garden full and I haven't got any at all.'

'That's *really* bad.' I know how much she misses her hens.

'They've even put fairy lights on the henhouse like I had. *Fucking fairy lights!*' She lets out a long, low moan then she carries on. 'I'm jealous of everything they've got and I haven't. Whatever we said before, when he drove off in his rental van he left this gaping hole in my life. I hate living on my own. I know I'm a fraud because I'm always encouraging other people to get together. But I can't face putting myself out there, and having it happen all over again. I just can't get over that someone I thought I knew as well as myself could lie to me like that.' It's as if now the tears have started, she can't stop them.

Even with my limited experience, one thing sticks out a mile. 'Nells, I'm so sorry. But you can't seriously let one bastard stop you getting on with your life. You're the nice one here, you deserve to be happy. As you say yourself there are some great guys in St Aidan, we just need to find you one of the good ones, one you can really trust.' It's meant to be a leading statement.

She takes a breath and completely misses my suggestion. 'Obviously, I had my one-off revenge shag straight away. There was no point messing about, I got that over really fast.'

I've got no idea why I'm so surprised. 'And how was that?'

'Absolutely fucking amazing.'

I'm grinning in the dark. 'Any clues as to who that was?'

She chokes. 'Absolutely not.' She gives a sigh. 'I was bloody discrete. I chose the guy very carefully, booked a room at The Harbourside, we had one drink at the bar, and left six hours later. Bish bash bosh, all done.' Not judging here, but that sounds like a long time for a quickie.

'Wasn't that a bit public?' This is St Aidan we're talking about after all. People here know what you're thinking before you've thought it.

Nell laughs. 'It wasn't like we met up at Jaggers or the Hungry Shark. Everyone we know drinks in town early doors, so I knew I'd be as good as invisible up at the Harbourside.'

I'm treading carefully. 'You didn't consider going back for more?' If it was so spectacular, some of us would have been tempted. Even Plum goes back for seconds in exceptional cases.

Nell lets out a groan. 'It's not fair to get involved when you're falling apart inside. In any case, it was too embarrassing.'

Now I've heard it all. 'Would it help to share why?'

I can sense her shudder. 'There was way too much screaming and crying all round. I could *never* go there again, ever. End of.'

It makes sense to sound her out. 'So let's go with a more general question. In your opinion as a proven matchmaker, if there was someone really nice you got to know gradually, the kind of person who's empathetic and fun and decorative *and* gives you a butterfly storm – if you'd been out of the game a while, would *they* be worth taking a chance on?' I've always had Nell down as a butterfly girl rather than a fanny flutter person. Although if someone's had her screaming, we may be revising that.

From her tone, she has to be rolling her eyes here. 'I suppose you're asking this for a "friend"?'

I'm straight back at her. 'Obviously.' I hope she isn't twisting this.

She sniffs. 'True butterflies are rare. If they're there, you have to be brave. Tell her from me – this one's worth it, Clemmie. She has to go for him.'

It's my duty to say this, however much it's screwing up my insides. 'Charlie mentioned you'd been chatting earlier.' Then I move on lightly to the only other place I can immediately think of. 'So, were we *really* looking for my dad the day we walked to Oyster Point? Because I can't remember that bit at all.' Too late I remember, custard sandwiches would have done the job here.

From her intake of breath, I know she's got my meaning. 'Of course we were searching for your dad. We were five, the rest of us had dads, we got it in our heads we should find yours.'

I'm puzzled. 'But why on the beach?'

She laughs. 'I've no idea about that. Other than we were there, and we were using our initiative searching the crowds. It must have affected your mum deeply though because before that she'd never dated, and she got together with Harry not long afterwards.'

I shake my head as I think about it. 'I suppose you never really know if what you remember is real, especially if other people remember it differently. My brain doesn't flash up clear cut pictures to order like with you and Plum and Sophie.'

Nell shifts in her chair. 'People's memory triggers vary. Going back to Laura's and making her sweets has brought a lot of things back for you.'

I laugh. 'But usually there's just one huge blank.' It's very frustrating not having a great memory. I always accepted it as one of those things I couldn't change, and it was a bummer when it came to exam time. If only I'd had a better memory I might even have got some decent grades instead of always bumping along the bottom of the class. 'When I think back to being a child, saying that something was missing is putting it too strongly. But I always had a vague sense that something indefinable wasn't there.'

Nell nods. 'Twins often say they feel something similar if they were separated at birth. Your mum did a great job. Before Harry came the two of you were a rock-solid unit. Apart from her crappy cooking she gave you everything you could have wanted and more. After the walk to Oyster Point your mum was so upset I think it stopped your curiosity. Maybe that was a bad thing.'

'Mum and Harry are brilliant parents; I couldn't have been any more loved. But when we used to build those huge sand castles with a moat around, it only took the tiniest part of the outer wall to collapse, and the water all flooded away. For me it's as if a tiny part of my outer wall isn't there and that gap lets me drift.'

Her hand lands on mine on the chair arm. 'This could be the whole reason why you've found it hard to find anyone you wanted to commit to until now. What with you feeling you don't measure up for a relationship, and Sophie endlessly trying to prove herself, these absent fathers have a lot to answer for.' This is more Plum's kind of summing up than Nell's.

I'm gobsmacked by what she's implying here. 'I'm still a fully paid up member of the Foot Loose and Fancy Free Club, thanks very much.'

Nell's laugh is throaty. 'My bad. I was forgetting, it's your "friend" who's getting fanny flutters for the guy next door.' She comes in close and drops her voice. 'Did you notice how sweet Charlie was with Levi?'

I can't help agreeing about Levi. If she's right about the other, I'd never say. 'They were so cute with Levi asleep on Charlie's stomach.' If the tender expression on Charlie's face has etched itself onto my brain uninvited, I'm not going to let on.

She sniffs. 'It turns your toes to syrup every time when you see a guy being so good with a baby, doesn't it?'

I'm going to have to play this down. 'It's probably an age thing, the alarms on our biological clocks go bonkers the second we pass thirty.'

Nell's laugh bursts out. 'Tell that one to your bestie. I reckon that thump in the solar plexus has a lot more to do with lust than alarm clocks.'

Even though I'm not exactly sure who's talking about who here I let out a loud guffaw, to show I totally get the joke. Then as a scrabble of paws hits the balcony outside Charlie's open doors, it turns to hysterical giggles in case he's heard.

'Everyone get home okay?' Even if it's a relief for me to move on from talking about fathers, I'm surprised to see him back, because we did the 'goodnights' earlier.

Charlie's eyes are narrow, glinting as the rising moon lights up his white shirt. 'Ben and Rach are home safely, they spent the entire journey telling me how grateful they were. Then as I got out of the car at theirs they gave me this.' He digs in the pocket of the jeans he changed into before they left, and as he wiggles his fingers, the note he's holding up twitches. 'It's fifty quid, they said it was a tip. Does that mean anything to anyone?'

'Damn.' My throat goes so dry, even though I'm opening and closing my mouth no more words will come out.

Nell jumps in. 'No worries, they gave me one too. Some people express their gratitude in words, other people shower fifty quid notes around.' She gives him an extra hard stare. 'It was a *proposal*, Charlie, life events don't get more momentous. We made it marvellous, they're showing they're happy. End of.'

If we're talking gratitude, I want to fling my arms around Nell for taking the flap out of Charlie.

'Great.' He's still holding up the note between his fingers. 'Well as you seem to have missed out on the shower, Clems, I'll give this to you.' He leans over and tucks the fifty quid under the prosecco bottle. 'Careful you don't lose it. As Nells says, proposal windfalls don't happen every day.' The way he leaves it hanging is loaded with implication.

I'm quaking because we're a whisker away from paying party guests here. I rack my brain for a reply. 'So, while we're talking cash, I've been meaning to ask you about Airbnb.' It's not the greatest timing, but it's the truth and it moves us on to safer ground. As the first part of my strategy for getting what I want it's good to get it out there.

He shrugs. 'Fine, it's a big subject, what do you want to know?'

I try to make it sound casual. 'Well, it's still up in the air, but I'm trying to find extra ways to earn. Not wanting to tread on your toes, but I was thinking about Airbnb?' Maybe letting my bedroom while I sleep in the smaller room. Or I could stay with Plum or Nell and let out the whole flat for weekends.

Nell's straight in there. 'So would Airbnb give Clemmie a better year round return overall than a longer let? Could she do occasional nights? What are the pros and cons? And do Dainty Dusters give you a special Seaspray deal?'

Now we've both said our piece, we're waiting expectantly.

Charlie does one of those tradesman's blows. Not that I'm familiar with them first hand, but my mum's a bit of an expert. I'm talking about the kind of moment where the plumber expels every bit of air in his body, then tells you your boiler's frigged. Or the garage mechanic's snort that almost whooshes your rust heap off the forecourt but actually means you need a new car.

If I don't hurry him up, we could be here all night. 'So, Charlie?' I'm ready for my bed so I'd like to get this over as soon as.

His second, smaller version of the tradesman choke comes out as a sigh. 'I'm sorry to be the one to break bad news, but you'd be jumping the gun to plan any type of let on the flat as it is.'

I can't help flaring up. 'If you think you can get all proprietorial and stop me letting, you ... you ... you've got another think coming.'

He takes a step back. 'Come on Clems, you *know* I wouldn't stand in your way like that.' He sounds wounded rather than cross. 'It's more about the state of the flat.' So now the truth's coming out.

True, it's not had the arse designed off it, but I love this place and I'm not going to sit back and let him slag it off. 'I know the colours are a bit wild and it's shabbier than chic, but *everyone apart from you* seems to love it.' My party regulars, for example.

Although, obviously, I'll be keeping them out of this. I stick out my chin. 'If maximalist really is the new minimalist, you could have a white elephant on your hands next door.'

He's shaking his head. 'Clems, it's not the decor that's the problem, it's the Electrical Safety Certificate. To get a that you'd probably need a full rewire. And it would make sense to re-plumb and re-plaster at the same time. Realistically you end up doing a full refurb.'

'Excuse me?' If I'm honest he lost me at the word 'Clems'.

He gives a resigned sigh. 'I know these flats inside out. The Residents Committee need that certificate too. In the long term, you'll have to sort all these things out, regardless of whether you live here or you let.'

'Hang on ...' Mentally, I'm running to catch up, and howling silently. 'So is this *as well* as the ten grand you mentioned back in April?' Not that I've actually got that yet. I'm clasping my stomach, because I feel like someone just kicked me in the guts.

He nods. 'The ten grand is for exterior work. Inside the cost would vary depending on the work. Even though your flat is small you're still talking tens of thousands.'

'I can't afford that.' Somehow my scream is happening on the outside not the inside.

Charlie closes his eyes and his voice is calm and resigned. 'The thing is Clems, you can't *not* afford it. Unless you close the flat up you *have* to have *some* work done.'

So much for my wish list. I'm totally scuppered before I've even begun.

Nell's patting my knee. 'Why don't we talk about this again tomorrow?'

'Or …' Charlie folds his arms and leans his shoulder against the wall. 'Better still, George and I have bills for work that's been done here already, and Nell's great with figures. If the three of us put our heads together on this, we'll be able to work out some rough costings. Then you'll know where you stand, Clems.'

I'm taking in that he's throwing me a lifeline here, but I'm way beyond being saved. I already know I'm shafted. 'Brillibobs, that sounds *fab*.'

He tilts his head at Nell. 'Is that okay with you, Nellie Melon?'

I wrinkle my nose at how cute that sounds as he says it. 'So who told you she was called that?'

He laughs. 'Sophie mentioned it earlier, but I might have heard George say it too.'

I can't help smiling at how Sophie's suddenly embracing Charlie, welcoming him into the inner fold telling him our kiddie names.

'I know you have a lot on in the evenings. Would seven Thursday morning at George's work for you? I'll pick up breakfast for the three of us from the bakery on my way down. Then we'll thrash some numbers around over coffee,' Charlie finishes.

I know there's nothing I can bring to this meeting. So, if for a fleeting second I'm feeling disappointed at not being included to thrash along with them, I give myself a hard kick, and remind myself not to be so damned hungry. Let's face it, I have croissants for lunch most days anyway. What *am* I going on about?

'Great.' From the way she says it she means anything but. 'In that case, see you Thursday, Charlie, thanks for all the help tonight.' As she gets up, she looks at me, then comes in for a kiss on each cheek and a hug. 'Clemmie, you're more than a star. Don't forget, remind that friend of yours to man up.'

I laugh back at her as she leaves. 'No worries, I won't.'

I expect Charlie to follow her as she leaves.

'Before you go, Clems ...'

I jump up as I realise he's still there, because I thought he'd have padded away. 'Yes?'

He slides a bag onto the table next to the prosecco bottle. 'These are for Sunday. They're old denim cut offs, feel free to hack more off if you need to.'

My heart slithers down to the decking, then carries on two more storeys to the ground. 'I have to wear shorts?'

He sends me a grin. 'Not compulsory, but they're more practical than a dress.' He takes in my pained groan. 'Cressy hates shorts too. She usually wears hers with a tucked in vest and some kind of mid-calf cardigan. Dusky pink would work well with your Converse, it's a cool way to avoid feeling too exposed.'

'Shit, Hobson.' I'm shaking my head. First baking, now fashion tips.

He's not moving. 'You saw what I meant about Nell and Levi?'

'I did.' As I'm nodding in the shadows, I'm thinking more about him and Levi. Then as I remember what he said about Nell and good timing suddenly it hits me. He's almost forty, guys have biological clocks too and he did say she needed a push. 'Are you thinking of getting together with Nell just so you can have a baby?' It's such an appalling thought it's out of my mouth as it forms.

'Sorry?'

This is about so much more than me being jealous. 'Please don't do that to her, Nell needs to be truly loved not grabbed because she's broody. Of everyone I know she deserves to find her penguin.'

There's a couple of seconds where all I can hear is the sound of the breeze, then there's a loud protest. 'Jeez, Clemmie, tell me you aren't serious? *I'm* not her penguin and I don't want *her* baby. Why do you always assume the worst?'

This blunder is going to take some coming back from. 'I'm sorry, I'm just looking out for her, she's a lot more vulnerable than she looks.'

He's staring down at me, towering above me and for some reason there's the lilt of a smile on his lips. As I watch the shadows on his face, his chest is inches from me. Then as I let my gaze trail down over the shadows of his forearms his hand stretches out and brushes back the strand of hair blowing across my forehead.

'Well, it's a relief we've cleared that one up.' His voice is low and grating as he tilts my chin upwards. 'This is why I love living next to a mermaid, I never know what you'll come out with next.'

I'm shivering, jolting with every bang of my heart as it hammers against my ribs. As I watch him bite his lip I'm aching to pull his head towards me so I can brush my lips on his, plunder his mouth. How long have I been aching to know how he tastes? As I slide my palm up his chest his skin is hot through the silky cotton then as his thigh bumps mine I remember. If I let this happen, I'll never be able to come on the balcony again. Or even open the door. Even if I can't stay here forever, this is a terrible idea. If I were adding snog with Hobson to my wishlist, it'd have to be the last thing I did before I disappeared for a very long time.

I take a jump backwards and clear my throat. 'I–I need to let you go. It's late, you're in with George at nine, remember.' So am I for that matter. Too much prosecco and a sky full of stars are a bad mix. If I ever took him to bed, I'd need at least two weeks before I got up again.

'Clemmie ...'

I point my finger to his end of the balcony. 'Okay, thank you – for everything. Now go to bed.'

He's still staring down at me. 'What about you? If you're not going yourself I could stay ...'

My fists are clenched by my sides so I don't change my mind. 'It's fine, good night, I'll go very soon.'

As I watch him slip off into the darkness I need to take a moment, because it's been a big day. When I woke up this morning I had no clue how to make pastry *or* host a romantic dinner, and now I've done both. For the first time in my life I've decided what I definitely want and where I want to be. Then three hours later I find it's impossible. From what Charlie said back there, however much I love this place and want to stay here, this balcony and the sea views might not be mine for much longer. As I stare out at the moon light sparking off the water and watch it breaking into a thousand fragments as the wind whooshes across the bay, I try to imagine *not* being here. There's a twist in my chest and the sourest taste in my mouth that's nothing to do with flat prosecco. If my heart hadn't already dropped through the balcony, I'd swear it was being ripped apart inside me.

29

In Clemmie's kitchen
Vital statistics
Saturday

On Saturday afternoon, I'm in the kitchen at the flat, singing along to my Solid Gold Bangers list, drizzling dark melted chocolate onto white chocolate gateaux ready for this evening's LCK chocolate fest. I've been doing so many choccie evenings lately, I'm less of a Little Mermaid and more like St Aidan's female embodiment of Willie Wonka. Somehow yelling the song words so loud my throat hurts helps to blot out that my life is unravelling as I watch. Obviously, the words 'I *can't l-i-i-i-ve, if living is without you …*' have absolutely no relevance to me personally, but I'm still giving it rock when I feel a gentle tap on my shoulder.

As I look around a wet black nose collides with my leg. 'No Diesel, you know it tickles when you lick my knee. And hello Charlie, how can I help?' I already know the answer to that so I lean over and turn the music down. Then as his nose for icing is unfailing I push the empty bowl towards him and go back to piping my chocolate zig zags. 'That's buttercream with Baileys. Quick as you can with the bowl please, I need it for my melt-in-the-middle fondant puddings.'

So much for me worrying about the embarrassment of whatever happened on the balcony late on Tuesday evening. It's been so universally not mentioned I could almost have dreamed it.

Charlie deposits his usual pile of shite – for want of a better word, he always comes with it – on the table. Then he grabs a spoon and starts on the icing remains. 'I'm actually here to work.' He nods at the heap.

'Baking business?' I'm not sure I can fit in any extra cooking today.

He laughs. 'Not with a Fat Max builders' tape and a laser rangefinder, Clems. I'm here to take a few measurements.' The corners of his eyes crinkle more when he takes in my blank stare. 'For the repair estimates?'

'You're taking them *that* seriously?' I should have made it clearer: *any* cost is going to be too much. Every time I think I might have to sell the flat my heart goes into freefall. The only way I can cope is by blanking it totally.

His face falls. 'Why wouldn't I be?'

'Is this going to take long? It's just I've got a party to prep for and my berry chocolate cheesecake takes a while to set.'

'No time at all.' He's already holding his beeping gizmo on the wall and noting down numbers.

As I collect the dirty bowls and the washing up water splashes into the sink I can't help feeling that the kitchen has shrunk since the last time Charlie was here. The windows are open to make the most of the cooling breeze while the oven's on, but as he squeezes past me, moving backwards and forwards with his tape and clipboard, my skin is on fire. By the time I'm done with the dishes and collecting the pudding ingredients together I'm wiping slicks of sweat off my forehead. However much I lust after him I know nothing can ever come of this. The day he made my mental list was when it turned from wish list to impossible fantasy.

As Charlie springs up onto the work surface, I pull a face. 'What the hell are you doing up there?'

He sniffs as he peers along the top of the high cupboards. 'Checking the ceiling to see if you need a new one.' He's staring down at me. 'Do you have a problem with that?'

'I was expecting a few new plugs and switches, not full blown demolition.' Not that it matters as there isn't any money for either.

As he goes back to his prodding and poking I can't help thinking, breakfast meetings as excuses for get togethers are fine. But when he's going to this trouble, I feel guilty because I'm wasting everyone's time.

The sad thing with my finances is I'm so close to what I *thought* I needed to hang on to the flat, which makes it agony that it's being pulled away from me. Another month of parties and the ten grand will be in the bag. Thanks to the amazing and unstinting help of the mermaids and St Aidan Singles we're close to pulling off what seemed totally impossible back in April. Admittedly, the local appetite for chocolate puddings is bound to wane eventually, although learning to make pastry has opened up the recipe options a lot. By popular request we've even had a *Return to Laura's Rhubarb* night. The rhubarb season's over in Sophie's garden now, so we had to order it in bulk from the market, but I'd never have predicted that. I know it's all down to luck. The secret with the pop-up evenings is we accidentally hit on an untapped market who were happy to devour what we were offering. Thanks to concepts like new ceilings I'm going to have to get used to the idea that it's going to end as fast as it began. By Autumn everyone will have moved onto something else and forgotten all about their evenings at Seaspray Cottage.

However well my Little Cornish Kitchen luck was holding this far, and however well my first dinner for two went, my time is almost over. I turn around to get the scales at the exact moment Charlie springs down from the work top. There's a groan from the floor boards as he lands, and next thing I spin straight into his chest. As my cheek collides with his shirt my heart's tapping faster than Michael Flatley's feet after six cans of Red Bull.

He puts a hand out to steady me. 'Jeez, sorry, Clems, squishing the star baker is a sackable offence.'

This close, I'm totally engulfed in the heady Hobson scent again. 'Go ahead, fire me, I reckon I'm on borrowed time anyway.' I shiver as my eyes lock on the bare triangle of tanned skin where his shirt neck is open. Then as I let them slide upwards past the lump of his Adam's apple to the stubble shadows on his chin I catch the rhythmic thud of his heart on his rib cage and I shudder. He's staring down at me again. And yet again I've got this indescribable urge to lift my hand and rub it over his face. To wrestle his head downwards and bury my mouth in his. As I take a step backwards to get the hell out of here, his grip tightens on my arm.

His voice is low. 'You're the star here, Clems, not me.' His lips stretch into a half-smile and he inclines his head. 'There's something I've been meaning to ask you ...'

There's a crazy voice in my head. *Will I sleep with you? So long as we talk about it first ... maybe the night before I go ...*

His throat clearing breaks the voice in my head off in mid-sentence. 'These parties you've been having, Clemmie ...'

My stomach does a somersault. And then another. I consider asking which parties, but that's futile. 'Yes?'

He scratches his head, screws up his face and stares at me very hard 'Were they a commercial venture?'

He's letting me off the hook here with his business jargon. 'I'm not sure I'd put it that formally.'

He sighs. 'Okay, play it your way. In words of one syllable, have you been making money from these Seconds evenings of yours?'

How did I ever think I'd got away with that proposal tip? My chest deflates. I can't compete with smarty pants; I know when I'm beaten. 'Occasionally. From time to time. Possibly.' I feel his glare boring into my skull like a truth drug, but I'm not going down without a fight. 'Shit, yes, I made money from every bloody one. We aren't all minted like you, I was desperate to get cash for the roof bill. Do you have an objection to that?'

His voice is high with indignation. 'On *every* level.' No surprise there then.

I can't believe I'm saying this. 'Name some then?'

'You're unregulated, uninsured, you've got no planning permission ...' He's spluttering now and falling back on speculator-speak. 'You could land yourself in *so* much trouble here, Clemmie.'

I'm about to whip the proverbial rug out from under his complaining butt. 'Technically, they're private parties for friends from the Singles' Club. If people want to make a donation towards costs and effort we're not going to stop them.' I give a sniff. 'As Nell says, there are a lot of lonely people in St Aidan who are only too pleased to swap an evening alone watching TV for a riotous couple of hours at mine tucking into mocha mousse or Eton mess or white chocolate boozy roulades and copping off with people. We're actually offering a public service here, so don't be such a kill-joy. In any case Nell ran it past George, and we're completely above board.' My last minute after-thought isn't strictly true, but he can't possibly know that.

His expression slides to a new level of scepticism. 'I sincerely doubt Nell did, seeing as she and George weren't actually speaking until recently.'

Now I'm the one sounding incredulous. 'When were they not talking?' That has to be bullshit.

Charlie shakes his head. 'Never mind that now. But what if the neighbours complain to the council? They'll be down on you like a ton of bricks.'

I can't believe he's being so hypocritical. Or even worse, that I was about to snog his face off. 'In case you're forgetting, you *are* the neighbour. You actually accepted a tip the other night too.'

His nostrils flare. 'Slagging me off isn't helpful, Clems, so let's stop this now.'

'Actually, I've barely started. This should be about give and take. From my side, I provide with you enough sugar calories to keep a lumberjack going, your dog comes in and eats my sandwiches, your mum's cat's been living here for months ... *and* I empty her litter trays ...'

He snaps back. 'If Pancake's a problem, give me the food, she can come back to mine now.' He makes a grab for the shrimp and quinoa gourmet pouches he dropped on the table earlier.

I'm shooting myself in the foot here. Pancake used to purr on the pillow and block out the sound of the sea so I could sleep. But these days she's been curling up under my chin or in the hollow of my stomach while we happily drift off together with the crash of the waves in the background. If it's low tide and the waves are distant I often toss and turn until the tide turns. Without her the bedroom would feel so empty I doubt I'd be able to sleep at all, so I need to back pedal here, and fast.

I screw myself up for a climb down. 'Pan-pan's actually fine. I'd like her to stay.' However cross I am, the quickest way to get what I want here will be to beg. 'All I'm asking is a couple of weeks' more parties, so I'll have enough to pay for the roof. Then I'll be out of your hair.'

He takes a moment to consider. 'Okay, I'll go with that. But don't be too blatant. You're the one I'm concerned about here. I'd hate you to come unstuck over this.'

And this is the tester. 'I'm assuming you're no longer interested in payment for your trouble in puddings?'

His appalled expression is a picture. 'There's no need for the puddings to stop.'

And we're almost back where we started. I have to throw one last thought out there, without giving too much away. 'And seeing I'm still not on the *Sunday Times* Rich List, I'm thinking I might have to offer you first dibs on the flat after all. Just so you know.' I'm expecting him to jump and punch the air, then come and knock my hand off. But he doesn't even flinch.

Instead, he frowns. 'We don't need to rush into anything. See what Nell and George put together next week, and we'll take it from there.' He finally let's go of my arm, and a minute later he's gathered his shit pile and he's in the doorway.

I'm rubbing my elbow and trying to drag in some oxygen because he seems to have taken all the air with him. 'Thanks, Charlie.'

'Keep the noise down tonight.' He's almost grinning. 'And if you're doing melt in the middles make mine a double. With pouring cream, please.' And then he's gone.

It's only half an hour later that I realise Diesel's still with me, curled up under the table.

30

On the quayside at St Aidan Harbour
Webbed feet and sea scouts
Sunday afternoon

It could have been worse. If Charlie had found out the truth about the parties earlier, we'd never have got the ten grand together. This way, we just might. And when you think of all the times we almost gave ourselves away we've done well. I've always known it was precarious hiding behind the Singles' Club front. With the flat not up to standard we could never do that in the long term, but it's one of those maddening situations. If the flat was done, I could use it to earn back the cost of the work. But without the money there won't be any repairs. Whenever I think of having to leave all my newfound memories behind I understand why people talk about bleeding hearts. That's the way mine feels.

Whatever wizardry the Breakfast Club work with their figures, I'm pretty much stuffed all ways. The best I can hope for is to pay the ten grand off and make the flat more salable. Although I think we all know who's going to end up buying it. When I think of Charlie the day he told me about his loss, I'm happy for him to be the one to have it. When he comes in ranting about regulations, not so much.

As for today's boat trip, despite spending the last five days thinking up more and more outrageous reasons *not* to come, it's two on Sunday afternoon, and I'm here on the quay, waiting for my turn to get ferried across to the boat, on a dinghy of all things. I'd rather express my mermaid connections from the comfort of a sandy beach or a rock pile. Back in the day us mermaids did all our swimming badges so we're like proverbial fish in the sea. Actually, being *on* the ocean in a heaving plastic tub has much less appeal.

Note to self: when it comes to getting what I want I've got a lot to learn.

'Hey, cool cardigan, it looks great over the top of your buoyancy aid.' As I stuff my strappy heels into a bag and hold it out to Plum she's tweaking the long bit at the back of my cardi, hanging on to Diesel's lead with her other hand. 'If that's the kind of stuff they're selling in the Cats' Protection shop I need to go in.'

I laugh and pull it closer around my bare legs. 'I didn't notice any overalls in there when I was last in.' It's a relief she's commenting on the cardi rather than my shorts or the Converse I'm finally tying up now. Despite the shimmer they still make my legs look like they're stocky enough to hold up the jetty. As for the buoyancy aid, no one can look sylphlike in one of those so that's a leveller in a good way. I'm not about to let on, but this particular cardi hasn't been anywhere near a charity shop. It's yet another piece of pricey Hobson kit, whipped out of a carrier like a rabbit from a hat in my kitchen a mere half an hour ago, leaving no opportunity for me to find an excuse not to wear it.

'The crushed pink is perfect with your hair, it's like Pantone Pale Dogwood. Is it cashmere?' Plum always identifies colours in terms of her artist materials. She's spot on with the fabric too, but I'll fudge that.

'Cashmere from a charity shop, you are joking me? It's probably cotton and viscose.' I give Diesel's ears a tickle and look back at Plum. 'Is Diesel going to be okay up at the gallery?' As looking after Diesel was my main ploy to miss the boat trip, I was miffed that Charlie talked Plum into doing it instead, in another last-minute strike. That's the trouble with Charlie being an all-round do-gooder these days. What with him stepping in to buy Sophie's farm *and* commissioning Plum, everyone's bending over backwards to do whatever he asks. And now I come to think about it late ambushes seem to be a recurring theme for him too.

Plum's squinting at the dinghy bobbing its way back towards the stone steps that lead down to the water. 'Diesel will be fine. I bumped into Joe in town last night and he said he might wander down and help keep an eye on him.'

'Great,' I say, keeping my eye-roll to myself. I'm not taken in by casual words like 'might' and 'bump' and 'wander'. Plum's been 'accidentally' colliding with Joe on an hourly basis since Tuesday. The official line is she's on Operation Siren Phase 2, finding out what *his* game is, and she couldn't be putting any more effort in.

She can't stop gushing about him either. 'He loves animals. Apparently, his family have the same Portuguese Water Dogs the Obamas have. They have webbed toes and love to swim in the sea because they were bred to help fishermen ...' She breaks off and stares at me, startled, then frowns. 'Jeez, sorry, Clems, they're your family too. Shit, that's *too* weird, isn't it? Me knowing about them when you don't.'

I pull a face. 'It's my choice, but maybe that's why half-brothers should be off limits? At least for the time being.' While I love how the flat has brought me closer to Laura, the photos and the letter turning my insides upside down is the part I like the least. The more I want the Marlows to go away, the faster they're closing in from every side. Somehow I wasn't prepared for Joe to be a three-dimensional person with backstory and details and dogs with duck feet. Complete with gallery owners in – cliché alert here – hot pursuit. With the emphasis on the heat.

Plum sighs. 'He's really nice, you'd like him.' She shakes her head. 'I'm sorry, that's not what you want to hear. It's uncanny though – that frown you're doing now, he does the same.'

This time around I'm ready for it. 'I don't frown.'

'Not much, you don't.' Her face splits into a grin.

To move this on I give Plum a nudge and point at the boat with windows and a blue stripe around the top that's anchored twenty yards away from the quay. 'Look, Nell, George and Charlie are out on the back now.' I move closer to point them out. 'How the hell am I going to clamber from that tiny dinghy onto the big thing?' When the others went on ahead with the cool boxes, I dipped back to the end of the queue hoping I might get overlooked and left on the shore. Changing into my Converse at the last minute turned out to be a great tactic.

Plum gives a throaty chortle. 'Good thing you've got your pretty plimmies on, imagine making that leap in your platforms. You can't put it off any longer, there's only three of you left to go now.'

She pulls me into a hug then gives me a determined shove towards the steps. 'You'd better hurry, you don't want to get left behind.'

'Don't I?' I give Diesel a pat and flash her a rueful grin as I go down the steps.

She laughs. 'Careful, don't fall in before you set off.' She swaps the shoe bag into her other hand so she can wave. 'You might love it. You didn't want to come to St Aidan remember, and look how well that's worked out.'

I ignore the irony of that and grin at Jed as he hangs onto a rope holding the boat steady. 'Hi, I'm Clemmie.' Then I take a deep breath and lunge for the dinghy. It gives a lurch as my weight hits it and as I collapse on the plank seat my cardigan tails land in the water sloshing around in the boat bottom.

As I hold one side up and wring it out into the harbour, Plum shouts: 'Good thing it's not cashmere.'

I'm scrunched up with my chin on my knees so it has to be said. 'I was hoping it would be more like the *Rio* video.'

Jed laughs. 'Wait 'til you get aboard, the shipmates on *Gone with the Wind* make Simon Le Bon look sad and boring.'

'Fab.' I wring out the other side of my cardi and look back to shout to Plum again, but she's turned away. Ten yards along the harbour I spot the reason why. He's wearing a crumpled flowery shirt that could be made from my favourite daisy dress and his dark ginger curls are caught up in what George would call a 'man bun'. And whatever Plum's saying about frowns, I can't see any evidence of any as he drops his hand on her shoulder and comes in for a peck on the cheek.

Two other hapless singles flop on board, and find a dry corner to stow their back packs. As they bump down onto the plank next to me from their shrieks it's obvious it's the nervous ones who've hung back until last.

Jed picks up the oars and pushes off from the side. 'Welcome aboard, ladies. Everyone ready?'

As the women next to me wail their replies I only hope Nell knows what she's letting herself in for having these two on her crew. Being deafened by banshee screams and exchanging 'What the hell?' eye rolls gives Jed and I an immediate camaraderie. He's pushed off and he's rowing backwards now, and after a final wave to Plum, Diesel and her plus one I turn around with my hands clamped over my ears to see Charlie, George and Nell still waving madly from the back of the cruiser.

It's only when the banshee screams subside halfway across to the cruiser that I pick up the barking on the shore. Back on the quayside Diesel's pulling furiously on the lead, woofing wildly while Plum waves her arms. Then Diesel makes a mad lunge and as Plum falls forwards my shoe bag flies through the air and splashes into the harbour. But there's no time to call out because a second later in a blur of paws and legs Diesel accelerates towards the edge, hurls himself off, and nose dives downwards in a graceful arc.

'Diesel!' I couldn't be wailing louder if it was my child who'd done a kamikaze off the quayside. There's a huge splash as he hits the water, then as the wake of waves spreads outwards he disappears under the oily brown surface. For the first time in my life I'm actually glad I spent all those months when I was sixteen almost getting my lifeguards' certificate. After miles of batting up and down St Aidan swimming baths wearing trainers, Clueless pyjamas and Harry's towelling dressing gown, swimming in denim shorts and a vest will be a piece of pee.

As the banshee screams start up again I wrench off my Converse, whip off my cardi, stand up, note where the bubbles are. Then I fling myself over the edge of the boat. Freezing doesn't begin to cover it. My gasp as the water closes over my head drives every bit of air out of my lungs and for a moment I'm blinded by the cold. I push my way back to the surface and get my head together. Then as I shake back my hair and start to swim towards the spot where Diesel sank, he surfaces too and starts paddling towards me.

'Clemmie, Clemmie! Diesel! Clemmie!' The shouts are flying from the cruiser and the dinghy. There's yelling from the shore and screaming too. Then more splashing as another figure plunges off the harbour edge and starts streaking through the water.

Jed's shouts are calmer than the others and clearer. 'Swim towards the dingy, Clemmie, the dog's coming to you, we'll pull him in.'

He's right. As I circle round, Diesel comes towards me, his head, whiskers and black nose poking out of the water, his legs doing slow motion running under the water. By the time we get close to the dinghy we're doing a laid-back breast stroke and we're so relaxed we could be out for an afternoon leisure swim.

'Okay, Clemmie, you're doing well, not far now.' Jed sounds like he's got this.

The other jumper is slicing through the water, and he arrives at the dinghy seconds ahead of us. As Diesel paddles alongside and gives him a lick on the face, he shoulders Diesel out of the water. There's a scrabbling of paws, and a shower of shimmering water droplets as Jed hauls him aboard.

'Great work, Clemmie, he's in.'

I hang on to the dinghy's side and swipe the water out of my eyes. 'Phew. It's probably easier if I swim back to shore.' If I clamber aboard, I'll probably capsize them all.

Jed laughs. 'Swim alongside us, we don't want him jumping again. It's definitely you he was swimming to.'

'Brill.' As I look sideways and see the other jumper hanging onto the dinghy next to me my stomach lurches. It's like I'm looking at myself in the mirror after a shower. And even though the fabric clinging to his super muscular shoulders is soaking there's a definite trace of flowers. Of all the harbours in all the world, my half-brother has to end up with me in this one.

He wipes a strand of hair off his forehead and grins. 'So *you're* Clemmie?'

The whole harbourside has been yelling my name. I could swim out to sea or maybe, just maybe, it's time to own up. 'Yep, I am.' I need to make my position clear here so I stick out my chin. 'If you're here for the flat I'm not giving it up without a fight.'

Joe squints at the sun. 'I'm not here for fights or flats, all I want is to hand you something.'

The surprise takes my force away. 'That's why you jumped in to save Diesel?' If it were anyone else, I'd want to hug them. For that alone I'll speak to him.

He shrugs. 'That bit had nothing to do with you. Diesel could have been in trouble, I had to check he was okay.'

We're in the middle of the harbour, we're soaking. Any guy

who has just jumped in without a thought to help my favourite dog can't be so bad. Maybe it's time to come clean.

I sniff. 'Actually, I think I'm your sister.' I'm kind of pleased we're already dripping, because for some weird reason there are tears sluicing down my face.

He laughs and pats me on the shoulder. 'And, finally, hi, Clemmie, I'm Joe. I can't tell you how good it is to meet you at last.'

I'm laughing and crying at the same time, because it's so huge and at the same time it could be any other meeting. 'Back at you, Joe.' The surprise is I mean it. After fighting against this for what feels like my whole life, now it's happened it's less awful than I anticipated. Two sentences in, Joe's like any other normal laid-back guy who's jumped into the harbour. It sounds like a cliché, but it's almost like I already know him. I'm also looking around at the crowd of people on the shore and on the boats, all of whom are still dry. 'You do realise we're the only two who were mad enough to jump in after Diesel?'

He lets out a laugh. 'It must run in the family. I'm used to fishing dogs out of harbours, we've got Portuguese Water Dogs at home. One sniff of salt water, they're in.'

I'm biting back my smile. 'I've already heard about your dogs.'

There's a note of disappointment in his voice. 'I hope Plum left something for me to tell you.' Then he's beaming back at me and grimacing, like he's got the same 'can't stop smiling' thing I have. 'Hey, you're shivering. When we get back to land you will be okay if I make my delivery?' His eyes narrow slightly, and there's a hesitant note in his voice.

My teeth are chattering. 'Try me, and I'll let you know.' However euphoric I am because we saved Diesel, I'm not totally unguarded.

He pulls a face. 'I've got it in my pocket now. Which means it's much wetter than it's meant to be.'

I can't help laughing. 'That sounds like my kind of stuff up.' Obviously, the ginger genes and the frowning genes aren't the only traits the Marlows have donated to me.

The corners of his eyes are crinkling. 'Come on, you're cold, shall we swim back together, then we can dry off?'

If someone had told me six months ago I'd be swimming across St Aidan harbour with my half-brother, balling my eyes out, I wouldn't have believed them. But there again, if they'd told me I'd be making espresso roulade I wouldn't have believed that either. Life takes you to places you never plan to be. And sometimes you have to forget the enormity and go with it.

31

On Plum's deck
Making waves
Sunday afternoon

'As icebreakers go, they don't get much better than jumping in St Aidan harbour.'

This is Charlie summing up that I'm finally talking to Joe. He's here with us on Plum's decking rather than on *Gone with the Wind* because somewhere along the line he also hurled himself into the water. He was too late to save Diesel but was ruled 'too wet to make the voyage' and didn't want to delay the departure while he nipped home for dry shorts. Which was an excuse he borrowed from me. There will always be another outing. And even though I'm not telling him, I'm pleased he's here for backup because he's a natural at handling tricky situations

It was Charlie who suggested we come straight to Plum's for cake, coffee and drying out, whispering something about neutral territory at me under his breath. Plum's hardly neutral when it comes to Joe, but I get what Charlie means. Seaspray Cottage is where all our dry clothes are but he's right when he says we need to check what Joe's here for before we invite him round.

After bumping into Joe in the harbour there's a feeling that this whole long-lost family meeting couldn't get any more surreal. But then Charlie, Joe and I end up plundering Plum's rag bag for dry clothes so it does. Due to the heat of the afternoon the guys reject an assortment of ripped boiler suits and end up in paint-splashed shorts and ragged shirts while I'm in a spotty pyjama play suit Plum's – much bigger – younger sister accidentally left behind on her last visit. Things to like about that are the Topshop label, and that it's wide enough to cover a multitude. The other good news is I'm re-united with my strappy platforms. So, thanks to some passing sea scouts who came to the rescue and fished them out of the harbour at least my legs are back to normal length again.

While Plum and I make coffee, Charlie and Joe go two doors up the hill to raid the glass cabinet at the bakery and buy the entire stock of strawberry tarts. We sit out on the decking, looking out at the sun glittering off the turquoise dapples of the bay, brushing the cream and pastry crumbs off our chins. And in my case shaking my head to test I'm actually here and it's real. It's the strangest sensation of being hugely momentous and completely normal all at the same time.

I have to comment. 'Diesel must be feeling embarrassed about earlier; he hasn't dived straight on the tart plate.'

Charlie laughs. 'You noticed he didn't give a damn when I rowed off across the harbour, but the second you pushed off he went ape?'

There's an obvious explanation for that. 'That's because I'm the woman with the cake.'

Charlie shrugs. 'It's more about total devotion than sponge;

he knows if he flashes those dark brown eyes at you now, he'll crack you in two seconds max. Although I suspect he thinks *he* rescued *you*, not the other way around.'

It's unnerving they both know me so well, but comfortable to know I can count on them. 'Okay, you win, Diesel, but only because your stare is so soulful.' I'm so grateful he saved me from the boat trip I'll give him my last piece of pastry. Although when I hear what's coming next from Joe I might wish I'd gone with *Gone with the Wind* after all. My visible shudders are more about nerves than still being cold from the water.

Joe's wiping his hands and he looks like he's ready to talk.

As we all look at him expectantly he raises his eyebrows. 'I'd better start by explaining – I'm here because of our grandmother, who we all call Laura.'

I glance at Charlie and try to ignore the knots in my tummy. 'We call her that too, don't we?'

'We do.' Charlie gives me a nod of encouragement.

Joe smiles at that, then presses on. 'Laura was not only lovely she was also exceptionally knowing. When she found out she wasn't going to grow old she went to great lengths to ensure her influence extended long after her life ended. She left everything to her grandchildren, but she wanted to keep the goodies out of our reach until we were old enough to handle them.'

I can't help dabbing my eyes at this. 'I'm just so sad she's not here now. Spending the last few months at her place has made me remember so much more about her.'

Joe nods. 'Thirty seems to be the crucial age when she thought we'd be mature.' He turns to me. 'I'm thirty but I'm not that sensible, I don't know about you, Clemmie?'

I smile through my tears. 'Me neither, but I'm better now than when I was eighteen.' I can't help noticing we're staring at each other through identical curtains of wavy hair strands.

He flicks his back, sending a shower of diamond drips into the sunlight. 'We actually only found out about you just before she died.'

'Really?' I'm not sure why I've cut in or why it comes as a shock.

He pulls down the corners of his mouth. 'We're all used to the idea now but hearing about you was a huge surprise at the time. Laura always longed for you to be part of our family, and she's used her will, her grandchildren and a small amount of bribery to do that.' He gives an uncomfortable squirm.

'Okay.' I'm intrigued now.

He pauses to give what looks like a nervous swallow. 'I'll put this bluntly – my brothers and I are old enough to get our hands on her cash, but the first catch is we can only spend it buying property in St Aidan.'

Plum joins in. 'That's harsh when you don't live anywhere near.'

Joe nods. 'It is. But without that clause I'd never have come. As it is I've just spent weeks of my holiday viewing houses and looking for you. So, I can see how Laura's mind was working.'

I might as well come out with it. 'So you haven't come to contest the will and claim the flat she's passing on to me?' That first day in George's office, I'd have been almost pleased to hand it over. Now I'm way more reluctant.

Joe frowns. 'That was what you meant in the harbour? You thought that was why I was here?'

I have to be honest. 'It crossed my mind. Not knowing about your conditions, I couldn't see why else you'd suddenly appear.'

'That was why you didn't want to see me?'

I let out a long breath. 'Not *only* that. Before I fell in love with the flat, I actually thought you deserved it more than me. But I'd never spoken to anyone in the family other than Laura.' I'm reluctant to wave the word 'rejection' out in the open even if it is how I feel. 'For thirty years I'd been fine without contact. I saw no advantage in changing that.'

He raises his eyebrows. 'I get that, and I think Laura knew that too. That was why I wasn't allowed to approach you, you had to agree to talk to me. My only hope was to hang around so if you saw enough of me, eventually you would.' His brow wrinkles. 'You did make the first move back there ... didn't you? You are okay with this?'

Plum's laughing. 'From the shore it looked a lot like you pursuing Clemmie across the harbour.'

I wrinkle my nose. 'You jumped in after Diesel, that gets you a chat over a cup of tea.'

'That's a relief.' He wipes his hand across his brow. 'Basically, it sounds awful, but the second catch is that Laura's legacy will only be released to us when you've agreed to see one of us brothers and we've delivered something on her behalf. This was Laura's way of bringing us together.'

No wonder he was sounding so tentative in the water. 'I'll admit I was very reluctant to talk to you before, but now I have it's not half as bad as I imagined. So, in that way Laura was right.'

He looks genuinely delighted. 'I completely understand why you wouldn't want contact, but when George Trenowden told me you'd refused, I was gutted. It wasn't only about the money; it was more that I was sad for Laura.'

'So what have you brought me? You said it got wet?' I'm not being impatient, but the faster he hands it over the sooner he'll complete his conditions. And I'm aching to know what's so important.

He rolls his eyes. 'It's a letter. I've been carrying it round in case I met you so it's very smudged. Laura definitely didn't mean me to swim to deliver it, blunders go don't get any more spectacular than this one.'

I wrinkle my nose. 'If you hadn't swum, I most probably wouldn't ever have accepted it, so I'm happy to take the ink runs.'

Joe nods at Plum and she slips inside, then comes back out and hands Joe a small soggy envelope which he passes over to me. 'We were drying it on the desk, I don't know how much has survived.'

It crosses my mind to let it dry properly first, but I can't wait. I glance up at Joe as I undo the envelope. 'Dark pink, that's so Laura. That spiky writing is so familiar; I use her hand-written recipe cards every day.'

Joe nods. 'That was Laura, always scratching away with her pen making all those little triangles.'

I sigh, because I'd overlooked how comforting it would be to talk to someone else who knew her. 'And sea blue paper too.' The single page is soft and felty in my fingers as I ease the folds apart.

Plum's leaning in to help. 'It's handmade paper so it shouldn't rip, would you like us to leave you on your own to read it?'

I shake my head. 'You're all as much a part of this as I am. If it wasn't for you meeting Joe at the harbour, I wouldn't even have it, and if it wasn't for Sophie I'd never have visited the flat. In any case, it's very short.' I can see now, it's just a few lines. The way my heart dips, I must have been hoping for more. Although realistically ten pages wouldn't be enough to answer the questions in my head now. As I screw up my eyes it takes a while to make out the first washed-out words:

Clemmie, my little penguin,

I pause and look up. 'Oh my, Clemmie penguin, that's what she used to call me. Like the penguins on the bookshelves.' I wipe away a tear from the outside of my eye. When I start to read again my eyelashes are as clumped and wet as when I surfaced in the harbour.

You were the one who couldn't be with us and because of that you will always have a very special place in my heart.

By the time this reaches you (and I hope it does), I will be long gone. But my forever wish is that one day you will get to know our family, and better still become a part of it. If you're holding this letter in your hand reading these words, you're already part way there. I am willing your heart to be big enough for you to leave the past behind and move on to a new beginning.

Life doesn't always work out as we'd like it to. The flat is my way of making up for a tiny part of what you missed out on. I like to think of you there, living your life, cooking in the kitchen like we used to do. If it makes you half as happy as I was when I looked after you there, that's enough for me.

When you were small you and I would look out together at the moon shining on the bay and you used to say ... I love you more than rainbows, to the moon and back, as deep as the ocean, to the edge of the sky ...

It broke my heart that I didn't get to see you grow up but my love for you never changed. You were far away from me, but I want you to know, you could not have been any more loved. All that love is here for you now, and more.

Always, Laura xx

Some people cry quietly. When I begin to read, my tears are streaming, but by the time I reach the end I'm letting out loud ugly moaning sobs and I don't even care. And somewhere through my sobs some strong arms close around me and hold me. It's only as my wails subside and the grip loosens that Charlie's scent breaks through my haze. If I've got my cheek rammed hard against Charlie's pecs and I'm keeping it there for longer than strictly necessary simply because it feels like the right place to be, hopefully he'll overlook I'm hanging on for so long.

Then Charlie gently lets me go and the others read it too, and one by one they all join in with the sniffing and eye wiping and hugs.

Plum's blowing her nose on a paint rag and her face is all red and streaky as her arm flops around my shoulder. 'It's just so sad, Clemmie.'

My stomach is contracting as I dab my nose on my napkin. 'It is sad ... but it's uplifting too.' It's making my chest ache and want to burst all at the same time. Just for now I feel like I could conquer the world, and even if it's fleeting you don't get much better than that.

Charlie squeezes me all over again. 'What did I tell you, Clems, it's lovely.'

Plum turns to Joe. 'Did you know what was in it?'

He sniffs. 'No, but Laura had a huge heart and she always wanted to make things right.'

Plum sighs. 'Just a few lines, but there's so much in there and she says it all so perfectly. It's beautiful, Clemmie.'

I turn to Joe because this could be my one chance to clear this up. 'So do you know what happened all those years ago?' I'm holding my breath as I wait for his answer.

Joe's shaking his head. 'Sorry, Laura only ever spoke about you to us just before she died. We didn't rush to find you because Laura was very specific, she wanted us to wait until now.' From the way he apologises he knows he's disappointing me.

It's my turn to explain my side. 'I've found pictures in the flat, and another letter. But the more I find, the less I understand.' I sigh. 'I never wanted to ask questions before, but now I do there's no one left I can ask.' I'm discounting my mum and his dad here, because they're obviously no use. I know I hated that Joe was in St Aidan, but Laura's letter puts everything in a different light.

Joe's shrugs. 'I wish I could help more, there's nothing else I can tell you. But you will meet up with me again?'

Charlie cuts in. 'How about we all go for lunch at the Harbourside tomorrow? My treat. You've a lot of catching up to do and it's very relaxed on the terrace there.'

I know I hate the way he's always on the case, but today I'm truly grateful he is. Just this once he couldn't have done better.

32

At the office
Cups and sorcerers
Thursday

It's already Thursday and the week's whooshed by because we had a chocolate evening Tuesday, and in between times we've been out in town with Joe. Then yesterday evening, Charlie insisted on getting his barbie out on the balcony, with the lame excuse that it was Joe's last night, and we all hung out on the top floor at Seaspray Cottage. It just shows how fast things can change. This time last week I was rigid at the thought of the half-brother I didn't know wandering around St Aidan. After five days of hanging out together, I'm thinking of him as the guy who makes us all laugh without trying when he puts on in his broad Norfolk accent, who balances biscuits on his nose then lets Diesel lick them off, who made a fire on the beach so we could toast marshmallows when we were looking for shooting stars. Who turned up at mine with an armful of red and yellow and purple tulips tied with a floppy blue satin bow, and one of Plum's seaglass hearts to hang in the window to remind me of Laura.

Having spent time with him, knowing how much we both love Laura and hearing more about her has been lovely. I'm waving him off back to Norwich with an ache in my chest, looking forward to him coming back. He imports food, so he's promised to bring us lots of delicious olives and cheeses and candied walnuts and chocolate when he comes back for the auction next Thursday. Knowing he's a foodie made me so nervous I could hardly make yesterday's puddings for shaking. But it turned out he loves Laura's lemon meringue as much as I do. It's as if another part of my past fell into place. But at the same time, he's so much more than that.

After so many crowded parties it was funny to have only eight of us. All the mermaids came, plus Joe, and Charlie, who is so often here these days you'd think he was trying to get honorary merman status. Then because Joe is in the running for Siren House, Sophie got her mum round to babysit so Nate could come too to scope out the opposition. Apart from the briefest mention we mostly stayed off the subject of the auction, but when there's a new family member in town after thirty years it pays to be open about stuff. Then Charlie invited George along too because considering he's been getting up at the crack *and* eating croissants for England, all in the name of creating a work schedule for my flat, it seemed only fair to include him.

Sometimes it does seem like my life is a lot fuller of croissant flakes than other peoples'. As I'm accidentally in the office ten minutes ahead of any clients this morning I treated myself to some pastries to have with my first cup of coffee. I whizz through to George's office to take him his nine o'clock coffee then I settle myself down at my desk to dunk. When the main door opens, I'm about to drop my croissant into the drawer in the interests of professional standards, but stop when I see it's Charlie.

'Back again so soon after brekkie?' Realistically, he can only have left half an hour ago at the most.

For a second he looks at me like he doesn't know what the hell I'm on about, then he twigs. 'With the farm purchase on-going there's lots to sign.' He sniffs the air. 'The coffee smells good this morning.'

'There's plenty in the pot if you'd you like some?'

His eyes light up. 'Yes, please, don't get up, I'll help myself.' He looks at his watch then makes a dash for the kitchen. 'I've got five minutes before I'm in with George so I'll drink it with you. What do I have to do for you to let me steal one of your croissants?'

As he comes back and slides onto a chair, I'm looking at my pile of three, considering. 'If I absolutely can't find a way to keep my flat will you buy it? Tell me that and I'll let you have one.' It comes out so fast I take myself by surprise, but I don't want to waste the moment. What Laura wrote in her letter and getting to know Joe has made the flat even more important to me. But if I can't make it work, and I put in all those conditions Charlie once mentioned, at least if he bought it maybe he'd let me come and stay sometimes.

He hesitates for a long time. 'You're putting me on the spot here, Clems, hasty decisions aren't good business.' What ever happened to Mr Infallible Hobson, favourite mantra, *Every decision I make is intuitive and immediate*?

It's in my interest to work with him on this one. 'Have a croissant while you decide, or even two?' This is me getting my back up plan into place, so if I have to sell it can be as fast and painless as possible. As he takes the first and digs those perfect teeth straight into it like he hasn't eaten yet this month, I can't help commenting. 'How come you're so ravenous when you've been here stuffing your face since seven?'

For a second his eyes go wide, then they relax again. 'You know me, always hungry.'

'So how's the Hawthorne Farm purchase going?' I had every last detail from Sophie when she came to help on Tuesday evening, so I doubt he's got anything to add.

If he's surprised I'm talking like a pro, he doesn't show it. 'We've agreed the price, fast-tracked the searches, and we're preparing the contracts so they're ready to sign immediately if Nate and Sophie buy at the auction. That should guarantee them enough to bid way over the guide price so they're in with a good chance. But if they don't buy we won't proceed and they get to keep the farm.'

This is what's been bugging me. 'That's a win-win for Sophie, isn't it? She sells if she needs to and gets to keep her house if she doesn't. So, where's the catch?'

Charlie rubs his jaw. 'The skew in their favour is reflected in the price. But apart from that, there isn't one.'

'So why the hell do it? Why not force them to sell if you want their place so much? That's what most people would do in your position.' Sophie told me as much herself.

Charlie lets out a long breath. 'I wouldn't do this for many people but I'm doing it because they're friends of yours. Whatever you might think, I care what they think of me.'

So, that's what he's up to. 'So you're proving you're a nice guy, and not just an evil developer?'

He does another exasperated blow. 'Not quite that.'

If he's due in with George at nine, I'm going to have to push this. 'So do you have an answer for me?' This is where I could do with being like Dakota and having a teensy waist and a pink frill to make my chest look more noticeable.

As it is he's looking nowhere near my boobs. In fact, he's looking at the ceiling. 'Thanks for giving me first refusal, I'll get back to you in a couple of weeks. A month, tops. Although, for the record, you shouldn't be selling.'

'That's it?' I can't help the shrill. It's a long way from the speed fallback deal I was hoping for.

'It's the best I can do for now.' As he gets up he's looking distracted. When he reaches George's door he hesitates and tilts his head. 'I don't suppose Nell ever mentions that date she had a couple of years ago up at the Harbourside?'

I give a gulp. 'The time when she ...?'

He butts in and saves me from the rest. 'That's the one.'

My eyes have to be popping out of my head. 'That was *you*?'

He raises an eyebrow. 'That would be telling.' His eyes narrow. 'So was there a reason she didn't go for another?'

I put my horror to one side. 'She was in pieces after her breakup.' I never betray confidences but her future happiness could be hanging on this. 'Also, she was worried she'd been too enthusiastic.'

He drops his voice. 'So she *did* enjoy it?'

I wouldn't be telling anyone else. 'Best night of her life, from what I gather ... but for chrissakes, don't say I told you.'

Charlie's smile stretches right across his face. 'That's exactly what I needed to hear.' He's beaming as he pushes into George's office. 'I'll catch you later. Thanks, Clems.'

I return his wave. 'You're welcome.' Then I take the croissants back into the kitchen feeling sick to my stomach.

33

At Siren House
Going, going, going, going
Thursday afternoon, a week later

It's not every day a mermaid tries to buy a castle by the sea, so when Sophie does it's a no-brainer – the afternoon of the auction we're all there at Siren House to support her. The agents have flung open the French windows of the main drawing room so the sun is making the mustard and green carpet even more bilious, and the airy entrance hall is full of people wandering around talking to each other behind the programmes we've all been given.

As Sophie hands over a sleeping Maisie in her push chair, she's almost wailing. 'Have you seen the crowds? There's *so* much competition.'

Charlie lifts up his programme and tilts his head towards her. 'Don't worry, they aren't all buyers. You're here with a party of eight don't forget.' It's the same gang from Charlie's balcony barbie, with Maisie instead of Joe. He nods across to where Nate is filling in forms with George at the estate agent's table. 'Nate will know how many serious bidders there are when he gets his bidding number.'

Sophie wipes the sweat off her forehead and shoves her cardi into the bottom of the pushchair. 'Everyone looks so smart, and I'm in my fifth T-shirt of the day, looking like something off the bloody *Vampire Diaries*.'

She's right on both counts. The women from the estate agents have ditched their usual polo shirts and chinos and are strutting round in pinstripe dresses and navy jackets with heels the height of the castle turrets. Meanwhile Sophie could have been in collision with a ketchup factory.

Nate's as laid back as ever as he sidles up with George, his number card in hand. 'Maybe giving Maisie ripe raspberries on the way here wasn't the best move, Soph.'

Sophie looks like she's about to blow steam out of her ears. 'I didn't *give* her them, she helped herself while I was busy doing my "Siren House will be ours" affirmations.' As she flaps her hands in front of her face she's talking so fast it's as if she can't stop. 'What number are we, Nate?'

Nate looks up from licking raspberry juice off his finger. 'Twenty-four.'

Sophie lets out a shriek. 'Twenty fucking four?' Her Sophie May foundation fades to white. 'We've got no chance; we might as well go home now.'

Nate gives a shrug. 'It's not that bad, they only started at eighteen.'

As George gets his phone out, Nell leans in for a look. 'Only ten minutes to go.'

Charlie rolls back on his heels. 'So are we all off to the Harbourside for a drink afterwards?'

I'm expecting Nell to react to the mention of the Harbourside but she doesn't flinch.

All she does is to wrinkle her nose. 'Sorry, I'm here on late lunch, I thought they'd have a sandwich van in the car park. I'll head back to town for some food the second it's over, then I'm off back to the office.'

I throw my apologies onto the pile. 'I'm rushing off to prep for tonight's Chocolate Truffle Fest. And Plum will be hurrying away too, the gallery's packed out.'

George lifts an eyebrow. 'Where is Plum, anyway?'

Nell grins up at him. 'I'll give you one guess.'

George's other eyebrow lifts too. 'Hanging out with the opposition?'

Nell nods. 'Although the up side of that is if the Marlows win today at least Clemmie and Plum will get to be mermaids in residence from time to time.'

I'm ignoring what she's implying about Plum's connections. 'I'm sure Joe will invite us *all* to his parties.'

Sophie lets out a moan. 'I'm not going down without a fight. Now I'm here again I'm just *so, so* desperate for it to be ours.'

I should be taking notes on determination here. If she pulls this off today, I'll definitely ask her about those affirmations she does. As I lean across and give her a squeeze, there's a waft of berries and when I get my hand back from her arm it's so sticky I have to dive into Maisie's changing bag for a wet wipe. When I rejoin the group, Charlie's talking them through it.

'So they'll start very soon; the auctioneer is the blonde woman in the black suit and fishnets holding the hammer. She's very good at spotting bids, and very clear at checking if you're in or out.' If all the auctioneers are this racy, maybe this explains Charlie's interest in speculating.

As the room fills up, Joe and Plum slide in a few yards away, and Joe grins at Nate. 'Good luck, let's hope one of us wins this.'

The auctioneer clears her throat. She's so businesslike and focussed she's making Sophie look like a light-weight. 'Hello and welcome, ladies and gentlemen, today we are selling one lot, a delightful castellated and turreted dwelling with lots of potential, known locally as Siren House. Just to let you know we have some proxy bids and some telephone bidders too.' Beside her there's a cluster of staff all holding their mobiles to their ears. 'So I'd like to outline a few conditions ...'

As she goes through her preamble, Charlie's feeding instructions into Nate's ear. 'Don't worry about the phone bidders. Your tactic is to hang right back, let the others bid it up, and only go in when everyone else is finished.'

Sophie's the colour of the clean parts of her T-shirt and her heart is banging so hard I can hear it from two feet away.

'Who'll start me at five hundred thousand ... do I have four hundred and fifty anywhere?' The auctioneer's looking around the room, and Joe's card flashes up. 'Thank you, number twenty-two at the back there, do I have four hundred and sixty anywhere? Thank you, number eighteen at the side. Do I hear four hundred and seventy ...?'

I'm staring at Nell, open-mouthed as the bids jump backwards and forwards across the room. 'Oh my, it's so fast.' The price has jumped up by two hundred thousand in a matter of seconds. It goes up and up, Joe's still in there, then it stalls at just under seven hundred and thirty.

As the silence is broken by a loud snore from Maisie in her pushchair, the auctioneer says, 'We won't take that as a bid,' and everyone laughs.

Then Charlie gives Nate a nudge. 'Okay, in you go.'

Nate sticks his card up, and the auctioneer says, 'I'll take seven hundred and thirty from number twenty-four.' And off they go again.

As they nod backwards and forwards between Joe and Nate, it's intense. I desperately want Sophie to win, but at the same time now I know him more I hate the idea of Joe being disappointed.

Then at eight hundred thousand to Nate, Joe shakes his head. 'No, I'm out.'

Sophie's eyes are shining and her fists are clenched as she nods at me and hisses, 'Yes.'

The auctioneer then says, 'And we have a phone bid at eight hundred and ten thousand.' She looks at Nate. 'Will you go to eight twenty?'

Nate nods.

The auctioneer's cutting in again. 'I have eight thirty on the phone.' She goes back to Nate. 'Will you go to eight forty?'

Nate hesitates. Then shakes his head, and hisses at Charlie. 'Eight thirty's our absolute max.' He looks at the auctioneer. 'Sorry, no. We're done.'

'And I have a second phone bidder, in at eight forty. Do I have eight fifty on the first phone? Eight sixty on phone two?'

Nate and Sophie have visibly flopped, and Joe creeps over and gives Nate a silent punch on the chest and mouths, 'Bad luck for both of us, it wasn't meant to be.'

We're all standing and the auctioneer is winding it up. 'Okay, so I'm at eight hundred and sixty-five thousand pounds now, for the first time, for the second time ...'

Charlie's voice is low. 'This is it, it's selling now.'

It's totally silent, then as the auctioneer raises her hammer high and starts to sweep it down there's a sudden flurry. Sophie dives in, grabs the card from Nate, and the second before the hammer hits the table she jumps in the air and shouts, 'Eight hundred and seventy ...'

Nate's hissing, 'No, Sophie, stop, we agreed we wouldn't, we can't ...'

The auctioneer nods and gives a smug smile. 'And we have eight hundred and seventy in the room. Eight hundred and seventy-five on phone two. Eight hundred and eighty back in the room?'

Sophie stares straight ahead and shouts, 'Yes!' She turns to Nate and hisses. 'I'll use the cash from the company, I'm not stopping until I get it.'

My eyes are open so wide they could be about to pop out, and shit knows where Sophie's getting her oxygen from, because I haven't taken a breath since my gasp when she started bidding.

There's more to-ing and fro-ing as they check if there are any more bids, then the auctioneer's calling. 'For the first time ... for the second time ... for the last time, at eight hundred and eighty thousand pounds.' She lifts her hammer, and then it slams down on the table. 'Sold to number twenty-four, the lady at the back in the – er – Chainsaw Massacre T-shirt.' She rushes across to

Sophie and snatches her hand first, then Nate's. 'Congratulations, you'll soon be the proud owners of St Aidan's most unusual home.'

'Yes! It's ours!' Sophie throws back her head, punches the air and lets out an ear-splitting scream.

George is standing, blinking, then he turns to Charlie. 'Which means you will soon be the proud owner of Hawthorne Farm. Congratulations for that.'

As Sophie and Nate get ushered across to the agent's table with George to sign the papers, I release the brake on the pushchair and spin Maisie round to where Plum and Joe are standing.

I'm shaking my head at them. 'That has to be the craziest five minutes of my entire life.' The single leaps they were making back there were equal to my annual salary. 'My head's exploding at the thought of so many zeros.'

Plum nods. 'Totally bonkers.' She looks at Joe. 'So are you gutted?'

He pulls down the corners of his mouth then laughs. 'I'll survive. It's straight back to Rightmove for me, there are a couple of others we're interested in.'

Nell wanders over and she's shaking her head too. 'I hope Siren House is ready for the Higgie storm that's going to hit it.' She's mispronouncing on purpose.

It's hard to think of real life after the dizziness of the last few minutes. 'Are you off?'

She shakes her head. 'I'll give Sophie a hug first. She'll be doing B&B forever and a day to pay for this.'

'She will?' I'm frowning at Nell, then Charlie comes our way too and tucks in behind her.

Nell nods. 'Contemplation and serenity weekends, that's her plan, we talked it through last week. I didn't actually believe she'd have the bottle to go through with it, but good on her for holding out for what she wants.'

I can't help worrying on her behalf, but at the same time wishing I had half her guts. 'You don't think she's over stretching?'

Nell laughs. 'You and me would be out of our depth but she'll be fine. We all started out with the same amount of nothing and look where Sophie is now. She sees what she wants and she works her ass off to get it, it's a great way to be, if that's the way you're made.' She pauses for a shrug. Where the rest of us are pale with the tension of the auction, Nell's cheeks are extra rosy. 'Anyway, seeing as we're talking like property moguls, where are you at with your flat?'

I'm only too aware that, unlike Sophie who clawed her way up from zero, the flat's being handed to me on a plate and I *still* can't make it work. Also, it should be me asking Nell that question with all the work she's been putting into the schedule.

I lean and hiss in her ear. 'I actually offered the flat to Charlie and he's "getting back" to me. What kind of developer doesn't bite your hand off to get the last flat in a building?'

Instead of looking horrified like she should, Nell laughs. 'The bottom line isn't *always* the most important thing, Clems. Maybe he likes having you living next door.'

That's no kind of answer, especially from someone as figure orientated as Nell. I go back to my normal voice. 'So how's the schedule coming along? You've certainly had enough meetings.'

Nell looks up at Charlie, who's suddenly back in the conversation. 'Actually, we've got a confession to make about that.' The smile they exchange is so fully charged my stomach implodes.

'But you must have hammered out *some* figures?' I've counted ten meetings at least.

Charlie rubs his chin. 'There have been a few – er – distractions – a serious lack of concentration even.' He couldn't look more sheepish.

Nell chortles. 'I don't know why we haven't done early morning singles' events before. Breakfast's a great time to connect – at least it was for us.'

Charlie's beaming down at her. 'This could be the moment to come clean and tell them?'

Nell's smile is so light and wide she doesn't need to say anything else. All I can think is that Charlie must have been lying when he said he wasn't her penguin. The tiniest sea breeze would blow me over, but at least Nell looks radiant. If I feel like I'm about to throw up when I look at Charlie pushing the dark waves back off his forehead and smiling along with Nell, I need to get over it, and fast. I gulp back the sour spit in my mouth and rush to fling my arms around her. 'I couldn't be happier for you both, you *so* deserve this.'

Plum's laughing next to me. 'And we *truly* forgive you for taking so long over this.' She shouts across to Sophie who's turning away from the agent's table. 'What did we tell you, Soph, Charlie and Nell are an item. Whoohooo or what?'

'Hang on a second.' Charlie's putting his hand up. 'Someone's got their wires crossed here.'

Plum's frowning at him. 'What's that?'

Nell's laughing so much can hardly get the words out. 'Me and *Charlie*, that *is* hilarious. Why the hell would *we* hook up when he's completely committed elsewhere.' She breaks off, snorts into her fist then wipes a tear from the corner of her eye. 'Go on, tell them, Charlie.'

He's cracking up slightly less than Nell. 'It's not me, it's George. George and Nell are the item.' He gives me a significant sideways glance. 'They actually go back a long way. But I'm sure we'll all forgive them for waiting this long to make it official.'

The knot in my chest is unravelling as I turn to Charlie. 'So what about the dawn raids on the office?'

He gives a shamefaced grin. 'I went to the first couple of meetings then left them to it. When I wolfed your croissants at the office last week I thought you'd be sure to guess.' As he comes in close he drops his voice. 'Thanks for that inside information you passed on that morning, it made all the difference.'

As Sophie, Nate and George make their way back over we're engulfed in the scent of sticky raspberries all over again.

Sophie goes over to Charlie, and kisses him on the cheek. 'This wouldn't have been possible without you. Thank you so much, you're a total star.' For a moment, she looks as if she's going to burst into tears, and Nate puts his arm round and squeezes her.

Charlie's smile couldn't be any warmer. 'You're welcome, I'd have hated to see those mood boards go to waste.'

Nell slides her arm around George's waist and as she tilts her face upwards he comes in for a kiss. Then she beams at us. 'See, I've got my very own solicitor to snog now, I'm liking how that feels. And Mr Hobson is rivalling *me* with his matchmaking skills.'

Sophie's looking so smug, it's has to be about more than the fact she just nabbed herself a castle. 'It's a great alliance.' She sends me a wink. 'You see, Clemmie, there *is* more to love than matching shirts.'

I get the feeling Plum and I are arriving late to this party and that Charlie and Sophie have known for days. But there is one thing I need to add because George and Nell's shirt fabrics are practically identical. 'Pale grey checks, Sophie. Just saying.' As for me feeling so relieved it's George not Charlie, that makes no sense at all. If I don't up my game with the flat it's not even as if I'll be around. And as Nell just reminded us, Charlie will always be in love with his wife. If he was ever going to move on he'd have done it years ago. Stupid of me not to think of that earlier.

Nell's grinning at me. 'This isn't the end of the Singles' Club; I love all those members too much for that. We'll get straight onto those breakfast events I mentioned, Clems.'

Sophie's wagging her finger at me. 'Oh my, that reminds me, I've been collecting names for a Mums and Bumps afternoon garden party at Seaspray. There's thirty of us mums, I've said you'll do a week next Thursday?'

This is Sophie, getting carried away again. All I can think of is how often Tilly and Marcus ask to pee, and how many kids thirty mums will have in tow in the school holidays. 'That's a lovely idea, but with one bathroom up two flights of stairs how it would work?' If I was Sophie with her bulldozer business drive, I'd probably stay quiet and let them wet themselves. But however much I want to try out this market I couldn't do that and live with myself.

She's shaking her head at me. 'That's all sorted.'

'Sorted how?' However gutted I am at the lost opportunity, other than rolling in a bank of portaloos off the harbour I can't see a way around this.

Charlie's chipping in now. 'I'm opening up the ground floor

flat for the afternoon. You know Sophie, she won't take "No" for an answer. She's a damned good business woman too, it's not often I meet anyone who's good enough to teach me about negotiation.' He's folding his arms, resting his shoulder on the wall, with a very thoughtful look on his face. 'It's a great idea of Sophie's, the garden's lovely, we don't use it enough. I've sourced some bunting; you just have to choose the colours.'

Talk about done deals. 'Apple green, gold, cerise, peacock blue, please. To go with the flat.' I'm going to have to stop my heart squishing when I see that look of his.

He isn't stopping there. 'The Harbourside have some tables and chairs in their store they don't use any more, so I'll blag those too.'

There's no answer to that. 'Lovely, in that case I'll stick it in the diary and we'll talk about food over the weekend.' It'll only be a few cupcakes and who doesn't love making those.

'And while you've got the diary out ...' Charlie's still leaning. 'Save Saturday morning for me.'

I take a deep breath. 'Okay, will that be breakfast, eleven o'clock puddings, or a speculators' club lunch with tap dancing auctioneers?'

That makes him grin. 'Only you, me and Diesel. Oh, and bring your Converse.'

After the last time, that's just what I don't want to hear.

34

In Charlie's car
Close shaves and salad plates
Saturday morning

After a late night with my *Laura's Summer Puddings* evening, despite a full ten minutes out on the balcony on Saturday morning letting the sea mist seep over my face, I'm still zombified. An eight o'clock start with Charlie is too early, and the excuse of missing the traffic isn't helping my head any. After three cups of coffee, and a glass of yesterday's gooseberry fool I can open one eye. Two bowls of soft buttery sponge and fruit from the leftover apple pudding topped with cold custard do the rest. Then Diesel bounds, Charlie walks, and I stumble along to the quayside where we locate his car, which is one of those pricey jobbies that's sleek, shiny and chunky all at the same time. It's a sign of his love for Diesel that he lets him jump straight onto the leather back seat. I clamber into the front, ease myself back against the deep, cream upholstery, then squint at my skirt seams and let out a relieved sigh when I find my dress is on the right way out.

Charlie jumps in and sends me a querying glance. 'Why are you peering on the floor, have you lost something?'

I send him a grin. 'Just checking my ankle boots match.'

'Is there a chance they won't?'

I have to be honest. 'They don't always. But they do today.'

'So we're good to go?'

Considering the way the heady mix of body spray and newly showered man is making my head spin since he closed the car door, I wouldn't be that upbeat. 'As soon as I've got my music on. If you're dragging me off to some mystery destination at the crack of dawn, your penance is my playlist.'

'Let me guess. "Boum !"? Alternative eighties?'

I laugh because although we hear it most evenings, the French tunes seem like they almost belong to another life. 'No, this one's for chilling, not working. Adele, Rag'n'Bone Man, Ed Sheeran.' After three months listening to Radio 1, for the first time since I was eighteen, my playlist's from the here and now.

So, Charlie turns up the volume, and we head out of town and drive south across country for an hour. By the time we cut back to hit the coast again, the sea's so pale and shimmery I have to comment.

'That's what I'm going to miss, if I go, the way the sea changes all the time.'

He gives a sniff. 'So you're still planning to leave?'

'You know I don't plan.' I might as well remind him. Although since we're being honest with each other lately, I relent. 'But I could hear from my job in Paris any day.'

I'm crossing my fingers we'll fit in the garden party first. And I admit I'm in denial. But Maude will be back from her study leave any day and calling for her *salade* and *soupe au poisson*. I was talking to George yesterday. If I want to keep the flat, my simplest option is to go back to work for Maude then I get to keep what she's paid me. So long as I close up the flat and postpone any upgrades, if I add in a bit from my salary every week that cash would be enough to pay the service charges and Council Tax and give me a year or two of breathing space. But if I stay here and return Maude's money I'll have to run the flat and upgrade it as well as restarting the Little Cornish Kitchen in a new venue. And that's a lot more outlay than George's part time work will cover. To do all that I'd need loans and business plans. And a lot more courage than I've got.

When I think of packing, I can't bear to think of going without my penguins and my musical box and Laura's basket of recipes, so this trip I'll be traveling heavy rather than light. And however horrified I was the day it arrived I'll find it hard to leave without my mixer. As for Laura's silk bathrobe, I wear that every day. And there are so many pretty cups I've become attached to, and piles of books and photos. And my sea glass key ring with the silver star fish and Joe's sea glass heart.

Charlie's tapping his fingers on the steering wheel. 'What about the market you've built up in St Aidan this summer?'

'I'd probably put that on hold for now.' Hopefully that will put an end to it. I roll my eyes because this is all I'm hearing lately, although admittedly when Sophie, Nell and Plum say it they sound less like bank managers. 'So what are your plans? Will it be autumn at Hawthorne Farm for you?' We all know he'll be chopping Sophie's place into smaller units to sell on, but asking again takes the heat off me.

There's more of the same finger tapping. 'It's very exciting. Yesterday afternoon the planners told us they'd be open to proposals for a small number of new-build units at the farm.' He says it as cooly as if he'd said he was going to eat a cupcake.

'What?' It comes out as a shout because I don't believe what I'm hearing.

'We're working towards a development of twelve super-insulated homes with zero carbon footprint in the top field.' He's still staring straight ahead at the road, which is good in one way, but could go down as avoidance tactics. There's a smile playing around his lips. 'When we looked into it around the time Sophie bought, we got the knock back. But there's a national directive for new home building now, so fingers crossed, it'll probably get the green light.'

I can't believe he's pulled such a low-down trick. 'Have you told Sophie?'

He drags in a breath. 'She knows, and we've written it into the sale contract that if the houses go ahead they'll get extra payment.'

It comes out as a moan. 'She adored those meadows, all the bunches of flowers she brought for the parties came from there.' We all loved them especially when they were filled with bees and drifts of blue and yellow petals.

He blows out his cheeks. 'The point is, Sophie loves Siren House more. If it wasn't us, someone else would build the houses. At least this way we know they'll be done in the most sensitive way possible.'

I can't help but feel angry. Just when he seemed like he was human he wrecks it by doing this. 'So where are we going now?' I'm past playing games here.

'I'm actually taking you to one of our developments now. Hopefully then you'll see for yourself, modern buildings can add to the landscape. I personally think these ones are beautiful from the outside and to live in. But you'll have to make up your own mind on that.'

As we round the corner we come across a cluster of white boxes, clinging to the hillside and overlooking the sea. I'm biting back my agitation. 'So you got me up at stupid o'clock just so I could admire your effing houses?'

As he draws up into the wide windswept car park with views straight down to the beach he's looking at me at last, and his brow's all furrowed. 'Not entirely.'

I take in the smooth stucco walls, marigolds bending against the wind from the sea, succulents in roughhewn planters and sleeper steps winding up the gaps between the buildings. 'It's kind of Greek and Cornish all at the same time.' When his eyes are sad like this they go extra dark and have the same melting effect on me as Diesel's. The only positive in going away is that at least I won't have to look at him and lust after him any more.

'You can decide for yourself when you've been inside. We're actually here to see Laura's friend, Jenny.' It comes out in a rush.

I remember who she is. 'The tenant who used to rent the flat?'

'That's the one.' He's talking more slowly now. 'Thanks to Diesel, we got to know each other quite well over the years. Jenny loved him as a pup.'

I hadn't realised they'd known each other so long.

'When Jenny was sorting out the flat to leave, I was actually drinking tea with her when she came across the letter in the pocket of the dressing gown.'

My stomach drops. 'So you knew about that all along?'

He gives a perplexed sigh. 'Only that it was there, not what it said. The first day on the balcony I tried to point you towards it, but when you didn't pick up the lead I decided it was best to take a step back. The flat is full of things from the past. I suspect Laura wanted you to discover the truth for yourself.'

I blow with the frustration of it all. 'Her letter still doesn't tell me what happened.' The one thing that has come to light is that Joe is a few months older than me. But that makes it all the more complicated.

He sighs again. 'You were supposed to work out there was one person who could help you. If you're thinking of leaving, I wanted you to have the last piece of the puzzle so you could close the circle before you go.'

There are tears rolling down my face and I don't even know why I'm crying. 'Jenny knows?' It feels like the wall I've been bashing my head against is falling away.

He nods. 'I think she'll be able to answer your questions. Something else came up too; I hope I've made the right call on that ...' As he reaches for a tissue from the glove box and hands it to me he's searching my face with his gaze. 'If you're ready, shall we go?'

I couldn't be more ready. Except when I come to climb down from the car my legs are too wobbly to walk.

35

At Jenny's flat
Ginger nuts and clenched fists
Later on Saturday morning

Obviously, Diesel had to come too. From the way he goes leaping ahead he's been before and knows all the short cuts to a biscuit. We follow him along the narrow winding paths to a sea blue door, tucked away from the breeze at the side of a long low white house towards the end of the cluster of buildings.

When Jenny answers the door her smile and laugh are warm, although as she leads us into a light living room her limp gives away how stiff her hips are. We spend a few minutes gasping at the views across the water. They're almost better than from Seaspray Cottage because the house is set higher above the beach, and the floor to ceiling windows stretch the full width of the living area. Jenny's got her Bonio dog biscuits ready although Diesel is polite enough to give her a greeting that almost knocks her over before he starts asking for them. While the kettle's boiling, I get to admire the airy bedroom, and whistle at the super-slick bathroom with its waterfall shower, and all the storage space. And then suddenly we're sitting on the bright blue linen sofas, with mugs of tea and slabs of ginger cake, and Jenny's smiling across at me.

'So you want to know about Jill and Robbie?' Diesel's chin is on her knee and she rubs his head.

I'm pursing my lips as I nod. 'Please.' I reach into my bag and pull out the photocopy of Laura's letter that's been tucked in there since the day after the boat trip, along with one of the penguins. I didn't want to risk losing the real one, but there are times of every day when I want to get it out just so I can read it again. 'Joe gave me this note from Laura, it's so full of love, but it still doesn't tell me what happened.'

Jenny's nodding. 'Not many people know the circumstances. Laura and I go way back; I'd known Rob since he was a baby, which was why Laura confided in me.'

As I think of the photo of Laura and me from the musical box my eyes fill with tears. 'I came across a picture of me on Laura's knee. There was another of my mum and Rob on the beach the summer before I was born. Do you know about that?'

Jenny smiles. 'Originally, the flat belonged to Laura's mum and when Laura's boys were small the family used to come for holidays. When her mum died and the kids left home she moved down here full time. Robbie was a chef; he'd landed the job of his dreams in Brittany and the summer before you were born he came to stay at the flat to look after Laura's cat for a couple of weeks before he went. That was when he met your mum.'

'So they did like each other?'

She nods. 'They did. Even though they'd only had a short time together your mum and Rob were head over heels, and when he left for France they wrote to each other every day. Back then we sent letters of course.'

'So that explains the picture.' I know what comes next. 'And she got pregnant with me when he came back for Christmas ... but because of his job he didn't want anything to do with us?'

Jenny shakes her head. 'If only it had been *that* simple, things would have turned out so differently. But when Rob first heard he'd landed the job abroad he and his previous girlfriend decided they didn't want a long-distance relationship and they broke up. By the time he went to his job in Brittany, he'd met your mum and was already making plans for her to go out and join him there. He'd organised for her work at the same hotel as him. Then just as your mum was about to set off for Brittany, Rob's ex-girlfriend got in touch to say she was expecting a baby.'

It's such a shock, I'm almost winded. 'Oh, no, how awful.' I can only think what agony that must have been for my mum. So, the travelling she never got to do was literally wrenched away from her.

Jenny raises her eyebrows. 'There were a few weeks when no one knew what was going to happen. But in the end your mum was insistent that Rob should go to be with the baby.'

My heart is aching for my mum. I turn to Charlie. 'So the letter we found at the flat was my mum's goodbye to Rob. That's so sad.'

Jenny takes a breath. 'At first, Rob couldn't or wouldn't accept her decision. So, he came back just after Christmas, but he couldn't change her mind. So, Rob went back to Brittany on his own, and later his first girlfriend went there too, and Joe was born in the April.'

'So I happened that Christmas?' It's strange to think if Rob had taken her first answer and stayed away, I wouldn't be here at all.

Jenny reaches across and pats my hand. 'You were extra precious because you were all your mum had left. She kept her pregnancy very quiet, especially from Rob, it wasn't difficult with him abroad. But he was committed elsewhere, she didn't want to get in the way of that, she was determined to be independent. The first Laura knew was when she met your mum in town with you when you were a baby. With your dark red hair and you looking so like Rob, it wasn't hard for Laura to guess what had happened.'

All the air just whooshed out of my lungs. 'So Rob didn't know about me at all?'

Jenny's shaking her head. 'He had no clue about the pregnancy or the baby and that was how it stayed. The only way your mum agreed for Laura to see you was if she promised to keep it from Rob. Once she was sure Laura was going to keep her word, she was happier to accept her help. Laura loved looking after you, the two of you got on so well. I can still see you now in that kitchen with your red curls and your little apron, tracing patterns in the icing sugar with your finger, and filling the bun cases. That recipe basket of hers was a favourite, you'd spend hours playing with it.'

I manage a smile as I'm taking it all in. 'I loved those the butterfly buns.' It's such a relief to know my dad didn't just walk away.

Jenny's staring out across the bay, wiping the corners of her eyes. 'Laura always hoped that once you were older your mum would relent and let her tell Rob. But Rob had settled and two more boys had come along, and your mum didn't want to jeopardise his family. The longer time went on the firmer she was that her secret should be kept rather than told.'

My fist is clenched so tight the penguin's feet are digging into my palm. 'That's my mum all over, she thinks things through very carefully. When she decides something, she sticks to it.'

As Diesel pushes his nose into her hand, Jenny rubs his ears. 'It must have been hard for your mum, taking you to see Laura and the flat, especially with you looking so like Rob. You always knew Laura was your grandmother, but your mum was always wary of you growing old enough to ask more searching questions. That time you all went off to Oyster Point, she knew time was running out.'

I let out a long sigh for everything my mum went through for me. For all her disappointment and heartbreak. 'She cried and cried after that. I never knew why that upset her so much, but I can see now.'

Jenny's brow is furrowed. 'Soon after that, your mum met Harry and, once she had that extra support, Laura decided it was time to step back. It seemed right to let you be a family without risking any more complications. It broke her heart to leave you, but that was when she moved away.'

As I slip off my shoe and tuck one foot under me on the sofa, I have to admit it. 'When I found that first letter I was cross that my mum let me grow up thinking something other than the truth about my dad. But maybe she never knew exactly what I thought. Maybe I was the one who decided he walked out.' The mermaids and I would have been very creative imagining scenarios. Knowing the pain she went through I can forgive her for not making it clearer that he didn't know about me.

Jenny's smoothing the linen on the chair arm. 'It was such a sad situation, especially for your mum. It was so selfless the way she gave up Rob even though she loved him. Not many people would have been strong or brave enough to do that. But because of that Laura forgave her for wanting to keep you secret from Rob.'

My insides feel like cotton wool. 'Joe said Laura told them eventually.'

Jenny purses her lips. 'Your mum used to write to Laura, she had all your photos in a special album. It was only when Laura told your mum she was terminally ill your mum finally agreed Laura could tell Rob and his family about you.'

I let out a sigh. 'I must have come as a bit of a shock to them.'

Jenny raises her eyebrows. 'It can't have been easy for Rob's wife. But she'd had seventeen years of Rob being a good husband to set against it.' She smiles at me. 'Your mum was very clear; she didn't want them rushing in and upsetting you when you were in sixth form. They had to wait for you to look for them.'

'And here we are, years down the line. It's all so sad.' I grab a tissue from my bag and as I blow my nose I realise Charlie's moved along the sofa, and his arm's around my shoulders. And Diesel has left his biscuits to sit on my foot. He's leaning back on my leg, resting his head on my knee.

Charlie's eyes are scouring my face. 'Are you okay, Clemmie?'

I let out an exhausted breath. 'It's a relief to understand at last.' I turn to Jenny. 'Thank you so much for being so honest. I feel different now I know.' There are so many clichés about weights lifting, I feel so light I'm almost floating up off the sofa.

There's an undertone of worry in Jenny's smile. 'I'm pleased you've come, Laura wanted you to understand. I suspect she meant us to meet when you took over the flat, but when you didn't arrive I had to hope that Charlie would bring you to me.'

I turn on him. 'So you knew?'

He's shaking his head. 'Jenny told me Laura's was a very sad story. I hoped she'd have the answers you were looking for.'

Jenny's got her troubled frown on again. 'Laura was always so worried you'd missed out. Her second partner was older, he left her well off. By leaving you the flat at least she gave you the opportunity to reconnect with your past, if that's what you chose to do.'

'It's funny to think I almost didn't visit the flat at all. It's great to finally know that Rob didn't walk away, I just wish I'd been able to see Laura.'

Jenny leans across and pats my hand. 'It's tragic that you and Laura missed each other. Laura's dream was always to get her four grandchildren together, so she's almost managed that at last.'

Spending time at the flat has changed so many things. The ripples of guilt that I've thought about letting it go are so huge I clutch my stomach. With everything I know now, even thinking about selling the flat feels like a betrayal. I *have* to find a way to hang on to it. 'I was going to say the views at Laura's flat are amazing, but you've got those here too.'

Jenny's smile widens. 'After going to Seaspray Cottage every day, when I moved I was looking for views, and Charlie came through with the perfect place. He doesn't often shout his own praises, but there are reasons his homes *all* win awards. Every detail is covered; I couldn't have asked for anywhere better to live.'

I grin at Charlie. 'This far he's been great at hiding his talent. I'm looking forward to seeing more.'

'Talking of more ...' Charlie's leaning forward now, his elbows on his thighs. 'We thought it would be easier if Jenny explained things first. But Rob is actually in Cornwall.'

My heart feels like it's stopped beating and my throat goes dry. 'Cornwall where?'

Charlie's voice is level. 'He's been looking at places with Joe and he was coming to see Jenny today anyway. If you'd like to meet up briefly you only have to say.'

My stomach has fallen through the floor. 'I–I–I ...'

Jenny's looking anxious. 'So long as you feel the same, he'd like to see you. But this is only if you feel ready. No one wants you to rush.'

'B-b-but I haven't brushed my hair ... and this dress has a rip.' It's not that I'm looking for excuses. But if I'd known I'd at least have tried to match my lippy to my cardi.

Jenny's smiling. 'Rob really wouldn't mind, Jordan used to have dreads. If it's easier for you, we could meet him down on the beach?'

It's the sand that finally gets me. 'I always imagined if I met him it would be on a beach. With the kind of sand where the saltwater has scored ripples across the surface as the tide went out. Where there's one or two rocks sticking up, with pools of sea at the bases.'

Jenny's voice is soft. 'With a wind off the sea. That would be nice.' She turns to Charlie. 'Shall I ring and ask him to meet us down there?'

The breeze will hide my hair tangles. 'How soon can he get here?' I'm suddenly worried it could be hours. Or days.

She smiles. 'A couple of minutes.'

My eyes widen. 'That quick?'

She looks slightly guilty. 'He's only next door.'

Charlie's searching my eyes for an answer. 'If you do it now it would be done, you wouldn't have to worry.'

And somehow, in spite of my split seam, I'm nodding. Furiously.

* * * *

'No time for doubts.' I'm yelling at Charlie into the breeze, and Jenny's tussling Diesel's stick.

Charlie's yelling back. 'That's good then.' Watching the lines of concern on his face, I'm wanting to hug him for caring so much as well as for making this happen.

It's only yards to the sand and there's no time to change into my Converse. We get there first, and I'm kicking off my boots, dipping to pick them up when I see a figure hurrying through the dune grass, hands in the pockets of his jeans, the wind tearing at his shirt. There's no need to hyperventilate, it's no big deal, I'm talking myself through this, telling myself all I'm doing is meeting Joe's dad here. Even so my heart is battering against my ribs and despite the chill there's sweat coursing down my cleavage. Despite the sand, this meeting is nothing like I've imagined all the times I have. But that doesn't matter, because this time it's real.

'Clemmie?' His hair is salt and pepper grey, and his broad face is weathered and a generation older than on the picture with my mum. And from his expression as we dip in for air kisses and he pats my back briefly he's feeling as stiff and as shy as I am.

I'm brushing back my own hair and hanging onto the hem of my dress with my spare hand. 'Lovely to meet you, Rob.' It sounds way too formal. Another stranger with my eyes and ear lobes. Then

I can't help blurting: 'Hey, you've got that same little finger as Joe and me that sticks out.' The Billabong T-shirt I glimpse puts me at ease because it could belong to any of the million surfers around the coast. When I take in the same broad shoulders as Joe, it's no mystery why I'm built. I'm already panicking I've run out of things to say.

Then he comes in closer. 'I'm truly sorry I'm so late to the party.'

'It's not a problem. I'm just pleased we're both here now.' It's my turn to shrug, because we're both caught in the cliché rut.

There are crinkles at the corners of his eyes. 'You're just as pretty as your photos but in real life you sparkle more.' As he lets out a sigh his eyes are shining. 'I can't tell you how wonderful it is to see you at last.'

Sparkle I can live with. When he comes in for another hug, a longer one this time, I find myself hugging him back. 'I'm sorry too, I had no idea you were waiting. Or even wanting to see me. It's only come up since I came back to Laura's place.'

When he finally lets go of me a long time later he's smiling. 'Laura particularly wanted you to have the flat because she knew how much you'd enjoy it. After all, it was a bigger part of your history than it was for any of my lads. She knew as soon as you got back to the flat you'd start to ask the questions you never got around to when you were younger. I've been holding my breath these last few weeks since you got there.'

'Really?' It's so strange to think of it and feel it from his side.

His smile is warm now. 'I hear you're as talented as Laura in the kitchen.' From the way he glances across to Jenny and Charlie, they've been filling him in. 'Laura was so good at baking, although she never bothered too much with savouries. She'd be so happy to know you're getting so much out of the flat.'

I'm pursing my lips, swallowing back my tears. There's a dull ache in my chest. 'I'm so sad not to have spent more time with her. I can see she gave me so much when I was small, and the last few weeks it's been amazing getting to know her again.'

He nods. 'Laura was lovely. But most of all she'd be ecstatic to know her plan to bring us together has finally come off.' He laughs. 'For me it was a bit like Sliding Doors.'

I can see exactly what he means by that. 'There were two lives and we ended up in different ones?'

He pulls a face. 'It took me the best part of twenty years to find out there were two, and I waited another ten to cross the gap. I appreciate why your mum wanted to keep them separate, it was a lot simpler that way. But I'm very happy we've collided at last.'

I'm clinging onto my hair in the wind. 'Me too.' That's a good way of putting it.

Jenny's beaming at us. 'If you'd like to drink to that with tea back at the house, I've made some of Laura's special toffee crispie.'

'You have?' Rob and I both turn together.

I'm thinking of the recipe cards. 'With the marshmallows in?' Another of my childhood favourites.

Jenny nods. 'That's the one. It must be fifty years since she gave me that recipe, it seemed like the right choice for today.'

Rob's smiling. 'I always licked out the saucepan for that.'

'Me too.' My mouth is watering as I recall the taste. There was nothing quite like that sticky sweetness. Colliding is a good way to put it. Even though he's a stranger, we've got Laura in common and now I'm feeling less tongue-tied there's so much to talk about. Like all Laura's recipes. It'll be a dead cert he likes lemon meringue pie too.

Charlie's eyes are lighting up at the thought of toffee crispie. 'And then after we've had a drink, maybe we could go out for a pub lunch?'

We're all nodding at him madly, relieved that Charlie's got this.

'There's a great place a couple of miles away called the Pack Horse Inn. I booked a table, just in case.'

As Diesel pushes his stick into my hand, I pause for a second to throw it up the beach. Even meetings with long lost family have to stop for dogs with sticks. And as we wander back up towards the house, we're all chatting like we've known each other for years not minutes, and once again I couldn't be more grateful to have Charlie with me. Today is all down to him. How do you say thank you to someone who not only sets up something this huge, but also smooths it through?

As for meeting Rob, five minutes after bumping into him on the beach this morning, I'd find it hard to pinpoint what it felt like when I didn't know him. It has to be the family similarities. It's as if me knowing Laura already paved the way for Rob. Laura's brought me to Joe and Rob, and I'm hoping that Joe and Rob will take me back to Laura too.

Sometimes events are so huge there are no words, and this is one of them. However much I see Rob in the future I'll always look back on that last hour we spent together as the time when the tilt of my whole world shifted – very gently, to a better place. There weren't any thunderclaps or even any sobbing. In the end, there was nothing momentous or earth shattering about what is, after all, simply right. It's crazy to think something so easy and natural could have caused so much worry and fracture across so many different lives for so long. As we walk back up the beach and across the gravel to the house, to anyone watching we'd look like any other family hurrying off a windy beach, heading for a hot mug of tea.

36

On the beach
Puddles on the sand
Saturday afternoon

'So this is the part where you get to wear your Converse again.' It's late afternoon and Charlie's pulled in by a quiet beach along the coast and he's dipped into the back of the car for my shoes. As he dangles them off his finger Diesel's dashing around barking.

'Are we walking?' I kick off my boots and bob down to tie the shimmery pink laces.

'After being well behaved for so long, Diesel's got a lot of energy to run off. A blast along the beach might be a good for all of us.'

As I look up at Charlie, I don't know where to start to tell him how much I owe him for today. 'I'm still floating, a walk will be a great way to come back down to earth.' There are alternating happy tingles and shock waves rippling through me and in my head I'm writing the email to tell Mum. And even though we've dropped Jenny off at home and said goodbye to Rob for a couple of weeks at least, the day's still got a special glow about it.

Just before we left, Jenny held Charlie's hand and told him how pleased she was he was looking so well, and how proud he should be of everything he's achieved. Then she took me to one side very discretely to suggest I could help Charlie. At first I was taken aback, but when I stopped to think about it I realise she's right. As we wind down the muddy hillocks onto the sand, Charlie picks up a piece of driftwood and flings it along the beach for Diesel.

I have to tread carefully here. 'Jenny's so grateful to you for her house. It must be amazing to touch people's lives with your building.'

His sigh is dismissive. 'It's only what I do.'

So far today's been all about me, but now it's his turn. 'You can't shrug it off, those houses are amazing. But I could tell Jenny was worried that you push yourself too much.'

His laugh is dismissive. 'I don't work that hard, you didn't even realise I had a job.' He lets out a long breath. 'I have to do it for Faye. It's the only way I can halfway live with my guilt for her not being here.' And that's the problem.

Our hips are level, but I'm jogging to keep up with his long strides. 'If your other schemes are anything like this one, it seems like you've created the most amazing legacy to her.'

As he sniffs there are lines on his face. 'That's been my only purpose, along with caring for Diesel. If I've achieved that my time hasn't been wasted.'

My heart is aching to see him so raw. 'I don't know anything about grief, but I'd guess if Faye loved you enough to sign up for a lifetime with you, she'd want you to be happy now.'

He has that faraway look in his eye. 'You're right, she was very selfless.'

It's hard to know how to put this. 'Have you thought that maybe now Faye would want you to put a little bit of effort into yourself as well as the building? Maybe you owe it to *her* to give yourself a break, because she'd want you to live again.'

He's frowning at me now. 'Okay, Clems, so what are you saying?'

'When I first arrived you always looked so, so sad.'

He sighs. 'For years that's how I've felt.'

'But ...' I have to encourage him here. 'Since you've been forced into seeing people more, you've actually cracked the odd smile. It's a bit like Rob and his Sliding Doors. You can stay locked away and dedicate your life to someone who isn't here any more. Or you could make the leap and let yourself back to a place where there are other people too. After nine years it isn't wrong for you to allow yourself to be happy.'

His lips are twitching as he looks down at me. 'When people tip meringue over their hair and borrow your metal detector because they've lost diamond rings in buttercream, I agree it's harder to dwell on the sad stuff. If you've got any suggestions, I'll give them a try.'

With Maude due back I'm not looking too far ahead. 'How about your own personal tour of the fun places in St Aidan to pay you back for today?' It'll be less daunting for him than a wild night with the Singles' Club, but at least then he'll know where to find a good time when he's ready.

That's made his lips curve. 'So will that count as my "journey back to Happy Land" first date then?'

That sends my stomach into a nose dive. 'It might be more like tourist information.' However much I want to help, I can't cope with thinking of it as a date.

He's straight back at me. 'Is Tuesday good for you?'

I nod. 'So long as I'm still here.' It's the truth, but to hide how much it aches when I think about it I make it sound jokey.

'About your plans ...' He's frowning again. 'Rob being here today was a stroke of luck, I took a risk on that, and I hope it helped. It's bad to leave things like that hanging.'

I have to point it out. 'I managed fine for the last thirty years.'

He doesn't reply straight away. 'Or so you think. But if someone leaves, the people left behind often feel it's their fault for not being good enough. They often end up not trying, if good stuff happens they throw it away because they feel like they don't deserve it.'

'And you think that's me?'

He shrugs. 'Maybe you've felt like that in the past because you assumed Rob left.' He loops his thumbs through the belt loops of his jeans. 'You do deserve good things, Clems. You talk about me, but I can't think of anyone who deserves good things more than you.'

I'm staring down at the sand clumps on my glittery toes, facing up to the truth. 'Of all of us mermaids, I'm the one who's achieved the least.' It has to be said.

Charlie's shaking his head. 'You've achieved different things, you put your energy into travelling. They've only got more material things because they stayed in one place.'

The pace has slowed and our hips are almost bumping. 'They all have more drive than me, they've always tried harder.'

He's staring down at me like he's peering into my brain. 'But mainly it's because they settled when you didn't. What was it that kept you moving on?'

It takes a while staring at the place where the sea merges into the sky, to think that through. 'There was always this tiny thought in the darkest part at the back of my mind, that maybe the next place would be the place I'd bump into the dad I didn't know. I absolutely never wanted to look for him, but maybe I was hanging onto this fantasy that if I went to enough places, one day we'd accidentally coincide.' Walking along the beach now, I know. 'I've never talked about it before, I'm not sure I was even conscious of it.' Maybe now I've met him, saying this out loud is like breaking the spell, setting myself free.

Charlie's raking his fingers though his wind-swept hair. 'Of all your friends you're the free spirit, none of us want to stop you flying, but this could be the right time for you to stay. Now you've met Rob you should find it easier.'

There's a sudden flash in my brain and I turn on him. '*That's* why you brought him here?'

Charlie's shaking his head, and his eyes are as sad as Diesel's again. 'Not only that, I hoped it would help in other ways too.'

As my agitation subsides I know it's time to explain. 'I've had a talk with George, about my best way forward.'

His voice rises. 'Shit, Clems, why the hell did you turn to George of all people?'

I hide my shock under a shrug. 'He's super professional, and he's dealt with the flat for years.' Not that I should need to justify it. 'He was very helpful.' I'd say we explored every option.

Charlie's face is like a storm cloud. 'Jeez, Nell, Plum, me and Sophie are bursting with strategies and working our butts off to sort things out for you, and you turn to the most cautious man in St Aidan?'

I'm pursing my lips. 'We talked through my priorities and found the most appropriate solution.'

Charlie's eye roll is higher than the breakers crashing along the bay. 'That sounds about right. And what did you decide?' He's spitting out the words.

I drag in a breath and try to sound decided and in control. 'What I want most is to keep the flat, and going back to Paris will let me do that.'

His frown is disbelieving. 'But what about the Little Cornish Kitchen and staying in St Aidan to see Joe and Rob?'

I'm going to back pedal here. 'Mostly it's about the cash flow, Paris makes it work that's all. Nothing's set in stone, my tickets haven't come through yet. But George understands I'm not a powerful capable business person like you. I've lived out of a backpack for the last few years, the flat is enough to start with. Even that feels like I'm a mermaid coming to live on the shore. I'm sorry if I've gone back on my offer to you.'

Charlie dismisses that with a head shake. 'You lecture me about letting myself be happy, then think about clearing off to live with Misery Maude? You love cooking and your Little Cornish Kitchen. Truly, you're choosing the wrong side of the sliding doors here.'

My voice turns to a wail. 'My St Aidan wish list is so long, if I try for all of it I could end up failing at everything. This way at least I keep the flat safe.'

His gives a snort. 'That's total bollocks. Life is about taking risks.'

'That's fine for you to say. I'm not that brave.'

He stops and spins me around to face him. 'We can re-think this, there could be better options coming along. There's so much love for you here, you *can't* go away again, Clems.'

'Love?' For a fleeting second I feel like I've found the explanation for my somersaulting insides. The ache in my chest is about so much more than lust. Then I look up at the base of his neck, and the shadow of stubble on his jaw and my tummy tumbles all over again. I catch my breath and stare up at his teeth cutting into his lip and my heart is banging. As he stares down at me it's as if the world has stopped.

I'm holding my breath, closing my eyes, parting my lips, almost ready for the kiss, when Nell's words ring in my ears. *He's completely committed elsewhere* ... Damn. He's not talking about *his* love; he's talking about Laura's and the girls'. How could I have misjudged this so badly? *He's* always going to love Faye, he just told me as much. Which is exactly understandable and how it should be.

I swallow and take a leap backwards. 'True love is about letting go, the girls know that.' I drag in a breath and try to avoid his eye. 'They'll understand if I go, they always do.' There's one sure way out of here to save face and a second later for the first time in years my feet are running.

As I hare back off along the beach and snatch a glance over

my shoulder, he's still standing staring at the space I was in. I've got at least a fifty-yard start. 'Race you back to the car!'

By the time my hands hit the silky metal of the car boot my throat is burning and my chest is exploding. I'm kicking myself, and not just for my mistake back there. How the hell could I have been careless enough to fall in love? As I catch a glimpse of the pink toes glistening on the gravel I add my Converse to my mental 'can't leave behind' list.

When Maude's email drops in my inbox, I'm going to need an enormous bag.

37

Out in St Aidan
Definitely not a date night – strawberries and other queries
Tuesday evening

It's eight and as I turn into the mews and hurry towards the Hungry Shark to meet up with Charlie, it's official – I'm on my way back to Paris. Maude sent my flight number this morning, and I pushed a few things into a rucksack this afternoon. Then while I ate a hasty dinner of jam doughnuts, Plum printed out my ticket and she's insisting on driving me to the airport first thing tomorrow. Nell and Sophie know how much I hate goodbyes, so they're popping in for a speed hug before work and have promised to clear the fridge later. Now it's all happened so fast, I can't imagine how I ever hoped I'd still be around for Sophie's Mum's and Bumps Garden Party. That's still ten days away and has now been downsized to a picnic, and the Singles will have to live without Laura's Coconut Heaven and the Meringue Revisited nights we'd lightly pencilled in for later this week. Even though I've been expecting this, now it's real my chest is aching. All that's left now is to break the news to Charlie. But as tonight is supposed to be about fun I'll leave that until the very end.

'Charlie!' As I catch his eye over a hundred salty surfer heads and push my way into the bar, I'm trying to pull the creases out of the vintage dress I grabbed this afternoon from Cats' Protection. I know orange is a risk against my hair, but the fabric is wonderfully swishy, and when I'm far away the tiny stars on the print will remind me of the sky and the beach at Seaspray Cottage.

'Nice dress.' He raises his eyebrows as I wriggle in next to his elbow. 'If you'd prefer dinner up at the Harbourside, they'll always make room for us on the terrace?'

I ignore how much my head is spinning as his scent wafts up my nose. 'No, Hobson, tonight's about showing you *new* places. Picking the default setting in your comfort zone central isn't going to help.'

There's a flash of amusement around his lips. 'If you say so.'

I'm trying to sound as knowledgeable as Nell did when she rattled off the itinerary for me. 'The Hungry Shark is famous for their local bottled ciders, and they do fab warm apple punch in the winter.'

He's holding back that smile again. 'Great, I'll bear that in mind for December. Would you like a drink before then?'

I'm killing this. 'It's fine, I'll get these, my treat, what would you like, the Kopparberg is nice, or the Rekorderlig?'

'Whatever you're having.'

I catch the eye of the guy behind the bar. 'Two mango and raspberry ciders, please.' When the bottles arrive, they're frosted with condensation and the liquid is icy sweet as it hits my throat. 'We used to drink here a lot in the Sixth Form because they never bothered with ID's. Do you want a glass?' I take in Charlie's head shake and hope he doesn't guess I haven't been in here since. As I take a swig he's looking at his label. 'Everything okay?'

'Great, so where exactly is this Cornish Rekorderlig brewery?'

I'm not sure Nell went into that much detail. 'Over near Truro?'

There are crinkles at the corners of his eyes. 'Would that be Truro in Sweden, then?'

I'm staring at my own bottle and kicking myself for the gaffe. 'Shit, that's not very local, is it? I do have other better, less flawed gems to pass on.'

He's almost laughing now. 'Such as?'

I'm racking my brain, using the time to check the size of the palpitations as I focus on his tanned wrists and the open neck of his soft faded polo shirt. 'Avoid the quinoa and kale at the Yellow Canary, it's truly gross.' Despite my off the scale heart problems, I have to do better than that. 'And Jaggers cocktail bar does great offers. Sex on the Beach is two for one, day and night, three six five. And this week any cocktail with strawberry is half price so long as you buy the biggest jug. The hangovers are truly awful though.' Even years on from when I last drank there I can personally vouch for that.

Charlie's shaking his head. 'Said with feeling. I'm noting all this down, Clems. So how does Jaggers compare to the Harbourside?'

It's amusing that he's only got one benchmark, but this one I know. Jaggers punters are eighteen rather than eighty, they're way more dedicated to mass drinking, the chairs are purple and red perspex. And there are dedicated chill out areas; the Harbourside probably doesn't even know what they are. We'll be going there last because it's at sea level. Is that useful?'

He nods. 'Totally. Can't wait to visit. But don't stress, I'm already having the best time. So, where's next?'

I'm squinting at the screwed-up cheat sheet I've pulled from my dress pocket. 'Definitely not the Crab and Pilchard. That's where I collided with the gravy urn back in the day.'

When he lets out that low laugh there are slices down his cheeks. But way worse is when he tips back his head to swig from his bottle, and I watch his throat contracting.

I take a deep breath. 'So I thought we could do the Hub, the Balcony Bar, Hot Jacks, the Ship and the Jolly Sailor, then move on down to the Beach Hut and Jaggers via the Smugglers'. I'm leaning strongly on Nell's singles' pub crawl, with a couple of extras thrown in. So long as we keep moving and drinking, I'll stay focused on the job.

He's more engaged with this than I'd expected. 'I don't mean to sound like a light weight, but it's a shame to use up all the pubs in one go. We could do this again later in the week. Showing me the sights could be your project.'

As if there weren't a thousand and four reasons for me not to leave already, here comes number a thousand and five. 'That might be difficult.'

He's grinning like he's got me. 'You can't cook *all* the time. With your new rules on finding happy places I expected we'd be out in town every other night at least?'

I refuse to spoil the evening by thinking about tomorrow, so I grin back. 'We're training you up to be independent here. At least we could walk through the bars then you know what they're like.' My fallback coping mechanism here is blocking out the reality of what's careering towards me at a million miles a second. If I actually considered how much I'm going to miss Sophie and Milla and Maisie and Nell and George and Plum, I'd scream. And that's before I even get on to thinking what it's going to be like not to have Charlie and Diesel popping their heads in every ten minutes. I've come far enough this summer to know I'd like the grown-up stuff, but I haven't quite made it all the way. George and I both know if I had I wouldn't be going. I'd still rather choose the easy way out than stay here and tough it out to get the goodies. To do that I'd have to be another, better, stronger person. As it is, I have to live with the limitations of who I am.

Charlie looks at his watch. 'How about you speed talk me down the hill, then when we get to Jaggers we'll bag a chill-out space and drink ourselves under those on-trend perspex tables.'

He's catching on fast but I'm not giving in that easily. 'Fine, so long as we pull in a late night hot chocolate at the Surf Shack on the way home.'

He's already leading the way towards the door, forcing a path through the crowd of surfers and their board piles. 'I thought we were sleeping under tables not going home? You won't have great times if you don't put *all* the effort in, I thought you'd know that.'

He's joking here, but for a second I'm letting myself wake up on the deck at Jaggers, sand drifts in my hair, curled up against the heat of his body. Even the sensation of an axe-in-the-skull hangover head doesn't take away the thrill. That's how badly I've got this. And as if to underline the problem, accidentally rubbing elbows as we dodge the crowds of summer holiday makers along the High Street is sending crazy tingles through my torso.

I'm not under any illusions. I'll miss everyone here like crazy, because I'll be one person in a city of strangers, missing a whole bunch of people. But when I leave, I'll be one tiny person gone from this buzzing place. The water will close over the space I was in, and there won't be a trace. The strangest thing is that I'm going back to a place I once loved so much I didn't want to leave it. Those few short months ago when I first arrived here I'd have swapped St Aidan for Paris in a heartbeat. Remembering that is what's getting me through. The minute I've done it, going back again should be a-okay. Really, why wouldn't it be?

At some point, I must have inadvertently let Charlie take the lead. You know what guys are like once they set their minds on a mission. Before I can say Swedish cider, we've been in and out of every bar on my crumpled paper, had a few proper local ciders along the way, stampeded down the cobbles to the sea front and grabbed ourselves a velvet sofa in an alcove at Jaggers. Halfway down our second giant pitcher of strawberry daiquiri I decide there's no point in holding back and swap my teensy cocktail glass for something bigger.

I wave my full jam jar at Charlie, then I chug my way to the bottom. 'This is pretty much like drinking strawberry smoothies, I might as well try for my five a day.'

He's laughing more easily now. Or maybe that's me. 'Go for it. So long as you don't have anywhere to be tomorrow.'

'Nowhere important.' It's barely eleven. I'll think about the flight later.

He eases back against the plush lilac cushions. 'We'll come here next time, it's very civilised.'

Of all the surprises, Charlie embracing Jaggers is unexpected. I stare across the empty bar. 'I'm not sure where everyone is, it's usually busier.' Like my Sardine evenings, times a hundred and then some. Then as if on cue, a crowd surges in.

As Charlie tips the last drips from the jug into my jar, he's yelling in my ear over the noise. 'What happened there, a pitch invasion? Shall we drink up and head home along the beach.'

I throw down the last syrupy mouthful, follow him out of the bar and down onto the sand, dragging my feet, not wanting the evening to end. Then I kick off my ankle boots, loop them over my fingers and try to take mental screenshots of the soft cool sand trickling over my toes as I walk. The inky glitter of the water. The muted splash as the frill of the tide rushes up the beach towards us.

His voice is soft in the shadows beside me. 'It's cloudy tonight, there are more stars on your dress than in the sky.'

I'm trying not to remember that everything I do and see here is for the last time. As we come to a standstill and stare up at the dark clouds moving across the crescent of the moon I can sense the heat of his body radiating to mine. That last-night snog I fantasised about weeks ago has never been far from my mind, and it's there again now. But however much I'm aching to touch him the woman who would grab what she wants on impulse is the same one who'd be staying. Whereas the real me wraps my hands around my chest instead, and shivers. In any case, I can't shake off the feeling it's best to save it for a long way down the line.

'Are you cold?' Charlie's voice is low, but he doesn't wait for an answer. He simply steps in front of me, and the next minute he wraps his arms around me and all the air whooshes out of my lungs. His body is hard against mine, and I'm staring up at the planes of his face in the darkness. And then out of nowhere, his fingers are clasping my hair, his face is coming towards mine. As I open my lips, close my eyes, and drop my shoes, I've done this a thousand times before already in my head. Except the heat and the strength of his body is so different from anything I'd imagined and this time my head's spinning and I'm seeing stars even if they aren't there. Even though I know I should push him away, my hand slides up his cheek and around his head, and I'm pulling him towards me. When his mouth collides with mine, his kiss is deep and velvety and delicious. It's like swirling salt caramel and chocolate strawberries that goes on forever and makes my whole body thrum. And when he finally breaks away, I'm left clutching my lips, staggering backwards.

He brushes my hair off my cheek. 'Okay, Clems?'

I'm still dizzy. 'Yes ... I'm really sorry, I didn't mean to ...'

'Didn't mean to what?' He lets out a low laugh. 'There *were* two of us involved there.'

It's like the kiss has acted like a truth drug. 'You see, you're actually on my Wish List ...'

That amuses him more. 'I'm pleased to hear it. I'd put you on mine – if I had one.'

I'm shaking my head. 'But I never meant to grab you now, I promised I'd save you for the very last night when I was definitively never coming back, in the world ever. Not the night before I went away for a while when I did want to come back at some point.' Out loud it sounds a lot more incoherent than it did in my head. When people say 'never apologise, never explain', this is why.

He's still laughing. 'Why, who's going away? I thought we'd cleared that up – you knocked it on the head on Saturday.'

Even though I'm still leaning my hands on the heat of his

chest, my body goes cold. My throat's so dry my voice is a croak. 'Actually *I* am. Tomorrow.'

His body goes rigid. As he takes a step backwards he's holding me at arm's length, staring down at me.

'And you're casually mentioning this NOW? Were you even going to tell me, or were you simply planning to *vanish*?'

My insides are shrivelling and my voice has shrunk to a squeak. 'I didn't want to spoil the evening.'

'Well congratulations, you did a great job there. Where are you going?' He doesn't give me time to reply, and his voice hardens. 'Don't tell me, it's Paris, isn't it?'

I nod.

'So what the hell happened to talking through the options before you decided, like we agreed?' His hand is shaking on my shoulder. 'There are so many viable alternatives, if only you'd asked first.'

I'm keeping my voice level. 'Believe me, it's the only way that works for me. Otherwise I have to pay Maude back ... and get loans .... and it's all ... just too complicated ...' My words tail off and even though I clear my throat I still sound as defeated as I am. 'The truth is, I'm not brave enough for anything else.'

His hands drop and he lets out a snort. 'No, Clems, this is you ducking out, you're pressing the self-destruct button, yet again. Despite everyone believing in you and wanting to help you, you don't give enough of a damn to even try. You couldn't be surrounded by any more love and support. If you truly cared about *any* of this, and *any* of us, you'd stay and fight and make the Little Cornish Kitchen work.'

'I – I – I ...'

As he takes another step back his voice is like cold steel. ‘Don’t say anything more, you couldn’t be more clear. I’m sorry I read this so wrong. Now please let’s go home.’

He strides ahead and I stumble along the beach edge three yards behind him, swallowing back the sour saliva and cursing myself for messing up so spectacularly.

When we reach the top of the stairs back at Seaspray Cottage he pauses for a second by his door. ‘Have a great time, I hope Paris gives you everything we can’t.’ From the way he spits out the words, he means anything but that. And as I hear the scrabble of Diesel’s feet on the floorboards I catch one last glimpse of his face. Seeing his expression more tortured and angry and hurt than I’ve ever seen I feel like there’s a knife twisting in my chest.

Then I make a dash to my bathroom and wretch up two jugs of sickly strawberry cocktail into the toilet.

And that was my last night in St Aidan.

38

Paris
Balconies and chin rests
Tuesday, a week later

When I get back to my little room in Paris, the traffic's so much louder than when I was last here. I was counting on the twinkling outline of the Eiffel Tower at night to plug the gaping hole left by the view of the stars over the bay with the lights of random fishing boats bobbing far out at sea. But somehow it doesn't. Not straight away. Although the biggest hole of all is somewhere between my chest and my stomach and eating doesn't make that one go away. However many patisserie windows I look in, I'm not even tempted. All I want to do is curl up in bed with my head under the covers. But without Pancake's firm furry back to rest my chin on, without her purr blowing in my ear, and without the overlay of the breakers thrashing on the sand, my brain won't switch off. So, for the first few nights instead of sleeping, I lie with my eyes open and my heart aching.

I don't get the luxury of missing everything from St Aidan.

Before I get out of Charles de Gaulle airport, Sophie's emails are pinging in. Since she signed for Siren House she's been super-busy transforming her visualisations into orders, and she's running every one past me so I don't feel left out. She's asking what I think of artisan solid wood Swedish media units and Broste Copenhagen toilet brushes – yes, really. Basically, she spends every waking second *and* most of the time she should be sleeping scrolling through Scandi websites. The amount she's spending you'd think she'd bought a county not just a teensy castle.

Much sweeter, Milla's messaging for advice on colours for her new room. The Pinterest board she's made is vibrant and most of the pictures could have come straight out of Laura's flat. When Sophie finds out she doesn't want a million shades of white, I'll hear the howl from here. Meanwhile, Plum's Facebook messaging me, asking what Joe's up to, Joe's Facebook messaging, telling me what Plum's up to. Nell's Twitter messaging the goss about the latest singles' hook-ups in between tax returns, and for every cup of Liptons I make for Maude, I'm getting a selfie of Nell and George with their checked shirts running into each other. And George is texting to ask where I've put the sugar. So as far as the St Aidan crew are concerned, they're acting like I haven't left. All except for Charlie of course. I saw so much of him before, but now there's nothing. Which given what happened isn't surprising, but it still makes the chasm in my insides get huger by the day not smaller.

In other areas life moves on. Maude is adding honey to her vinaigrette, she's dumped artichokes and moved onto blanched chicory and she's added tuna steak to her favourites list so I'm visiting the fish and oyster caravan every day. But hurrying home from the market with a bag smelling like the quayside in St Aidan only makes me feel more homesick.

The mermaids must know I'm struggling because they're sending mini parcels. Every day there's one of Plum's tiny seascapes and something else too. There was a postcard wrapped in tissue with a picture of the bay saying *I've forgotten all about work in St Aidan* in blue splashy letters over the photo. Then there was a cockle shell, with sand from the beach still clinging to it. A starfish wrapped in a strand of seaweed. On Saturday, a strawberry tart in an individual Crusty Cobs box arrived in a million pieces but was the first food I've properly tasted since I got back. Then there was a tiny tin of Gourmet Kitty potted shrimps and pearl barley, which I didn't eat but which made me laugh.

It's a good thing there's so much interaction with St Aidan to distract me. After working for George and fitting in the singles' nights what I have to do here for Maude seems insignificant. I can see why the mermaids were dismissive when I once called it a career. I did try a batch of mini cupcakes to liven things up, but Maude simply pulled a face and asked for one of her individually wrapped apricot sponges instead. It took a double Porn Star Martini to get her over the shock.

Then on Tuesday, a week after I arrive, just when things should be getting better, my morning goes every kind of bad. First of all, the postman comes but there's no parcel. I know the seascapes couldn't go on forever, and they were only ever about settling me in, but for some reason when there isn't one I'm so gutted I could cry. Which isn't helped when Maude gets all pre-menstrual about her Liptons not being strong enough, when it's exactly the same it has been for months. Then I go to the fish stall and they give me a double load for being a loyal customer. Which in fairness I am. But it still means that by the time I call in for my usual coffee at the cafe, the smell of the sea floating up from under the table and is doubly evocative and makes me weepy. Then before my coffee arrives, an email from Sophie drops in my inbox with pictures of the serviettes and rugs she's bought for Thursday's picnic at Seaspray Cottage. Any of those on their own, even all of those together, I'd have coped. But a second email comes. All it says is *Wish you were here*, *Clemmie Orangina* but, when I scroll down to the photo of Milla's rainbow birthday cupcakes, I can't hold back the tears.

Mostly they remind me how much I miss Charlie. But once I manage to shut that out, when I think of everyone in the garden at the cottage, I know I have to be there too. Even though I can see the top of the Eiffel Tower in the distance from my tiny table on the pavement here, deep down I know that staying another week or another month isn't going to change how I feel. Back in April, Paris was the only place in the world I wanted to be. Now it's August there are still things here I love but there's somewhere else I'd rather be. I can sit here and be miserable, or I can take control and go and do what makes me happy. An email to George is a good place to start.

As soon as I've quashed my sobs and blown my nose I begin to I tap it out:

Hi George,

Paris isn't quite as fab as I remembered, so I'm looking at those options again ...

However professional I'm trying to sound, I can't bring myself to say re-visit.

If it's not too much trouble, please could you ring your bestie at the bank and grab me an appointment to talk about loans…

Paying back Maude is just the start. I'll have to borrow more once I get a business plan. I have to stop and fan my face when I think about that. But what's that old saying, 'You can't make an omelette ...'?

Which reminds me to break off to text Nell.

Coming home tomorrow to bake for the garden party, please can you bring me eggs xx

She texts straight back:

Will do. Good woman. Bring on Laura's School Dinner Nostalgia nights!!! x

Then I go back to George:

... and could you possibly ask your insider contact at the estate agents if there are any teensy properties suitable for a 'pop up' kitchen that aren't up on Rightmove ...

I'll be looking for a beach hut rather than a restaurant, but if I'm serious – and I am, even if the word does make me go rigid – I need to look under every proverbial stone on the proverbial beach

... and please, please, please can I have my job back?

Obviously, I save the biggest one for the end.

Big love, Clemmie x

I add a kiss for mermaid luck. Then I give a silent 'eeeek', press 'send' and collapse back against my chair. I've done it. It's symbolic. I've crossed the line from being a person who takes the easy way out. And I'm one email closer to being a person who takes responsibility for shaping my own destiny and is fully prepared to deal with whatever shit that entails. In that one hugely long sentence I accept that maybe life won't ever be simple again. But at least I'll be working my butt off to be where I want to be, doing what I want, with the people I love.

Then I email Sophie and tell her I'll be back to bake for Thursday and please will she send me some menu suggestions. I'm on the FlyBE website booking a flight when my coffee arrives. Then the post van squeals to a halt by the kerb and the postman winds down his window and throws a parcel onto the table along with a long explanation that is possibly about it getting lost in his footwell.

By the time I've got a seat confirmed on the plane tomorrow teatime, I've opened another teensy seascape, and a tiny piece of drift wood plank, with some painted words on ...

Life takes you to unexpected places, love brings you home

Which makes me go all teary all over again.

If the postman had delivered that in the first place … I'd still be doing exactly what I'm doing. So, seeing I'm on a roll here, I ring Plum and ask her if she can pick me up from the airport. She says *Yes, great, thank jeez you're coming home, woohooo*. Then I say, *Less of the wooohooooos, I'm on fifty pence a minute here, oh and thanks for all the seascapes, they really helped*. And she says, *Seascapes? What seascapes?* She sees so many I don't blame her for getting confused. So, I say, *Never mind, we'll sort it tomorrow, I can't wait. And can we please stop off at Waitrose on the way back?*

At which point the waiter comes over, and I order a huge hot chocolate and a ham salad baguette, because facing Maude is going to take a massive protein boost. One minute I'm licking breadcrumbs off my finger, writing lists of Little Cornish Kitchen school puddings down on my serviette. The next there's a scramble of paws, a strangled bark, and a cold wet, black nose is pushing into my ear. Then my sandwich whooshes of my plate and hits the pavement. A second later it's gone. There's only one dog I know who's as fast as that at swiping sandwiches. But he should be in …

'Diesel?' I'm still looking down at the pavement, so it's the deck shoes I see first. Then the soft faded jeans and that flash of tanned torso between the low-slung belt and the polo shirt. 'And Charlie?' I'm shaking and dizzy but I manage a croak. 'What are you two doing here? Apart from stealing baguettes.'

Charlie pulls up a chair and Diesel curls up in the teensy space between the table and the café window. 'We're here on a flying visit, the ferries were doing special summer offers.'

'Really?' I'm blinking in disbelief because August is peak time.

Charlie pulls down the corners of his mouth. 'No, actually that's not true at all, it cost an arm and a leg to get on the tunnel.

We hated it so much without you we had to come. But most of all I want to say sorry.'

I let out a sigh. 'I should be the one apologising, you were right, I should have told you earlier.' Funny how I thought I'd never face him after a kiss, and yet as I stare at his lips it's hard to believe it ever happened at all.

He shakes his head. 'I should have respected your choices. I was only angry because I was so desperate for you to stay. Especially after the beach.' His forehead crinkles. 'You do remember the bit before the shouting?'

So, I didn't get away with it. 'When I jumped you?'

'If that's how you like to remember it, it didn't feel like that to me.' He's almost smiling. 'You might not realise, but that very first day you yanked me and Diesel in off that balcony everything changed for me. It was as if I'd been living life in black and white for years and suddenly you turned the colour back on. I've come to tell you that too.'

I let out a breath. 'That's such a lovely thing to say.'

He's leaning towards me, his lovely face lined with tension. 'You're not like anybody I've ever known before, Clems. You're quirky and feisty and funny and unique and beautiful and you amaze me every single minute that I'm with you. That's why I've been trying so hard to make things work in St Aidan, I had no idea you'd disappear so fast.'

I can't help remembering what Nell said, and I have to clear this up before I get my hopes up. 'I know we were trying to get you to have fun, but are you really ready for someone else?'

His face softens. 'That's the funny thing. When you lose someone you love, eventually the people who care about you tell you it's okay to move on. Even you were saying that's what Faye would have wanted me to do. But it's hard to fall in love to order. Then when you do it's harder still, especially when you're still carrying the guilt.'

'My poor, poor, Hobson.' My heart is twisting at the thought of the pain he's been through.

He shrugs. 'I'd written myself off. But when I saw you and all your mermaid hair at Sophie's launch it was like a thunderbolt hitting my world. And after that I couldn't stay away.'

I want to take him in my arms and rock him and never let go. 'I did notice you came round a lot.'

He's shaking his head. 'I'd try not to, then I'd find myself walking along the balcony. Baking was the perfect excuse to hang out with you so you got something out of it too. At first I was wracked with guilt for even thinking about it.' As he closes his eyes for a second his lashes are soft and sooty. 'When I baked with Cressy the first time around, I was hurting so much. Doing it all over again with you made me see how far I'd come. But somehow doing it with you was the final step in putting me back together again. At the start, I didn't trust the thunderbolt was real, but by the end I knew for certain. I had fallen in love with you that first day, but every day I love you more.'

I swallow back tears stuck in my throat. 'I pour egg white all over my head and you still say that?' If I helped him to be happy that's amazing. There's a tiny voice inside my head telling me I can't have this, but there's a louder one. It's Charlie's from the beach, saying, *You do deserve good things, Clems, there's no one who deserves them more*. This is everything I'd thought I couldn't have, everything I want so much. But there's a reason why I've only got one night with Charlie on my wish list. I haven't got the first clue how to handle more.

He laughs. 'It's exactly the reason I love you.' His voice is low. 'You can't tell me you don't feel it too? And, obviously, Diesel adores you.' He gives my foot a nudge to show he's teasing.

As Diesel rolls over onto his back and prods me with his paw I rub his stomach. 'And I love you too, Diesel.' For the time being, I'm hoping Charlie will know he's included in that. I'm screwing up my courage finding a way to tell Charlie I love him so much he makes me feel like throwing up. 'Obviously, I'd love you more if you didn't steal my elevenses.'

Charlie is dipping into his bag. 'We also came to deliver these.' There are three small packages wrapped in tissue paper, and he slides the smallest flattest one towards me.

Before I open it I already know what it is. 'Another seascape?' I sigh because as I look at it I can hear the roar of the waves. 'And the others came from you too?' I'm kicking myself for not realising sooner.

That makes him laugh 'No one else would have sent you Pancake's potted shrimps.' His smile is rueful. 'That's the last picture in the series. They're supposed to make you want to come back.'

My lips are twitching. 'Thank you, they're beautiful, they were actually what kept me going. Until this morning's one didn't arrive.' I move on from that. 'So what's in the next one?' When I pull off the tissue there's a small green pear.

Charlie clears his throat. 'It's not quite ripe, but it's from the tree in the garden.'

I sit up and try to breath in his scent. 'That's amazing. When we sat under that tree in the spring the blossom petals were falling like snow and I was squished under your arm pretending to be your girlfriend.'

He nods. 'Back then you wouldn't commit to any more than two days ahead and summer was too far away for you to think about, and yet here we are. It's already August, the pears are almost ready. It hasn't been *that* painful, has it?'

I'll let him have that one. 'Nope. Give or take a disaster or two.'

He's clasping my hand across the table. 'I'll let you into a secret.' He takes a breath and rubs his thumb over my nail. 'Settling down isn't hard if it's what you choose to do with the person you love. If you're happy and life's filled with love time flies. You don't feel tied.'

I let out a sigh. 'The most I've got my head around this far is a night with you. What if I mess up?'

His eyebrows lift. 'You'll never know if you don't try. The thing is, I don't want to end up like that Adele song we were listening to in the car. It's no good us meeting up years down the line and thinking about what we might have had, I want us to be together now. So, I had to come and say that.' He's shuffled his chair around and he's resting his temple against mine. 'But you know what, Clems? The last thing I want is to persuade you to come home if it's not what you want. I'm in love with you, I couldn't love you any more, whenever you come back, I'll be waiting.'

I'm glad I kept it in until now. 'You won't have too long to wait.' I'm biting my lip. 'When the postman accidentally missed delivering my picture this morning, I was so gutted it jolted me into realising I had to take control of my life. I've already started working on that.'

'And?' He's squeezing my hand very tightly and the stubble of his face is pricking my cheek.

'Maybe to start with I'll take it one night at a time. But I'd love to be with you.' I can't hold back my grin any more. 'I fly back tomorrow.'

He's laughing now and he pulls me towards him into the sweetest most delicious snog. When he finally lets me go, my toes have turned to syrup and all I want to do is snog him again.

'That's brilliant, Clems. We'll work on that wish list of yours. Turn a night into a lifetime, and we'll be all good.' He rubs his lips. 'You might be back before us; with the pet regulations, it could take us a while. I hope there's time for lunch before we leave, but you've one last present to open first.'

This guy and his stomach. I'm glad he doesn't change, because I love him just as he is. 'Is it a lipstick?' The last package is smaller, and I'm frowning, then as I see what's emerging I can't help smiling. 'It's one of your penguins?'

He's nodding. 'I didn't want to risk posting him. You are my penguin, aren't you?'

For some reason my face is wet with tears as I laugh back at him. 'Actually, Hobson, I think I am.'

He sighs. 'And seeing as we're in the most romantic city in the world, we need to have a proper kiss.'

And it's a long time before I hear the noise of the traffic again.

39

In the garden at Seaspray Cottage
Fancy dress and planning officers
Thursday

Coming back this time was very different. Every other visit I've been plotting my escape even before the plane touched down. This time I spend the flight checking my shopping list over and over again, and when I land in Exeter my legs are so wobbly I almost fall down the plane steps. Charlie wasn't joking about me getting back first. Plum and I do a late-night shop and we're already pushing our loaded trolley across the Waitrose car park in Exeter and Charlie is still only driving through Dorset. As Plum and I make our way along the path from the harbour there aren't enough words to say how wonderful it is to see the moon rising up the twilight sky over the bay and hear the gentle rush of the breakers in the background. As we haul the shopping bags up to the kitchen the thyme and beeswax smell of the hall and the familiar creak of stairs are like the house welcoming me home and wrapping itself around me. By the time Diesel bursts in from the balcony a couple of hours later the night air is heavy with the scent of sponge, and there are trays of tiny cupcakes cooling on every kitchen surface. Then Charlie saunters in with that soft smile and my heart melts. This time I don't have to fight to keep my hands off him. I slide my fingers through his hair, throw myself against his chest, and bury myself in the longest sweetest kiss of my life.

When Charlie wakes me next morning with a snog and a tray of coffee, bacon and scrambled eggs, he's already dressed and ready to leave for a ten o'clock meeting. As soon as I'm showered I start putting plates and china cups into boxes ready to take downstairs for this afternoon then I start to work my way down Sophie's final menu list. Every item has the word 'mini' in front, except the drinks, which say large. According to Sophie, so long as food's small enough to fit in a child's mouth it has zero calories. Obviously, the low-level food will be healthy veggie sticks and cheesy chunks and teensy wholemeal sandwiches, and she mentioned a higher picnic table to keep the chocolate, cakes and twiglets up at mums' level.

When I nip down to the garden for mint sprigs at twelve, it's still just the usual grass and trees. It looks like Charlie and Sophie gave up on the tables, but realistically this is kids playing on the lawn. Sophie's left the stripy blankets in a pile on the patchwork sofa and they'll be fine to sit on. So, I dash back upstairs and while the extra small vegan sausage rolls are cooking, I chop the veggies and I'm just finishing slicing up the fruit for the drinks when Sophie, Milla and Maisie arrive.

Sophie comes in for a huge hug. 'I'm so happy that you're back.' She beams and pushes a sleeping Maisie in her car seat under the kitchen table. 'Right, Milla's going to help you upstairs, Clems. My Dainty Dusters ladies are here to carry boxes of cups and plates down, then we'll come back for the food and drinks. The ground floor flat's open, we'll pop things in the fridges there.' She sounds like her mind's on the job, although a carrying team of six sounds like over-kill for a picnic, but maybe that's how you think when you're heading for life in a castle.

As I grin at Sophie, I'm so happy to be back too. 'Brill, the fruit cocktails are in the fridge here. There's strawberry, and watermelon and lime, we'll add more fruit pieces when we serve them.' As Sophie grabs the first box and rushes out, I hand Milla the packs of blue gingham serviettes last seen on Sophie's photo. 'Would you like to fold these while I pipe some icing?' As I finish the swirl of turquoise, I hand Milla the first cupcake. 'Here, you'd better be my tester.' I take the second for myself. One mouthful, and the sweetness of the buttercream melting onto my tongue and I'm truly back in the game. However hard it's going to be to find a new home for the Little Cornish Kitchen to pop up in, it's going to be worth it.

'Yummy.' She's brushing the crumbs off her lips. 'And I love your dress, Clemmie, it's nearly the same as the bunting.'

I'm frowning down at the sprinkling of white stars across my orange dress that I've put on for good luck. 'Which bunting?'

She clamps her hand to her mouth. 'Actually, my bunting ... that I'm choosing for my bedroom. We mustn't go downstairs, Mum's putting the food out, you know that, don't you?'

I laugh. 'With two hundred bite-size cakes to ice, and a thousand baby sandwiches to fill, we aren't going anywhere.' It's funny how Milla's already just as on top of things as Sophie. And with

Dainty Dusters here on the job it flows like magic. As fast as we prepare things, they're whisked away.

As Sophie dips in an hour later I'm shaking my head. 'You've made so many trips up and down, when you first suggested this I only thought of the loos not the carrying.' I'm going to have to be sharper when I'm searching. Then I remind myself, I may not have much choice. When I think I may not find *anywhere* suitable I shiver, then block that thought. From now on I've got to tough it out.

Sophie's cheeks are flushed as she pushes back her hair. 'That's why we've got the helpers, my little treat, they're staying to clear away too.' She picks up Maisie who's snored her way through all the preparation. 'So if you're ready with the last of the sandwiches, the first mums will be arriving any minute. Nate's here already, Plum's bringing Marcus and Tilly, and Joe's on his way.'

'I didn't know dads came too.' I'm kicking myself for sounding so sexist.

Sophie's cheeks are pinker than ever. 'Some of them are today.'

I take off my baking apron and give Sophie a squeeze on the way to the door. 'I feel like a fraud here, all I've done is make the food.'

She hugs me back. 'We can't bring Dainty Dusters to every event, but today's special because it's like a whole new beginning for you.'

As we wind our way down the stairs, I'm hanging on to the excitement surging in my chest, to stop it fast forwarding to fear.

As we reach the half-landing the sunlight's slanting through the tall sash window but Sophie tugs my skirt and whisks me past. 'No peeping; wait until we're down. Don't worry, it's looking lovely, but I want it to be a surprise.' As we reach the ground floor hallway she takes my hand. 'Close your eyes, I'll lead you out.'

There's a gust of warm salty air as we move towards the open door. I shuffle along next to Sophie thinking it's a lot of fuss for a few carrot sticks on a kiddies' table.

She guides me down the last step and out onto the herringbone brick path. 'Okay, you can look now.'

As I open my eyes the first thing I see is bunting ... bonkers amounts of bunting. It's trailing down in parallel lines from the eaves to the garden wall, fluttering against the sky like an outdoor ceiling, draped between the fruit trees, along the fence, across the walls.

I spot the starry fabric Milla was talking about, and send her a grin through my happy tears. Then I shake my head to make sure it's real. 'There's more bunting here than for the Fish Quay Festival, and the colours couldn't be more perfect.' There's orange and blue and pink and green flags with flowers and stripes and shells. 'And look at the lawn ... How did you do this so fast? A couple of hours ago the garden was empty.'

Sophie's laughing across at Nate and Charlie. 'One mention of cupcakes, you should see these guys go.'

I'm looking past the bright splashes of rugs spread out across the grass. 'Oh my, you brought furniture too?' At the far end of the lawn there are pale green metal chairs with curly bits, and tables with parasols and mums sitting around them. 'It's all *so* pretty.'

Nate gives me a wink. 'She did promise us *all* the cakes.'

My knees are sagging. 'It couldn't look more beautiful.'

Charlie gives a low laugh and comes over and gives my hand a squeeze. 'It'll be even better when the food comes out.'

As if on cue, the French windows to the ground floor flat swing open, and the first wave of Dainty Dusters ladies proceed across the grass carrying tiered cake stands laden with the teensy cakes and snacks I've been making. The second wave follow with the pink and orange fruit cocktails in big glass containers with taps and take them over to the table where Laura's second-best flowery china cups are spread out in colouful lines. Then as the ladies move around the tables with drinks of cups on trays lots more mums and children arrive.

Some of the kids settle down in huddles on the rugs, others run around chasing balls, the mums dig in for buns and chocolate shortcake and mini lemon meringue pies, and Sophie pulls me across to a table by the apple tree.

Her eyes are shining as she fills my plate for me. 'So, what's the verdict?'

I can't stop smiling. 'It couldn't be any more picturesque. It's beautiful, I can't thank everyone enough.'

Her smile couldn't be wider. 'I know it's sad to say "au revoir" to Laura's teensy top floor, but it's *so* exciting to say "bonjour" to somewhere new.'

I pull a face. 'It will be when I find it.'

She leans forward and clasps both my hands. 'Look how pretty the garden looks with the cafe tables. Imagine it at dusk, decked out in fairy lights, with the echo of the surf ebbing and flowing along the beach, all our friends from the Singles' Club lazing around, slinging down their gin fizz, knocking back chocolate torte like there's no tomorrow.' She's quivering with excitement. 'We mermaids have been working with Charlie on this, it's why we were so gutted when you rushed off, and why we're so excited you're back. Truly, when the Little Cornish Kitchen pops up again down here it's going to be amazing.'

I can't help laughing. 'The garden's looking fabulous, but there are a couple of catches.' I'm counting off my fingers. 'One, the complete absence of a kitchen, and two, there's no roof. Considering Cornwall is the rainfall capital of the world on many days, that might be a drawback.' To be honest, as I snaffle a mini cupcake and chomp on it, I can't think how a razor-sharp business brain like Sophie's has overlooked such crucial points.

She's straight back at me. 'That's where the genius masterstroke surprise comes in.'

I'm staring over the heads of the children zig zagging across the lawn playing tag, past the fence to where the boundary wall sits alongside the sandy beach path. 'What's that guy doing?' For my money, he's driving in a stake with a mallet, and attaching a yellow notice to it.

Sophie follows where I'm pointing, then she punches the air, and grins at me triumphantly. 'And it's happening as we speak. That's the planning application notice.'

'What?' My fourth cupcake disappears in one gulp.

'Charlie's applied for a change of use.' The breezy way she says it, she could be talking about a trip to the hairdressers.

'I'm really not getting this.' That's putting it mildly.

She's back to shaking her head. 'Charlie, come over here, it's time to explain to Clems.' Charlie saunters across towards me, Diesel close behind, and when he arrives he piles a plate with cupcakes then gestures with his head. 'Come on, let's go and sit under our pear tree.'

My heart squishes as I hear him say 'our'. I follow him past the line of trees and four trunks along he sits down and pats the grass beside him.

He pushes back a lock of hair falling over his forehead and slings his arm around my shoulders. 'What we've come up with is a way for you to work your magic in the kitchen and keep the population of St Aidan fed, happy and in love. And I get to safeguard my pudding supply too.'

I'm frowning. 'This is St Aidan we're talking about, al fresco won't work like it would in St Lucia. At the very least we'd need a covered terrace. And wind breaks for when there's a force ten howling in off the bay.'

The corners of his eyes crinkle as he smiles. 'No, no, you've got this all wrong, the garden's not the venue, it's secondary space you spill out to.'

'What?' I'm still confused.

Charlie's grin couldn't be wider. 'A few weeks ago when Sophie first asked about opening up the flat for today, it hit me. If we drop your venue down to the vacant ground floor flat, you get the same allure of views and location, with more space, easier access and the garden too.'

I can't help wailing. 'Why didn't you tell me?'

'If we'd talked about it I'd have said. But I didn't want to make empty promises until I heard back from the planners. They have finally come off the fence and said they'll be happy for part of the ground floor of the cottage to be commercial. The yellow sign is the formal application.'

'Wow.'

I'm almost lost for words but Charlie's buzzing. 'The flat's newly wired, alteration would be minimal. A month tops, and you'd comply with every regulation out there, and be up and running. You can even paint and furnish it like Laura's place if you want.'

It's so well worked out, I can't believe what I'm hearing. 'So is there a catch?'

He bites his lip. 'Nope. If you're actually living at Laura's, you can keep the upgrades there to a minimum. If you work at George's, and get extra income from your Little Cornish Kitchen events, we'll all help you set up the business.'

I'm thinking of it from every side. 'I still owe Maude.'

Charlie waves his hand. 'A week of deprivation has worked wonders. St Aidan's even more desperate for your cooking than it was before. You'll pay Madame Misery back in no time.'

I might not be a business Einstein, but even I've worked out there's a problem here. 'Brilliant except for one thing – you haven't mentioned the rent?'

He gives a rueful grin and fondles Diesel's ears. 'That's where Sophie wiped the floor with me. As soon as I suggested you using the flat, she included two years of the rental on the flat here as part of the Hawthorne Farm deal. So, the minute Sophie bought Siren House, you scored yourself two years here rent-free.'

I'm scratching my head. 'So who's actually paying?'

'No money is changing hands. It was a sweetener, one of the reasons I persuaded her and Nate to sell to me at the right price.'

'Is speculation always that convoluted?'

He laughs. 'The best deals are never easy. That's why they're so satisfying when you get them right.' He's doing that thing where he stares deep into my eyes looking amazingly hot, and vulnerable and hopeful all at the same time. 'So is that everything?'

'No, there is something else.' I shied away from it before, but my heart is bursting, and I have to tell him.

'And?' He cocks an eyebrow at me.

'Thank you. Not just for this. Thank you for always being there for me, for teaching me to bake, for making me understand about my past, for bringing me to Rob, for helping me see what I want, and supporting me to become the kind of person who dares to reach for all those things.' It's already a very long list. 'But most of all, thank you for being your truly awesome self. I've never said this to anyone before. But Charlie Hobson, I love you.' I'm sniffing as I say the words and it hits me how much. When he pulls me into a snog it's salty with tears.

He's sniffing too. 'Thank you. I love you too, Clemmie penguin.'

I brush my hand across my eyes. 'You did make my heart flip that first day when you were eating macaroons. And a lot when we were baking. But the more I got to know you, the more I thought I couldn't have you.'

His voice is all low and gravely. 'Thank you for coming home, Clems. I promise you won't regret it.' He pulls me into the lightest of kisses, that makes my body explode into rainbows, and leaves me aching for more. If there weren't so many people wandering round us, I wouldn't let him go this easily.

Then he gets up, sidesteps a hurtling toddler, and pulls me up off the grass. 'Come on Clemmie Kitchen, let's get you back to your garden party.'

As we walk back across the garden to Sophie and Plum, they're grinning at us. And I know this is why I'm home. With friends who go to these lengths for me, how could I ever have left?

40

Sophie's house warming party at Siren House
Driftwood and bottle tops
Sunday, three weeks later

'I knew you two were destined to be together the night you hooked her tail.'

This is Nell, and somehow she's managing to hang on to George, hold a handful of cupcakes, swig her alcoholic pink lemonade *and* beam at Charlie and me across the garden terrace at Siren House.

Charlie's laughing at her as he swigs his Peroni. 'Funny you should say that.' The bottle is glinting against the line where the cloudless autumn sky merges with the deep blue of the sea. I shift my feet as I watch because the way his throat moves as he swallows always makes my knees feel like they could collapse at any moment. Even when I'm sitting down.

Nell laughs. 'That first glance you shot across the room at Clems said it all, Charlie. It's *so* exciting when that happens.'

Plum and I are glossing over our brief spectacular misreading of Nell's enthusiasm for Charlie. Okay, we hold our hands up and admit it – maybe we aren't the world's best matchmakers. At least we did our bit with George and Nell. Although Charlie was the real mastermind there.

Charlie grins. 'Clemmie dressed as a mermaid, it gets me every time.' He leans over and adjusts the starfish in my hair.

There's no point hiding it. Another party of Sophie's, and whatever we said after the last one, we're all here again in our bridesmaid's dresses, with our netting, seaweed and starfish tail additions. Because even if the dresses are even tighter than they were back in April, we mermaids could hardly come to the mini housewarming bash at Siren House dressed any other way. As Sophie was the bride she doesn't have a bridesmaid dress so she's tied her tail net over aqua capri pants.

I have to point it out. 'These tails are an upgraded design, Plum's added elastic this time so we can move our feet.'

Plum's laughing. 'We couldn't risk you falling over this close to the cliff edge.'

Nell's teasing Charlie. 'I've never known you take so long to seal a deal.'

He's straight back at her. 'Clems was very slippery to catch, but now I've got her I won't be letting go.' He loops his hand round my neck and comes in for the kind of teasing kiss that makes me glad I'm a girl not a mermaid.

I smile up at him. 'You might have to hold on tight.' I'm joking, obviously, but it's good to tease him. 'Not really, now I've swum home, I'm here to stay.' I didn't know what I was missing out on all these years, but I'm so pleased I've found it now. As for not being able to keep my hands off Charlie, we've barely left the flat since I got back. Obviously, I've been nipping downstairs to decorate the Little Cornish Kitchen's next home. Milla's been helping me with colours, and even if Sophie's proud of the way I'm stalking vintage interiors sites so far I'm buying my velvet sofas from eBay and finding my mismatched chairs on Gumtree. I can't bear to take anything from upstairs because somehow it's important for Laura's flat to stay as it is forever. However much Charlie teases me about making it a media room extension to his flat, I won't be giving in.

Sophie and Nate got the keys to the castle last week. They stripped out the carpets and ripped off the wallpaper, then sent in Dainty Dusters and their floor scrubbing machines – oh, yes, those really are a thing. It's as far as they can take it for now, and they're going to live with it. And to celebrate moving in with the basics until they save up for the bigger restoration work, they're throwing a lovely relaxed 'at home' afternoon for the mermaids and close friends. Sophie's flopped on one of the sun loungers from the farm courtyard, Maisie in her arms, Tilly and Marcus kneeling playing scissors paper stone across her legs – or should that be tail – while Milla's in her own mermaid outfit, headphones on, tapping out a dance at the edge of the decking.

As the late afternoon sun pops out from behind a fluffy cloud, Sophie holds up a macaroon and nods at me. 'Blue and lavender, for old time's sake.'

I have to point it out. 'There's a lot fewer macaroons than last time.'

Sophie laughs. 'When you spent all afternoon putting the buttercream in the last lot, who'd have dreamed you'd be making them all yourself for the next party?'

'Certainly not me.' I take one from my own stack and sink my teeth into it. 'I think we need to blame Charlie for that.' I lean back against him and look up into his eyes and he grins back. The rainbow cupcakes for today aren't our best work, because we got distracted halfway through, then ran out of time.

Sophie smiles. 'Well done, Charlie, but Clemmie's the one who really deserves the cheer.' She finds a glass and whooshes it upwards. 'While we're all here, lets drink to Clemmie coming home, and to Charlie for making her want to stay.'

Nell's staring at her lemonade. 'We've all tried before, and none of us have managed. So, well done, Charlie.'

Plum lifts her glass. 'To Clemmie and Charlie, and the wonderful Little Cornish Kitchen at Seaspray Cottage, or wherever else it pops up.'

It takes me so much by surprise, I've hardly got time to protest. But when they've finished cheering, and swigging and patting me on the back, I'm wiping the damp bits in the corners of my eyes.

Sophie spots I'm the colour of Nell's lemonade, and moves the conversation on. She picks up another macaroon. 'Plain, simple and beautiful, that's what we're about now.'

I laugh. '... simplicity is the essence of happiness ... all you need is less.' After all her emails, I should know.

Plum chimes in: 'Mindfulness is easy in empty spaces ...'

Sophie pulls a face as we chant her sayings back to her. 'Have I been going on?'

I shake my head, because none of us blame her. It takes guts and more than a few mantras to swap a state of the art kitchen for an ancient gas stove and a scrubbed table. 'It's fine, we understand, and even if it's empty, the house is already looking amazing.' The sparsely furnished rooms with their mottled walls and splashes of sunlight are shabby but lovely to be in, and Sophie had the vision to see that.

She's leaning forward, anxiously. 'You can feel it, can't you? There's so much well-being here on the edge of the ocean.'

Nate shakes his head. 'Put it another way. It'll be great when we've distilled the energy to decorate, Soph.'

Even though we're all laughing with Nate, I have to hand it to her. 'You're right though, Sophie, it's mega amounts of work, but it already feels like you belong here.'

As if to second that Maisie takes the rainbow cupcake she's holding, and grinds the buttercream into Sophie's hair and down her pristine T-shirt.

Sophie lets out a squawk. 'Mai-sie.'

Nate laughs. 'How many shirts is that today?'

Sophie's nostrils flare like they do when she's doing her calmness affirmations. 'Only six.'

I'm sitting looking out over the bay. 'So what else do we need to drink to? Nell and George.'

Nell chips in: 'Nate, Sophie, Milla, Tilly, Marcus, Maisie and Siren House.'

Charlie grins at Plum. 'How about Plum and Joe?'

Plum looks at me. 'Joe's on his way, but for now we're just good friends.'

Nell coughs. 'We won't write you off yet – look how long Charlie and Clemmie took.'

Charlie laughs. 'You may think we're only together because I want someone to cook my puddings for me, and to get my hands on her flat, but that's not true.'

Two can play at that game. 'And I'm not only with Charlie because I want to be related to Cressy Cupcake.' I turn my head around to laugh at him. 'Oh my, I'll get to have Cressy Cupcake as my bridesmaid, won't I?' Then I realise what I've said and screw up my eyes. 'Oh, shit, sorry.'

Charlie's laughing. 'This is exactly why I love you, Clems.' He takes a moment to smile down at me. 'Whenever you're ready, I'm sure Cressy will be delighted.'

I'm laughing too. 'Even though I was only away a week, it's so lovely to be back here with you all.' Then I remember. 'Oh, oh, Laura. We need to drink to Laura too.' How could I have forgotten? Saying her name brings tears to my eyes because I owe her so much. 'Laura brought me home to begin with, she helped me learn to bake, Laura's why I met Charlie, she brought my brothers and Rob back to me, and so much of the Little Cornish Kitchen was down to her.' I'm sniffing into my hand, and Sophie passes me a tissue, and I blow my nose.

Charlie looks down at me. 'You know Joe's bringing Jack and Jordan round later?'

'Yes.' I met them last week, and although they're less like me than Joe, the little resemblances are still fascinating.

Charlie's smiling. 'Someone else is coming too ...'

This time it's less of a surprise. 'Rob?' At first I wanted to get to know him on my own before we went out in St Aidan together. Even if they haven't gone on about it, I know the mermaid's have been longing to meet him.

Charlie nods again. 'You are okay with that?'

I can feel everyone watching me, holding their breath and waiting. And when I start nodding, it's hard to stop. 'Actually, I am.'

41

PS

It's strange. Now Rob and the half-bros are in and out of my life, it's hard to think there was a time when I didn't know them. However big or small the question mark was before, now it's not there any more. Instead of a blur there are four real guys who are working their way through every beer Roaring Waves brewery brews, bringing lemon meringue pies to compare, and agonising over estate agents' details. And that can only be good.

My mum and Harry are going to find a lot has changed when they come back. But first they'll have to get their heads around a daughter in St Aidan, who's all grown up and settled, with a job, a flat, a dog, a cat, a boyfriend and a Little Cornish Kitchen.

Yes, Pancake gets to stay. And it's the same with Charlie. Now we're together I can't imagine it any other way. He's right. Settling down isn't hard at all when you're with the person you love.

And we get to eat pear tart too. Sitting on the balcony at

Seaspray Cottage, listening to the sound of the surf rolling up the beach and the thump of Diesel's tail, watching the stars come out, over a bottle of Freixenet. Planning our next trip to Waitrose. And we couldn't be any happier.

Clemmie and Laura's Recipes from *The Little Cornish Kitchen*

Clemmie spends lots of her time in the book baking, so here are a few of her recipes in case you'd like to try them for yourself at home.

Clemmie's Meringues

In the book everyone loves Clemmie's meringue sweets. If you'd like to try your own, here is the recipe. If you don't have time to make your own meringues, you can use bought meringues instead.

For the home made meringue mixture:

- 4 large organic egg whites, at room temperature
- 115g caster sugar
- 115g icing sugar

For this recipe it's very important to keep everything very clean and use a bowl that's not plastic

Pre-heat the oven to 100°C for a fan oven, 110°c for an electric oven, or Gas 1/4. Line two baking sheets with baking parchment.

Put 4 large egg whites into a bowl and beat with an electric hand whisk on medium speed until the mixture stands up in stuff peaks when the whisk is lifted out. The mixture should be glossy and thick

Now turn the whisk speed up to fast and add the caster sugar a desertspoonful at a time. Beat for 3–4 seconds between each spoonful.

Next add the icing sugar a third at a time, and fold it gently into the mitxture with a metal spoon.

Drop spoonfuls of the mixture onto rounds on the baking parchment (or if you're feeling very fancy, you can pipe them from a piping bag).

Bake for one hour thirty minutes in a fan oven, and one hour fifteen minutes in an electric or gas oven, until the meringues sound crisp when tapped on the bottom. Leave to cool on the trays, or on a cooling rack.

The meringues stay fresh for two weeks if stored in an airtight container.

For sandwiched meringues:

Serve two meringues sandwiched together with whipped double cream.

If you prefer buttercream filling ...

Cream 100g soft butter with 200g icing sugar. Add vanilla or chocolate powder if you'd like the buttercream flavoured.

Clemmie's Pavlova

For individual Pavlova bases spread two to three scoops of meringue mixture into a circle.

When cooked and cool, top with whipping or pouring double cream, whipped, and top with piles of sliced strawberries (or other fruit in season).

Clemmie's Eton Mess

Serves four

500g strawberries
400ml double cream
3 x 7.5cm ready-made meringue nests, crumbled
Lemon curd (optional)
Mint sprigs to garnish

Puree half the strawberries in a blender and chop the rest. If you'd like strawberries to top, put four to one side, and slice the rest.

Whip the double cream until stiff, then add the strawberry purèe, and crumbled meringue. Then fold in the sliced strawberries.

Serve in chilled glasses or pretty tea cups. Put a spoonful of lemon curd in the individual serving glasses. Then share the cream and strawberry mixture equally between the glasses, and top with a strawberry and a mint sprig.

Clemmie's Quick Chocolate Brownies

If you're looking for a brownie recipe, this one is fast, easy and foolproof for beginners

The beauty of this one is that it uses Nutella chocolate spread–pause for a drool–which contains lots of the ingredients for brownies, already combined. So all you have to do is to add flour and eggs to Nutella, mix it together, and bake. Easy peasy, the brownies really are mouth-wateringly delish – and there's plenty of opportunity for brownie mix tasting too. If Bryony can do it, so can you! :)

300g Nutella
2 eggs (free range ones if you're going to taste the mixture!)
60g self raising flour

Put ingredients in a bowl. Mix it together until smooth. Spoon into greased baking tin (20cm square) or muffin/bun cases.

For extra pizazz sprinkle on a few chopped hazelnuts.

Bake in oven at 350°F (180°C) for 30 mins if baking as a cake. If cooking muffin/bun case brownies cook for 10-15 mins, or until centres are baked through, depending on the size. (Check by sticking a sharp knife in, it comes out clean when they're done, although they are also nice slightly sticky in the middle.)

Eat when hot, or leave to cool. Cut into squares for cake.
And enjoy ...

Love, Jane xx

Acknowledgements

A big thank you ...

To my editor Charlotte Ledger, for her unending talent, support, brilliance and fairy dust supplies. I love writing, but Charlotte's the one who makes the magic happen, I couldn't do this without her. To Kimberly Young and the team at HarperCollins, for their fabulous covers, and all round expertise and support. To my agent Amanda Preston for non-stop brilliance, and for always being there to talk me off the cliff edge next to my Aga. To Emily Ruston for her amazing editing, help and cheery emails.

To my writing friends across the world. To the fabulous book bloggers, who spread the word. To all my wonderful Facebook friends and readers – I love hearing from you and meeting up with you.

A very special thank you to fabulous cake baker, Caroline Tranter, for bringing the baking in my books to life, designing the recipes, and for letting us use her fab pictures and recipes in our blog pieces. If ever you get the chance to taste Caroline's cakes, grab it!

Big hugs to my family, for cheering me on all the way. To my wonderful dad and my lovely mum. To my grandmothers whose baking bowls gave me my taste for buttercream. To Anna for our lovely spa days and for being amazing, to Indi and Richard for delivering Eric. To Eric for reminding us how it feels to be happier than we could ever imagine. To Max for still being the man about our house, for the chats, for cooking my tea and bringing me cake. To Caroline for the cake and all the baking talk. And big love to my own hero, Phil ... this year I promise to come on more bike rides. And thank you for never letting me give up.